Sisters of Gold

Birmingham Rose

Birmingham Friends

Birmingham Blitz

Orphan of Angel Street

Poppy Day

The Narrowboat Girl

Chocolate Girls

Water Gypsies

Miss Purdy's Class

Family of Women

Where Earth Meets Sky

The Bells of Bournville Green

A Hopscotch Summer

Soldier Girl

All the Days of Our Lives

My Daughter, My Mother

The Women of Lilac Street

Meet Me Under the Clock

War Babies

Now the War is Over

The Doorstep Child

ANNIE MURRAY

Sisters of Gold

MACMILLAN

First published in 2018 by Macmillan
an imprint of Pan Macmillan
20 New Wharf Road, London N1 9RR
Associated companies throughout the world
www.panmacmillan.com

ISBN 978-1-5098-4150-9

1 3 5 7 9 8 6 4 2

A CIP catalogue record for this book is available from the British Library.

Typeset by Ellipsis, Glasgow
Printed and bound by CPI Group (UK) Ltd, Croydon, CR0 4YY

Visit **www.panmacmillan.com** to read more about all our books
and to buy them. You will also find features, author interviews and
news of any author events, and you can sign up for e-newsletters
so that you're always first to hear about our new releases.

For my sister, Julia

A Week's Work in Birmingham

A week's work in Birmingham in its aggregate results is something wonderful. It comprises the fabrication of fourteen millions of pens, six thousand bedsteads, seven thousand guns, three hundred million of cut nails, one hundred million of buttons, one thousand saddles, five millions of copper or bronze coins, twenty thousand pairs of spectacles, six tons of papier-mâché ware, £30,000 worth of jewellery, four thousand miles of iron and steel wire, two tons of pins, five tons of hairpins, hooks and eyes and eyelets, one hundred and thirty thousand gross of wood screws, five hundred tons of nuts, screw bolts, spikes and rivets, fifty tons of wrought-iron hinges, three hundred and fifty miles length of wax for vestas, forty tons of refined metal, forty tons of German silver, one thousand dozen offenders, three thousand five hundred bellows, a thousand roasting jacks, one hundred and fifty sewing machines, eight hundred tons of brass and copper wares, besides an almost endless multitude of miscellaneous articles of which no statistics can be given, but which, like those enumerated, find employment for hundreds and thousands of busy hands, and are destined to supply the manifold wants of humanity from China to Peru.

Birmingham Weekly Post, 9 July 1892

'All that is needed for a workman to start as a master is a peculiarly shaped bench (known as a Peg) and a leather apron, one or two pounds' worth of tools (including a blow-pipe) and for material, a few sovereigns and some ounces of copper and zinc. His shop may be the top room of his house, or a small building over the wash house at a rent of 2s or 2s 6d a week and the indispensable gas jet . . .'

J. S. Wright, 1866, member of the Local Industries Committee of the British Association at Birmingham

'The pursuit of technique for itself leads to mere mechanism, but being tempered by an artistic idea, it is humanized and becomes beautiful.'

R. Catterson-Smith, 1901, Headmaster of the Birmingham School of Jewellery and Silversmithing, 84 Vittoria Street

I

One

Birmingham, 1904

Jack Sidwell arranged himself beneath a Bovril advertisement on the platform at Snow Hill station and waited, fidgeting and fretting about his hat.

On a dandyish whim brought on by the sweltering August weather, he had treated himself to a second-hand straw boater. The speckled mirror in the wardrobe dealer's cramped room, where he tried it on, had flattered his boyish features into looking their full twenty-six years. Even with his neat blond moustache, Jack never looked his age. He paid his one and six and set off along the street with a swagger.

Now that he had agreed to come and meet these two young women off the train, he was beginning to long for the familiarity of his old cloth cap. Bet I look a proper Charlie, and other demoralizing thoughts, started to pester at him, along with the heaviness of his jacket in the heat, the moistness of his back and armpits. He might be a young man with a business all his own – he even employed another lad now – but still, he just felt like a sweaty chump in a silly hat.

Several trains arrived and departed. Sidelong beams of sunlight lit the smoke and steam as it unfurled towards the iron roof beams. There was a feverish feel to the afternoon. The stenches of horse muck and industry blooming in the heat, light glancing off the tracks in the distance, the talk all around of the hanging this morning at the gaol over in Winson Green. He shuddered. Made you feel queer, thinking about that. Jack tugged nervously at his collar and drew in a hot, smut-laced breath.

What were these two women doing, anyway, coming to Birmingham? He'd picked up rumours in the house – some trouble, them needing a bolt hole. But he hadn't dared ask Mr Watts. It all seemed a bit rum and he was curious to see what these wenches would look like. Not that they were 'wenches' exactly, not by the sound of it.

The Bristol train came steaming in, pulled by a magnificent, thudding beast of an engine. By the time the air had cleared and the bulk of passengers began to disperse, halfway along the platform he saw two young women in plain grey clothes and straw bonnets standing, uncertainly, close together. They had to be the ones. In outline, he saw that the taller of the two had a stately bearing, her dark hair fixed in a sober style and fastened low on her neck. The other was smaller, almost elfish in appearance.

Jack, while theoretically intensely interested in women, found that few of these real, alarming creatures seemed to cross his path. His heart began to pound like one of the pistons turning the engine wheels.

'Here goes, m'lad.' Pulling his shoulders back, he strode towards them.

Four eyes fixed upon him: two of them wide with some emotion which, oversensitive, he mistook for snootiness. The face of this taller girl was grey-eyed and sternly beautiful, though even Jack could recognize that at this moment it looked hollowed out by exhaustion. The smaller girl's eyes were set in a heart-shaped little face with strong cheekbones, slender but definite brows, and brown hair hauled back under her hat. These greenish eyes blazed at him with an expression of burning defiance which he found most intimidating. That look she was giving – it was fit to blow you over. She wasn't pretty exactly, not in a pin-up way – but my goodness, what a girl!

Heart palpitating, he managed to raise the hat with self-conscious aplomb.

'The Misses Hanson? Mr Ebenezer Watts sent me to meet you.' Pompously he added, 'He found himself unable to leave the works this afternoon.' As an after-thought he held his hand out to the elder, less intimidating sister. 'I'm Jack Sidwell. I, er . . .' It seemed a lame finish. 'I work upstairs.'

The two women nodded. Neither of them spoke, which was even more disconcerting. They seemed com-pletely bewildered. Jack wanted to stare at the fascinating younger one, but didn't dare.

'We've got to take the tram,' he said, trying to keep up his courage. 'Let me carry those.'

He took their old leather grip bags, one in each hand, and led them out of the station. One thing had become immediately clear to him: they both had a lot on their minds, and whatever it was, they were not thinking about him or his hat.

Each time the tram slowed, even a fraction, Margaret tried to look out between the swaying bodies in the packed carriage, to see this great city which was to take them in.

'It won't be yet.' Annie, her younger sister, nudged her painfully in the ribs. Everything about Annie was sharp – her pointed chin, her elbows, her temper. 'Stop fretting. He'll *tell* us when to get off.'

She nodded towards the rear of the carriage, where they could just see their round-faced guide, Mr Sidwell, who had become separated from them.

Margaret did not have the energy to reply that she was just trying to *see* the place. What she could make out, however, was overwhelming. All those buildings – all the traffic and people! As the tram crawled along, she stopped trying to look out. The high collar of her blouse, her cuffs, her corset, all made her feel imprisoned. In the stifling heat, a sick panic rose in her. If only she could get out. She was shut in here, in this strange place with the hot stench of all these people.

'Anyway,' Annie went on, seeming unaffected by the heat and having, as ever, to be right, 'Birmingham's a big place.'

'Oh, do just be quiet, Annie, *please.*'

Closing her eyes, she clung to one of the leather straps, pressing a handkerchief over her nose and mouth. *I need thee every hour, most gracious Lord . . .* She kept praying the words of one of her favourite hymns to give herself strength. But the tune brought back Sunday mornings at home in their father's church, the swell of organ and cello, the things she had always known, that she had never expected to leave – not like this. Tears threatened to overwhelm her and she forced the thoughts away. Be strong in the Lord . . . Pray without ceasing. She must find courage.

There was enough to sicken the stomach: the stale stink of garments imbued with grime and chemical smells of industry, of sour breath, decaying teeth, cigarette smoke. She was used to the poor – as a minister's dutiful daughter, much more accustomed than most of her class. For many of her nineteen years, she had visited villagers in their dank cottages, tending to their sickly children and elders. Nor did she look down on any of her fellow children of God.

But this was different – the city with its looming, soot-blackened buildings, streets going off in every direction which somehow seemed dark, even at this time of day, the rush of people, some now pressed tightly up against her, the pallid faces, clothes patched with sweat and dirt. And the noise! Even walking to the tram, amid the clanging bells, the press of people, the clatter and thump of the place, she had been almost overcome. All this, added to her distress, seemed about to tilt her back into illness again.

It felt like weeks since they had left the village, though it was only this morning, the bus chugging between fields where lapwings settled on the dewy grass. Already, she had been sick with fear and shame. The events of the past days had propelled them out of all that was dear and familiar – into this huge, unknown place. The fact that it was the city of her mother's birth did not, at this moment, bring much comfort.

As she fought a rising sensation of nausea, beside her a thin man with a drooping moustache spoke to his neighbour in a grim, gloating tone.

'So – they done another'un this morning.'

'D'yer go over there, then? The nick?'

'Nah. Would've if I 'adn't been on early today. See the bastard hang.'

'You don't see nowt these days. It's all done inside.'

The first speaker made a sound of annoyance. 'Well, as good as. I'd've gone all the same.' There was a pause before he went on. 'They've got a condemned cell there now. I know a bloke 'elped put it in. That's where they spend their last night, like. Last meal, before they tek 'em out in the morning, get the rope around their neck . . .'

Margaret pressed her hand to her mouth, screwing her eyes tightly shut. Perspiration was soaking through her clothes. She tried to block out the man's whining voice but it pierced through all her other thoughts.

Hanged by the neck until you are dead . . . Dear God, dear sweet Jesus, stupid, *stupid* Annie. What might have happened . . . Annie in a cell, Annie being taken out early one morning . . .

The heat rose in sickening waves, overwhelming her. A few seconds later, she was overcome by blackness.

There were voices, the faintest breeze tickling her face. Margaret could feel the hard ground beneath her, but from behind someone was supporting the upper half of her body.

'I think she's coming to,' a woman's voice said. The gentle sound of it brought back her mother and filled her with longing.

She felt queasy. Smells came to her – smoky, putrid . . . And sweat . . . The sweat of someone very close . . . A man's arms holding on to her!

Her eyes snapped open and she tried to leap to her feet.

'Maggs – don't!' Annie was squatting beside her, fanning her with a newspaper. Someone else was pressing her down by the shoulders.

'Don't rush it, bab,' the comforting woman said. 'You've had a bit of a turn. Just get up slow, like, or you might pass out again.' To someone else, she added, 'Poor thing – 'er looks ever so washed out.'

Margaret struggled to sit up, breathing deeply to force away the nausea. A ring of faces surrounded her, interested in the spectacle.

'Those two ain't from round 'ere,' a man's voice said. 'Couple of lookers though, ain't they?'

For a moment Margaret could see only strangers. Where was she? she thought, panicking again. A street, a horse and dray going by, crowds of people surging past . . . Then her sister's face again, swimming into view. Annie was squatting beside her now, careless of her skirt hem in all the muck.

'You fainted on the tram,' she said. 'Lucky we were nearly there, and Jack – Mr Sidwell – and I managed to get you off. Other people helped.'

Annie, being Annie, sounded quite excited about this turn of events. Margaret shrivelled inside. She wanted to pass out again with the shame. The humiliation of finding herself collapsed on the filthy brick pavement of a Birmingham street, surrounded by a crowd of interested strangers, only added to the burden of all her other emotions. She could not say a word.

'You'll be all right now, bab,' the kindly lady said. Margaret realized that it had been Jack Sidwell holding her up and that he had now retreated. She saw his dull black shoes planted beside her.

'Thank you all,' she managed, as hands helped her to her feet. 'I'm sorry . . .'

'Oh, there's nowt to be sorry about,' the woman said, squeezing her arm. Her thin, prematurely aged face smiled at Margaret. 'Could happen to anyone in this heat. And you look new around here.'

'That's what a visit to Brum does for yer!' someone offered, which provoked laughter.

'Where've you got to get to?' the woman asked Jack Sidwell.

'Only Chain Street.' But he sounded flustered. Picking

up the bags, he said to Annie, 'Can you help her?' He gave a helpless look as if to say, *what can I do?*

Annie took Margaret's arm. Jack led the way and Margaret saw him straighten his shoulders. She found something faintly ridiculous about him. Was it that hat?

'Come on,' he said. 'Nearly there.'

Two

Annie, supporting Margaret by the arm, looked about her with eager interest. Jack Sidwell walked ahead of them, carrying a bag in each hand.

Annie's lips turned up for a second at the sight of Jack as they wove along the busy pavement. There was a rash creeping up his neck and every time he looked at her, he blushed furiously. It was like Adam Blake all over again, she thought contemptuously. Adam, a lad in the village, was forever gawping at her yet couldn't manage to get a coherent word out of his mouth. She seemed to have this effect on boys, but from her point of view they (and men in general) were all rather ridiculous.

Annie, aged seventeen, had a grand view of her life and how it was going to proceed, and this towering vision did not particularly involve the presence of males. Especially not if their father or most of the other men she knew were anything to go by.

They were walking along the busiest streets she had ever seen: narrow, cobbled, the blue brick pavements teeming with people. On each side rose buildings, elegant under their coating of soot, some ornately patterned with carvings, and in various colours of brick. Some were obviously large manufactories from which issued metallic clangs and crashes. You could feel the vibrations of thumping and banging through the pavement. Some of the warrens of terraces could have been mistaken for dwellings alone, had it not been for all the signs and plaques announcing that they contained a host of businesses. And everywhere, on each floor and in every available space, were windows, long and light-welcoming, elegantly shaped, some arched, some decorative. Every now and then she caught a glimpse of someone bent over a bench behind one of the ground-floor windows and here and there glowed a bright finger of flame. Smoke poured from chimneys, adding to the stenches of the fetid summer air.

Annie looked about her, finding it all most exciting. She had always wanted to get out and see more of the world, and now this was a chance to begin. All the same, she was concerned about Margaret, who was much frailer than she was. Her sister did seem to be reviving though, now that they were out walking in the air – even this balmy air, thick with smoke and grit, so different from the freshness of their village home.

All around was an astonishing commotion of people, some talking, others silent and hurrying down the street. The girls had to keep alert to make sure they did not collide with anyone. Annie found herself twisting this way and that. A barefoot boy forcing a barrow bigger than himself along the pavement passed so close to her that he brushed her skirt; people scurried in and out of buildings; carts clattered past, horses leaving piles of their doings on the road, clouds of flies shifting about them. That, at least, was a smell that was familiar.

'Are you feeling better?' Annie asked, squeezing Margaret's arm.

Margaret nodded bravely, though she was still pale. 'Those people were kind,' she murmured. 'Like mother used to say.'

Margaret and Annie's Birmingham-born mother had

died six years ago and they longed for her every day. As children, they had asked her for stories about when she was growing up, in the city, before she met their father.

'There're plenty of good people in Birmingham,' she used to say. 'Don't let anyone tell you different. Some of them may be rough and ready, but most of them've got hearts of gold.'

In a few moments, they reached their destination, another road of high terraces and smut-coated bricks.

'So, this is it,' Jack Sidwell said, stopping outside numbers twenty-four and twenty-six Chain Street.

Margaret looked up at the buildings, a pair of adjoining three-storey houses, their front doors side by side. At number twenty-four, to the left, the flat sash windows were flush with the building, but at number twenty-six, these had been replaced by wide bays dustily reflecting the sky.

Screwed to the side of this front door was a brass plaque which read 'Ebenezer Watts & Son, Goldsmith & Jeweller'. Below it were two very small ones advertising 'J. Sidwell, Enamelling' and 'Sidney R. Cole, Gem Setting'. At number twenty-four, the largest sign read 'P. Tallis, Silversmith, Engraver' and below, almost too small to read, was 'C. Turner – Die Sinker'.

'Mrs Watts?' Jack called out as he led them into number twenty-six. 'I've got 'em!' Realizing too late that this made them sound like parcels, he tried again, pompously. 'Your nieces are here!' Margaret glanced at Annie and saw her smirking at his clumsiness.

'Oh, girls, at last!'

In the brown light of the hall, they heard Aunt Harriet before she appeared from the first door to their right.

Margaret felt the tension inside her ease in relief and pleasure at the sight of their aunt. She had met her only once as a small child and then not again until their mother's funeral in '98, which felt like a long time ago. Now she was meeting a woman with the loveliest, kindest face she thought she had ever seen.

Harriet Watts was a small, comfortably rounded woman with vivacious brown eyes and dark chestnut hair twisted back in a soft, becoming style. There was something exotic about Aunt Harriet which appealed immediately to Margaret. She was wearing a dress of dark crimson with a white collar, and in the gloom, points of golden light glittered from her ears and from a brooch at her throat as she hurried to greet them.

'Margaret – oh, look at you!' Aunt Harriet stood on tiptoes in her elegant little shoes, to kiss her cheek. 'Well, I never – you're taller than me now!'

Margaret felt the tears come at this warm welcome, even though she did not mean to cry.

'And little Annie – oh, my word. You're – seventeen, is it – already?' Annie was kissed and pressed for a moment against Aunt Hatt's sturdy, lavender-scented form. Their aunt stood back and gazed at both of them again. The gold earrings glistened as she moved her head.

'Both so lovely. Oh, Eb'll be delighted to see you. He'll be through in a little while – he's got a bit of a rush on today. Come through to the back . . . Oh, Jack!' He was still lurking in the hall, holding his hat. 'You can go now, thank you.'

'I, er . . . Oh . . . Right.' He disappeared up the staircase in front of them, the straw hat pressed to his chest.

'Thank you, Mr Sidwell!' Margaret called after him timidly, feeling that he had not been given quite enough credit for his efforts.

'He's a good lad,' Aunt Harriet said, rolling her eyes comically. 'Now, the front room here is the office.' She put her head round the door for a moment. 'Girls – these are my nieces, Margaret and Annie. I'm just going to settle them in.'

Margaret saw two young women, not much older than themselves: one, handsome and dark-haired, seated at a small desk; the other, a plump girl with round cheeks and spectacles, standing at a bench which ran under the window.

'These are my right-hand women,' Aunt Hatt said. 'This is Susan –' she indicated the seated woman, who bowed her head solemnly – 'and Bridget.'

She looks nice, Margaret thought, as Bridget said hello and smiled at them. The room was very crowded, crammed full of desks heaped with papers and shelves full of ledgers. On the bench was a pair of weighing scales.

'Now, this is *our* room.' Their aunt led them along the passage. In a recess in the wall to the left were pegs, on which hung coats and hats. 'I try to keep it nice. So much of the house is given over to the business, but – anyway, we'll soon have our *new* house, away from here! Did you know we are moving out – we're *building* a house! I'll take you up to your room presently – but I expect you'd like a cup of tea?'

'Oh, yes, please, Auntie,' Annie said. She was always hungry. She ate like a horse and seemed to burn off food like one as well.

'Fanny!' Aunt Hatt said, calling commandingly, and a thin young woman with pale hair under a cap appeared from another room further along the passage.

'Make us all a pot of tea, will you, please?' Aunt Harriet said.

Fanny muttered, 'Yes, Mrs Watts,' and disappeared

towards the kitchen, peering curiously at the sisters as she did so.

'Come on in . . . We've a cook, Mrs Sullivan – she and Fanny come in during the daytime. Now, you come and sit comfy, my dears, and we'll have our tea.'

The room smelt strongly of lavender mingled with coal dust from the grate. Margaret felt she had stepped into quite another world from that of their own puritanical home, in which any superfluous clutter or possession was forbidden.

The visible parts of the walls were covered in deep red paper patterned with gold-and-white flowers, and the curtains were in a similar shade. The mantelpiece was draped in velvet of the same warm red and crowded with a dense array of knick-knacks: candlesticks, china vases with lavender sprigs poking from them, ornaments and photographs, all competing for space with a large and loudly ticking brass carriage clock. The polished wooden floor was overlain with rugs and the room crowded with furniture.

Aunt Harriet left the room for a few moments to supervise the maid. As promising rattling sounds came from the kitchen, the girls removed their hats and, as instructed, settled in the leather chairs beside the unlit fire. The polished fender and mellow tick of the clock were homely and soothing.

Margaret sat back in her chair with a sigh of relief. They were here at last. Things felt safe and welcoming and she was eager to get to know her mother's brother and Aunt Hatt too. But just now, she felt a sudden longing to sit back and go to sleep.

Annie, still alert, was looking curiously about her. There was a gilt-framed mirror over the fireplace, and on the wall opposite the window hung a painting of two little blonde children hand in hand in the waves of a sunlit beach.

'You look like a bird in a new nest,' Margaret remarked. She nodded at the painting, thinking of their own rare holidays by the sea, when they had a mother as well as a father, and of the golden innocence of the children. She was still fragile as a reed with shock after all that had happened. 'That's what we used to be like.'

'We still *are*,' Annie said, turning to her passionately. But her face creased with concern. 'Are you all right? Not feeling . . . ill?' She was always so worried, so protective after Margaret's years as an invalid.

Margaret drew in a deep breath. 'Yes. I'm quite all right. It was just the heat, I think.'

'And all that talk about the hanging.'

'Yes.' Margaret lowered her head. Her voice came out brokenly after the silence that had stifled them all at home. 'Oh, Annie, shouldn't we be on our knees, repenting?'

'*We*, repenting?' Annie erupted. 'Why, in heaven's name . . . ?'

'Here we are, dears!'

Aunt Harriet's voice silenced her. She swung in through the door bearing a tray with a crockery teapot, cups and saucers, and a plate holding a generous-sized fruit cake, all of which must have taken some strength to carry. Aunt Hatt showed no sign of a struggle. She laid it on the table, which was covered in a white lace cloth.

She looked round at them, obviously sensing an atmosphere in the room.

'Are you all right, dears?'

'Yes, thank you, Aunt,' Margaret said, fighting to slow her breathing.

Aunt Harriet had a calm warmth about her which was

a balm to their frayed emotions. But Margaret knew that their aunt must be wondering what on earth was going on. Why they were here, needing to stay.

'Now,' Aunt Harriet said, pulling out a chair from under the table and seating herself gracefully on it. 'I'll just let that brew for a moment.' She placed her hands in her lap, crossed her feet in their neat black shoes, leaned a little towards them and said, 'Well, it's very nice to see you both. How is your father?'

'He's well, thank you,' Margaret said, managing a normal tone. 'At least, his rheumatics trouble him a little, but he is very uncomplaining.'

'He is,' Aunt Harriet agreed. 'A stoic soul, your father. Not neglecting himself for his flock, I hope?' She was speaking cautiously, Margaret could see. Being tactful. Neither Aunt Harriet nor their mother's brother, Uncle Ebenezer, were religious people.

'No more than usual,' Annie said.

Margaret gave her a look for the tone in her voice.

Aunt Harriet smiled warmly at them. Margaret thought how lovely she was to look at, but she could also see the uncertainty in her aunt's eyes.

'When you wrote and asked if you could come to us for a little while . . .' She stopped, obviously not wanting to pry, but her confusion was clear. 'Whatever the reason, dears, you're welcome, especially now our Georgie has set up his own home. Only –' she lowered her voice further – 'I had the impression from what you said that there had been a spot of bother between you? I should hate to think of there being a rift of any sort in the family.'

Margaret and Annie exchanged glances. Margaret gave her sister a powerful look which said, *Don't you dare say anything. Not now.*

'No, Auntie, it's not that . . .' Margaret ran out of words; the blood was rushing to her face. I can't just come out and tell her, she thought. Overwhelmed, she pressed her hands to her face and began to weep.

'Oh, my dear –' Aunt Harriet leaned forward. 'I'm sorry for asking. Don't get upset. We won't talk about it – not unless you want to.'

'I'm so ashamed,' Margaret blurted, between her sobs. 'I'm so sorry, Auntie – for putting you to all this trouble.'

'She's got *nothing* to be ashamed of!' She heard Annie's voice, low and fierce. 'Margaret's not the one at fault.'

'All right, dear,' Aunt Harriet said, seeming perturbed by Annie's tone. 'But we don't need to go into anything now, do we?'

There was a silence in which Margaret managed to control her tears. She wiped her eyes and looked up.

'Come along – tea.' Aunt Harriet got up and they heard the comforting sound of pouring tea. 'Here – have a piece of cake and let's not be miserable, eh? Whatever it is, it can wait until you're more rested.'

Three

There was a brief interval of calm in which they sipped cups of strong tea. While Margaret composed herself, Annie told Aunt Harriet about their journey: the bus to Bristol, the train from Temple Meads station, the tram journey with Jack Sidwell. She did not mention the fainting fit on the tram, for which Margaret was grateful. She marvelled again at her little sister's energy. Annie did not seem at all tired.

As Aunt Harriet was pouring them a second cup of tea, they heard faint sounds from the yard, voices and the clump of boots.

'Ah – they're coming out,' Harriet said. Seeing their puzzled faces she said, 'Eb's shopping is at the back – that's what we call the workshop where we make everything. There's an entry –' She nodded towards the back window. They could hear footsteps and voices, passing along the side of the house. 'At least they don't have to come through the house all the time. Although there're Jack and Sid with their rooms upstairs, tramping in and out. That's another reason we want to move – keeping the place clean is the devil.'

There came the sound of a deep, warm voice 'pom-pomming' tunefully somewhere along the passage at the back. A moment later the voice boomed, 'Hatt?'

'All right, love, we're in here!' Aunt Harriet smiled. 'It's Eb. He'll be pleased to see you.'

'So – have those young ladies . . . ? Ah!' Their uncle stood at the doorway. 'Here you are!' Margaret smiled, the sight of him warming her heart. Although Uncle Eb and her mother did not exactly look alike, she could see Leah, her mother, in him and it was a great comfort. She knew for sure then that it had been right to come here and seek refuge with these kindly, reassuring people.

Uncle Eb was a solid, cheerful-looking man, his fleshy face topped by grizzled curly hair and, beneath a bulbous nose, a bushy grey moustache. Over white shirtsleeves he wore a dark weskit, shiny with age, curving at the front to cover a bow-window belly which protruded over dark-clad, also bowed, legs. He held his arms out, beaming.

'So – our Young Ladies have arrived! Come on, wenches, come and give yer uncle a kiss!'

The girls got to their feet to be kissed and embraced. Uncle Eb smelt of chemicals and pipe tobacco.

'Well . . .' He held each one of them by the hand and gazed into their faces. 'Look at you both! Is that you then, our Maggie – my word, she's the image of her father, isn't she, Hatt? And little Annie – gracious, I've never known who you take after, bab. You don't favour your mother much, do yer?'

Annie shrugged, smiling. 'I must be from under the gooseberry bush,' she said and her uncle and aunt laughed.

'Oh, I doubt that very much!' Uncle Eb laughed. 'Any road – you need a bolt hole? I can't believe you young missionary wenches could be getting into too much mischief. What's going on?'

'Eb.' Harriet's voice was sharp. 'Don't start on the poor girls now. They've only just arrived.'

'Oh, pardon me.' Eb held his hands up in surrender.

'There I go, both feet in as usual. Don't mind me. What lovely wenches you are! Bit on the scrawny side, though – need feeding up, the pair of yer. Have a bit of cake? Make yourselves at home – our home is your home – Liberty Hall, eh, Hatt?' He squeezed their hands, then let go. 'Any tea left in that pot? Georgie's still here – he's coming in to see you as well.'

Seconds later their son Georgie, a tall, slender man, appeared at the door, and stood watching them, smiling. He was handsome, with dark hair and a sallow complexion, very obviously his mother's son. He must be twenty-six now, Margaret thought, startled.

'Margaret and Annie, isn't it?' He came and shook their hands shyly, but his brown eyes gave off liveliness and interest. 'Nice that you could come – how long are you staying?'

'They don't know for sure yet,' Aunt Hatt said as they looked at each other awkwardly. 'Now, Georgie, stay for once and have a cup of tea with your cousins, won't you?' She looked at Margaret and Annie, pulling a face. 'He's always off somewhere, this one – for the firm, I mean.'

'Can't, Mother.' He rolled his eyes comically. 'Clara wants me home – or there'll be trouble. He smiled at the girls. 'I'll be in tomorrow. Hope to see you then.'

'Well, if you've really got to rush off again,' Aunt Hatt said long-sufferingly, 'before you go, you could carry these young girls' bags upstairs for them.'

'Of course,' Georgie said, with a smile.

They heard his fast steps climb and descend the stairs and with further goodbyes, he disappeared.

'He does most of the travelling for us because Eb won't budge from home if he can possibly help it. Georgie's even been to America!' she said, clearly full of pride. 'Mind you – I'm rather hoping, him being a married man now . . . Oh, and you'll meet our little Jimmy . . .'

Aunt Hatt regaled them with stories of their grandson Jimmy, with whom she was obviously besotted. They would soon come to realize that most of the photographs on the mantel were of either Georgie or Jimmy. Georgie was Eb and Hatt's only son and now he and his wife Clara had little Jimmy, they had decided to move out of their shared attic at number twenty-six. They had a newly built little house outside Birmingham, in a district called Handsworth. And it was close to there that Aunt Hatt and Uncle Eb were soon to move as well.

'You're lucky you caught us when you did,' Aunt Harriet told them later as they ate Mrs Sullivan's meal of brown stew with beans and potatoes which, Margaret found, went down very comfortingly. 'Since Georgie got his own place we decided to move out ourselves – into the country. So we'll be gone in a few months. We'll have to take them out there and show them while they're here, won't we, Eb?'

They were all seated in the soft lamplight of the cluttered, cosy room. It was very warm and stuffy on this hot night, even with the window open on to the yard. Eb sat in his place at the head of the table, his napkin tucked into his collar almost as if he was at the barber's.

'Lucky for you we hadn't rented out Georgie's room!' he said, through a hearty mouthful.

'Do you need more space, Uncle?' Margaret asked. She was increasingly aware of a painful throb in her temples; she felt utterly exhausted and was struggling to keep up a conversation. Eb chewed mightily and swallowed, wiping his moustache on the back of his hand.

'Napkin, Eb! What do I give you a napkin for?' Harriet scolded.

'There's always someone wants a workshop,' he said, making apologetic use of his napkin. 'I've got my shopping out the back, as you can see . . .' He held his arm towards the window where another building loomed very close to the house. 'But when we move out we can have all these extra rooms bringing in rent.' He smiled jovially at this thought.

'And we can extend the office into here,' Aunt Hatt said, looking round the room.

'Hmm.' Her husband's mouth was presently occupied with potato.

'No, Eb – you're not renting this out as well – we've hardly room to turn round in there,' Aunt Hatt said heatedly. 'We're practically sitting on each other's knees . . .'

Eb, still chewing, looked round at them all and gave a wink.

'Don't mind him – he just likes to mither me,' Aunt Hatt said.

'So these houses have a good many different businesses in them?' Annie asked. She looked much revived, after food. Margaret was grateful to her for keeping up the conversation. 'Mother used to tell us about it.'

They had grown up hearing stories from Leah Hanson about this district spreading north from the heart of Birmingham, on what was once the old Colmore estate – also known as Hockley.

'We're very interested to see,' Annie went on. 'There are so many different trades!'

'Ar – there's a fair few,' Eb agreed. 'Some places round here have a different firm in every room. Next door, see – downstairs is all Tallis's place. He's a silversmith. Bit of an oddity, Tallis.'

Margaret wondered about this description. 'What does he make?' she managed to ask.

'Oh, a variety – condiments sets and napkin rings, candlesticks, all sorts,' Eb said.

'He does very nice silver-backed dressing-table sets,' Aunt Hatt added.

'Yes, and there's a sports line – tankards, trophy cups. He's an engraver so they do a line in that. Any road, that's Tallis – smaller outfit than we've got here but he does fine work. Then upstairs, there's – Caleb Turner, he's a die sinker. Good lad, Turner is – does quite a bit for us. See, us, we live at the back of this house. So up there –' he nodded towards the ceiling at the front – 'there's Sid Cole. We gave 'im the front room for the light. Gem setter, 'e is. A good'un. Does a lot for me an' all – lives in there too, he does. And there's Jack the lad in the back attic, who you met. Enamelling's his line.'

'Does he live here as well?' Annie asked with a twinkle at Margaret.

'Our Jack? Oh, no – lives round the corner, with his mother. I think she's hoping he'll find himself a lady sooner or later – poor old Jack. He don't seem to have much luck in that department.'

'We saw the plates on the wall next door,' Annie said. 'Die sinkers . . . What's a die sinker, Uncle Eb?'

Eb finished his mouthful, swallowing with dignity and setting his knife and fork down; then he pulled his pipe and a leather pouch from his pocket and began to stuff the pipe bowl with tobacco. 'Well,' he said, 'anything you make, out of metal, like – see that brooch Hatt's wearing?' He pointed the pipe at his wife.

Aunt Harriet leaned forward to show them a gilt-edged brooch, intricately designed with a classical-looking head wreathed in leaves, and more flowers and tendrils around it, all in vivid-coloured enamel.

'Anything like this that you're going to make, first you've got to design it – just on paper, like. Then, to get it so you can stamp it out of metal, you've got to have a punch and a die with the design engraved in it – two bits of metal that fit into each other. The patterns in 'em are all cut by hand – that's what being a die sinker is. I've got shelves of them. You put your bit of metal on – copper or zinc and the like – between the two sides and you stamp the design into them. You can come and see the workshop tomorrow.'

'It's so small and so complicated – however do they do it?' Margaret exclaimed. The colours seemed to call to her, their brightness reviving her the way the vividness of flowers did in the spring. 'It's beautiful!'

'It is.' Eb took a sip from his glass of stout – its appearance a shock for Margaret and Annie. Alcohol never crossed the threshold of their own home. The drink left a milky froth on Eb's moustache. Then he lit up the pipe, puffing with obvious enjoyment.

'There's no shortage of skilled men around here – and a few wenches, at that. They say there's about thirty thousand people working just in this part of Brumma-gem. Oh – and while we're on that subject –' He sat up straighter and looked at his nieces with a twinkle. 'There's the question of what you young ladies are going to do while you're here? Extra pairs of hands – we can soon put you to work . . .'

Margaret felt dismayed. She had not thought of this. What on earth did Uncle expect them to do? But Annie sat up straight.

'Oh, yes!' she began, but Aunt Hatt cut in.

'Eb! Not now, you terrible man. These poor girls have

28

only just arrived. Their heads must be spinning! There's no earthly need for them to work – surely they won't be here long enough for that? And we certainly don't need to talk about anything like that tonight.'

'All right.' Eb held his hands up in surrender. 'Very good, very good. Eh – you wenches . . .' He leaned forward with a grin. You tell me this then: what's the difference between a tube and a foolish Dutchman?' He paused, triumphantly. 'No idea? Well – I'll tell you – one is a hollow cylinder and the other a silly Hollander!'

Their baffled faces and Aunt Hatt's severe look dared him to say another word.

'Don't mind him and his jokes,' she said.

'But I *want* to do something,' Annie insisted, as if there had been no interruption to the conversation. 'To earn my keep, for a start. And I want to see what life is like for . . . for people who work in factories, for people outside the village. I want to know about *life*.'

'Annie!' Margaret interrupted. 'Don't be so silly. You can't seriously be thinking about . . .'

But even Margaret found Aunt Hatt's glare directed at her and she subsided. An awkward silence had grown up in the room.

'Now,' Aunt Hatt said. 'What about some plum pudding and custard?' And then you girls can have another nice cup of tea and we'll let you go up to bed. You look ready to drop, the pair of you. I'll put some water on the boil for you.' She smiled at them with concern and said kindly, 'It'll all look better in the morning.'

Four

Aunt Hatt led them up to 'Georgie's room', where they were to sleep, in the bigger of the two attics at the front of the house. She had prepared hot water for them to wash with and Margaret enjoyed the warm weight of the basin as she carried hers up the narrow stairs.

'There we are, dears,' Aunt Hatt said, rather out of breath as they entered the low-ceilinged room. 'I think you'll find it comfortable. It was Georgie's room – and then his and Clara's.' She sounded wistful, Margaret thought. She could see that Georgie had been a much-loved boy, and now Jimmy, his son, would be surrounded by loving family as well. 'You can put your things in the chest of drawers and that little cupboard.' These two items were squeezed along the back wall.

A window, lined with deep red curtains, looked out over the street. Aunt Hatt – for already she had become that, not Aunt Harriet – drew them together. There was tan-coloured linoleum on the floor covered by a small rug each side of the enormous bed which took up most of the room.

'There are towels for you, look – and a po'.' Delicately she added, 'You can bring the water and so on down to the yard in the morning. By the way – we have our baths in the scullery. When we get to the new house, we'll have a bathroom!' Joyfully, she clasped her hands together under her chin. 'Hot water from taps – can you imagine!

But for now, I have mine on a Sunday morning – and we'll make sure you each get your time.'

Aunt Hatt came and kissed each of them and Margaret smelt her lavender scent again. Tears filled her eyes at this motherly gesture.

'Just get your heads down, girls. It's a nice comfortable bed. Goodnight, dears.'

Margaret and Annie unpacked their modest number of belongings. A light coat and spare dress, a skirt, blouse and underwear, a face cloth and a nightdress each; a cake of soap, and for cleaning their teeth strips of willow and a little pot of salt.

'We look very down-at-heel compared with Aunt, don't we?' Margaret said, wistfully holding up her grey dress with its frayed hem. Their boots were quite literally down-at-heel. There were so few occasions when they could go and buy cloth or find time to get their shoes mended. Life at home was full of the stern purpose of God's work, with no fripperies.

Annie glanced round. 'I s'pose so, yes,' she said, shrugging. Clothes had never been high on Annie's list of priorities.

Margaret had brought letter-writing things and her little Bible with onion-skin pages. Annie had brought her favourite book, *The Mill on the Floss*. Modestly they turned away from each other to wash in the candlelight. The familiarity of the bedtime ritual was soothing in this strange place, the feel of the warm water against their cheeks, the folding back of the sheet . . .

Yet the room seethed with things unsaid: a continuation of the atmosphere that had grown between them during these last days.

Margaret stood plaiting her thick hair. Annie could never be bothered. The brass bedstead creaked as each of them climbed on to it. Margaret started to pull the heavy bedclothes and gold-coloured eiderdown over them.

'What're you doing?' Annie threw them off irritably. 'You can't put all that on us – we'll cook!'

'Oh, yes,' Margaret said. 'Sorry.' She sounded dazed. Annie, lying with her hair spread on the pillow, looked sorry for being so sharp.

'We should say our prayers,' Margaret said, an edge of desperation to her voice.

'Just the Lord's Prayer,' Annie said. 'We haven't got Father breathing down our necks here.'

'Annie,' Margaret said in a desperate tone. '*Don't* talk like that, please.'

They recited it together, but it brought neither of them peace or stillness. A moment later Margaret, staring up at the cracked distemper on the ceiling, said crossly, 'What on earth were you talking about getting a job for?'

'That's what I want to do!' Annie sprang up to lean on one elbow. Her eyes blazed at Margaret as they had so many times in their lives. 'I must go out and work! Lots of women have jobs here – didn't we see them, in the street? And anyway, if we're to do the Lord's bidding, we have to be fearless as lions.'

'But I thought . . .' Margaret sounded amazed. Annie was always the rebel at home, the one chafing against their father's rigidity. It was Margaret who had been his disciple. 'I thought you didn't want . . . You were always talking about getting away.'

'Away from the *village*,' Annie said. 'That small life. I want to get out and see the world, God's wide world!' She swung her arm as if to paint a vision. 'There's so much more to see and do – and I want to do something *great*. Not like Father, all those years with farmers and

32

sheep . . . Why was he there? Instead of in London or . . . or here in Birmingham, at Carrs Lane?'

'Father couldn't help it,' Margaret said stiffly. 'You know that. It was his sensitive nature.' She knew they were circling round it all, round everything that had happened.

'Sensitive?' Annie raged, so that Margaret shushed her. Annie sat fully upright and went on in a fierce whisper. 'All this talk about him being sensitive! Who was he ever sensitive to? Hardly ever anyone but himself – and *him*! His protégé. Bringing him into our house like that – after what he'd done!'

'But Annie . . .' Margaret sounded tearful again. Her tears were only a blink away these days. 'You know what it was like for him, losing John, then Mother . . .'

As the elder of the two she had a clearer memory of the father they had known before his infant son succumbed to fever, followed four years later by his wife.

'I know – but we lost them too,' Annie said furiously. 'And just because someone keeps *saying* they're sensitive doesn't mean they *are*. What sensitivity has he shown to you? You've got to stop believing everything he says.'

'You can't just think you can do what you want.' Margaret desperately wanted to move the conversation away – from home, from Father, and from those last days – and nights – when she and Annie had resolved together that they had to get out of there. All this was the source of her agony. 'Aren't you frightened of what it would be like, working here? And you'd cause Aunt and Uncle all sorts of worry . . .'

'But it was Uncle who suggested it,' Annie argued. 'That's what people do here – they work. And I want to do *God*'s work. Not just in the village, but in a big city like this! All those things Mr Rowntree wrote about how poorly people live . . . How can society be improved if we don't go and see what it's really like?' She was burning with impatience. 'It's not going to get better by itself, is it? God needs *our* hands; *our* lips to speak his word.'

She waited for Margaret to say, *and why would not country people and farmers be as worthy receivers of the Lord's word as anyone else?* That was what she would have said before – Father's words, repeated to justify his life in their small backwater. But now, in an unsteady voice, all Margaret said was, 'Are you ready for me to put the light out?'

Annie nodded. Margaret blew and they settled down in the familiar, comforting whiff of candle smoke. Margaret turned on her side, her back to Annie, her whole being aching.

'Maggs?'

'Yes.' She didn't move.

'Are you going to tell them?'

There was a silence. Margaret was sure she could hear her own heart thudding. 'Tell them what?'

'All of it. You'll have to. They're putting us up – and we don't even know how long for. I mean, I'm not just going to go back with my tail between my legs, whatever he says.'

Margaret struggled to speak but her throat seemed blocked with tears. 'No,' she managed. 'I can't.'

'How can you even think that it was your fault?'

'I don't know!' She burst into sobs. 'That's just the trouble. I keep going over and over it all and I know that somewhere I did something terribly wrong. And Father said . . .'

'But he was *wrong*, Maggs. He's not *God* – he's not always right about everything. He was wrong and cruel and ridiculous . . .' She stopped for a second, thinking about how they could explain to Eb and Harriet Watts. 'I don't really think Aunt Harriet likes Father much, anyway.'

'Annie!' Margaret snapped, lifting her head from the pillow. '*Please*, leave me alone, will you? Just go to sleep.'

'But we'll have to—'

'Not tonight,' Margaret pleaded. 'I can't talk about anything tonight. Just *be quiet*.'

On the floor below, Eb Watts stood by the bed in his vest and underpants with a bemused expression on his face, one hand held out in front of him as if he was about to do something and had completely forgotten what it was.

'Eb?' Harriet was sitting up in bed, carefully fixing a net over her thick braid of hair. She wore a delicately embroidered nightgown. The room itself was a haven of ladylike pieces of furniture – her dressing table with an oval looking-glass, a little upholstered stool in front of it, and a silky bedspread in her favourite shade of light plum. Every inch of the house that was their living space, she tried to make as pretty and homely as possible.

'What're you doing, love?' she said. 'Are you coming to bed, or what?'

'Oh – ar.' He climbed in beside her.

'Eb – you haven't got your nightshirt on!'

'Never mind – won't hurt for once. Too darn hot for that.' Blowing out the candle he said, 'Come 'ere, you beautiful wench.'

With a giggle Harriet Watts snuggled up against the comforting girth of her husband.

'Funny having those two Hanson girls here,' he said. 'Solemn wenches though, the pair of 'em.'

'They seem very nice,' Harriet said. 'It'll be a change to have some girls about for a bit and perhaps it'll do them good as well. They've come from a very strict home, Eb.'

'Oh, ar, I'll say. They do seem rather strait-laced – 'specially the older one,' Eb said. He curved a hand stealthily round his wife's warm breast. 'You don't think they'll try and convert us, do yer?'

'Eb . . .' Hatt said, warningly.

The hand receded.

'Margaret's the image of the old man,' he said, suppressing a sigh. 'But that Annie – funny little thing she is. Looks a handful to me.'

'D'you think she meant it – about getting a job?'

'Well – why shouldn't they?' he said. 'Can't have them just sitting around here. They can get weaving – see a bit of life instead of all this religious claptrap.'

'Your sister was a good woman,' Hatt said. 'She believed in it, proper like.'

'Ole Lil? Oh, ar. She was – can't think why she married that stuffed shirt of a husband, though. *Leah*. Changing her name as if her real name and her own family weren't good enough or summat. I never could get used to calling her that. Hardly saw 'er after she moved down there anyway.'

'She changed it when she got married, dain't she? I suppose it sounded more religious. Not many Lils in the Bible, are there?'

'There's nowt wrong with the name Lilian,' Eb said, stroking his wife's full hip, still hoping pleasantly that there might be more on offer tonight, if he was lucky. 'And what's gone on there, d'yer think – them coming running here to us?'

'I don't know.' Harriet's voice was troubled. 'It seems

as if it's summat to do with *him* – their father. I'll see if I can get them to talk to me. Margaret, at least. The girl looked quite poorly when she arrived and things aren't right – I can see by the look of her. Be gentle with her, Eb.'

'I will!' he said, indignant. 'What d'yer think I'm going to do?'

'And don't be rude about their religion. It's important to them. There are some very kindly religious people. Just because you don't hold with it.'

'Well, you know what I always say,' Eb said, pressing his body hopefully against his wife's. 'Too much religion can make you go off pop!'

'I know that's what you always say,' she said. 'Just don't say it in front of these young ladies, that's all. Oh, Eb – get *off* me, will you? It's far too hot for all that carry-on.'

Five

By the next evening, Margaret felt she had lived a year instead of a day.

Far from the grilling with questions she had expected the next morning, her uncle and aunt asked nothing, were both very busy and seemed intent on keeping her and Annie busy all day as well.

That first morning she woke to the warm glow of light through the curtains, confused for a second by the sounds. In place of the quiet of home, broken only by the vociferous cockerel along the lane or the distant cows protesting, she could hear horses' hooves and cartwheels from the street below, the ring of something metallic being dropped on the ground, clattering sounds and shouts and the tread of many pairs of feet.

It all came flooding back to her. She was not at home – she was here, in Birmingham. And she lay in the curtains' light, red as if seeping through blood, thinking of her father, the pain of it all filling her once again.

Even before they had got downstairs, they could sense that the house was already in full swing. They were hit by a cocktail of smells: whiffs of acrid fumes mingled with milky porridge and the sour smell of a wet mop. The maid, Fanny, a bony, ginger-haired girl about Margaret's age, was busy cleaning the landing on the middle floor. Fanny's job, they would discover, as well as washing and general cleaning, was to wage war on the stairs and passages, which Aunt Hatt was determined to keep clean and respectable, despite the number of feet passing through each day.

Coming down the linoleum-covered attic stairs to the first floor, they could see that the door of the workroom at the front was ajar. They looked at each other, then crept closer for a moment. A man was sitting with his back to them, bent over his workbench in the bright morning light. They could see an array of tools in front of him. Margaret realized he was one of the people to whom Uncle Eb rented a room and she would have liked to go and see what he was doing, but it might have seemed rude. They said good morning to Fanny, stepping apologetically over her handiwork in the corridor. Good-naturedly, she mopped it again.

The banister of the main stairs felt smooth and well-polished under Margaret's hand as they went down to the ground floor. The back door was open in the warmth and from the workshop out at the back of the house came sounds of thuds and voices. Doors opened and closed.

'Good morning, Aunt Hatt,' Margaret said, leading the way in. Aunt Harriet was already at the desk in the office, at the front of the house, leaning over a ledger. The girl called Susan was at her desk and Bridget turned and smiled at them once again, saying hello softly.

'Ah, you're awake!' Aunt Hatt looked up over her wire spectacles. Margaret saw that the dress she was wearing today was in a deep, sea green. How lovely it was, she thought. How elegant her aunt looked. She was taken aback by the worldliness of her thoughts.

'We left you to sleep a bit,' Aunt Hatt said. 'Now – there's breakfast for you. Mrs Sullivan will boil you an egg apiece. And after that, Eb says he'll show you about the place. Then you can go and have a look around the district if you like. I'll have to get on, I'm afraid. There's so much to do . . .' She drifted back to her work.

'Does she mean us to go out on our own?' Annie whispered, thrilled, as they sat at the neatly laid table.

'I suppose she does,' Margaret said uncertainly. She could see that Aunt Hatt could probably do with the pair of them out of the way for a while and felt guilty for burdening her. Her aunt and uncle seemed to be so busy! 'I mean – she's not going to send us with a chaperone, is she?'

'Jack Sidwell,' Annie grinned, knocking the top off her boiled egg. 'In that hat!'

Margaret looked reproachfully at her. 'Poor man,' she said. 'He was kind. You're so mean.'

'Right, you two wenches – you can come and have a look round out 'ere.'

Uncle Eb led them out to his long, brick workshop in the yard. Only a narrow alley separated its back wall from the house. Stepping inside, they could see that the place was packed full of such a variety of activity and people and machines that Margaret hardly knew where to look.

Male faces turned briefly to look at them, then hastened back to their work. The workshop was full of hammering and banging and from the back, with rhythmic regularity, came much heavier thumping noises. A pungent, chemical smell stung their nostrils.

Margaret and Annie exchanged glances. They were both dressed in sober clothes, grey skirts and pale blouses, buttoned high at the neck. But in this entirely male environment it was difficult not to feel self-consciously female. Margaret found herself blushing uncomfortably. She thought of her aunt, at the heart of all this grime and graft, in her jewel-coloured clothes like an exotic little bird.

'Right.' Uncle Eb beckoned them to a desk in the corner which seemed to be his territory in the workshop. 'I'll give yer a quick run-through, all right? It all starts with these – designs.' He picked up one of several notebooks which were on the table. They saw drawings of bracelets, all beautifully executed. 'See that? That's our Christmas special this year.' The design showed a slender twist of metal with holly leaves and berries around it. Flicking pages, he showed them other inked drawings.

'Any road – once we've approved the design . . .' He was already on the move. 'Come over here with me . . .'

A young man at the side bench was working one of a row of presses. It was about three feet high with a crossbar at the top, weighted at one end with a black iron ball. They watched as their uncle spun the bar round and there came a thud from below. Turning the bar back round he extracted something from the flat jaws of the machine and held it out to them. Margaret saw a dull piece of metal, but when she looked closely it was stamped with an intricate floral pattern.

'Don't go near them presses,' Eb warned, before she could comment. 'You want to mind your heads. I've 'ad a few knocked out cold in my time. Now – these two lads are my apprentices. Tom, here –' he indicated the boy at the press – 'and that young feller over there –' Another boy was seated at the end of the table. He kept his head down, sawing at something which he held pressed against a sliver of wood fixed above the curved bench. The saw was about six inches long, its teeth so fine that all they could see was a thin strip of wire.

'He's learning how to use a piercing saw,' Eb said. 'In six months he'll be able to turn any shape I ask 'im. Now – see this?' He bent and pointed out through one of the grimy windows at the side of the building.

Margaret looked out to see a wall ahead of them. She was not sure what she was supposed to be looking at.

'All these works've got as many windows in as you can get,' Eb said. 'And see them tiles, all along the wall there?'

The tiles, though lightly covered in soot, were a creamy colour beneath, giving off a soft gleam.

'Glazed, see? You put tiles like that opposite the windows – brings more light into the room. Now – along this side, we've got cutting and stamping machines.' He waved an arm as if this was all the explanation needed. Margaret saw blanks of flat shapes lying on the workbenches – the oval beginnings of brooches, cut in wafer-thin metal.

'We do plated gold and pure gold – mostly nine and eighteen carat.' Seeing Annie's frown, he said, 'Gold's too soft to work well, you see, until you've heated it and mixed it with another metal. Twenty-four carat's pure, one hundred per cent gold. Eighteen carat's seventy-five per cent gold with a bit of silver or copper or zinc mixed in. The colour depends on what you mix it with – you mix gold and copper and you get a rosy pink colour. Mix it with silver and it's a white gold. The nine carat's thirty-seven and a half per cent. Got it?' He grinned at their serious faces.

'You mean, it's more than sixty per cent *not* gold, but you still call it gold?' Annie said rather severely.

To Margaret's relief, their uncle's grin widened. 'You don't miss much, do yer? That's about it, yes.' He stood with his hands at his waist, flexing his back for a moment.

Course, I'll do fine work if the order comes in. But nine and eighteen carat's more affordable for your man or woman in the street. And the more can afford 'em, the more we can sell. And why shouldn't anyone be able to have a pretty brooch or bracelet or a cigarette case if they want one, eh?'

'So what do you make here, Uncle?' Margaret asked.

'Oh – all sorts. Jewellery – that's bracelets, brooches, rings, pendants, cufflinks and studs, speciality picture frames – some like their pictures with jewelled frames – we've got a bit of a name for them.'

'What about chains?' Annie said. 'In Chain Street?'

'We don't do them – there's plenty of chain makers about. We don't set the gems either – not yet. I send that out to be done. One day . . .' He smiled. 'Best thing is to have everyone working under one roof, but –' He shrugged. 'At the moment this roof ain't big enough.' He walked on, beckoning.

'Right, to tell yer quick, 'cause I need to get to work.' They stood to one side of the workshop. 'The bullion gets delivered here . . . So, three mornings a week, before you young ladies've even prised your dainty eyes open, I'll be down under there in the cellar.' He pointed to the far end. 'Well away from the house. You don't want to live over the furnace if yer can 'elp it 'cause it makes a fair old stink. I were down 'ere at half past six this morning, getting it ready, see. We roll it out, or pull it through a machine to make it into wire – depending what it's for. It's kept in the safe over there . . .' He pointed at a huge, solid iron thing. 'And then . . .' He reached for a metal box that was lying on one of the benches. 'Every morning when they come in, they get one of these – everything's in here that they need for the job. Every box is weighed

43

and recorded. At the end of the day we weigh them back in.'

'Why?' Annie asked, frowning.

'Well, why d'yer think, my dear?' Eb leaned towards her, his face serious. 'We don't want any gold going missing, do we? Course – there is a bit of wastage allowed for. It happens when you're working. We sweep everything – the machines, floors, the lot. All the sweepings go back in the furnace to burn off the dust and I sell the lemel back to the metal dealers. Lemel – that's all the shavings of waste metal.'

'I suppose you have to employ very honest people,' Margaret said, trying to digest all this information. 'As gold is so valuable.'

'Oh, we work on trust – have to. And all my lads are good'uns, aren't you, you lucky lot?' He addressed his workers jovially. 'You get wise to all the tricks. No turn-ups on trousers in here – and no hair lacquer. You'd be surprised how much gold dust you can stick in yer hair if you keep running yer hands through it all day long! And all these sinks –' He pointed. 'That water don't go out into the drains – oh, no. It goes down into sawdust in the basement and we get the gold out of that an' all. Aprons, overalls – all washed here and the dust strained out.'

'Gracious,' Margaret said. 'I'd never have thought of all that.'

'Oh – it soon comes, with time,' Eb laughed. He hurried them through the rest of the workshop – the shelves of dies for stamping out shapes for decoration, the drop stampers at the end, working the machines, each using one leg to work the long rope, raising a heavy metal weight and letting it release with force to stamp out the metal.

'The deeper the cut, the more difficult the work,'

Uncle Eb said. The men kept working steadily. The boss was there and they had work to do. The weight of the stamp came hurtling down and crashed on to the dies below.

'Right – there's a few girls up in this end room.' In a narrow side room, four women sat working at various machines, the straps whirring round large cogs close to the ceiling. 'They do finishing and polishing in here – women's work, that.'

'Why?' Annie asked, in her challenging tone. Margaret gave her a look – not that she took any notice.

'Just is,' Eb said, ignoring her tone.

As their uncle steered them back along the workshop, they saw a man pouring liquid into a shallow bath in a kind of cupboard, with an outlet pipe above it leading out through the roof. The constant, overpowering stench seemed to be coming out of there. It was not something Uncle Eb had mentioned. Margaret didn't like to ask as her uncle seemed in a hurry now, but Annie said, 'What's that then?'

'Oh – that's the pickle,' he said. 'Vitriol – an acid, that is. It gets all the muck off the gold – solder and such. Right – last thing, I've got to get on.' He indicated the work tables on the other side from the presses. 'These on this side are the pegs.'

Each table had semicircles cut out all round it, each with a leather pouch fastened to it which Margaret guessed must be to catch any gold waste. Beside each semicircle a man sat on a stool, bent over his work, a leather apron tied across his lap. Most of them had a tube of some kind in their mouths and were working with a gas flame which burnt at the end of a cable fixed to the bench.

'Birmingham sidelight, we call that,' Eb said hurriedly. 'And them things in their mouths, those are blowpipes.

That's how they direct the flame exactly where they want it to go. This thing . . .' He picked up a long tool in the shape of a cross, with strings attached from the top to each end of the crossbar. 'The Archimedes Drill – look . . .' He twisted it round and pumped it up and down, drilling a hole in a little piece of brass scrap. 'Old as the hills, that is – still the best way of doing it.'

Margaret and Annie exchanged smiles. There were a whole host of tools at each workstation and Margaret found herself fascinated by all of it. Each man was working away, one or two alternating a drag on a Woodbine with blowing into the pipe.

'So – you've got the gist of it. I must get on. If you go and see yer Aunt Hatt, 'er'll give you an idea what to do next.'

They thanked him and went back into the house. Fanny was sweeping the passage and she pressed herself against the wall to let them pass. They caught a glimpse of Mrs Sullivan in the back kitchen, a gaunt, severe-looking woman, bent over a board of chopped onions.

'What shall we do?' Margaret whispered to Annie. 'I feel as if we're in the way.'

'Let's go out,' Annie said. 'We'll go and ask Aunt.'

They were walking along the passage to the office when scurrying footsteps came down the stairs and Jack Sidwell, who had brought them from the station, squeezed past them.

'Mornin'!' he said chirpily. But he was blushing furiously and hurried out of the front door.

Margaret and Annie looked at each other.

'D'you think he's sweet on you?' Annie whispered.

'*Me?*' Margaret said. 'You, more like!' Annie made a scornful noise at this and Margaret smiled. 'I think you've got an admirer – heaven help him.'

Six

'You've done *what*?' Aunt Hatt sank into a chair in the back room later that morning, looking up at Annie with plain horror on her face. 'Annie Hanson – you've only been out of my sight for a couple of hours!'

'Well, you did say you were going to toughen us up,' Annie said. She could not help the triumphant grin spreading over her face. Margaret was mortified at Annie's forwardness, seeing that her aunt looked genuinely upset. They had already quarrelled about it on the way home.

'Couldn't you have stopped her?' Aunt Hatt looked at Margaret. Aunt Hatt didn't know Annie, Margaret thought. If there was ever a born crusader it was her. Annie thought she was going to convert the world by sheer force of personality.

'I didn't know she was going to do it and then it was too late, Auntie – I'm sorry,' Margaret said, very dismayed by what had happened.

'Whatever would your father say? He'll think I'm letting you run wild – or worse, making skivvies out of you.'

'Oh, no – he won't,' Annie assured her with her usual forceful confidence. 'You don't need to tell him, do you? And Mother used to say, *Perfect love casteth out fear*...
One John, chapter four, verse eighteen. How can you

take the message of God's love into the world if we're afraid to be in it in the first place?'

Aunt Hatt stared at her nonplussed, this being a dilemma with which she was not especially familiar.

'I just want to get some experience, Aunt,' Annie said, more appeasingly.

'Well, you'll certainly get that,' Aunt Hatt retorted. 'And a lot more, if I know anything about those places.'

After their tour of the works of Watts & Son that morning, the girls had gone into the front office where Susan was seated at her desk, Bridget standing at the bench by the window, surrounded by little boxes, and Cousin Georgie leaning over his mother's desk, the two of them talking shop. Aunt Hatt looked elegant as ever, a gold brooch pinned to the high neck of her dress.

Georgie greeted them in his friendly way and said he would bring Clara and little Jimmy over to meet them as soon as they could all manage and that they must come to Handsworth and visit the house.

'We thought we might go out for a short while,' Margaret said tentatively. It now felt as if she and Annie were in the way in the office as well as in the rest of the house. With all this business carrying on around them it felt as if the only place to go to was the attic.

'D'you think it's all right for them to wander about like that?' Aunt Hatt asked Georgie.

'You'll be all right,' Susan piped up. She had a brisk, confident manner. Bridget was nodding her agreement.

'People always think there are thieves and robbers on every corner in this part of town,' Georgie said. 'There're always some who are out for what they can get, but it's quite safe just to walk about in the daytime – don't you worry. Just don't go wandering too far off – and mind the horse road. You won't be used to as much traffic as we have here.'

Margaret could see that Aunt Hatt was torn between needing the two of them out of her hair while feeling responsible for their safety.

'We'll be all right, Auntie,' she said. 'We go out and about at home all the time, visiting people and so on.' A pang of homesickness gripped her as she said this. If only they could be there today, in the peace and beauty of the countryside, serving the people of their own village as they had always done.

'Well, if you think you'll be all right,' Aunt Hatt said. 'You needn't get lost – just ask for Chain Street and any-one'll tell you the way. Mrs Sullivan puts our dinner on the table at one o'clock, all right?'

Straw hats on, they set out into the humid morning and the stench and clamour of the streets at the heart of the jewellery quarter.

'Oh, dear – I do feel we're in the way,' Margaret fret-ted. 'We can't stay long, can we?' She felt in every way out of place, a country bumpkin with a gentle West Country accent, not knowing how to go about anything.

'I don't know,' Annie said. 'I think she likes having us – but it would all be so much easier if we had something to do.'

'How can we?' Margaret said. 'There's so much to learn. I can hardly even remember the name of anything Uncle told us about this morning, can you?'

'No!' Annie laughed. 'Never mind – let's just have a look around and see. It's not as busy as yesterday, is it?'

'I've never seen so many people as then,' Margaret agreed.

Margaret was glad of Annie's steadiness, when her

own heart was aflutter with nerves. She felt queasy – partly from having to eat porridge which always turned her up a bit. But this seemed to be how she felt all the time now, shocked and trembling inside, as if she was horribly changed and life could never be the same again.

The streets were not as thronging at eleven in the morning as they had been at going-home time. All the same, there was still plenty happening. They linked arms and walked the blue brick pavements, gazing about them. They passed along Frederick Street, Vittoria Street and Vyse Street, reading the signs and plaques over the doorways, trying to take in the sheer number and variety of trades: the silversmiths and goldsmiths; the factories making buttons of brass, bone and shell; the pen makers, enamellers and die sinkers; the badge makers, spectacle and false-eye makers; the gem setters and engravers and makers of church metalwork. Each street was a warren of doorways, entries, overhead passageways linking buildings with ramshackle parts added on to them and protruding out of them, looking as if they must fall at any moment. The roads were busy with horses and carts.

Margaret felt a rank taste building in her mouth. To walk was to move through smells: here the sudden stench of horse urine, or a pungent acid whiff from the nearby buildings; coal dust forever on the air, horse muck lying on the cobbles with flies swarming over it, and in the heat, which was becoming oppressive, the rot of refuse collecting in the backyards.

Everyone seemed to be in a hurry. Barrows rumbled along the pavements, pushed either by men who seemed impossibly old and bent or boys who appeared just as unfeasibly small, looking like tiny, barefoot men. They saw two lads who had discarded their barrows, the basket containers piled with parcels and bundles, and were setting about each other with their knuckles.

Annie, used to being a Sunday-school teacher and bosser of children, immediately went up to them.

'What d'you think you're doing?' she said. 'That's no way to go on, is it? You stop that and get back to your work!'

'Annie!' Margaret protested, horrified – and too late. 'You can't just . . .'

The boys stopped for a second, bemused. The smaller of the two, perhaps nine years old, was ragged and filthy, a cap on his head at a cock-eyed angle. He moved his jaw, spat into the gutter, shot Annie a look of insolent indifference and the two of them went back to punching each other with renewed enthusiasm.

Annie was not used to people not doing as she said.

'Come away, Annie.' Margaret pulled her arm. 'For goodness' sake, you're not in charge of them.'

Annie glanced back at their barrows. 'I wonder what they've got in there.'

'Whatever it is, it's probably worth a king's ransom,' Margaret laughed. 'No one seems to take any notice!'

For some reason she had enjoyed the boys not doing as Annie said, as if there was a devil in her that warmed to flagrant disobedience in someone else. And, to her surprise, now she had got out, it felt exhilarating walking the streets like this, discovering new things. They had lived in the small village ever since they could remember.

They seemed to be walking towards the edge of the quarter now. The buildings became shoddier. Instead of the ornate, variegated brick buildings with beautiful windows, everything felt more drab and mean and the road was quieter. 'Camden Street', they read, 'Pope Street', 'Craig Street'.

'I think we're going too far,' Margaret said. She had started to feel uneasy.

The eyes of the few people on the street who turned to look at them, strangers in the area, seemed to fix on them with hostility. A woman stood at the end of an alley, leaning against the wall, looking up and down as if waiting for someone. A very old man shuffled along in the distance and another, younger, came along the street supporting himself on a crutch. He had a peg leg and was wincing at every step. His hair was long and straggly, his face unshaven and, Margaret thought with a tense feeling of dread, he looked the worse for drink.

'Good morning,' she said as they passed him, bent over his rough crutch.

He half raised his head and stared at them, saying nothing, but the expression in his eyes chilled her already troubled heart. A cold, male gaze. Like *his* gaze. That look she had once mistaken for love. She wondered if she would ever be able to look into the eyes of a man again. A shudder went through her.

'Annie – let's go back now,' she said, suddenly afraid.

'But look –' Annie was peering along a narrow slit between two buildings. 'All along there are these passages. I want to see what's behind – it must be where people live. These are just the sort of places that Mr Rowntree was writing about.'

'Annie, you can't go intruding on people's privacy!' Margaret said, trying to grasp her sister's arm, but Annie shook her off.

'You just wait there one moment. I'm going to see.'

'Annie, no!' But there was no stopping her. She slipped into the dark passageway, leaving Margaret standing on the corner feeling conspicuous and furious. She lowered her head, hiding in the shade of her hat brim. Why must Annie be so headstrong and arrogant? What did she want with nosing into such places?

After a few moments left waiting there to be stared at by the few passers-by, Margaret thought, I can't just stand here. It seemed easier to follow.

The passageway was like a tunnel through the houses, arched overhead so that the only light was what filtered in each end. As she stepped into it, the air was suddenly cool and dank, even in the summer warmth. The bricks she was walking on were rough and potted with holes. She felt her way carefully so as not to rick an ankle, having to steady herself with her hand on the slimy wall. The passage took her along the length of the building and she soon joined Annie, who had paused at the far end.

'Oh, my goodness,' she whispered.

The alley opened into a yard, its atmosphere so overcast and sunless that it felt almost like dusk even at midday. Never in her life before had she seen so cheerless a place. All along one side were the doorways of small, shabby houses built up against a wall and all facing a blank, soot-encrusted wall the other side. There were slates missing from the sagging roofs, windows broken or boarded up. One had no door, only a gaping black hole for an entrance. Several washing lines were suspended across with a few items hanging limply from them. There was a tilted lamp in the middle of the uneven bricks. At the far end they could see some other low buildings, an upended barrel standing in front of them. A rank smell drifted from somewhere. No one was about in the yard. Everything looked and smelt mean and demoralizing.

'Come away,' Margaret said. She pulled Annie's hand and the two of them hurried back to the street, which felt like another world of light.

'There must be yards like this all along behind here,' Annie said. Even she seemed sobered by what they had found. 'You'd never know they were there, would you, unless you went in? I wonder if the whole city is full of places like that?'

Margaret looked along the street, imagining the dank yards crammed in behind the frontage facing them.

'How do people live?' she said as they walked away. The place had oppressed her. 'Even the washing was grey with soot.' She thought of their washing line in the garden at home, the clothes billowing in the fresh country wind.

'How can souls flourish in a place like this?' Annie said. 'It's bad enough in Watery Lane.'

In the worst and poorest lane in the village, the water level rose during the winter months so that the path became a stream or a swamp of sucking mud. The cottages were damp, their thatch covered in moss and mould, and the inhabitants and their children were afflicted by coughs and wheezing chests. But on summer days it could look quite pleasant and even Watery Lane felt cheerful compared with the yard they had seen.

The girls walked side by side in silence. Margaret felt a sense of despair wash through her at the enormity of the Lord's calling. Were they not charged to bring the word of Jesus to all people in this wretched world? It was enough of an uphill struggle in a small village, where she had usually felt unequal to the task. Where did anyone begin in this dark warren of Birmingham streets?

Annie, walking fast, her head down, did not share her sister's despair. God had brought her here for a reason, she knew. Her father and mother had met through the Congregationalist Church and God had been the air they breathed through their upbringing. William Hanson, their father, had spoken to them of the work of Quaker See-bohm Rowntree, the clarion call he had sent up about the poverty on which he had reported in York. His book, *Poverty: A Study of Town Life*, sat on their father's shelves.

Their parents' work, Annie knew, was God's work: the work of souls as well as material welfare. And Annie was sure she had a mission in life. She knew right from wrong. She knew the word of the Lord and it was her life's work to take it to others. Any quarrel she had was with her father, and the puritan gloom and rigidity into which he had sunk after their mother's death – not with God.

I have to find a way of meeting people and being able to talk to them, she thought. If the Lord is to use me in his work, I need to know their lives – what it is that blights them, how they are wrong and sinful in their ideas, how they might be saved . . .

As they headed back the way they had come, Annie looked around her more carefully, full of a passionate zeal. She stopped suddenly, her attention caught by a sign on the wall next to the entrance of an imposing and decoratively built factory. Along its frontage, of varie-gated colours of brick, curlicue lettering announced 'Masters, Hogg & Co., Steel Pen Works'. The hand-painted sign read 'Stampers and piercers wanted'.

This was it. She stood for several seconds. Surely this was the Lord speaking to her, calling her to follow . . .

'I'm going to see,' she announced to Margaret, and before Margaret could grab hold of her, Annie, looking as bold as she dared, an elf in her neat black boots, was already tip-tapping up the steps.

'Annie – don't be ridiculous!' Margaret was aghast. Now what was the wretched girl doing!

But Annie was already disappearing inside. In the dark entrance hall, she felt suddenly small and girded herself with thoughts of Daniel walking into the den with a lion. Of David and Goliath.

'Yes?' A man's head appeared at a hatch in the wall.

'I've come about a job,' she said, as boldly as she dared. She was suddenly aware that her well-spoken voice, slightly tinged with West Country, must sound out of place, but he did not react. He was picking at his teeth with a little stick and his pouchy eyes regarded her in silence, seeming wholly unimpressed by this announcement. At last, after a period of cogitation, he removed the toothpick from his mouth and said, 'Done it before?'

'No – but I'm sure I could learn. I've only just come to Birmingham.' Annie felt foolish now, but was damned if she was going to show it. Haughtily, she added, 'Is there someone else I should apply to?'

Again, he stood looking at her for such a long time that she wondered if he had been suddenly struck dumb. Eventually he straightened up.

'Come in tomorrow. If ye're unskilled, Miss Hinks'll start yer on stamping. Eight sharp.'

As she went to go out into the street, a bell rang and there came a sudden sound like a wave breaking behind her. A tide of feet were descending stairs somewhere in the building and as she emerged to the street which was now thronging with dinner-time busyness, women began to pour out past her, through the door. She barely got a look at any of them as they were all rushing so fast. She just had an impression of drab clothes and a variety of faces, all pale, of varying ages, all intent on getting out of the building. Annie managed to move out of the way and found Margaret pressed against the wall, trying not to be pushed along by the surge of people.

'I'm starting tomorrow!' she cried, in triumph.

'But Annie, you've never done any such work before.' Aunt Hatt looked disturbed and cross at this news.

'I told him I'm a fast learner,' Annie said. 'He said there's nothing to it – I'll be stamping out pen nibs.'

'I know it's unskilled work, but they have to work very fast – your fingers'll be cut to ribbons.'

'I want to try it,' Annie insisted. 'And Uncle did say he wanted us to work. We'll be in the way otherwise, won't we?'

Aunt Hatt did not argue with this, but her eyes were full of doubt.

'Well,' she conceded. 'I can see you're a determined young madam so on your head be it. Everyone's got to start somewhere. If you're no good, you'll be out. But I really don't know what your mother would have said.'

'I'm sure Mother would have said it'd do us good to see a bit of life,' Annie argued. Their grandfather, Mother and Eb's father, had been a jewel setter a few streets away and Leah – or Lilian – had started her working life in his workshop. 'She said honest work never did her any harm.'

Aunt Hatt stared back. There was not much she could say to argue with this.

By that evening, their arrival the day before seemed years ago to Margaret. They all sat round the table for the evening meal and Uncle Eb chuckled heartily at the news that Annie had gone and found herself a job.

'Well – you're a one, aren't you?' He looked at Annie with amused admiration. 'There's still the offer of a job for you here, Margaret,' he said. 'I could do with one more polisher out the back!'

Margaret blushed, not knowing what she should say.

'Oh, leave her alone, Eb,' Aunt Hatt said. 'Our Margaret's too delicate for this sort of thing. I can find her plenty to do without that. We're rushed off our feet in the office.'

Margaret looked up to see her aunt looking very directly at her along the table. 'I thought, Margaret, that perhaps you and I could have a little talk when we've finished our tea?'

Margaret's chest tightened and she felt her face burn with embarrassment. The thought of having to talk about what had happened filled her with horror. She would have to say *something* to Aunt Hatt. Their aunt was being so kind. She looked down, giving a faint nod.

During their meal Aunt Hatt held forth on her two favourite subjects: her grandson Jimmy and the decoration of the new house, both things, they were soon learning, she could talk about almost endlessly. And to Margaret's surprise, once they had finished their meal Uncle Eb, who, she had the impression, would usually have sat on at the table smoking his pipe, got to his feet and left the room, with a rumbling sort of announcement that he was 'Off out for a bit . . .'

'Is Uncle going to a meeting?' Annie asked, this being the only kind of evening outing with which they were familiar.

'Oh,' Aunt Hatt said, seeming amused. 'You might say that. He's off to the Jewellers' Arms – his favourite watering hole. Quite a bit of business goes on in there, though, so it's a meeting of sorts!'

Neither Margaret nor Annie was sure what to say to this. Annie got to her feet, pushed her chair under the table and said she was going upstairs. As she passed behind her, Margaret felt her sister's hand on her shoulder for a second. The hand gave her a squeeze before leaving the room. Margaret was warmed by Annie's tact and support, even though she had driven her mad earlier in the day. Annie often knew to do just the right thing even if she argued about everything else.

The room settled. The clock ticked. Aunt Harriet cleared her throat and poured herself another cup of tea, offering Margaret one, but she shook her head.

She sat, head bent, hands clasped on the cloth, and stared at the frayed grey cuffs of her dress. She couldn't do it, she knew. The very idea of having to find words to describe the shameful thing that had happened was utterly beyond her, however kind Aunt Hatt was.

'It's really nothing much, Aunt,' she said. 'You've seen what Annie's like. She's very headstrong and . . . Well, we had a bit of a falling-out with Father and we thought it might be best if we were out of the way for a while, that's all. And we've always so much wanted to get to know you both as well.'

Her cheeks burned with remorse at the inadequacy of this explanation, but it was all she could manage. She looked up to see Aunt Hatt eyeing her over her teacup. Clearly, her aunt strongly suspected she was not hearing the whole truth.

But she put the cup down and said, 'Well – it's lovely to have you here. We never had any daughters, dear. I had a difficult time with that side of things – one of my great regrets. So you've no fear of not being welcome. But if you'll be staying a little while, we'd better get you both settled in with summat to do, hadn't we?'

Later, Harriet Watts climbed into bed beside her beerily snoozing husband.

'That all seemed a bit serious,' Eb murmured as his wife arranged the covers over herself, throwing the eiderdown off. He lumped about, turning on his back and yawning loudly. 'She tell you what's been going on? Can't be anything that bad in that house of virtue, surely?'

'I can't exactly say she did,' Hatt said.

'What d'yer mean?' He spoke through another yawn. 'What's the problem?'

'I don't know.' She settled on her back, sounding uneasy. 'Whatever it is, she wasn't letting on. Said summat about a falling-out with their father.'

'Oh – that old stick.'

'He wasn't so bad – not in the beginning,' Hatt said. 'I think it was that babby dying, little John. His only son – and then Lil, of course.'

'Yes.' Eb sighed. 'All the same – our Lil changed once she was with him.'

'She was a lovely lady – you know she was. Even then.'

Eb sighed. 'All that religious claptrap. You know what I say about—'

'Yes, dear, I do. Every time.'

He chuckled, hands starting to explore the warm, soft body beside him. In a wheedling voice, he said, 'Come on, Hatt – as we're both so wide awake. D'yer fancy a bit of – you know . . . ?'

'No, Ebenezer Watts, I don't,' Hatt said, firmly removing a wandering hand. 'It's late enough already and we've got to be up early.'

'Never mind. It won't take—'

'Eb – *no*.'

There was another defeated sigh from beside her, as her husband gradually sank back into sleep.

Seven

The West Country, 1887

There were hushed conversations in the passage outside Mother's room: Lucy the maid and Mrs Berry, the lady who delivered Annie to the world, their heads close together. They did not know that Margaret, aged two, could hear, tucked just inside the next room.

'I don't know if it'll survive, it's that small.'

'It?'

'A little girl. Scrawny as a rabbit.'

Days later, on a breezy April morning, Margaret gazed into the pram, hungry to see her new little sister. In her memory she was looking down from a great height. Mother must have picked her up to let her see.

'There you are, lovey-dove – your baby sister, Annie,' their mother said. 'She's had a bit of a time of it, but she's here – and one day she'll be able to get up and play with you.'

Margaret saw the tiny, mauve face of her sister, cradled under the billowing elm leaves behind the modest house attached to the Zion chapel, to which they had recently moved and of which her father was minister.

Leah, their mother, spent what seemed hours holding her tiny child. And Annie survived like fury.

'She's a little fighter,' Mother said happily. 'We shall all need to look out.'

Their brother John was born in the summer of 1891 and was a sunny, easygoing little boy.

Annie, despite her astonishing appetite, always remained a miniature, wiry version of the other, more substantial, members of the family. Of all of them, she was the one who seemed to have endless energy and was seldom ill. Their father called her 'our miracle, our little sprite'. Margaret had always felt large and stolid in comparison. Her health was more fragile and she was more afraid of life.

Margaret did not remember their move to the village and the Zion chapel, a small backwater of Congregationalist service. Nor did she remember her father before that time, or what had changed. Only as she grew older did she begin to pick up the threads of history.

William Hanson and Lilian Watts had met when he was serving as an assistant at Carrs Lane church in the centre of Birmingham. Lilian, the youngest and only member of the Watts family to have her soul lit by religion, attended the church. She was employed by her jeweller father at that time, in Regent Place. Soon after they became close, William – Annie and Margaret's tall, good-looking father – had been moved to a mission on the Tottenham Court Road in London, from where he had wooed their mother with heartfelt letters. The two of them married and continued to work in London, where Lilian changed her name to Leah; it seemed to have been a symbol of her commitment to her faith.

Soon after Margaret was born, when her father was in his early thirties, he had suffered a breakdown – some sort of crisis. The church elders had deemed it sensible to send him to somewhere quieter, a village deep in the countryside, where he could restore himself. And after that, they had never sent him anywhere else.

Margaret had always known that her father was sensitive, fragile in emotion and crushingly hard on himself. He was a man of urgent convictions of black versus white, right versus wrong. It was their mother who could laugh at things – how could she not, being a Watts? – and keep a balance, a flexibility more characteristic of Congregationalism. She seemed less in dread of the wrath of God which seemed to pursue her troubled husband. Leah was in awe of William and always deferred to him as a good Christian wife. But Margaret remembered her mother's religion as that of service and kindness to others, of light and laughter, rather than the need to purge her soul.

They grew up as a happy household then – outward-looking and kind. Margaret idolized her father. He was a tall, striking man, wide-shouldered from his childhood labouring on a farm. It was in his father's Shropshire fields that he had first experienced the strange visions which had made him so certain of being chosen by God. Every Sunday he stood in the high pulpit, urgently entreating his congregation of villagers and farmers to the path of righteousness. So far as Margaret was concerned, he was the source of all direction and rightness. She saw how he spent himself to do good. And she even looked like him, with his large grey eyes and wide, upturned mouth which gave him a permanently amiable look and tempered his severity.

The family prayed together. Leah read to her children as they grew and all of them were vividly affected by Dr Barnardo's book *The Children's Treasury and Advocate* of the Homeless and Destitute, full of inspiring stories. As soon as they were old enough, they taught in the Sunday school, visited the sick and troubled in the area and went to the village school.

It was only John who, had he lived long enough, would have been sent away to the Congregationalist school at Caterham. There were such schools for girls, but their mother refused to let them go.

'I can't see any point in having children if you're just going to send them all away,' she told her husband. 'It's bad enough sending John, but I want my girls close to me – they can learn plenty here and make up their minds where the Lord calls them to.'

So all this particular hope was invested in the boy. Margaret remembered the terrible sense of anguish which laid itself upon the house when John died of a fever at the age of three. They all ached with missing the sweet-natured little boy, but it was William Hanson who seemed to take it as a personal affront, a challenge to the force of his commitment. He became more silent and severe.

Annie, as she grew older, thrived on teaching. She had a towering personality and was happy to boss and command even when a number of the village children were nearly twice her size. Margaret liked the company of children. She was gentler and more hesitant, but she did her part, with Bible stories and nature walks. She wondered whether she should be a missionary teacher. They grew up with the idea that they were supposed to be something and when God had decided what that was, He would deliver His message.

Their mother fell ill before the Christmas of 1898. The doctor called every day, treading softly as his patient lay on white pillows, the nightcap sliding from her greying hair as she twisted restlessly. Her lungs heaved and rattled. She took the girls' hands and smiled at them, hardly able to speak.

When the pneumonia stopped her breath, it doused the family's joyful flame for good.

Margaret was thirteen, Annie eleven. Their father became silent, forbidding. He employed a housekeeper, Alice Lamb, a straightforward woman from the congregation who, in her late forties, was grieving her own lack of husband and family. The minister's children were never a substitute she could love as her own but she did her best at least to feed and clothe and pay attention to them.

William Hanson wrapped the Lord about him. But he seldom seemed to feel any joy. Margaret, sensing all his sorrow and being in awe of her father, tried to reach him by pleasing him.

'Father – would you like a little walk down by the river?' she might ask on a Saturday afternoon. 'The air would do you good.'

She would walk with him, trying to get him to talk to her. He strode in his long black coat, head bowed, hands clasped behind his back. Sometimes he spoke about his calling as a youth, standing in a summer field and feeling the mantle of God falling upon him.

'I knew,' was all he would say. That kind of knowing would brook no argument. 'I felt God's presence and I knew I dared not refuse.'

She would ask him things – about the grandparents in Shropshire that they had never known, about the Bible. Things which would please and soothe him.

But as the years passed, he became more rigid. Graces

at mealtimes grew longer; he could not bear the girls to wear bright colours and insisted they reduce their clothing to seemly grey and black and read only religious books on a Sunday. He became overbearing and flew into a rage at the slightest sign of anyone crossing him – as, increasingly, Annie did.

'What can possibly be wrong with me reading George Eliot?' Annie argued. 'You couldn't find a more moral storyteller if you tried.' She would sneak off to hidden corners to indulge in the novels she loved while Margaret felt duty bound to stay in with *The Pilgrim's Progress* or Foxe's *Book of Martyrs*.

'How does he always know what God wants?' Annie often grumbled. 'I can pray just as well as he can.'

As they grew older, Annie's clashes with their father increased by the year.

Eight

When Margaret was fifteen, she fell ill, an ordinary sickness at first, a fever and bad chest. But even once the worst had past and she should have been fresh and on her feet again, she could not seem to reach a point of feeling well.

'I'm so tired all the time,' she kept saying. 'But I just can't sleep.'

School became a torment of headaches, of a cloudiness in the head making it impossible to think or remember things and a desperate struggle to keep awake over a page of arithmetic or a reading of Greek myths. The slightest exertion exhausted her. Eventually she had to stay at home. Day after day there was the same dreary sense of unwellness and aches and pains, of fogginess, of being unable to sleep while being bone tired, so that she would lie there, wide-eyed, for hours while the rest of the household slept, then be unable to wake in the morning.

Her father came and prayed at her bedside, trying to exercise patience. But she also remembered lying in bed, the curtains drawn as the light hurt her eyes, and being so limp that she could barely move. Her father was pacing her and Annie's room, still in his outdoor boots. He had come in from some errand in the village and the sight of her shrouded room had sparked rage in him.

'We've all had quite enough of this, Margaret. It's not like you to be so self-indulgent! I don't want to see you lying in that bed again. Renew your prayers! Ask for God's help, and strength will be granted you. Come along –' He stripped back the bedclothes, baring her legs which she found mortifying, and seized hold of her hand, his eyes blazing at her in the gloom. 'I say to thee – pick up thy bed and walk!'

He hauled her to her feet and she did her very best to obey him, her legs shaking.

'Now get yourself dressed and come downstairs. Discipline yourself. I don't want to see you languishing up here again.'

Through her fog of unwellness, she managed to dress painfully slowly and get down the stairs. When Annie came in from school at dinner time, she found Margaret collapsed on the couch, fast asleep again.

The sickness dragged on for three years, swallowing up her young life. The only people she saw were Alice Lamb and her family. She had not the strength even to attend church and began to be nervous of going out.

Despite her father's remonstrations and the baffled attempts of the village doctor who suggested tonics, she just could not seem to get moving. Unlike Annie who was almost always full of an electric energy.

In gentler moods, her father would sit and read to her. They were sweet times. He would fold himself into the little wicker chair beside her bed, one long leg crossed over the other. She could feel his worry and care. They would say a prayer, he might read to her from scripture or some other improving book. (Annie read to her from different, more exciting books.) And sometimes she could not help weeping in despair.

After she had been ill for two years, Annie, ever sharp,

said one day, 'I think it's that you're sheltering from the world.' It was not said in accusation. Annie was fifteen by then. The two of them spent a lot of time in each other's company, were each other's mother as well as sister. 'One day, you'll just emerge – like Lazarus.'

'I'm not dead,' Margaret whispered.

'That's not what I meant,' Annie said, sitting on the edge of her bed. 'I just mean, you'll get better. As if you're in a box and you have to find where the handle is to get out.'

Annie's energy and force of belief could make her believe it too and Margaret tried to cling to that. Some days though, it felt as if that time would never come. Her sentence of illness entered its third year. She was a young woman, soon to be eighteen, and still confined to her childhood bed.

'Father,' she sobbed to him one afternoon. 'I long so much to do the Lord's work, like you. But how can I know what He wants when I am like this?'

Her father was silent for a moment. His leg moved gently, rhythmically, as if he was trying to think what to say.

'The Lord works in mysterious ways, Margaret,' he began wearily.

But all the frustration and disappointment which she usually tried to accept or hide came pouring out to her father, whom she had seen as her pattern, her friend. She railed against this narrow, invalid life to which she had been reduced when she felt she surely must be called to much more. All her life she had been told that there would be a calling!

'I thought I was to be a missionary,' she wept. 'I want to be like you, Father. I am ready – my mind and my heart. But my body fails me all the time. And I'm so tired of it.'

To her astonishment, her father did something he had never done before. He reached across and took her hand in his huge, warm one. It was a while before he said anything. She heard him swallow several times and she had the awe-inspiring realization that he was trying not to weep himself.

'My dear,' he managed eventually, in a choked voice. 'My own life has not run smoothly in the ways I thought the Lord wanted for me. That is how I came to be in this . . . in this place, doing the Lord's work among simple country people.' He added swiftly, 'People who, of course, are God's children as much as any other.'

Margaret realized then the extent of her father's disappointment; that the word he had managed not to say was probably 'backwater'. He had regarded himself as destined for the great city missions, but he had not the constitution for it. Something in him, as a younger man, had broken down and the Church authorities had never thought him strong enough to be moved again.

'I know your sister is likely to be destined for the missions.' He gave a faint chuckle. 'I had hopes for John, of course . . .' He looked down for a moment, but then raised his head, his mouth turning up. 'Annie seems to have the constitution of an ox and is full of certainty.' He looked into her eyes and she was moved by the emotion in them. Never in her life had she loved her poor father so much or felt so close to him. 'Perhaps some of us have to walk the quieter paths, where the trumpets of glory are heard but dimly.'

She still could not see him as having failed as he seemed to feel he had. She lay looking at him, this tall man who loomed so central in her life, and her eyes were full of love.

Her father laid his free hand on her forehead. 'I pray hourly for your healing,' he said. 'Try and believe that all shall be well, my dear child. The Lord loves you abundantly and so do I.'

As he left the room, she let the tears run down her cheeks.

Soon after her eighteenth birthday, she began to feel a little improved. Having been shut away for so long in the house, she was frail, nervous of going out and uncertain of everything.

Annie, now sixteen, had completed her schooling and was busy in the village – Sunday school, running a Bible class, visiting and helping. She was already chafing to get away, a free spirit who argued with their father over almost every point, and seemed sure that some great mission awaited her.

Margaret had lost any certainty she ever had. Even walking along the lane that summer, trying to regain strength in her legs, seemed a challenge. She felt a floating sense that everything in life was unsure; her own being – even God – and it frightened her. No other option had ever been shown to her than marriage or the missions and there seemed no one she could ask or with whom she could share her uncertainty and loneliness. She ached for her mother. The only things she could do, she decided, were to remain obedient and pray and all would be revealed to her.

That summer, one evening when the three of them were seated around the tea table, their father announced that an assistant was to join him to work beside him in the church.

'His name is Charles Barber,' William Hanson told them. Margaret could hear a tremor of suppressed emotion in his voice that startled her. 'He is a young minister who has been working in Salford. But lately, he has been struggling.'

'A crisis of faith?' Annie asked, not beating about the bush.

'Annie,' her father said sternly. 'When Mr Barber comes, you must be gentle with him.'

'I will,' Annie said, spreading butter energetically on her bread. 'I only asked what was wrong.'

'I believe it is something like that, yes,' their father said austerely. He seemed uncomfortable discussing it. 'So far as I have heard, he has been working very hard and is feeling the strain. They have sent him here for a quieter ministry for a time.' He told them that a Mr and Mrs Davis, members of the congregation whose sons had now left home, and who lived nearby, had offered to let Charles Barber lodge with them.

'He will be arriving this weekend,' William Hanson said. 'And I know you will do all you can to care for him and make him welcome.'

Nine

August 1904

Annie was downstairs by seven the next morning. Her whole body felt electric with nervous excitement. Her job started today – she was to be a worker in God's vineyard, an explorer of social conditions like Dr Barnardo and Mr Rowntree. It felt as though her real life was beginning at last!

Uncle Eb had been up a good while, busy with the furnace in the cellar under the workshop, preparing the gold for working. His clothes gave off an acrid whiff of smoke and chemicals.

'So,' he said as they all stood crowded into the kitchen which smelt of the porridge bubbling gently on the range. 'Off to work for Messrs Masters and Hogg then, eh? Very wealthy men of the city, those two. Very fine house that Mr Masters has, out towards Worcester, I believe – comes into the works in a top hat in his own carriage. And I believe Mr Hogg has got a fine collection of paintings in his country mansion.'

Annie heard the admiration in his voice for these two successful manufacturers, but it seemed to her that Uncle Eb was laughing at her. There was a definite gleam of amusement in his eyes and she was not sure she liked this.

'Don't you think it's a good idea?' she asked, rather pertly.

'Oh, I do, I do,' he agreed, holding his hands up as if to defend himself. But again, there was a teasing note in his voice.

'Well, *he* might think so – but I'm not so sure,' Aunt Hatt said, pouring water into the teapot, steam billowing round her. 'I don't know what you want to go and work in a place like that for. You won't find it easy, I can tell you. But if you're that set on it, you'll have to see for yourself.' She turned, holding out a bowl. 'Go and sit down. Sugar on your porridge?'

'Salt, please,' Annie said, settling at the table.

'You can come out at dinner time if you like,' Aunt Hatt said. 'You're not too far away. Or I can get Margaret to bring your dinner over to you. That might be best.'

Annie was startled. She had not thought about these practicalities. Aunt Hatt stood over her in her apron, arms folded, her lovely face rather stern.

'You'll have to step out and get it off her. They won't just have anyone wandering into the works.'

'Have you worked in a pen factory?' Annie asked, hurriedly eating her porridge. The last thing she wanted was to be late on her first day.

'No,' Aunt Hatt said, with an air of being a cut above that sort of thing. 'Of course I haven't. I worked for my father, God rest him. But I know one or two who have. I just hope you can keep up.'

Of course I'll be able to keep up! Annie fumed inwardly. When in her life had she not been able to keep up with something? But she held these thoughts to herself. Aunt Hatt was still standing looking solemnly at her.

'It's not going to be the life you're used to, you know.'

'I *know*, Aunt,' Annie said, trying to hide her irritation. That was what she wanted – a life that she was not used to! Demurely, she said, 'I'll do my best, though.'

She had dressed in her oldest grey frock and black shoes, carelessly combed her hair back into a low bunch on her neck and plonked her hat on. When she stepped outside the house, she found that the weather had changed. It was cooler, the sky a heavy grey over the rooftops, the streets wet and mucky beneath the many feet that were moving along them.

She was standing on the step of number twenty-six Chain Street, when Jack Sidwell appeared out of the sea of unfamiliar faces, at high speed, turning to come into the house.

'Oh!' He was so startled to find her standing there that he almost fell back down the step and had to recover himself. He pulled his cap off, revealing tousled blond hair. 'I, er . . . Morning!'

'Good morning,' Annie said pertly.

Jack stood.

'Did you want to come in?' She stepped out of the way.

'Er . . . I . . . Yes.' He fled past her and she heard his feet hurrying up the stairs.

Annie stood tall and took a breath of the smoke-filled air. *I must put upon me the armour of God, that I may be able to stand against the wiles of the devil . . .*

Full of a sense of responsibility for making disciples of all nations, she stepped out into the bustle of the street. Most people had their heads down, hurrying towards the working day. There were carts halted at various points along the road and the crowds poured past them like water.

Thine is the Kingdom, the power and the glory . . .

The Masters, Hogg & Co. manufactory seemed a bigger, even more imposing place than she remembered. By the time she arrived a soft rain was beginning to fall. Everything appeared doused in grey; the entrance was thronging with people trying to get inside out of the wet and for a few seconds Annie's bullish confidence began to ebb away. She was used to being a queen bee, but here there were so many people, all strangers, that she felt suddenly small and defenceless. How was she to manage and where was she supposed to go?

Nearby she saw a gentle-looking young woman standing aside from a group of others who were cracking jokes in what seemed to Annie rough, intimidating voices. Going up to the girl, she said quietly, 'I'm new today. Can you tell me where I'm supposed to go?'

'D'yer know which room ye're in?'

Annie shook her head.

'I'll take yer to Miss Hinks,' the girl said. ''Er'll tell yer.'

She delivered Annie inside where there was another girl waiting to start work that day; skinny and frail looking, the same height as Annie. She looked anxious, dark rings under her sad-looking blue eyes and mousey hair scrailed up into a bun.

Miss Hinks, their forewoman, was a gaunt, unsmiling person, an apron tied over her straight black skirt. She already seemed to know the other girl and called her Lizzie, though not with any particular friendliness.

'So – you've not done press work before?' Miss Hinks asked Annie in a sharp tone.

Annie was about to announce that she was sure she could pick it up in no time, but for once feeling compelled to be humble, admitted, 'No.'

'Right. Come with me then.'

She walked off, clearly expecting them to follow, up a stone staircase and into a long upper corridor which echoed with the sound of many women hurrying along it. Through its high, arched windows, Annie could see that this factory, one of the bigger ones in the area, occupied three sides of a rectangle. In the yard enclosed by its walls was a small building with a clock facing her, which now said five to eight. Close to it soared a brick chimney, a flag of smoke coming from it; beyond, other chimneys of the nearby works were belching out thick swirls of filth. She remembered their train journey into Birmingham, the way the countryside had died away, built over by a seemingly endless vista of factories and smoking chimneys until the train was so shut in between them that all they could see was blackened walls and, occasionally, a glimpse, for a second, of a ribbon of canal winding between them.

A moment later they entered a long room, beams arching across the ceiling and windows all along one wall through which fell the morning's dull light. There were benches down both sides with rows of cast-iron machines, each with a handle on one side and a ball counterweight at the other, similar to the ones she had seen in Uncle Eb's workshop. Each had a stool positioned by it, on which the women were in the process of settling themselves in front of their machines.

'Come along here,' Miss Hinks instructed.

Annie could sense heads turning to stare at them but she did not meet anyone's eyes to see if they looked friendly or hostile. She heard one woman whisper, 'Hello, Lizzie – how's your mother?' Lizzie was slightly behind her and Annie did not hear the reply.

'Here you are – you can work here.' There were two machines, side by side, with no one seated at them.

A moment later, the clock struck eight and a bell rang. Annie was aware of movement, like a sudden rustling of trees, followed by a metallic clatter, then thumps and bangs as the women around them started working the presses. She only had a second to glance, because Miss Hinks was starting to tell her and Lizzie what to do. But in that second her confidence that she would learn easily, that she would certainly be better at the job than this little worn-out rag of a girl Lizzie, began to slip.

The women were pushing something into the press, stamping it, spitting it out and starting on another at such speed that it was as if the work was a natural part of the movement of their bodies, like breathing or walking, which could be done without thought or effort.

Dear Lord, Annie thought, a knot of dread tightening in her belly. How on earth do they do that so *quickly*?

She and Lizzie stood as Miss Hinks instructed on one of the machines. She could see that Lizzie already seemed familiar with the work.

'These are blanking presses.' Miss Hinks nodded towards the nearest black iron machine on the bench. They looked much like the presses in Uncle Eb's workshop, with a round counterweight at the other end of the handle. She directed her instructions mainly at Annie, and went over to pick up a flat strip of metal. 'So what we're doing is pressing out blanks to make the nibs. Some are brass and some steel – these ones are steel. You press out the shape of the nib like this.'

She laid the strip in the machine and tugged the handle briefly back and forth and showed them the nib-shaped hole in the strip.

'Keep 'em as close together as you can – the less scrap left the better.' She picked up the remains of a strip, showing them the thin metal lacework remaining after as many blanks as possible had been cut from it. 'The blanks drop down into here.' Reaching under the machine, she pulled out a flat, nib-shaped piece of metal and handed it to Annie. It was rough at the edges and felt almost weightless in her hand.

'These ladies,' she waved an arm towards the feverishly stamping women all about them, 'can cut out a hundred and twenty or more of these a minute when they're really going. There's some can do a hundred and sixty a minute.'

Annie stared at her. 'That *can't* be possible.'

'Oh,' Miss Hinks's expression grew a fraction grimmer, 'it's possible. For them that are used to it. Any road – your quota's thirty-six thousand in your shift – you won't make that today, nor tomorrow neither. If you still can't make it in a week or two you'll be out that door, all right?'

Annie's mind was calculating furiously. Thirty-six thousand a day! That was . . . Nine hours, so in an hour it would be four thousand . . . Per minute, sixty-six . . . Still more than one a second on average, but at least not as bad as one hundred and twenty . . .

'Most of this lot're on piecework,' Miss Hinks was saying. 'Which you won't be until you've got quicker at it. You'll be on eight shillings a week to start. So –' Her face softened fractionally. 'You two're lambs to the slaughter today.'

Annie did not like to admit that she did not know what piecework was. But another problem had already presented itself.

'Go on, then – have a go,' Miss Hinks ordered.

'I'm sorry,' Annie confessed, as Lizzie went to her press. 'But I'm not sure I can. I'm left-handed.'

'Well, why dain't yer say so?' Miss Hinks said, rolling her eyes. 'You all right, Lizzie? Wait there,' she said to Annie. 'I'll have to fetch someone to turn it round for yer.'

Annie stood feeling foolish as Lizzie began work. She already seemed to know what to do and have a feel for it. All the other women were thumping away, managing to chat to each other at the same time, and there was a busy hum in the room.

'What's up wi' you then?' The woman the other side of her seemed very old to Annie, as well as very stout, and her voice sounded aggressive. Her face reminded Annie of a big angry dog's. Several of her teeth were missing and her tone was not friendly.

'I'm left-handed,' Annie said.

'Ooh, left-handed,' the woman mocked.

'My old man's left-'anded,' someone said from the other side of the room.

'I 'ope 'e's good with both 'is 'ands, bab, whatever 'anded 'e is!' the first woman cackled, all the while working at the speed of a turbine.

'Dirty girl, Doris!' the other woman called back amiably. 'That's what you are. Dirty-minded.'

Annie looked down, her cheeks flaming. She was not

entirely sure if she had guessed what the woman meant but she had a nasty feeling she had. She was not sure how to deal with any of this.

'Ooh – brought a blush to yer cheeks, 'ave I, bab?' Doris said, in a rude, mocking tone which Annie did not like. She chose to ignore her.

'Don't you mind 'er,' the other woman called over. ''Er don't mean no harm. New to it, are yer, bab?'

'Yes,' Annie admitted.

'You'll soon pick it up – nothing to it.'

Lizzie looked round at Annie and rolled her eyes. But she gave a little smile.

'You wanna keep yer eye on the job, Lizzie Poole,' Doris shouted to her. 'Or you'll 'ave the end of yer finger off. And that goes for you an' all,' she nodded at Annie.

Miss Hinks appeared with a middle-aged man at her side and all the chatter quietened down. In a few skilled movements, screwing and unscrewing bits of the press, he had converted the handle to the other side.

'There yer go, bab. Left-handed press,' he said, rushing off before she could thank him.

Annie, fumblingly, copied what Lizzie was doing, with Miss Hinks peering over her shoulder. It was not too difficult, but she felt unexpectedly overawed by the thought of how fast the other women were working.

'Well,' Miss Hinks said in an unimpressed way that punctured Annie's pride, 'you'll do, I s'pose. You're going to have to get quicker than that, though.'

Lizzie, who had deft little fingers, seemed to fare better. As Annie struggled to get going, she could feel her cheeks burning with humiliation. She was used to being the one telling other people what to do and being the fastest and cleverest at everything!

'Rules're on the door. Work starts at eight, and two

after dinner. That's when they shut the doors. If you're late it's a penny stopped from your wages.'

Annie wished Miss Hinks had chosen to tell her all this before she tried to operate the press at the same time. She half listened, struggling to take in the information.

'Dinner at one. Lavs are down in the yard. Only for in the break. I'll show you how to weigh your work in later – that's if you have any,' she said acidly. 'You can read the rest for yourself. On you go then.'

Lizzie already seemed to be pressing out the blanks as if she had been doing it all her life. Annie set to, at first trembling with the effort to hurry, inserting the metal strip and cutting blanks from each end of it until the metal ran out. Her little box of nib blanks seemed to be filling terribly slowly. She was concentrating so hard that she was barely aware of what any of the women were saying around her, which she soon realized was just as well. Any thought of finding energy to preach the word while she was working had been pushed right out of her head. At this moment she had far more basic things to worry about!

She eyed Lizzie, who was definitely working faster. The girl must have felt her look and she glanced back, a faint smile lifting the anxious set of her face. This warmed Annie, who was already wondering what she had done by coming here. She felt as if she had been fed into a huge, devouring production machine with which she would never be able to keep up. And the fragments of talk which reached her were of a character far riper than she was used to. Five hours stretched ahead of her until Margaret was to come to the gates with her dinner. It felt like an eternity.

I'm not going to let this beat me, she thought, clenching her jaw. If this is the first of God's challenges, I must not fall at the first hurdle. She was sure there was something immense she was meant to do. And her competitive spirit did not want to be beaten by all these women around her, some not much different from her in age. A hundred and sixty a minute? It seemed beyond imagining. Even a hundred and twenty – two every second! But it had set light to her determination. All she had to do was get to seventy-five a minute, and she was damn well going to show them she could work as well as anyone!

Ten

'How did she seem?' Aunt Hatt asked when Margaret returned, having delivered a dish of stew to the entrance of Masters, Hogg & Co.

'Well – she looked all right,' Margaret said, doubtfully. 'She was more interested in eating than talking.'

'She won't know what's hit her in there,' Aunt Hatt observed. She sounded concerned, but added with a laugh, 'She's a character, that one, I must say.'

Margaret gave a wan smile. 'She's that, all right.'

She was worried for her stubborn little sister, but Annie had not said much except that she was *starving* and that work finished at six. She looked pale and tense and Margaret saw that she had a lot of little nicks on her fingers, one or two even bleeding. Annie seized on the bottle of water and the plate of stew and potatoes that Margaret had carried to her, and ate it there and then, pressed against the wall of the factory, and not seeming to care who saw her as the seething dinner-time crowds jostled past.

In any case, they had other things to think about. Soon after Annie left that morning, Aunt Hatt had handed Margaret an envelope addressed to 'The Misses Hanson'. With a jolt, Margaret saw their father's hand-writing. She ran up to the attic and read it perched on the side of the bed, tears running down her cheeks. Every-thing in her life that had seemed so certain had been shaken at its very foundations and the pain of it had crouched as an ache inside her all the morning. At dinner time, she brought the letter to show Annie. They stood out of the way, close to the wall of the factory while Annie read it.

'My dear daughters,' William Hanson had written. Even in that greeting Margaret sensed a stiffness, the way he had not used their names. She watched Annie's face. The letter began calmly enough.

> I was pleased to receive your note saying that you are safely arrived in Birmingham. Please convey my greetings to Ebenezer and Harriet. I know that having imposed yourselves upon them you will do everything in your power to be considerate and helpful to them. I do not suppose I shall be calling on them myself.
>
> It has been hard to explain your absence and I have had to rely on Alice Lamb a good deal. This has forced me into a position of untruths, since CB is convalescent under my roof. I'm sure you will be gratified to hear that our patient is recovering well. He seems to remember nothing of what has passed and was at first at a loss in finding himself abed in our house. He is quiet and at peace and has not spoken of the incident at all.

'Well, how could he!' Annie burst out, her face alight with fury.

Their father seemed to have been working himself up as he wrote.

> I am only thankful that your good mother is not here to witness the events of the past days. Never, in

86

all my days as a father, have I thought to feel such shame on behalf of my offspring for the bitter lies with which you have presented me. I feel the devil prowling about my home like a wild beast.

I only pray that you will soon return both to your home and your senses, governed by the contrition that these shameful events demand. It is a further humiliation to me that you have put other family members to such trouble on your behalf.

I shall not persist in writing to you. You know my view on what has happened.

Until you see fit to return,

Your father,

William Hanson

'"The devil prowling about my home",' Annie said, her fury evident in every line of her body. 'That's because he's got that *black soul* under our roof.' She slapped the letter back into Margaret's hand. 'Mother would have believed us. Oh, Maggs, don't! You mustn't take this on yourself – he's arrogant and wrong!'

Margaret found her sister's intense gaze fixed on her and was touched to see tears in Annie's eyes as her own also filled once again. The letter had torn at her inside. In all of this, their father, the father she had idolized, had felt such sorrow for, had betrayed them and this was the most painful thing of all.

'Are you *absolutely* sure he didn't see you?' she asked, her lips close to Annie's ear. 'That he didn't know it was you?'

'I don't think so,' Annie said. 'How could he have? And what does it matter? He can't *say* anything even if he did.'

Annie wiped her eyes fiercely on the backs of her wrists. 'I'll have to go. See you later.'

Margaret watched her sister's proud, passionate little figure disappear back through the factory gates. Annie was always so strong, so sure, and she was grateful for that. She tried to push away her unworthy, raging thoughts that she was the one hardest done by, in the face of her father's unjust blame.

She hurried back to eat her own dinner with Eb and Hatt, joined also by Georgie, who seemed quietly amused that Annie had gone out to work at Masters, Hogg & Co.

'We'll see how long she lasts, won't we?' Eb chuckled.

'Oh,' Margaret told them, 'if Annie's determined to do something, she'll cling on for grim death.'

'Sounds like my Clara,' Georgie said wryly, rolling his eyes.

'Now look,' Aunt Hatt said, when the men had gone back to work. 'Let's sit and have a talk about what you are going to do while you're here.' She turned her chair to rest her feet on the fender and sat back wearily, sipping the tea Mrs Sullivan had made after dinner.

Aunt Hatt had been busy in the office all morning and Margaret had kept out of the way, feeling at a loose end, her mind full of dark thoughts made all the worse by her father's letter. She knew she needed to be occupied. She wondered if she should do what Uncle Eb had suggested and learn to work the polishing machine.

'I know your health is not very strong,' Aunt Hatt began.

'But I'm much better now,' Margaret protested. 'I'm sure I could work. Uncle Eb said—'

'No, no –' Aunt Hatt waved a hand dismissively, almost knocking her cup from its saucer. 'I don't think that's a good idea at all. I've got plenty for you. We could certainly do with another pair of hands in the office. Susan does a lot of the paperwork and Bridget's on packing – but we're ever so busy. There's always the post needs doing . . .' Aunt Hatt seemed to be going through a list of tasks in her mind. 'And I can show you how to do some of the paperwork and you can help Bridget when needs be. Yes –' She looked pleased. 'I think we can squeeze you in for the time being. The more I think of it, you'd be a godsend!'

'I hope so,' Margaret smiled gladly. 'Any help you want, Auntie, you just ask.'

'Oh – and if that sister of yours stays the course, there's her dinner every day . . . You can take it if she doesn't want to have to come back here.'

'I'll do that, of course.' Margaret had been glad of the chance to get out of the house.

'Well, there you are. Plenty to do and you'll earn your keep. We'll pay you a few shillings on top of that, though.'

Margaret felt Aunt Hatt looking closely at her. She could tell she was dying to ask her more questions, especially after the arrival of the letter that morning.

'Whatever it is has gone on between you and your father,' she said carefully, 'you're probably best out of the way for a bit. I can see you need to get over it.'

'It won't be for long, I don't suppose,' Margaret said. In truth, she had no idea how any of this might be resolved, but she was quite sure she was not going home while that man remained anywhere near the place.

Aunt Hatt leaned forward to pat Margaret's hand and their eyes met. Margaret realized that her aunt already felt fond and protective of her and she was so grateful for her warmth.

'It's nice to have you here, bab. Bit of life in the house. And you'll be a help to me, I can see.'

Annie walked into number twenty-six that evening utterly worn out, with a throbbing head, aching back, and hands burning from handling the rough pieces of metal for all those hours of the day. She had also endured a certain education and suffered a painful dent to her pride as she had sat in that long room amid the rows of women, most of whom she hardly even caught sight of. And her work was so much slower than most of them – even Lizzie, who had deft little fingers and picked it up much faster.

But Annie was not going to show any of this to any-one and she forced herself to hum a tune as she opened the door.

'All right, Annie?' Aunt Hatt called from the office.

Annie put her head round the door, forcing a smile on to her face. Aunt Hatt, seated pen in hand at her desk which was piled with ledgers, looked up over her spectacles. To her surprise, Margaret was also in there, sitting close to Aunt Hatt. Both of them looked busy.

'Yes, thanks, Auntie,' she said brightly, though feeling as if she wanted to collapse on to her bed and never get up again.

'There's tea in the pot in the back – help yourself.'

Annie smiled. A hot cup of tea – never had that sounded so welcome!

'Oh – and Annie? How about the pair of you having a bath tonight?'

At this blissful idea, Annie could only nod, having to

stop her lips trembling. Though Lizzie was quietly friendly, some of the other women near her seemed hostile towards her, as if singling her out as different, a stranger. She was overwhelmed by the impossibility of her task. How was she supposed to preach the Lord's word in such a place – to these women? There was no time, for a start! Everyone was always rushing, both in and out of the room, when the bell went and to get through the work while they were there. And all of it was so different from anything she was used to. She could not imagine the likes of Doris being receptive to what she had to say. The day had made her feel lonely and a failure, but she didn't want to break down and sob in front of her aunt. It's so *hard*! she thought. I can't do it and everyone's looking down on me!

Aunt Hatt was no fool. 'If you handed in your notice, no one would think the worse of you,' she said, eyeing Annie kindly.

But I would, Annie thought.

'No, no,' she said, turning away. 'It's quite all right. I just need to get used to it, that's all.'

Later that night, after tea and once all the workers had gone home, they helped Aunt Hatt boil pans of water on the range and pour them into the tin bath in the scullery.

'In our new house, we'll have a proper bathroom,' Aunt Hatt told them again, emerging out of a cloud of steam after she had poured a kettle of water into the bath. It fitted along the quarry-tiled floor, between the cupboards and stone sink. 'Just think – pipes through the house, water straight out of the tap! Heaven!'

In the village they had a simple bathroom with cold running water so the routine of pouring a hot bath was much like here. And to Annie, sinking her stinging hands and aching body into the warm water, no bath had ever felt more luxurious than this one. She tried not to think about the fact that in just a few hours she had to be back at the pen factory, doing the same thing for all those hours over again.

As she later sank into sleep, curled up next to Margaret, she thought, I'm going to get faster. I'm going to be the fastest one there. If they can all do it, so can I.

Eleven

Aunt Hatt gave Margaret the simplest tasks in the office at first: addressing envelopes, writing out invoices and helping Bridget pack up finished goods in boxes.

'Here,' she said, clearing a space at the end of her own desk. 'You'll have to perch here, Margaret. I'll bring a chair in from next door.'

Susan was a little in awe of Margaret as the niece of her employer, even though she was a few years older than Margaret. She busied herself with letters. Though she was pleasant enough, Susan was suffering from a heavy cold that day and it was Bridget, the packer, who Margaret found to be the friendlier of the two. Bridget was only two years older than herself.

Margaret had to sit sideways at the desk as there was nowhere for her knees to go and this was not very comfortable, but she was glad to have been given a job to do and to feel a useful part of the place. They all sat together that afternoon as the rain fell outside, her aunt in front of her with the account books. Aunt Hatt oversaw orders and accounts and her work was never-ending.

Even though it was summer, by four in the afternoon the light had faded in the room so that they could barely see what they were about.

'Right,' Aunt Hatt said, as the hands of the clock on the wall reached the hour. 'Tea. Mrs Sullivan'll be in any moment. And when we've finished, we'll have to light the gas. We have a little break every afternoon,' she informed Margaret.

Sure enough, within moments Mrs Sullivan made an appearance in her apron bearing a tray with a large pot of tea and a plate of buttered toast; Bridget cleared a space for her to lay it on the bench by the window.

'The others brew theirs up in the works,' Aunt Hatt said as Susan poured the tea. 'Eb stays out there for his.'

It was a nice little interlude, Margaret found. Ten to fifteen minutes in which they all sat round and relaxed and chatted. Aunt Hatt asked Bridget about her sister's forthcoming wedding and Susan said her father was better, yes, thank you. Margaret was glad they did not ask her any questions and she sat smiling and listening eagerly.

Soon the dregs were cooling in the cups and they were back to work again – this time with the mantles lit and hissing away, one in the middle of the room and two on the wall, and the room felt cosy and companionable. Bridget packed little boxes and rustled paper; Aunt Hatt's pen filled pages with ornately slanting blue writing and figures and Susan sniffed intermittently.

Margaret was writing out invoices which was not too demanding. Soon the work became quite mechanical and she could not still her mind. Her father's letter, the pain and fury lashing out from his words, had cut deeply into her and she was in turmoil. All her life she had worked to earn his approval. It was she who had felt tender towards him even though he was often severe. But since their mother's death he had become more rigid and dour by the year and now he had betrayed her, taken her for a liar by the word of someone he had known only a few months.

Her thoughts swelled in her mind, overwhelming her.

She was filled with a terrible ache of anguish at the rift with him, that he had so easily thought the very worst of her. Tears blurred the address she was trying to write and she got to her feet before any could spill on the ink, hurrying from the room, her head bowed.

'Margaret?' She heard Aunt Hatt's voice. She had hoped her aunt had not noticed her emotion but she heard her follow.

Margaret longed to go somewhere alone and weep until she could gain control of herself, but all she could think of doing was going into the back room. Her body shaking, she stood, arms folded, facing the fireplace. She heard her aunt hesitate at the door, then come hurrying in and close the door, as Margaret's sobs burst from her, uncontrollable.

'Oh dear, oh dear.' Aunt Hatt was beside her, guiding her to a chair. 'My poor dear – you come and sit down. That's right – now, you sit there and we'll have a nice little chat. Shall I ask Mrs Sullivan to make some more tea?'

'No, Auntie! You've got too much work to do!' Margaret sat trying desperately to control herself, but the tears kept coming. 'Just let me sit here a moment or two and I'll be back to work, I promise.'

But Aunt Hatt wasn't having it. 'You just sit there, wench,' she said firmly.

Margaret, while mortified at having made such a spectacle of herself, was overwhelmed by her aunt's kindness. She obeyed and Aunt Hatt pulled up another chair beside her, as if she had all the time in the world. Margaret could see that she would at least have to tell her aunt something.

*

'When he first came, I felt sorry for him.' Margaret spoke, leaning forward, her arms resting on her knees, looking down at the rug by the fire. 'And . . . I don't know. I had been ill for so long and the need to look after someone else, someone who was suffering, seemed to make me stronger.'

'How old a man is he?' Aunt Hatt asked tactfully.

'He is eight years older than me – so twenty-seven now. When he came, I liked him.' She drifted for a moment, almost overtaken by those early tender feelings which this memory roused in her. 'Though he is rather serious,' she added.

How could she explain it to Aunt Hatt, who did not share their faith? She had thought Charles was the message from God that she had been waiting for, the blazing sign like a burning bush, telling her what to do with her life.

'He came to see us the first day he arrived. Mr and Mrs Davis, the people he was lodging with, only live about a quarter of a mile away.'

In her mind she saw him, as she had so often, his long-legged figure striding the village lanes, a black top hat resting on his wavy hair, his black ulster unfastened and billowing in the breeze as if there was never time for such fripperies as buttons.

'Of course, we all made him welcome. He was . . .' A blush spread through her as she recalled how that visit had affected her. He was softly spoken, and fixed his gaze very directly upon anyone he was talking to with what seemed like startling candour. He had been so magnetic, yet so frail somehow, that within half an hour of his being there, she had known she would never be quite the same again. 'He was very nice,' she finished. 'And we could see he had been ill in some way.'

96

'Rather like your own father at the same age,' Aunt Hatt said.

Margaret looked up, startled. She had not realized anyone else knew this. 'Yes. A sort of nervous collapse. Charles – Mr Barber – was quite open about it. He had been working in Salford, had spent himself in his work for the poor. There was a slight twitch, a tremor at the outer corner of his right eye – and he was very pale. You could see he had been under strain.'

She realized that her hands had begun to shake and she pressed them together in her lap. For a moment she could not go on.

'So, you fell in love with him?' Aunt Hatt asked simply, as if falling in love was an obvious, everyday matter, not the overpowering, tormented thing that Margaret remembered.

Head down, she nodded. 'I . . . I don't know.'

'You don't know?'

She looked up again, her eyes filling with tears. 'Oh, Auntie – I thought I was in love with him. I was . . . I just . . .' She began to cry again, hands over her face.

'Oh, my lovey,' Aunt Hatt said. She leaned over and touched Margaret's shoulder for a moment, then sat back and waited.

How to tell her, tell anyone. From the moment Charles Barber appeared, he had fixed on her. That very first evening, their eyes met and she seemed to see in his intense gaze all the interest and understanding that she craved. He seemed a soul who shared her own ideals and longings to such an extent that she was overcome by him.

And her father saw Charles Barber as a younger version of himself – a young man burning with fervour for his faith who had fallen into a crisis of doubt, needing the help of an older man who carried the same scars but had endured. He also, Margaret's instincts had told her, needed the consolation and love of a woman. It was as if he had reached out to her and in doing so had healed her – she was another wounded soul.

'D'you know,' Annie had teased, that first evening after Charles Barber had visited, 'you've got roses in your cheeks all of a sudden. Now – I wonder why that might be?'

Margaret had looked in the glass in their bedroom. It was true. All this time throughout her illness her face had worn a sickly pallor. Now she saw that a glow had begun in her which she could feel through her body, arising from a sense of love and attention. From the mirror looked a beautiful young woman, her hair coiled back modestly, eyes wide and alive instead of dulled as they had been for so long before. She felt as if it was the first time she had seen herself for at least two years and what she saw was a woman who had had a flame lit inside her.

Charles shared her father's ministry and the two men would sit talking for hours at a time. Every other Sunday it was Charles, not William, who stood in the high pulpit of the Zion chapel, preaching to the villagers and farmers who rose early on a Sunday and rode to the village, stabling their horses behind the church. He preached with a quiet passion and urgency, and the sound of it seemed to vibrate through her. He had the power to make people attend on his every word. One or two people began to bring notebooks to jot down his phrases or references. For them, as well as for herself, there was a stunning difference between her father – feared, respected, perhaps distantly loved – and Charles. Her father preached austerely, sometimes dramatically, of sin and damnation. Charles's sermons resonated with charismatic passion for the love of God.

'This is the driving purpose of my life!' He did not have to raise his voice: he had them all attendant, his eyes rolling ceiling-wards as if he could see to something beyond this humble valley church. 'To proclaim the grace and the love of our Saviour Jesus Christ!'

As the weeks passed, when he delivered such lines his eyes would light on Margaret, below him in the congregation, marking her out as the chosen focus of that love. It was not that he did not ever talk to Annie, but she was sixteen and saw him as impossibly ancient. With Margaret it was different.

There was the talking, the walks she had shared with him. This in itself had been like being swept along by a force that was almost too much for her. Charles walked very fast and her unaccustomed legs strained to keep up. Quite soon it became less of a struggle. Her body strengthened and her health returned. And it was he, with his vigour, his vision and his favouring of her, who had brought her back to life.

One glowing day in late October, they paused together on a low hill facing the village. Charles stood with his hands in the pockets of that long black coat, his hair blown back and eyes fixed on the horizon as if all the world was his responsibility.

'I feel the Lord has asked things of me which are almost too much for my frame to bear,' he said, in his low, intense voice. 'Such responsibility can only be the charge of the very robust of body and faith – and sometimes I wonder if I am too weak a vessel.'

Margaret was unsure what to say. She was in awe of him, of the force of him. Even the sight of him made her whole body pulse faster.

'The Lord gives us only what we can bear,' she said, wondering if this was true though it was what she had always been told. At times, during her long illness, she had wondered whether she could really endure any more of the sapping of her young life.

'Do you believe that?' Charles had turned to her, speaking with such burning urgency that she blushed. It seemed so strange that he would place any value on her opinions.

She looked down at her black buttoned boots. Who was she? For a moment she felt she had no substance compared with this flame who stood beside her, whose physical presence made the hairs rise on her flesh. She had to find some conviction to match his!

'Yes,' she said calmly, staring ahead of her. 'We must not fear. *'There is no fear in love, but perfect love casts out fear . . . He who fears is not perfected in love.'*

She felt Charles's gaze like a ray of light on her cheek as the lovely words of John's epistle poured from her.

'Of course,' he said. His voice seemed to tremble with humility. 'Of course you are right. You in your quiet way, Margaret, have a faith more splendid than my own.'

'The thing was,' she said to her aunt, 'I had been poorly for so long and when he came, I got better. It was as simple as that. It was as if he had given me my life back. I felt as if I *had* to be with him.'

Twelve

Aunt Hatt cleared her throat and put her teacup down.

What more can I tell her? Margaret thought. She thinks it's just a simple case of falling in love . . .

Last winter, with her health recovered, Margaret had begun her life again. She felt left behind. Annie was still at home, still doing the work of the church but chafing at the smallness of the village. Annie, too, felt that God needed more of her in the great world out there. She read a great deal and was full of ambition.

For Margaret, whose world had for so long been confined to bedroom and parlour, the cold, crisp months were very happy ones. With Charles there as well, there was much talk and the liveliness that a guest can add to family life.

Margaret started visiting again, took up her beloved work with the children, and began, at last, to see that she had a future.

'Now that I look back to this spring,' she said, her right index finger tracing a small circle on the leather arm of Aunt Hatt's chair, 'I suppose I can see signs. You see, we knew really that Charles had been ill. But when he came, he did not seem *ill* exactly. I was caught up in him completely. He was like no one I had ever met.' The tears came again and she wiped them away.

She could not seem to speak, as if they were veering too close to the darkness of what had happened, the way

Charles had drawn her in until he could pluck her like a stringed instrument.

'I thought – and he made me think – that he was my destiny. He even used that word. And I was so unused to thinking about what I should do . . . I didn't know anything about myself! While I was ill there was no point in thinking about the future. It was as if I was pressed against a wall – there was no road I could take. We all thought of the missions because that's what people like us do – but I was never so sure, not like Annie. So to marry Charles and be the wife of a minister seemed to be what God was steering me towards.' She stopped and looked up again, her eyes wet. 'Not steering – *hurling*, more like. What could make more sense? Charles told me he loved me. I . . .' She stopped in confusion.

Into the silence, Aunt Hatt said, 'Nothing like someone telling you they love you to make you feel you must love them back, eh?'

Margaret looked up in surprise. 'Has it happened to you, Aunt?'

'Oh –' She brushed it off with a laugh. 'Only when I was very young. A lad mooning about who almost persuaded me. But then I met Eb. This other feller didn't stand a chance after that!'

Margaret smiled, but she could see it was not the same. Already fragile, she had lost herself to him. He was like the smoke and fire that descended on Mount Sinai; like the rushing wind of Pentecost, bearing her along.

The door opened suddenly and Uncle Eb's cheerful face appeared. 'All right, ladies?' he asked.

'Eb,' Harriet said in a warning tone. 'Just give us a few more moments, will you?'

Eb looked from one to the other of them, suddenly

solemn. 'Right you are,' he said, closing the door behind him.

But the mood had been broken. Margaret could not bear to go on, to put these things into words to Aunt Harriet. Not even about how it began, the afternoon when she and Charles had been alone in the house. Even this was not the beginning of how her feelings first caught light, because she had been fascinated by him from the moment he arrived on their doorstep in that sweeping black coat. But that day they were alone in the parlour was when he captured her, hungry and innocent as she was.

Charles was standing with his back to the fire as if deeply lost in thought, his gaze fixed on the trees beyond the window. Margaret had been about to ask him if he would care for some tea, but she sat respectfully, not wanting to interrupt. She ached for him to share his thoughts with her.

Suddenly seeming to come back to the room, he looked across at her and smiled.

'May I sit with you a moment, Margaret?'

She was on a stiff-backed couch on which there was only room for two and she was startled by this. Was it quite correct for them to sit so close, side by side? But of course, such a pure and holy man could not mean any harm – and in her father's house.

'Of course,' she said, shifting as far towards one end as she could. 'Please make yourself comfortable. Shall we have some tea?'

'Oh, in a moment,' he said. He gave a quick smile. 'That would be nice, yes.'

He moved the tails of his jacket aside with a delicate gesture and sat lightly beside her, on her right. Margaret's heart felt like a piston inside her, so loud she thought he must hear it. Blood thundered through her veins.

He turned and gave her that smile, looking carefully at her.

'You are an astonishingly fine young woman, do you know that, Margaret?' He laughed at her confusion. 'No – of course you don't. And that is one of the things that makes you so lovely.' He looked at her intently. Slowly he said, 'I can see things in you which I don't believe you even know are there . . . Such qualities . . .'

She was looking down into her lap now, overwhelmed by this attention, these compliments. Her face, for so long pallid, was hot with blushes.

'Do look at me, Margaret, will you?'

She managed to raise her head. His flinty eyes, which she had so often seen cast heavenward, were fixed on her. Here he was, so close that the creases of his black jacket, the pores of his pale skin and bristles of his beard, the sharp, well-defined nose, were all intensely visible. She could hear each of his breaths and the hairs on her body stood on end.

'Might you do one thing for me, Margaret?' he said in a tender voice.

She began to tremble. What did this mean? Did Charles . . . Was he about to put into words feelings which she could hardly believe he would ever feel for her? No, she told herself – what a fool she was. He would ask for some errand in the village, some assistance in his godly work. After all, she was so much younger than he. How could he possibly be thinking of her in any other way?

'Of course,' she said in a low voice. 'What is it?'

He sat back, resting his right elbow on the arm of the couch and still not moving his gaze from her.

'I always think a woman looks at her most lovely when she sits like this –' He laid his left hand on the small of her back and she straightened. 'Delicately upright. The hair perhaps like this . . .' Gently he lifted her long plait and laid it so that it fell forward over her right shoulder. 'And with the ankles crossed in front.'

Margaret crossed her ankles.

'There.' He gazed at her, seeming entranced. Margaret felt that no one had ever looked at her the way Charles Barber looked at her.

'But your father doesn't want you to marry him – is that it?' Aunt Harriet said, as if impatient to get to the crux of the matter.

Margaret lowered her eyes, unable to hold her aunt's gaze. This explanation, handed to her for the moment, was what would have to do. She just could not put into words the feeling of those nights, Annie and herself together in their bedroom, the chest of drawers shifted in front of the door, knowing that he was lying in the room next to theirs.

'Yes,' she whispered. 'That's the problem.'

Thirteen

September 1904

'Margaret?' Aunt Hatt said, looking up from her desk in the office. 'Could you go and deliver this for me, d'you think?' She held out an envelope addressed to a firm in Frederick Street. 'And on your way back, go next door and ask Caleb Turner to come in when he's got a minute, will you? Eb needs to speak to him.'

'Yes, of course,' Margaret said, turning to go. She had been to Mr Turner's a number of times now. Aunt Hatt had at first been hesitant about asking her to run messages.

'We don't want you overdoing it,' she said.

'Auntie, I'm perfectly well now, thank you,' Margaret said. 'I shall enjoy it. It's interesting.'

Three weeks had passed since she and Annie arrived in Birmingham. Margaret was moved by how kind and welcoming the Watts household had been. She realized, with shame, that she had not expected this in what she considered an ungodly household. She had settled into her tasks in the office and was finding all the work done in the quarter fascinating.

Georgie and Clara had come to the house to share a meal with them a couple of times. Clara was a lively, friendly redhead who both she and Annie liked immediately, and little Jimmy, just a year old, a beaming, freckled carrot top who made them all smile and was very happy to come and sit on her lap. Margaret was truly moved by the warmth of her mother's family.

They had also taken the cable tram out into Staffordshire, along the Soho Road. On the way Uncle Eb pointed towards the window and said to Margaret, 'Just over there's where Matthew Boulton's manufactory used to be. It would've been behind all them buildings – over on the heath – huge place, it was. They knocked it all down a while back – in the sixties. He was the feller really started all this jewellery trade here, yer know. Marvellous, all the things 'e did. He was the one who made sure Birmingham had its own Assay Office.'

'Its own what, Uncle?' Margaret asked.

'Oh – the Assay Office – it's where they check that everything's what we say it is – the right quality of gold. Everything we make has to go through there – say we send them a batch of a hundred bracelets, they test one to make sure it's got the right gold content, and then they mark all of them with the hallmark – that's an anchor for Birmingham. That feller, Matthew Boulton, got sick of having to send all his goods to Chester which was the nearest – so he got them to set up an Assay Office here.'

Only Margaret benefited from this as Aunt Hatt was in full flow to Annie about all the different-coloured curtains she was going to have made for the new house and how she was planning to arrange the new parlour . . . Annie, not being one for fripperies, turned to Margaret and rolled her eyes: Margaret could only hope that this had been discreet enough for her aunt not to notice.

They alighted from the tramcar and walked through the sunny afternoon to see the famous new house. Georgie and Clara met them there with Jimmy and they all stood outside a very promising-looking shell of a building.

Aunt Hatt was going into raptures once again about hot-water pipes and bathrooms and Eb stood in the scrubby earth at the front peering inside.

'Ooh, don't go in there, Eb,' Aunt Hatt said. 'You don't want anything falling on you.'

'It's very big, isn't it?' Annie said.

'I want us to have space for all my grandchildren to be here at once!' Aunt Hatt said.

Georgie nudged Clara, who had Jimmy in her arms, and Margaret heard him say, 'Best get to work then, hadn't we?'

'You watch it, Georgie Watts,' Clara said, elbowing him back.

Margaret thought of this, smiling, as she went out. She had been glad the house did not seem to be almost ready, because even though it was roomy, she felt that her uncle and aunt should begin this new phase of their life without two nieces in tow. And at the moment she did not want to think about going back to face her father. In fact, these days she tried as hard as she could not to think of him at all.

This was not too difficult during working hours as her uncle and aunt kept her busy. Every day she took Annie her dinner at Masters, Hogg & Co. She often delivered messages, which gave her a chance to explore, and there were plenty of trips to the post office. For larger deliveries of goods, Aunt Hatt used one of the messenger boys who loaded up their basket trolleys full of precious goods. But there were always plenty of letters to post in addition to this.

At first Margaret had been frightened walking the streets, as if she was in a foreign country, amid people who seemed tougher, more energetic and determined than she could ever be. But already she was getting used to walking around the quarter and starting to look forward to it. All the mucky blue pavements, the busy streets hemmed in by warrens of workshops – now she had realized why people called the place a 'hive of industry' – were starting to feel familiar and less overwhelming. And apart from a curious stare now and then, most people were far too busy to trouble about her. The sun lit the shabby sides of buildings at an autumnal slant today, but it was not cold as she stepped out into the morning and she found she was walking faster, like everyone else here in the city, a spring in her step.

Some of the streets were dotted with the businesses of any normal town: shopkeepers selling bread and groceries, banks and pubs, wardrobe dealers, fishmongers, butchers, beer sellers . . . But Frederick Street was like a poem to the crafts of the district and each day she learned more of its lines. William Caley, chaser; David Montagu, gold chain maker; Arthur Cohen, gold ring maker; Herick Emile, gem setter; Clarence Clutterbuck, diamond mounter; Sanders & Son, precious stone dealers; Harrison & Hipwood, metal spinners; David Levy, watch manufacturers . . . On and on along the street on each side, unbroken by any other sort of commerce. The air was acrid with smoke and vitriol and other chemicals used for processing precious metals.

And that morning she noticed a plaque at one property which read 'Dorothy Bradley & Son, Silversmith'. Surely that couldn't be right? She paused for a moment to stare at Dorothy Bradley's modest premises, full of a strange excitement. Could a woman really be a silversmith?

All her life, Margaret had never thought it possible to

be anything apart from a wife or a missionary teacher. But perhaps there were all sorts of other possibilities?

Margaret was suddenly filled with a sick feeling of doubt. Here she was in this place, allowing it to corrupt her. Was that what it was? The devil's seduction – in the crudest guise of gold and silver. A busy, energetic life, all geared to making money. How could she be lured in so quickly, so easily? Was this the City of Destruction from Bunyan's *Pilgrim's Progress* and was she being tempted away from the wicket gate of Christ's way? But – and this sickened her more – she had been so sure that Charles Barber was a message from God! She was going to marry Charles, be a minister's wife, honour and please her beloved father . . .

'Move over a bit, will yer, if ye're just gunna stand there,' a voice yelled at her. A lad was behind her with a basket trolley, trying to get it along the pavement.

Margaret stepped to one side, a hand over her mouth as nausea rose in her. She drew in deep breaths until it began to fade and walked on to deliver Aunt Hatt's message, a feeling of sudden, utter exhaustion coming over her.

'Dear God, no,' she prayed. 'Not this again – please don't let me be ill again . . .'

After delivering her message in Frederick Street, she returned slowly to Chain Street, gradually recovering as she walked. The door of number twenty-four, her next task, was open and she saw the middle-aged man, in what she had learned was Mr Tallis's front office, turn to look up at her over his spectacles and give her a brief nod before returning to his work.

Margaret climbed the dusty staircase. Apart from

Caleb Turner, she was not familiar with the people who worked here. And though she now knew by sight the man in the front office and a middle-aged woman who also worked there, of Mr Tallis, who seemed to have the run of all the ground floor including his shopping at the back, she had seen no sign. She had once or twice caught sight of a young girl with long fair hair, who Aunt Hatt said was his daughter.

Caleb Turner's workshop was on the first floor at the front. Uncle Eb thought highly of him, and though he was not the only die sinker her uncle employed to execute his designs, Mr Turner did a lot of work for him.

At her knock, Margaret heard a muffled response which she took to mean she should enter. As she came in, Caleb Turner turned from his workbench under the window. He was a middle-aged man, pale, with thin, grizzled hair and a temperament that could be described as unexcitable.

'Oh, it's you, bab,' he said. 'I dain't 'ear yer on the stairs, yer that light-footed. Yer old man want to see me again?' He always talked to her as if she was Eb's daughter, even though he knew perfectly well she was not.

Margaret nodded, attempting to smile. She liked and trusted Caleb Turner. He had a wife and four children and seemed such a mild person.

'You're white as a sheet, wench.' He swivelled round a bit more and peered at her, as if eyes so used to close work had to strain to see anything further away. 'You all right?'

'Yes, thank you.' Margaret fiddled with the bottom button of her cardigan, embarrassed by his scrutiny. To distract him, she said, 'May I see what you are working on?'

'All right.' He indicated with his head. 'Come and 'ave a look.'

She moved, intrigued, towards the bench which was littered with tools. Dust motes floated in the light from the window. In front of Caleb was a circular die. She was astonished by his work. He could carve the most involved-looking things in a day or two. Bending to look closely, Margaret saw, carved into the metal, a face, about an inch and a half high, the back of the head draped in a robe. The two halves of the die would fit together perfectly, with a thin piece of metal in between, into which the pattern would be stamped.

'It's for the coffin factory,' Caleb said. 'The Virgin Mary, that is – for the Catholics, like. I do a bit for them now and again – and one of their own fellers passed on last week, so they're short-handed.' She realized he meant what was called 'coffin furniture' – metal decoration for wooden coffins.

'It's beautiful,' Margaret said. In her upbringing, anything to do with Mary, the mother of God, was seen as alien popery, but the thing was so lovely that this did not seem to matter. All she wanted was to gaze at it.

'Oh, it's cheap tat they'll be stamping out of it,' Caleb said cheerfully. 'But there you go – it's only going under the ground in the end, ain't it? Any road, I've got to get this done. Tell Eb I'll be round dinner time.'

Fourteen

Another curt letter arrived from their father, telling them that Charles Barber was now recovered and a new appointment was being sought for him at the end of the year. William Hanson therefore expected his daughters home by the same date. The letter filled Margaret with pain. She was still under her father's influence so strongly that displeasing him felt like the worst thing she had ever done. On Sunday mornings, she and Annie walked to the Congregationalist church at Carrs Lane to hear the Revd Jowett preach. In the past, she would have written letters to her father telling him all about the services and sermons, assuring him that she and Annie were keeping up their night-time prayers. But at present she could not even truthfully write the words 'Dear Father'. And now, this letter, with its cold tone . . .

'But what if we don't want to go?' Annie said, on reading the letter. The two of them were sitting on their attic bed, Annie with her knees drawn up close to her. She looked even thinner and more tired about the eyes than when they had arrived, but seemed to burn with fiercer determination than ever. To the surprise of everyone except Margaret, she was still sticking it out at the pen manufactory.

'Whatever do you mean?' Margaret looked at her, startled. Wanting was never an option in their lives. Duty was the call – what *should* they do? She had scarcely ever asked herself what she might *want*.

Annie said urgently, 'Well, perhaps God is calling us for something else. Something greater! I feel God's call for me is bigger than the village – than Father's . . .'

'What – making pens?' Margaret could hear the sarcasm in her own voice.

'Not making pens. But being *here*. If ever there was a place God's work is needed it's here – far more than in the village. Think what the pastor said on Sunday, about all those dark places where God's light does not shine . . .'

Margaret turned away, sighing. Annie was always so sure what God wanted from her. Until recently, she had also been sure, not least because that was all that God seemed to offer. She ached to be home, to return to the quiet, undisturbed life she had known before, when walking in God's way in the manner of her parents seemed a certain and unchanging thing.

'Father wants us home,' she said quietly. 'We can't just stay here with Uncle and Aunt for ever. And I have to make things right with him.'

'*He* needs to apologize,' Annie said. 'Where is his admission of wrongdoing? Believing that *hypocrite*, that monster, instead of you!'

Annie, with her truth-telling, always seemed to manage to probe at Margaret's sorest parts, at the feelings to which she did not want to admit. That her father, until now Godlike in her eyes, had betrayed her, she still could not bear. She bowed her head.

'Annie, just be quiet – *please*.'

*

114

Long after Annie was asleep that night, Margaret lay in the dark, afraid to close her eyes because that was when it started. Not dreams exactly, for she was still wide awake, but images crowding in.

Even with her eyes open she could not prevent it. For months, Charles Barber had occupied her mind, waking and often sleeping as well. He had turned his attention on her and she had felt honoured and chosen. She had felt loved.

Most days, for an hour or sometimes more, they would walk together, along the river and up the surrounding hills. She trotted alongside his striding figure, tingling with excitement at being by his side. Villagers touched their caps, people greeted them. It had become very obvious that Pastor Hanson's eldest daughter was walking out with the assistant, Charles Barber. What an energetic and exciting young man he was, the other Congregationalists said. Marvellous to see young Maggie Hanson recovered at last.

Charles drew her out of herself by talking. He had a sweeping vision of God's plan, both for the world and for himself. He cast aside her doubts and filled her with excitement.

One damp winter morning they had gone together to visit an old lady called Mrs Orchard, who was dying. Her daughter had been very distressed. Charles prayed with old Mrs Orchard while Margaret sat with the daughter and listened to her sorrows. From where they were sitting, by a smoking fire, she could just see Charles in the next-door room of the tiny, brick-floored cottage. He was leaning forward, murmuring prayers. She was conscious of him, of his voice, every second of the time, as if they were joined by an emotional thread. She had a strong feeling that she was destined to be at his side, as if their lives could never now be separated.

In the afternoon they took their walk. They stood watching golden willow leaves floating along the river's glassy surface. Charles had a gentle smile on his face, as if he could see everything, was sure of everything. She was very conscious of him beside her: male, strange, fascinating, his black boots very large beside her button-up brown ones as they stood together on the bank. Being close to him had given her a whole new sense of her body – her femaleness, the melting excitement he could arouse in her.

'Don't heed those whisperings of the devil,' he said to her, suddenly.

Margaret was startled. She had been thinking about boots and the sweep of his coat and how nicely it hung; of the masculine form that stood beneath that coat . . . She looked up at him, trying to appear as if her thoughts had been rather more theological.

Charles turned to her, looking intensely down at her.

'If I ever saw a woman chosen by God it's you, Margaret. The ways of the Lord are always narrow. People – ungodly people at least – think we're fools or obsessives. But we *know*, don't we, the calling of the Lord in every atom of our bodies? You and I, together – we can move mountains.'

His gaze blazed at her. Her cheeks flushed and she felt a thrilling, shameful sensation of heat in the private parts of her body. She was astounded at what he seemed to see in her. There she was, a frail girl, soon to be nineteen years old, while he was closer to thirty, yet he appeared to view her as a grown woman and his – if not equal – at least potential helpmeet. Under this gaze she knew she

116

had begun to grow, to feel herself older and more substantial.

Another afternoon, bright and crisp, he was in a less
earnest mood. They tramped up the hill looking down
on the valley and when they had looked from the top,
over the frosty woods and fields, Charles seemed in a
wild, energetic mood. Suddenly he took her hand and
said, 'Come on – let's run!'

He set off, tugging her hand and she dragging behind
until her legs found their rhythm, dodging hummocks of
grass, trying to stay upright and not slip. She was frightened but exhilarated, almost flying in a way she had not
done for years, the downhill running almost effortless
until they were going so fast she was veering out of control.

'Stop!' she gasped, laughing so much she felt she
might become hysterical, as if something was trying to
break its way out of her chest. 'Stop – we'll fall! I can't
breathe!'

'You won't fall – I shan't let you!' he shouted, grasping her hand more firmly as she panted and gasped, and
at last, as the hill bottomed out, they slowed to a walk,
their breath gusting white on the air. She felt uplifted, in
a heavenly state of happiness and excitement.

'Oh,' Charles cried, laughing, 'it's a marvellous thing
to be outside! I can't stand being cooped up inside for
long.'

When they reached the stile, he said, 'Come – up
here.' He handed her up the step, then commanded,
'Stop! Turn around, dear Margaret. That's right. Now sit
on it and face me. That's right – one ankle crossing the
other . . .'

Feeling slightly foolish she obeyed, humouring him as
if posing for a photograph, though there was no camera.

'So lovely – that green scarf against your hair. So fine.'

After staring at her for what became an uncomfortably long time, so that she started to fidget because she felt silly, he stepped up on to the stile, suddenly very close. His eyes bored into her.

'My goodness, my dear, you are so lovely.'

She was leaning back a little, startled. Charles, who was not wearing gloves, laid his hand against her cheek. It was surprisingly warm. He tilted her face up towards him. Her gasp was stifled as his lips joined forcibly with hers and she realized to her horror that his tongue was beginning to push between her lips. She was paralysed with confusion. What in heaven's name was he doing?

And as suddenly he pulled back, his eyes burning into her. She sat trembling, looking back at him.

'You have never been kissed before?' he said, and there was something in the way he said it that sounded pleased. He watched her. 'You did not know . . . ?'

She shook her head, her pulse forcing hot blood into her cheeks. Was that kissing? All she had ever seen between her parents was a chaste kiss on the cheek.

'My dear girl, how sweet you are,' he said. He seemed about to say more, but he lowered his eyes and drew back abruptly, stepping down to the ground. 'Climb over,' he said, suddenly curt.

From then he was silent, seeming moody, and for Margaret the afternoon was spoilt. She felt she had done something wrong, but did not know what it was.

As she lay in bed that night she tried to train her thoughts away from him, from the excitement that had risen in her body when he came close to her. He gave off a feeling of pent-up desire that became more and more unmistakeable . . .

Blushing with shame, she forced her mind to pray . . .

If she did not, she knew where her thoughts would go, their steps taking her across the yard behind the church that evening, into the darkness which followed.

Fifteen

Each morning, Annie made sure that she clocked in at the works bang on time and was seated at her press ready for the bell to ring.

She was getting used to the hours of work, which in the beginning had felt like an eternity. For the first days she had gone home with pains in her back and neck, her fingers cut to ribbons. And her wages were always less than she expected. She was not as fast as the others yet and there were so many stoppages – for her overall; for the Sick Club; a penny for once not getting back inside on time when work began again at two o'clock; another penny, the first week, for wastage, which evidently went into the 'Waste Fund' to be divided up at Christmas.

There was a lot to learn. Firstly, to add to the exhaustion, she discovered that all the obligatory cleaning of their presses and workplaces was to be done on Saturday mornings. She was beginning to feel as if she lived her whole life at Masters and Hogg.

Gradually she came to understand how the factory worked. The room where they pressed out blanks for pen nibs was one of many. Whenever the bell rang and they knocked off work, women came streaming out of a host of similar rooms where they worked at presses designed for the many processes it took to produce a finished pen nib.

There were presses for stamping a pattern on to each

nib, for piercing a tiny hole in each to let the air through, for raising them into a curved shape, for splitting each nib at the tip. In another room, she saw long straps with wheels high up by the ceiling, the straps turning hour after hour, working machines which ground the nibs smooth. She learned, with increasing amazement, that on the lower floors, as well as the rollers for making the steel strips for her blanks, were ovens for annealing – or heat treatment – of the metal in 'muffles' before drenching them first in oil, followed by a bath of vitriol. Later the nibs were 'barrelled' – turned in large barrels with a grinding powder to smooth them. In yet another room some of them were coated with lacquer, bright silver or gold – and all to produce box upon box full of thousands of the fragile nibs in varying colours, which were then sold all over the world.

'It's astonishingly complicated for something so small,' she said to Margaret, in wonder. 'I can barely imagine how they even thought of it!'

Annie worked like a whirlwind, but still she was slow compared to the others.

'Not done many today, 'ave yer?' Doris would say to her smugly, when they did their daily weigh-in.

Doris always had a pronouncement to make about everything. Many of these outbursts were directed to the room in general, and some of them of the sort that made Annie wish she could block her ears. Since the room was so long, she only really became familiar with the women close to her – Lizzie, Doris and a few others. But Doris targeted most of her remarks at a girl called Hetty, not much older than Annie, a skinny wisp of a thing with a blotchy face. Hetty never said much, just sniggered a lot, showing off decayed teeth. She was the perfect audience for Doris.

121

At first Annie had wondered why Doris had not moved up to a more skilled job as she was well into her forties. But she soon saw that Doris was slow-witted – except when it came to being insulting. Hetty, though younger, seemed much the same. Annie even wondered for a time if Hetty was Doris's daughter, but learned that she was not.

All day the two of them exchanged filthy jokes, especially about the men in their lives – or rather Doris joked about 'the old man' and Hetty sniggered.

Doris gave Annie snooty, hostile looks if she ever turned Doris's way. Not that Annie was easily intimidated. She would look away, standing as tall as her petite height would permit, and go to her machine without looking to one side or the other.

I'll show them, Annie thought, driven by the need to prove herself. I'll show them I can be one of them and work hard. She didn't want these women looking down on her as an outsider, especially a pair like Doris and Hetty. They might be God's children, she thought, furiously, but they were still crude as tar.

During those first weeks, Annie did her best to keep quiet and take in what was going on around her. Some of the women entering the factory in the morning looked roughly dressed, only just managing to pass the regulation of being 'neat' for the work. They were a mixture of ages. One or two, in the blanking room, were hard-faced and intimidating, but they worked up at the other end from Annie.

Many of the girls were young and they talked to each other and to Lizzie, but never to her. One or two would give her a nod, but they were not welcoming or polite. They just ignored her, eyeing her from a distance as she went in to work. After a while she could see that they were not really hostile but just shy. They sensed that she was different and did not know what to say to her. The only one she had anything to do with was Lizzie, who would give her a hollow-eyed smile as they arrived at their presses and a 'see yer tomorrow' sometimes as they left.

But it knocked Annie's confidence. For the first time in her life she felt inadequate. How was she supposed to preach the love of God among these rushing, harried women when she could barely even manage a conversation? Once I prove I can do the work, it will be different, Annie thought, turning the handle of her press with all her energy, trying to get the blanks stamped out faster and faster. Sometimes, with a great feeling of triumph, she knew she had done enough – more than enough – in the hour. The problem was trying to keep this up for every hour of the day. Often, as they stood in the long room, light falling through the windows, her back, feet and head all aching and longing for a drink of water, she wanted to walk out, for it all just to stop.

But she had to keep going, she told herself. Somehow, she had to do God's work. That was what she had come here for, wasn't it?

The blanks poured from the machines into piles like metal chaff. Her fingers were raw but she ignored the pain in them. Each week, she was getting faster. She worked on, like a little dynamo, in the certainty of being an instrument of God's glory.

At the end of her third week, Miss Hinks approached her.

'Well,' she said stiffly. 'You've come on a bit since you started, I'll say that for yer. You're a good worker and you've reached your quota. You can go on piecework from next week.'

Annie nodded, lowering her eyes. She did not show it, but she was thrilled. She had proved she could do the job like the others!

'Thank you, Miss Hinks,' she said carefully, getting up from her stool to leave.

'Don't forget you've got to come in tomorrow,' Miss Hinks said, in her grim way. 'You've got your machine to clean – remember?'

'Yes, Miss Hinks,' Annie said humbly.

But she was not feeling humble. She walked home that night elated. She had proved something – she was on a level with all the others! Walking the streets that workers were milling along, she laughed at herself inwardly. What a funny thing most people would consider me, she thought. Being pleased at working well in a factory. But she was full of burning conviction that the meaning of her life was, somehow, to be involved with people – God's people. To do His work among them, wherever that might take her. It felt a bold and adventurous vocation, though she had no clear plan. She just assumed that once she was accepted in the factory, she would be able to teach the other women – perhaps preach to them in the break – and that she would go down in history as one of the great missionaries who had converted the slum dwellers and factory workers of Birmingham!

She stepped into number twenty-six Chain Street and was hanging her coat in the hall when she became aware of someone standing at the bottom of the stairs; she jumped, her hand going to her heart.

'Sorry, er, miss . . . Didn't mean to startle you . . .'

Heart thudding, she peered into the gloom, then turned away, uninterested. 'Oh, it's you.' Jack Sidwell, the young man who had brought them from the railway station.

'I er . . .' He sounded flustered. 'I wanted a word with you, Miss, er, Miss Annie.'

'Did you?' She was adjusting her sleeves, still wrapped in her passionate thoughts about the future. Surely he hadn't been lurking about in the hall waiting for her to come home?

'Yes, I, er . . . I was gunna ask if . . . Well, if you'd like to walk out with me, some . . .' He did not seem to have thought this through. 'Some . . . day. Soon.'

'Oh, *no*,' Annie dismissed him, walking towards the office. 'No, thank you. Absolutely not.'

Aunt Hatt, Margaret, Susan and Bridget were all look-ing up at her when she walked into the office. The gas was already lit, casting a soft glow around the room. They heard the front door close with a sullen click.

'Was that poor Jack?' Aunt Hatt said. Annie could not tell whether her aunt was trying not to laugh.

'Yes,' she said breezily.

'Well, that was telling him, poor feller,' Bridget said. Annie thought she seemed offended on Jack's behalf.

'Poor Jack,' Margaret said. 'You're such a heartless thing, Annie.'

'Is there any tea in the pot, Auntie? I'm dropping,' Annie said, secretly feeling sorry she had been so brusque. But walk out with Jack Sidwell? she thought scornfully as she went to pour her tea. Never in a month of Sundays – she had far more important things to do – she was on piecework!

The next week she worked with feverish speed. In her head she listened to the music of her favourite hymns, the more energetic the better! *When wilt thou save the people, O God of mercy, when?* boomed in her head and she was so absorbed that she did not notice the mutterings going on around her.

By the Wednesday, she was surprised, when the bell went for their dinner break, to find Lizzie standing next to her. Lizzie was looking round her anxiously, as if to check that no one else was listening.

'I wanted to say something to yer,' she whispered. 'Come outside and I'll tell yer.'

But as they made to leave the workroom, a number of the women, including Doris and Hetty, stood barring their way.

'I dunno what you're doing with 'er, Lizzie,' a younger, gaunt-faced woman sneered. 'You want to stick with yer own if you know what's good for yer.'

Annie felt truly intimidated, but she wasn't damn well going to show it. She drew herself up, straight-backed, and stared brazenly at them as if they were one of her Sunday-school classes. Who did these people think they were, coming and standing in her way? Annie Hanson was not used to anyone thwarting her!

'You're spoiling everything for the rest of us.' Doris was in the middle, arms folded. She was enjoying her power and her voice was menacing. 'Yer'd better cut it out – or else.'

'I was going to tell her,' Lizzie said. She seemed intimidated by Doris as well. Annie felt a lump come into her throat suddenly. For all her bravado, she knew she needed someone to stand up for her, because she was lost and had no idea what was going on. All the angry-looking eyes around her seemed to bore into her. And Lizzie, for all she looked a poor, worn-out little thing, seemed to have the other women's respect.

'Well, you'd better flaming tell her, or there'll be nothing for any of us – and God knows, you need it more'n most, Lizzie.'

Annie felt she must say something. What was this crime she had committed?

'Tell me what?' she asked, keeping her voice soft and timid.

'If you don't know, yer need to find out, quick.' A woman pushed forward. Annie knew her name was Hilda. She was handsome with black hair and a tough, forbidding expression, and Annie felt respect for her. She knew Hilda had six children and she was a hard worker.

'Yer on piecework now, right? If you keep on the way yer going now, they'll cut the rate and there'll be less in everyone's wages.' Hilda leaned forward and pushed her face close towards Annie's. Annie could smell her sweat. 'And my family ain't going 'ungry 'cause of you. Gorrit? You ease up – or else.'

Never had Annie felt so small and foolish and out of place. She was used to people deferring to her, as the minister's daughter. But here no one cared who she was. And she was frightened of Hilda, of the crowd of others behind her. What might they do to her if she didn't obey? She would surely lose her job one way or another. This first, humbling test faced her.

'I honestly didn't know,' she said, looking down at her black shoes. Her face stung with blushes. 'I'm sorry. I won't do it again.'

'You'd better not.' Hilda backed off, hands placed self-righteously on hips. Annie managed to look up at her. 'You never worked in a factory before, then? Don't sound as if you come from round 'ere.'

Annie shook her head. 'I'm from the country.' She could see it would be a very bad idea to tell them anything else about herself. As for any ideas about preaching to them . . . She was starting to realize that she might be the one with a thing or two to learn.

'Well,' Hilda said, a sneer in her voice, 'you ain't in the country now with a load o' cows and sheep.' There were sniggers from some of the others. 'So – got that straight?'

'Yes,' Annie said, looking down again to hide how close to tears she was.

Everyone faded away, in a hurry for their break.

'I was going to tell you,' Lizzie said as they walked out. 'I knew they'd be on to yer for working so fast. But it don't seem fair if no one'd told yer . . .'

'Thanks,' Annie said, swallowing hard. She felt very foolish. 'That's nice of you.' She could see Lizzie meant to be kind and Annie wanted to change the subject. 'How old are you, Lizzie?' she asked as they passed along the corridor.

'Fourteen,' Lizzie said. Annie was surprised. Although small, the girl seemed older.

'So why do they all know you?'

'Oh, they don't – not really,' Lizzie said. 'My mother worked here for a bit, that's all. Some of them know her.' She hesitated as they reached the doors and Annie could see she wanted to get away.

'Thank you for helping me, Lizzie,' she said.

Lizzie smiled faintly, but she already seemed to have other things on her mind as she hurried away.

Sixteen

Margaret walked out of number twenty-six Chain Street the next Monday afternoon, smiling to herself.

Before setting out, she had been helping Aunt Hatt in the house. Sometimes she had to go into the workshop at the back to give a message to her uncle. She loved the busy atmosphere in there, the banging and crashing, the glimpses of bright gems or of something shining and beautiful emerging in its mantle of gold from beneath the muck of dull, workaday metal.

Other times it was popping in to see Caleb Turner next door, working on his astonishing, intricate dies, or Sid Cole upstairs bent over at his peg, fastening shining gems into the clasps of rings. Sometimes it was tiny fragments of ruby, diamond or emerald. Others were set with semi-precious stones: delicate, glistening piles of pink rose quartz or malachite green, soft white agate or topaz.

She was coming to love this busy, productive household. Mrs Sullivan, the cook, was a bit of a stick but Margaret managed to get along with her all right. The maid, Fanny, was only a couple of years older than her. She was so chatty – as an excuse for long intervals of leaning on a mop handle and only active in the jaw department – that Margaret sometimes had gently to remind her that it might be time to get back to work.

The other person who she met in passing in the house was Jack Sidwell, who seemed to do a tremendous amount of running up and down the stairs for no purpose that Margaret could understand. There was also a lad called Horace who worked for Jack, but they hardly ever seemed to set eyes on him. She still felt embarrassed every time she met Jack because of her faint on the tram and the uncomfortable memory of him holding her from behind on the pavement. But Jack seemed even fuller of blushes at the sight of her and after a terse, 'Morning!' or 'All right?' he fled up or down the stairs, depending. It had become clear that it was Annie who Jack was sweet on, though any attempt he made towards her met with extremely short shrift.

'Oh, he's got his eye on you, that one has,' Uncle Eb had teased Annie the evening she had so brutally dismissed Jack in the hall. They were at table, with plates of boiled beef with carrots. 'He's a good lad – got his own little business, yer know . . . He's a bit out of practice with the ladies, like – but you could make a good marriage there . . .'

Annie's look of scorn could almost have burned a hole in the cloth.

'Marriage?' she said, sitting bolt upright, eyes fixed intently on her uncle. 'Oh, *no* – marriage is not for me.'

Uncle Eb sat back, confounded by this. 'Well, I'll be . . . What's wrong with marriage?'

To Margaret's horror, Annie announced, 'Marriage, for a woman, is to be a man's chattel. Which is something I have no intention of becoming.'

'*Annie!*' Margaret said, mortified.

Her uncle and aunt were so busy staring at Annie that they did not see Margaret's blushes. Annie was the absolute end, she thought furiously. She did not know Annie's views had gone this far – what an insulting thing to say to a married couple! And wasn't marriage supposed to be the pinnacle of human experience? What on earth had got into her?

Uncle Eb wiped his moustache with his napkin and peered at his niece as if she was a strange animal from a faraway country.

'You're not one of them suffragists, are you?' he said warily.

Margaret watched in trepidation. Whenever Annie started to argue with their father at home, she found herself in a state of horrible tension. She had never found the strength to take issue with him herself, not just because she was timid, but out of fear of wounding his feelings. She knew that her father was not a happy man.

And whenever they had tried to discuss women having the vote at home, this never developed very far because however much Annie argued, Father wasn't having it. Women were of course equal in the sight of God, but a woman in a loving and godly marriage did not require the vote.

'Husband and wife are at one in marriage,' he would pronounce. 'There is no need for a woman to have a separate vote when her will is that of her husband's.'

'But what about all the women who *aren't* married?' Annie objected on one occasion.

William Hanson looked disconcerted, as if they were a category of people that until this moment he had barely considered.

'Likewise – there is no call for it. There are enough men to decide the politics of the nation without women having to trammel themselves in it. Women have enough toil of their own.'

'Yes,' Annie announced now to Uncle Eb. 'I suppose I am a suffragist. Why should women not vote like men do? We are their equal in intellect and energy. And in some things, I'd say *more* than equal – certainly doing work that demands the same effort and intelligence. After all, look at the way Aunt Hatt runs the office here!'

Margaret was horrified. Uncle Eb looked stunned, wounded even.

'But –' He turned to his wife. 'You wouldn't want the vote, would you, Hatt?'

Margaret waited to see what her aunt would say. In the scarce times when her mind was not on the business, Aunt Hatt's main preoccupations were her clothes, the cleanliness of her house and her dreams of furnishing the new one in Handsworth. After the Hanson household, where most conversations turned upon the will and urgent mission of God, she found Aunt Hatt rather restful. It seemed shameful to admit this, though.

Aunt Harriet looked doubtful. 'Well – to tell you the truth, I've never given it a lot of thought. I mean, I have quite enough to do . . .' She frowned, glanced at her husband, then said uncertainly, 'No – I don't suppose so. Not really.'

'All I can say is . . .' Annie ploughed on, despite Margaret's increasingly desperate looks which said, *Annie, for heaven's sake, stop! Be quiet!* 'I can't imagine giving up my thoughts – or my life, for that matter – to a man.' Having dropped this thunderbolt on to the table, she went back to sawing up her beef with great energy.

'Well,' Uncle Eb said, with an outrush of breath. His moustache lifted as he smiled. 'Who's going to warn our Jack then? If this 'un started on him he wouldn't know what'd hit 'im!'

132

'Oh, I think he's already wondering that,' Aunt Hatt said.

At this, all of them burst out laughing and the tense moment passed.

This added to Margaret's smile as she walked along. She loved her uncle and aunt's good nature. Both of them could be sharp and irritable when pressed with the demands of the business, but it warmed her to see how united they were. They did not take anything too heavily and always ended up laughing their way out of any quarrel.

She delivered an order to the bullion dealer whose wagon regularly rolled up in front of Watts & Son, from where the raw gold was carried along the entry at the side of the house and down to the basement. Then she posted some letters, before looking for the shop where she was to buy buttons and two yards of grey serge for her aunt. The day was overcast, but she was feeling cheerful.

She found herself hard to understand. One moment she felt free and optimistic, as though released from all her inner torments. The next, she would be walking along amid the bustle of this busy place and something would come to mind and pierce right through her. Yesterday it was a memory of Charles as he had been when they first met – the quietly charming man in a vulnerable state who had drawn her to him. She was so fragile then, a sickly girl beginning to recover, and he, acquainted with suffering himself, had lured her gently, as if she was a shy bird. With an ache, she missed him, missed the harmony she had felt, the reviving excitement of his interest in her. Memories came of them sitting together by the fire in the parlour at home: the way he had reached forward to take up the poker and shift the coals; the upward wave of his hair; his strong legs close to hers; how he had turned when speaking, to look into her eyes. And suddenly she was close to weeping in the street.

Another time she was walking along Vyse Street when it had begun to drizzle. For an intense moment she was a child, standing beside the river at the edge of the village, her hand in her father's – her tall universe of a father – and the wet blowing against their cheeks.

'Come on, little Margaret,' her father had said, squeezing her hand. 'We'd best get home now the rain's coming on. Let's get back in the warm.' So sweet, such a memory of trust and innocence, that again she was almost floored.

But I'm not going to think about any of it, she decided today. She looked about her. A cart drawn up near an entry loaded with blocks of salt, a rook fluttering from a rooftop and the vivid jewellers' gas flames glowing behind the lower windows, all filled her with a sense of contentment. She started to hum to herself and two passing women stared at her. One said to the other, 'Well, someone's happy.'

But I *am* happy today, Margaret thought, blushing as she hurried onward – because she had caught the habit of hurrying and these streets were now so familiar that she hardly had to think to find her way back to Chain Street. And I'm not going to worry about any of the horrible things today.

When she was approaching number twenty-six, she saw a small figure sitting on the front step of number twenty-four, next door. The girl's dress was covered by a white pinafore, she wore a straw hat with the brim tilted back from her face, and her hay-coloured hair hung thick over her shoulders.

Since they had been staying with the Watts family, Margaret had seen the girl a few times going in and out to school and had smiled at her. She felt a swell of pleasure. Margaret liked children, felt a great sympathy towards them. Annie liked the young too – especially being in command of them. Annie had been keen to teach in the Sunday and other schools when she was hardly big enough to see over the table. But though Margaret taught as well, she preferred being in the company of one or two children and enjoying their playful imaginations.

As Margaret approached, the girl looked up. She was a self-possessed-looking child with a long, pale face and blue-grey eyes.

'Hello,' Margaret said. 'Do you live here? I've seen you before, I think.'

The girl nodded, drawing her knees in closer to her. A stout pair of brown boots was visible at the blue gingham hem of her dress.

'My name's Margaret Hanson. What's your name?'

'Daisy Tallis,' the girl said. There was a disconcerting directness to her gaze. Margaret had been taught to lower her eyes when addressing someone senior to her, but Daisy seemed to have had no such instruction.

'And how old are you, Daisy?'

'Nine – but I'm nearly ten,' she said. 'I live with my father. My mother passed away and I have no brothers or sisters. We have Mrs Flett who helps us, though,' she added, as if it was important that Margaret should know this. 'She does our cooking and things like that.'

'I see,' Margaret said. Mrs Flett must be the middle-aged woman she had seen coming and going. The girl was softly and politely spoken. She found herself unsure what to say next. Looking at the plaques by the door, she tried, 'So your father is Mr Tallis, the silversmith?'

Daisy nodded. Suddenly, she smiled. It was a sweet, sad smile and Margaret felt a pleasant tenderness, as if she had tamed a young horse and it had come trustingly to eat from her hand.

'I need to go inside now,' Daisy said. Standing up, she grasped a little canvas bag which had emerged from her lap. 'Goodbye.'

Seventeen

Everyone ignored Annie as she settled at her press the next morning. After all the business over piecework, she had looked around her cautiously as she clocked in. She was ashamed that she felt so wary of some of the women – afraid, in fact. She found it hard to admit, but she had made bad mistakes in her first weeks at the factory and now she was anxious to make up for them. It was an unusual feeling for her to have to be humble.

I mustn't work too fast, she thought. It cut against her pride, her competitive nature. But she could see she was only going to make trouble for herself. And the effort had also been truly exhausting.

Doris was blathering on as usual in her booming voice. The other women all greeted Lizzie and joked and chatted with each other. Annie felt a pang of loneliness.

Lizzie sat on her stool not looking from one side to the other. Annie wondered if the other women had warned even sweet-faced Lizzie not to talk to her and her loneliness increased until she remembered that Lizzie had been feeling unwell the day before, saying she felt sick, and she had not eaten anything at dinner time. She did look pale, Annie thought, glancing round at her.

The bell rang and everyone set to, the rhythmic stamp of the presses all along the room. Annie worked steadily but not too fast. Better to lose wages, she thought, than turn everyone against her.

It was hard to look about you anywhere when you were working and it was not until later in the morning that she heard a disturbance.

'No one's allowed out of here until one o'clock, you know that, Lizzie Poole.'

'I've got to, Miss Hinks.' Lizzie's voice came low but urgent. She said something else that no one could hear.

'Well –' Miss Hinks sounded very displeased. 'I suppose you'll have to then . . .'

Miss Hinks, though austere and usually unbending, let Lizzie out of the room.

'Well, I never,' someone else remarked. 'There's not many can sweet-talk old Hinky.'

Lizzie came back in later, head down, and carried on working.

When the bell rang at one, Annie stopped work, pulling back her aching shoulders. Lizzie's scrawny form was slumped over the bench next to her press, head resting on her arms.

'Hey, Lizzie,' Hilda called. 'What's up with you today then?'

There was no answer. Hilda and another of the women went over to her.

'I'll be all right,' Annie heard Lizzie say. She got to her feet, forcing a smile even though she was as white as a sheet.

'All right, then, bab.' Hilda and the other woman moved away. 'Get some food inside yer and you'll feel better.'

When Annie came back from her dinner break, she went out to the lavatories in the yard. There were two for the men, two for the women. Both the women's were occupied so she waited by the rough wooden doors. There was a gap under each and from inside one she heard the sound of someone being sick, followed by a wretched moan. It was a long time before the door opened and other women were coming up, complaining.

'Hurry up in there!' One of them elbowed Annie sharply out of the way and banged on each door. 'You ain't the only one as needs to go, yer know!'

The other door opened and as someone came out, the woman pushed in there without a backward look at Annie.

Charming, Annie thought, flushing with annoyance.

It was Lizzie who emerged from the second lavatory and Annie was shocked by the look of her. She was half bent over, her face pale and shiny with perspiration, seeming hardly able to get along. But by the time Annie had hurried in and done her business, Lizzie was back at her work place. Annie cast nervous glances at her when she could. She had often visited people who were sick in the village, taking gifts of food or remedies from their mother, offering to help in any way she could. The one thing she had never been able to get over was feeling sick in sympathy with other people and all afternoon her stomach was queasy on Lizzie's behalf.

It seemed an age until the evening bell rang. As soon as the presses were stilled and the others were hurrying away, she went over to Lizzie, who was sitting resting her forehead on her hand.

'Lizzie?' she said timidly.

'What?' Even though Lizzie's voice was faint, she sounded hostile, as if she just could not rise to another thing, even talking to anyone.

Annie felt foolish. Here she was, with big dreams of preaching, and she hardly had the first idea how to conduct even a simple conversation in this place! She found it impossible to join in with any of the chat about husbands and suitors, wedding plans and children – let alone the earthy sense of humour which was entirely new to her. But it did feel as if, by keeping quiet and just getting on with her work, she would gradually be accepted. One or two of the shyer girls had given her a nod in passing, as if in sympathy, and it warmed her heart. She was surprised how much she discovered she longed to fit into this strange place.

'I . . .' She struggled for the right words. 'I can see you're not very well. I just wondered if you wanted any help?'

Lizzie raised her head. Her eyes were sunken and she looked very pale and sick.

'What d'yer think you're gunna do to help me?' she said sarcastically. 'I just need to get 'ome, that's all.'

'D'you live far?'

A slight shake of the head.

'Perhaps you should have gone home earlier,' Annie ventured. She was trying to help. All her upbringing had conditioned her to help, but Lizzie did not seem in the least grateful for this. 'You look really poorly.'

But at this show of sympathy, Lizzie burst into sobs, clutching her face and her body shaking. Annie saw that her young hands were rough and chapped, the nails bitten to the quicks.

Scared of being rejected, but moved by this pent-up suffering, Annie gently touched her shoulder.

'We've got to get out of here. Let me help you get home, Lizzie.' She spoke very gently. 'I don't mean any harm to you. You do look very ill.'

Lizzie caved in like a rag doll. She slid from her stool and Annie took her arm. Slowly they made their way out to the street, where the lamplighter was already lighting up the dusk.

Lizzie told her she lived in Pope Street. The very name of it repelled Annie. She wondered if the street was populated by Roman Catholics, who to Annie inhabited a foreign country, full of dark superstition and lurid, bloodstained statues.

And Pope Street after sundown seemed to Annie the darkest, most threatening place she had ever been. They moved away from the main factories of the quarter into long, mean side streets, poorly lit, with rough, uneven cobbles in the road and the houses like black crouching shapes in the gathering dusk. It was a cool night and a stinking fog was gathering, yellow tinged, blurring the edges of everything. At intervals, she saw the blacker, yawning mouths of alleyways, or entries as they were called here, looking like places for deeds that the eye would not want to see. There were a few people, men mostly, standing smoking or slouched against the wall as if waiting, in a way that she could only think sinister. The light was fading fast now and she was glad of Lizzie beside her.

Arm in arm, they passed along the darkening pavements, amid the people hurrying from the factories and workshops towards hearths and evening meals. Lights were on in the many pubs and Annie regarded them with as much horror as she did Catholics. She had had to get used to the idea that her uncle spent several hours each week in his favourite watering hole, the Jewellers' Arms. Alcohol never touched the lips of her family who looked upon public houses as the cradles of evil deeds and family neglect.

She shuddered as a gust of air, loud with raucous voices and laced with beer and tobacco, burned inside her nostrils like the harsh stink of sin. The night-time streets shocked and frightened her and she held herself tightly as a defence against them.

Lizzie revived a little in the fresh air, but after a few minutes she had to stop and rest, leaning against a wall.

'I dunno how I'm gunna get in tomorrow,' she muttered faintly. 'I feel that bad.'

'Oh, Lizzie,' Annie said. 'You're very poorly – you must stay in bed.'

'Huh.' Lizzie made a bitter sound, almost a laugh. 'How d'yer think I can stay in bed? If I don't work, no one'll eat. Mom's worse than me.'

Annie stared at her in horror. Lizzie was bent over, pressing her hands on her thighs. Standing upright made her feel sicker.

'But Lizzie, what about your father? Doesn't he keep the family?'

'He's . . . gone.' It was costing her to speak.

Gone. Harsh, judgemental thoughts filled Annie's mind. An abandoned family!

'And . . . who is in your family?'

'Our mom – and my brother and sisters . . .'

Annie looked at the pathetic figure curled against a sooty factory wall and was filled with rage. A feckless man, no doubt drinking down his wages and taking off when responsibility no longer suited him – off to sow his seed elsewhere, leaving his family close to destitution. Hadn't she heard this sorry story so many times before! She felt as if the Lord stood in righteousness at her shoulder and she was filled with anger and exaltation. So – here was her mission, in a different guise! This was the beginning.

'Come on, Lizzie,' she said in a steely voice. 'Look, let me put my arm round your waist. We must get you home.'

Lizzie found her way as if the street was a part of her own body. Soon she stopped at one of the entries.

'You'd better loose me,' she murmured. 'It's not very wide.'

Annie obeyed, but to her relief, Lizzie caught her hand and led her along the black slit, where the fetid stenches seemed to linger and gather strength. She thanked God that she had at least already looked along one of these alleyways in daylight, or now she would have been utterly terrified.

There was dim light at the end. As they emerged into the yard, she saw a gas lamp bracketed to the wall in the middle of the row of back houses, giving off a miserly light, as if even the gas supply was poorer in this district. The air was so thick with the stench of dry pan lavatories, of chemicals and smoke, that the foreign concoction of smells was making her just as nervous as the dark strangeness of the place. She found herself glad of the shrouding dusk, afraid of what daylight might show her. Sounds came from the houses: voices, a rhythmic banging from the end of the yard like someone putting an axe through wood, and somewhere, a young child was letting out a grizzling cry.

'Watch it –' Lizzie pulled her away from a black pool gathered in a low point of the uneven brick yard. 'You don't need to come with me – I'm home now.' Lizzie pointed at the crouching row of houses. Even sick as she was, the girl seemed ashamed at the idea of taking anybody inside.

Only then did it dawn on Annie that she was somehow going to have to get home again through this dark warren. She had not paid much attention to where they were going.

'It's all right, Lizzie,' she said, bracing herself. 'I can come and meet your family. And you'll have to tell me the way back again.'

'All right,' Lizzie said doubtfully, but she had no energy to argue. 'My brother can go with yer.'

She pushed the door open. Inside, Annie saw the wavering light of a candle and the sound of the crying child grew louder.

Eighteen

'Oh, no!' As she stepped inside, Lizzie clapped one hand over her mouth and with the other tried to bar Annie's way. 'Stay there, Annie – you'd best not come in!'

But the combination of stenches unwinding itself through the open front door had already reached Annie, so awful that she quickly resorted to an old habit of breathing through her mouth.

'It's all right, Lizzie,' she said gently, sorry for the girl's shame. 'People can't help being ill.'

As Lizzie relented and they stepped inside, Annie, with shock, took in the sight of the one downstairs room, which was barely any lighter than the yard they had just left.

A stub of candle flickered on a saucer on the table which occupied most of the cramped abode and was littered with bits of boxes and cards. There were a few other pieces of furniture: chairs and a cupboard. Some heat must have been coming out of the black range at the far side of the room, for it was not deathly cold. The grizzling of the child continued and from somewhere was emanating the most terrible combination of smells.

'Lizzie!' What seemed a pile of rags occupying the one armchair close to the range, got to its feet in the shape of a boy, who was hauling up into his arms the crying child who had been on his lap. The lad sagged under the weight. The crying stopped for a moment as the little one noticed a change in things.

''Ve yer got summat to eat?' he demanded. 'Our Nellie won't shurrup – and 'er's sicked on me.'

Annie could see that the boy looked about eight or nine, the child in his arms more than a baby – perhaps as old as two years.

'Denny,' Lizzie spoke faintly. 'Go and empty out that pail – now. It's terrible. Give Nellie to me . . .'

'It's all right.' Annie stepped forwards. 'You've not the strength, Lizzie. I'll take her.'

The boy shot her a look thick with suspicion but Lizzie said, 'It's all right, Den.'

As Annie found herself holding a child, wet, stinking of urine, but at least no longer howling, she heard another faint voice say, 'Lizzie – that you?'

'Mom?' Lizzie said.

Annie could not see anyone at first. As Lizzie moved towards the fireplace, Annie became aware of two more pairs of eyes watching her. Two little girls who looked much the same size, with nests of pale, straggly hair, sat side by side on the bottom step of the stairs which opened out of one side of the room.

''Oo the 'ell's that lady?' the boy demanded, staring at her.

'Shoosh, Den – language. The lady works at the factory with me, 'er's a friend,' Lizzie said, having no idea how much this lifted Annie's heart and gave her fresh courage. 'Tek the pail out, Den – it stinks terrible.'

The boy picked up a bucket of ordure with a clank and disappeared outside. Annie saw with another shock that he had nothing on his feet. She stood rocking from side to side, trying to pacify the child in her arms. The smell of her was overpowering and at first Annie tried to hold her away from her body, but the little one squirmed and buried her face in Annie's chest. Poor little mite, she thought, giving up and holding her close. I bet she's sore underneath and famished as well.

'Mom – you feeling any better?'

Lizzie knelt by the hearth and as she did so Annie saw to her horror that there was someone lying there on the floor, on some sort of rough bedding, a dark garment bundled under her head.

'Lizzie?' She spoke in the slurred voice of someone feeling very unwell. 'That you? Oh, thank goodness. Help me sit up, will yer?'

As Lizzie pulled on her arm, Annie saw a gaunt-faced woman rise groggily from the floor and wrap her arms round her knees. Her long, pale hair was as tousled a mess as that of the little girls. She did not seem to have noticed Annie was there.

'Why dain't you go upstairs, Mom?' Lizzie said. Kneeling, she curled forward and as if drained of all strength, rested her head on her mother's feet.

'It's warmer 'ere,' the woman said. 'Denny's put a bit of his wood on the fire. And the babby . . . Pass her to me, Den . . .' She reached out an arm, not seeming to realize the boy had gone outside.

Annie took the infant, who was now grizzling again, over to her mother and laid her in her arms from behind. Mrs Poole did not turn round to look at her and Annie saw her reach into her clothing and latch the child to her breast. For a few moments it was quiet.

'You feeling bad, Lizzie?' she said, weakly.

Lizzie couldn't help it; bent over, still resting her head on her mother's body, she broke into sobs.

'I feel so bad,' she said. 'I could hardly keep going all day – I 'ad to ask Miss Hinks if I could go out to the . . .

147

to relief meself . . .' She sobbed even harder. 'And I kept wanting to be sick, even though there was nothing in me.'

'Poor babby,' the mother said. Her voice was thin but she reached out and stroked Lizzie's hair. 'You're a good wench. The babby's been sick all day again, and I can't . . .' She seemed to run out of strength to speak, and the baby began to wriggle and cry.

Annie looked about her. The two little girls, who appeared to be about six years old – were they twins? – had moved closer and were staring at her. The baby's cry was setting her nerves on edge. She wondered if there was any food in the house, or even the possibility of a cup of tea or something for Lizzie after her gruelling day.

The boy came back in with the pail.

'D'yer wash it out, Den?' Lizzie said, sitting up groggily. He nodded. He seemed angry, Annie thought. Poor lad was most likely hungry. Young boys always seemed to be hungry at the best of times.

Lizzie straightened up, wiping her eyes. 'All right, Nellie,' she said, caressing the baby. 'You feeling better, Mom?' Annie could hear the plea in her voice for her mother to recover, for all the weight of the family not to be on her own skinny shoulders.

Her mother nodded, but Annie could see this was not the truth. She was obviously still feeling very poorly.

Annie felt helpless. At home, she would usually have arrived at such a house with a basin of broth, or something to ease the family's cold and hunger. Or at least she would have known she could go home and fetch some such refreshment. But now she had no money and no idea of where she might go. And she couldn't just stand here all night. She was no help and Uncle and Aunt would be wondering where on earth she was.

'Lizzie,' she said. The girl seemed to have forgotten she was there. She saw Lizzie's mother's head turn in bewilderment.

'Oh, Mom – this is Annie. Works at the factory with me. I was feeling bad so she helped me home.'

A faint smile came over her mother's features. 'Thank you, bab. That's good of yer.' She peered more closely at Annie in the gloom. 'Ain't 'er got a pretty face?'

'Lizzie,' Annie said. 'Could I speak with you a minute?'

'Oh – yes. You'll be wanting to go . . .' Lizzie got up, with an effort.

'No – it's not that.' Annie led Lizzie back to the door and whispered to her. 'Is there any food in the house? Can I help you with anything?' She did not know how, but she knew it was her duty to help. And she felt so sorry for poor Lizzie.

'I couldn't eat, I feel that sick,' Lizzie said. 'Or Mom. But . . .' She looked round, helplessly. 'We got nothing, I don't think. I mean . . .' She hastened to reassure Annie. 'We ain't always like this. It's 'cause our mom's poorly. Den?' she called across to him. 'Ain't we got nothing to eat?'

'No.' He sounded angry. 'And not a farthing.'

'Where could we get something?' Annie said. She recalled seeing some little shops in the nearby streets. 'I could go – although I've got no money on me.'

Lizzie glanced anxiously at her mother. 'We've none – 'til I get my wages or Den sells some firewood. Mom does outwork, see, for the button factory . . .' She glanced at the cards and misshapen-looking boxes on the table. 'But she's not been able to.'

Annie felt despair wash over her. There were a hundred questions she wanted to ask about how they had come to these straits, but the most urgent thing seemed to be to get something for the children to eat.

'If we go down to Mrs Wills on the corner, she might let us have a bit of something, I 'spect,' Lizzie said doubtfully. 'We're a bit behind with paying 'er, though . . .'

Nellie, the little one, let out another shriek of hunger and frustration and Annie drew her resolve together.

'Let's go,' she said.

Everything was swathed in the sulphurous, evil-smelling fog. Mrs Wills's little shop was only a few yards away, the light inside a blur of yellow guiding them to the entrance.

'Don't you have gas in your house?' Annie asked, thinking of the candle.

'Oh, yes – we just ain't got mantles,' Lizzie said. Her voice was still faint and sick and she looked curled in on herself. Annie could see the effort it had cost her to come out again.

Mrs Wills was sitting, a mighty form, behind the narrow counter in her cluttered shop. She wore a huge brown shawl draped right over her head and from under its shadow peered a jowelly face, the eyes hard and calculating. The gas lamp popped away in the middle of the tiny room and Annie saw every kind of thing for sale, crowded on to shelves behind the shop's intimidating guardian.

'Evenin', Mrs Wills,' Lizzie said. Annie could hear that she was trying to get into the woman's good books.

Mrs Wills got up off her stool behind the counter and made a grudging 'huh' noise. Close to her was a loaf of bread that must have been sitting there all day by the look of it – if not more than one day.

'You come to pay your bill, Lizzie Poole?' she said. 'That mother of yours owes me more than anyone in the book.'

'Not today – but I'll get my wages on Friday,' Lizzie pleaded. 'Please could yer let us have summat – there's nothing for the babby . . .'

Mrs Wills folded her arms. 'What – more on the strap?'

Lizzie was nodding, looking sick and wretched.

'Could you please let us have that loaf?' Annie said, moving round in front of Lizzie. 'And anything else that you could see your way to advancing us? Tea, and a little jam, perhaps?'

Mrs Wills looked outraged. 'Who're you?' she said rudely.

'I am a friend of the family,' Annie said. 'I can guarantee that your bill will be paid this week in full – but we do need some things for tonight.'

A contemptuous look came over Mrs Wills's face; the bullying look of someone who has power over others.

'Them Pooles've pushed me as far as I can go,' she said. ''Er with her fly-by-night husband. I've never seen you round here before. Why should I believe anything you say?'

Annie could feel her temper beginning to fray.

'Look,' she said, in a clipped voice. 'There are children who need to eat and Mrs Poole is unwell. I will pay this bill. I am the niece of Ebenezer Watts, of Chain Street. I can guarantee you that you will get your money. But please – kindly fetch us some food so that these children do not have to go to bed hungry.'

At the mention of Ebenezer Watts, Mrs Wills's expression changed into something more uncertain.

'Mr Watts – 'im with the goldsmiths business?' she said, suddenly ingratiating. 'I see. Well – I suppose that'll be all right. As long as you do pay me . . .'

'I will pay,' Annie repeated acidly. 'I've just said so. Make us a parcel of what food you can – and I'll pay the bill. Have you any milk?'

'Not at this time o' night, no,' Mrs Wills sneered as if some unreasonable magical performance was being expected of her.

'All right – well, whatever you have. Oh – and while you're at it, put in a couple of mantles and some candles as well.'

Lizzie didn't say anything until they were outside but Annie could see she was bursting with curiosity.

'That told that old bitch,' she said, as they walked back to the entry. She seemed to revive for a moment. 'But how're yer going to pay her?'

'Like I said,' Annie told her.

'What – are you really Ebenezer Watts's . . . niece, was it?' Her voice held a tone of wonder, to add to the awe she already seemed to feel towards Annie.

'Yes,' Annie said. 'That's not so strange, is it?'

'But your uncle must be a rich man.' Lizzie hardly seemed to believe her. 'Watts is a good firm. Why're you working at Masters and Hogg?'

'Well – everyone has to earn a living, don't they?' Annie replied lightly. 'I can't just live off Uncle.'

As they walked back along Pope Street and down the entry, she thought about her own wages. She was working hard but not earning so much as to outdo the other women. Holding Lizzie's scrawny arm, she felt tender towards the girl, and resolved that Lizzie was going to have all the wages she earned that week. There'd certainly be a few shillings after all the stoppages for various things were deducted. But she knew it would be wiser to stay quiet about this intention for now.

Nineteen

As soon as they got back, Lizzie caved in and sat limply on a chair, her head resting on the table. Mrs Poole barely had the strength to thank them for going out to buy the food. She lay limply on the floor with Nellie, the baby, beside her, who for the moment seemed to have slipped into sleep. The room smelt a little less rank than before though there was still a sourness to it.

The boy, Den, stood watchful and sullen and the two little girls were back on the step again, eerily like two peas in a pod, saying nothing.

So Annie took charge.

She would have liked to do something for the baby – change her into something dry at least – but there seemed no point in disturbing her for the moment nor was there much hope of anything to change her into anyway.

Annie took off her hat and coat and found a hook on the back of the door. Going to the range, which was still warm, she saw the embers of a fire. At least we can boil some water, she thought, although it's going to take an age. She went into the scullery adjacent to the downstairs room, but though there was a stone sink, she saw that the waste ran out into a pail below and there was no pump for any water.

'Where do we get water from?' she asked Den.

With the air of an old man who has lived much, Den picked up the bucket and disappeared outside, staggering back in with it almost full. Annie looked dubiously into the pail, wondering why three members of the family were sick and not the others. We must boil it somehow, she thought. She had read about Miss Nightingale's work in Crimea and how to nurse people in the healthiest manner, keeping germs at bay and having plenty of fresh air. She eyed the one cracked window with a sense of despair. These houses each backed on to another, similarly cramped, in the street, so there was no back door. And she could hardly suggest keeping the only door open when it was so cold.

'Is there anything else for the fire?' she asked Den. He was staring at her and she thought she had never seen a child with such a hard gaze. His fierce eyes looked out from under an overgrown fringe of brown hair. There was something almost frightening about him. He shook his head.

'Nobbut that chair.'

Backless and dried out, it was pushed half under the table.

'It does look rickety,' she agreed.

As if to demonstrate, Den picked it up and one leg and the supporting bar under the seat fell off.

'Put it on the fire,' Annie ordered. 'We'll get another chair from somewhere if necessary. But we must get this water boiled. Can we break up the rest of it?'

Den tried, in a manly fashion, then shook his head. 'I'll ask Mr Blount,' he said gruffly, and vanished again.

They managed to build the fire and, after what seemed an eternity to Annie, who was worried about getting home, the water boiled for tea. Annie cut bread for Den and the little girls who came to the table, all three gulping the food down like hungry little dogs. She made black tea, looking round for anything to pour it into. There were two cups so she gave them to Lizzie and her mother.

'You can all have some after,' she promised, smiling at the children, who looked solemnly back at her. The two little girls, she noticed, at least had shoes on their feet. 'But we must wash the cups properly.'

She could see there would be nothing in the way of soap in the house, so very hot water would have to do.

There was nothing else to sit on so Annie stood by the table as the children ate. She had not fitted either of the new gas mantles and the light of the candle was dwindling now, so she lit one of those she had bought, seeing tiny flames reflected in the eyes of the little girls.

'Are you twins?' she asked them.

They glanced at each other, then nodded, mouths crammed. With their bird's-nest hair, grimy faces and cut-down clothes, there was something wild-looking about them, but they had a sweetness to them also, like Lizzie. Annie wondered what had happened to this family, but now did not seem the time to ask. She was about to enquire as to their names, when Den spoke up.

'That's Ada, that's Ivy,' he said. Some food had improved his mood a little, but he still had a gruff, angry manner.

'It's very good of yer, lady.' Annie heard Mrs Poole's voice from behind her, so soft that she only just caught the words. She was sitting up, sipping at the tea. Annie had asked Mrs Wills for an ounce of sugar and it seemed to be bringing the woman round a little. Annie had also put some water aside to cool in a saucer for the baby.

'Oh, everyone needs a helping hand when there's sickness about,' Annie said.

'I don't know as I can pay yer . . . I'm doing my best

to work, but . . . I'm not lazy, yer know – I wouldn't want yer thinking I'm . . .' She trailed off.

'It's all right, Mrs Poole,' Annie said.

'It's summat going round,' Mrs Poole said weakly. 'Next door've 'ad it . . . And I can't manage . . . Not like this . . .'

'Don't worry, Mom.' Lizzie was sipping her tea as well. 'I'll soon have my wages . . .'

'Please don't worry yourself,' Annie said, going to her. 'I'm happy to help.' And as she said it she realized that she did feel in her element, helping like this. Not preaching – but doing and being useful.

She smiled down at Mrs Poole. The baby girl, Nellie, was on her back, a lock of blonde hair across her forehead, sweet-faced in the gloom.

'I'll come in tomorrow after work and see how you are. But now I really must get home – my uncle and aunt will be worried.'

'Den,' Lizzie said. 'Take the lady back to her house. Chain Street, ain't it?'

Outside it was quite cold and the fog had thickened so that they could barely see a yard in front of them. Each gas lamp offered a blurred aura of light, making the dark around it seem even denser. The damp air, full of smoke and other effluents, stung her nostrils and made her and the boy cough. Everyone in the streets seemed to be coughing and hawking as well.

Walking beside Den Poole was like being accompanied by a swaggering little man. Despite walking barefoot, he moved at astonishing speed, so that even Annie, who was nippy on her feet, had to make quite an effort to keep up, trusting that he knew where he was going.

157

She prayed that one of her ankles would not turn on the cobbles or in some unseen hole as they crossed the road. But Den seemed to know every inch of the place, with all the certainty of a little dog. Thank heaven for him! How would she have found the way home through these invisible, sinister streets without this expert guide?

It was then she also realized that she was famished herself. She had no idea what the time was now. It felt like the middle of the night.

'How old are you, Den?' she panted, trying to be friendly as they scurried along.

'Nine,' he said, to her surprise. He was small for his age, she thought.

'And your sisters?'

'Ada and Ivy're six. Dunno about Nellie. 'Er's a babby.'

'And what about your father?' she said gently, somehow hoping to reach the young boy in him.

But it was like questioning a wall. He did not answer and she regretted asking. She had already wrung out of him the only words he uttered during their trot back to Chain Street. When they reached the end of the road, he stopped and pointed.

'Thank you, Den,' she said. 'You've been very helpful.'

But he swung round instantly and disappeared into the murk and Annie could not help but think of a young rat, vanishing down a hole.

'Where in heaven's name have you *been*?'

Aunt Hatt rushed to let her in. Annie saw Margaret's frightened face looking round the door of the family's living room. To Annie's surprise, her aunt fell upon her and pulled her into her arms.

'I'm so sorry . . .' Annie began, but had the air knocked out of her by the embrace.

'Oh, my dear – where on earth have you *been* all this time?' Aunt Hatt repeated. She sounded close to tears. 'If anything happened to you I could never look your father in the face again. Come in, come in – we've been waiting . . . We didn't like to start without you.'

Annie hurriedly took off her hat and coat and joined the others now seated at the table. To her horror the clock on the mantelpiece said twenty to nine!

'Annie, why're you so *late*?' Margaret hissed, furious that her uncle and aunt had been so put out. She had been frightened as well. 'We've all been beside ourselves.'

'Ah!' Uncle Eb greeted her. 'So you've not been sold into the White Slave Trade like your aunt was quite sure you had?' He was smiling, but she could see that he had been anxious.

'I'm very sorry to cause you worry, Uncle and Aunt,' Annie said, genuinely contrite as she took her place at the table. 'I really am. Only, there's a girl, Lizzie Poole, works in the factory with me – she was very ill. I took her home and when I got there, it was the most terrible place, on a yard, and her mother was sick as well and just lying there on the floor . . .'

She was gabbling, the shock of it coming to her now. In her young years of assisting people, she had never seen a household as abject as that of the Pooles'.

'So I had to help and it took for ever just to boil some water . . .'

'You've been in those backyards, a little thing like you?' Aunt Hatt stilled the spoon she was serving stew with for a moment and stared at Annie appalled. 'What did you want to go there for? They're filthy, dirty places, those yards. You never know what you might catch – or what sort of rough people'll be hanging about! You might've . . .' She decided not to share her thoughts about what might have befallen Annie. 'I've never set *foot* in one of them places – nor would I! Where was this?'

'In Pope Street,' Annie said, astonished by her aunt's reaction. Their parents had always told them that no place was too humble for them to visit, no person beyond the reach of the Lord's light and care. She knew Aunt Hatt was from a well-to-do family, but had she never set foot in a place where so many people lived close by? Didn't she *care* about the people around her?

'Ooh,' Aunt Hatt shuddered, rather like a bird re-arranging its feathers. 'I don't know how you could.' She passed Annie a plate piled with food. Kidneys gleamed in gravy. Eb was already eating urgently.

'There're five children and the father has deserted them,' Annie said heatedly, feeling harsh judgement on the man rise in her once again. 'He's left the poor woman with only one child old enough to do a day's work – just old enough, anyway. Poor Lizzie – and now she's sick herself. The boy, who should be at school, is selling fire-wood on the streets and there was not a farthing nor a mouthful of food in the house. And the baby is poorly as well.'

Annie could see her sister listening to her attentively.

'Oh, how dreadful,' Margaret said, her annoyance melting into sympathy now she could see Annie was safe.

Aunt Hatt was staring at her. 'Well, what did you think you could do about it?' she said rather tartly.

'Well, we – the boy and I – put one of the chairs on

the fire and I went to the shop nearby and got a few things for them – on the strap,' Annie explained, proud of herself for acquiring this expression.

Uncle Eb snorted, seemingly in amusement at this.

'And Uncle,' Annie said with renewed urgency. 'I think I must give the family my wages from the factory. After all, we are well fed and the money is not truly necessary for us, is it? I could hold a little back to cover my keep if you—'

'Give it 'em,' Uncle Eb said, with a wave of his hand. 'If that's the straits they're in – if they're on the parish they won't need to go shouting it about that someone's giving them a bit extra, though.' He gave Annie a bewildered look. 'I don't know why you're working in that factory in the first place. But you've a good heart in yer, wench, I'll say that.'

'It's what we are enjoined to do,' Annie said firmly. 'Matthew chapter twenty-five, *Lord, when did we see thee hungry and give thee food? . . . As you did it to the least of my brethren, you did it to me . . .*'

Eb stared at her, fork in hand. 'Ar, well, I wouldn't know about that. But it's a hard life for some and we're doing all right. So give 'em your bits of wages if that's what yer want.'

'But you mustn't go back to those awful yards again,' Aunt Hatt said, looking round the cluttered room as if it was a haven of safety.

'But I must,' Annie said. 'I've promised I'll go tomorrow. They are in the most terrible way, Aunt Hatt – it's my Christian duty to go.'

'Well,' Aunt Hatt said huffily, 'I believe in looking after my own, not chasing after every waif and stray. I don't know why you want to go running after these people as can't help themselves.'

'But Annie's right, Aunt.' To Annie's surprise she heard Margaret's voice speak up gently in support of her. 'It's what we believe in – and it's what we do.'

Annie looked across at Margaret and they both smiled.

That night Annie dreamt about Charles Barber. She fell into bed utterly exhausted, her mind full of the Pooles' house, the terrible smell of it weaving itself into her memories. But once she slept it was he, instead, who forced his way into her dreams.

This time it was herself he was coming for. His face wore the strange, livid expression she had seen as he had shoved Margaret against the wall of the stables, pushing her to the ground, his hands groping at her . . . An ecstasy of rage boiled in her and she wrestled with him, lashing out, fighting him . . .

'Annie . . . Annie, what is it?'

Margaret's voice came to her, very close, and she felt her sister's hand on her shoulder, soothing her. 'Are you all right? You're not sick as well?'

Annie scarcely knew where she was. Her nightclothes were clammy with sweat. Disarmed by the darkness, she said, 'I was dreaming about him.'

Margaret lay back with a sigh, but she kept her hand on Annie's arm. Annie found it comforting.

'I was dreaming about that night.' She drew in a shaky breath. 'I can hardly believe now that it was real – that I . . .'

'You were trying to help me,' Margaret said softly. 'You *did* help me – you rescued me.' She paused. 'Are you ashamed?'

The question pierced into Annie. *You could have*

killed him . . . their father had raged, when he saw what had happened. Yes – she felt shame. Yet there was also exaltation, at the time, a thrilling strength in lashing out at something so clearly, utterly wrong. As if it had not been Charles Barber, the fragile disciple of their father, but a wild beast. *Should* she feel ashamed? What she felt, lying there in the night's blackness, was frightened and sobered by knowing what she was capable of.

'Do you wish I hadn't?' she asked.

'No. Of course not,' Margaret said. After a long silence, still feeling her sister's hand on her arm, Annie heard her say, 'I don't suppose either of us will marry now, will we?'

Twenty

Lizzie came into work as usual the next day, looking wrung out, her gentle face seeming unable to raise any expression.

'You all right, wench?' someone called to her in a motherly way as they all poured into the workroom. Lizzie nodded faintly.

'Lizzie?' Annie said as they took their places at their presses. 'Have you eaten anything today?'

Lizzie turned and nodded faintly. 'Mom's a bit better. 'Er made me some tea. I don't feel like anything much.'

Annie wondered if this was just Lizzie making a virtue of necessity. She worried about the girl all day, glancing at her often as they raced through their work, pouring torrents of the shiny, sharp-edged blanks into the boxes below the press. She felt protective towards sweet little Lizzie as though she was her younger sister. To her surprise, she realized that she had not once thought of talking to Lizzie about faith, or asked if she ever read the Bible. She just felt sorry for her and wanted to help.

Lizzie kept her head down and worked. When the bell rang at dinner time, guessing that the girl would have no food and no one bringing her any, Annie said, 'Look, Lizzie, come out with me. You can meet my sister and we'll have a bite together.'

'I'm not really hungry,' Lizzie tried to resist.

'Come on.' Annie took her arm. 'If you're not still being sick, you'll feel better for something inside you.'

Margaret was waiting outside as usual, with a pudding basin filled with last night's stew. Annie felt happy and proud at the sight of her graceful-looking sister in her grey coat, and her lovely, reassuring face under her hat.

'This is Lizzie,' she said. 'Lizzie, this is my sister Margaret.'

Annie saw Margaret take Lizzie in and manage to quell her shock at how young the girl looked, how thin and ill. Lizzie nodded shyly at her, not seeming to have the energy to do anything else.

'Nice to meet you, Lizzie,' Margaret said, and Lizzie suddenly managed a smile, hearing the kindness in her voice. 'Here, look –' Margaret said to Annie. 'Mrs S has put plenty more potatoes in for you.'

'Good,' Annie said. 'We're going to share it, aren't we, Lizzie? I can't eat all this.' It was untrue but it seemed to make Lizzie feel a bit better.

They said goodbye to Margaret and went to the room in the factory where they were allowed to eat, sitting at old, deal tables. The room was full of chatter. Annie saw Doris and some of the others eyeing them as they came in but for once Doris kept her observations to herself.

'Go on,' Annie encouraged Lizzie. She held out the spoon to her. 'Have some. It's still nice and warm and the gravy's lovely.'

She saw Lizzie steel herself, as if she wasn't certain eating was a good idea. She shaved off a little piece of gravy-dipped potato and put it in her mouth. A look of pleasure came over her.

'That's *nice*.'

'Go on,' Annie said. 'Have all you like. I had some last night – your need is greater than mine.'

Annie took another mouthful and held out the spoon to Lizzie and so they alternated, Annie holding back from taking very much while trying to look as if she was really tucking in. Once she got going, Lizzie ate with relish.

'Does your sister come every day?' she asked.

'Yes. I've told her she needn't,' Annie said. 'But she likes getting out and about. It gets her out of the office.'

Lizzie took another mouthful. Now that she was eating she seemed unable to stop.

'She works in the office with our auntie, you see.'

'Have you always lived with your auntie?' Lizzie asked, frowning.

'Oh – no. We're just . . .' How could she explain this? Annie thought. 'We're just staying for a while. Getting to know them . . .' She wanted to get off the subject. 'And the others in the building. There's a gem setter upstairs – and an enameller called Jack Sidwell.' She rolled her eyes comically. 'I think he's sweet on me. Every time I'm in the house he keeps lurking about on the stairs. I avoid him like the plague.'

Lizzie's eyes widened and she put her hand over her mouth, bursting into giggles like a little girl.

Annie felt a bit guilty, joking about Jack Sidwell, but his keenness on her was so unsubtle and obvious that the whole household was aware of it. And it was fun chattering with a girl like Lizzie. It was so different from her childhood home where everyone was so earnestly purposeful and tried not to gossip, which was virtuous but dull. She had always had devilish thoughts about people and now she could let some of them out!

'Every time I go past he just flattens himself against the wall and stands there with his mouth open!'

Lizzie was giggling all the more and a couple of the others glanced over at them.

'What're you tittering about, Lizzie?' one of them called.

'Nothing,' Lizzie said, still grinning.

'I'll come and see your mother after,' Annie said as they got up to go.

'There's no need,' Lizzie assured her, looking anxious. It was as if a distance had opened between them again.

But as Lizzie was finding out, there was no arguing with Annie.

'Mom,' Lizzie said as they walked into the house. 'I'm back – and I've got the lady . . . Annie, with me again.'

Mrs Poole was at the table, in front of the scattering of cards Annie had seen the night before and a pile of tiny white buttons which she was bent over, squinting and sewing on to the cards. She also seemed to have a second task of glueing boxes together, but they looked rough and unsatisfactory and there was a horrible, rancid smell of glue in the room.

The little one was on the floor beside her, lying asleep on a coat, but there was no sign of Den or the twins. The woman, who Annie saw was younger than she had thought, looked up at her in a hunted way. Her face was very thin and sickly-looking and her fair hair hung in wisps. She did look a little better than she had the day before.

In the dim light through the one window facing the yard, Annie saw anew the poor state of the place, this cramped little room leading to a small scullery at the back. There was only a brick floor, pale green walls and a rough wooden staircase to one side curving up to the floor above. There was the range, the table and two chairs, the one armchair and a rickety-looking cupboard. Apart from a worn peg-run by the range there was little else. From outside in the yard came the sharp bangs – interspersed with curses – of the man chopping up lumps of wood, who they had passed on the way in.

'Good afternoon, Mrs Poole,' Annie said politely. 'I'm glad to see you looking better.'

'Was you the lady helping us last night?' As she raised her pinched face, Annie glimpsed, past the careworn and sickly look, a sweet girl who must once have looked much as Lizzie did now. 'I was feeling that bad I never even said thank you.'

'It's all right,' Annie said, wondering about the water supply again. She knew from her reading that diarrhoea was often a killer in these big city neighbourhoods, brought about by contaminated water. But not everyone in the family was ill, so perhaps this was not the cause. 'You did look very poorly.'

'We weren't the only ones in the yard,' Mrs Poole said. 'This one's not right yet, neither.'

Her face full of worry, she looked down at the sleeping child.

''Er's hardly keeping anything down. 'Er keeps crying and I can't get a thing done – it does for my nerves. At least 'er's quiet for the moment. I don't want . . .' Her voice trembled. 'I've lost a few, see, with the fever and that.'

Annie looked at her, horrified realization of what she meant dawning on her. How many children had Mrs Poole had altogether? she wondered. The woman seemed so helpless.

'You're giving her boiled water?' Annie said, kneeling

to look at the baby, trying not to wince as the floor hurt her knees.

'Yes,' Mrs Poole said. ''Er's had a bit.'

'Perhaps she should see a doctor?'

'No-o . . .' It was a moan. 'I ain't got money for food, let alone . . .' Mrs Poole's eyes filled with tears. 'Oh, lady – I don't know what to do. My little boy went – just at the age this one is.'

Annie gently touched Nellie's forehead. The child seemed lifeless and for a terrible moment her heart picked up speed, thinking that she had faded away. Then she heard the little body let out a breath. Sleep was probably the best thing for her, she decided. She glanced up and saw Lizzie watching, a stricken look on her face.

'Is there any heat in the fire?' Annie asked. 'To make tea – and water for the baby?' Some of the little ration of tea she had bought yesterday must be left, she reasoned.

'Denny'll be back soon,' Mrs Poole said. ''E's taken the girls with him to . . .' She cut herself off abruptly, as if aware of saying something she shouldn't, and kept her head bent over the scattered items of outwork.

More horrified realization came to Annie. Those three little children were out on the streets, and doing what? Begging for food or fuel? She held on tight to her temper at the sight of this household where some feckless, selfish man had left them in this dire poverty . . .

'Look,' Annie said, 'let me sit with you for a bit and help.'

The work Mrs Poole was doing seemed such a desperate attempt – unskilled and fiddly, taking ages in a way that provoked Annie's impatient temperament. And she guessed it would be very poorly paid. But she could stay at least until the baby woke and see how she was faring after a drink of water. She knew from experience that

169

small infants could go up or downhill very fast. If Nellie was seriously ailing she would flaming well pay for a doctor herself.

'There's no point me sitting here and watching you work, is there? Every little helps. And Lizzie, it's getting dark – how about putting one of those mantles in so it's not such a strain on the eyes?'

Mrs Poole looked back at her wonderingly, seeming not to have the strength to protest at them using gas she had no money to pay for. Annie quietly slipped Lizzie a couple of pennies for the gas meter and put some water on to boil. They sat round the table, Mrs Poole and Annie carding the buttons and Lizzie glueing boxes. She seemed to fare better at it than her mother. When Annie introduced herself properly, Mrs Poole told her that her name was Mary. Annie wondered whether Mary Poole was always so limp and hopeless looking. Her eyes were like two pools of resigned sorrow.

'I'm sorry to hear from Lizzie that you are in such difficulties,' Annie said. 'And I'll help you as I can.'

Mary Poole stopped her sewing for a moment and peered at her in the gloom. She looked as if she had a list of questions on her mind to ask, all competing. But in the end she said suspiciously, 'You ain't from the parish, are yer?'

'No, Mom! I told you – Annie works at Masters and Hogg with me,' Lizzie said. 'Her uncle's Mr Watts – the goldsmith in Chain Street.'

Mary looked even more perplexed. 'But – you're not from round 'ere?'

'No,' Annie said. 'My sister and I are just staying for a bit.' She did not want any more questions.

'But – why would you want to help us?'

'It's just what a Christian person should do,' Annie said firmly.

Mary looked taken aback. ''Ow old are you, then?' she said, bewildered. 'Tiny little slip of a thing.'

'I'm seventeen,' Annie said, growing impatient at all these questions. 'Mrs Poole – what has happened? Lizzie tells me that your husband has not come home for . . . for some time?'

At this, Mary Poole dropped the card she was sewing onto the table. She put her head in her hands and her shoulders started to shake.

'I don't know what to do for the best,' she wept. 'I don't know where 'e is – and I can't go on like this . . .'

Annie glanced at Lizzie, whose eyes were also full of tears. 'Don't, Mom,' she said, but she could not help crying as well.

Annie waited a moment, wondering what to say next. She was steeling herself to hear about the feckless Mr Poole's desertion of them. She was surprised that Mary and Lizzie showed no sign of anger with the vanished head of the family.

'Have you been to the police?' she asked eventually.

Mary sat up as if someone had knocked on her spine. She wiped her eyes with the backs of her hands.

'No. Not the coppers! I dunno where he's gone and I'm worried sick but I . . . I don't know what they might do to 'im.'

'Has he committed a crime?' Annie asked, looking from one woman to the other. Lizzie was watching her mother with wide, upset eyes.

'My Wilf? No – course he ain't. He just . . .' More tears ran down her cheeks. ''E ain't right. See, he couldn't keep a job even before he went off. 'E was all right before – before the accident, I mean. Worked for years, Wilf did,

171

and we got by. But 'e was working at Coopers, on the lathes, like, making saucepans. One of the belts caught 'im – threw 'im up against the ceiling. And then . . .' Weeping, she went on. 'When 'is sleeve tore off, it dropped 'im down and he hit his head again. 'E come 'ome all rags, blood all down him. Well, 'e healed up all right – on the outside. But 'e was never the same after – 'e just weren't my Wilf any more.' She shook her head despairingly.

'He tried to get back to work but he couldn't seem to do anything. Wouldn't go near the machines. He couldn't sleep – he wasn't right. And then one day, he just went . . .'

'How long ago did the accident happen?' Annie asked, appalled.

'Back last winter.' Mary Poole tilted her head, her eyes still wet. 'He tried to keep going, I gotta give 'im that. But 'e couldn't . . . 'E kept . . . They kept sacking 'im. I was at my wits' end because we wasn't gettin' his pay . . . So we started this.' She nodded down at the buttons and cards. 'I mean, we dain't 'ave much before, but we managed . . . And those people, at the parish – cruel, that's what they are.'

Again she put her head in her hands and wept weakly.

'Oh, Mom, don't,' Lizzie said again. Annie could see the pain in her eyes at the sight of her mother.

'I don't know where 'e's gone. He's like me – he ain't got no one else, no family. But I don't want the coppers on to 'im,' Mary said. 'They'd frighten 'im. He's like a lost little child. He ain't no good as a husband now, I've got to say. But I don't want them hurting him.'

She turned to Annie with desperate intensity.

'If we go on like this we'll end up in the workhouse. I can't go in there – I'll do anything to see that my children don't neither. My mother died in there when I was born.

But I don't know what to do. Help me – please, miss, can you help me? What can I do?'

Annie was about to promise that she would help, that they would somehow find a way, when the door burst open and Den and the twins came running in as if the devil was after them. Den, something clutched in his arms, turned and slammed the door shut with his foot. The girls stood panting.

'Denny?' Mary Poole half got to her feet, looking frightened.

'S'all right.' For the first time, Annie saw a smile cross Den Poole's face – a brief glimpse of youthful mischief. 'We gorrit!'

He went to the hearth and opened the grey, woolly bundle he held in his arms. A little cascade of coal fell into the fire bucket. Annie could hear what sounded like the fall of small, gritty bits and dusty slack.

'Ada – Ivy – show 'em what you got,' Den instructed.

The twins solemnly each reached into the little pockets of their dresses and brought out small lumps of coal, holding them out like offerings.

'I got a couple too.' Den emptied his own pockets.

'Where did you get it from?' Annie asked, puzzled.

'Down the wharf,' Den said. 'And we got a piece at Lucas's!'

This information was lost on Annie.

'What – between yer?' Lizzie asked.

'No – one each!'

'It's the Lucas factory,' Lizzie explained, getting up to tend the fire. 'Sometimes the men have the odd bit of bread to spare from their dinner. No wonder you look so cheerful,' she added to Den.

'I brung a bit back for Nellie.' Den fished in his pocket, and in his coal-blackened hand held out a corner of bread that by now had almost the look of a piece of charcoal.

Annie was about to remark that it was not likely to do Nellie any good, but Mary Poole said softly, 'Yer a good lad, Denny. Here – put it on the table 'til 'er wakes up.'

The sight of the coal and the merest scrap of food seemed to have cheered them all up no end.

Twenty-One

Daisy Tallis now made a habit of waiting out on the front step of number twenty-four. Although the air was full of autumn chills and the evenings closing in earlier, when Margaret stepped out of the house or was coming home along the street in the late afternoon, she often saw the young girl sitting there.

Daisy hardly ever looked straight at her. She would turn her head this way and that, seeming to look dreamily into the distance. Eventually, once Margaret drew close enough, Daisy's gaze would take her in, as if this was purely accidental.

'Hello, Daisy.' Margaret always greeted her with a friendly smile.

'Hello.' Daisy often looked solemn at first, but then her lips would curve up in spite of herself and suddenly she would change into an eager little girl.

Soon it became obvious that Daisy really was waiting for her and Margaret got into the habit of stopping for a chat. Aunt Hatt talked about Daisy as a poor, motherless thing and Margaret was drawn to the child. Annie, being Annie, had dived in head first and involved herself with the Poole family, feeding the hungry and clothing the naked – more or less. Talking to a lonely child was the least Margaret felt she could do. And Daisy only lived next door. Margaret never seemed to see her with other companions. Daisy, with her sad, watchful eyes, seemed marooned in a world of adults.

Margaret asked herself often these days whether she should not volunteer her services in some way at Carrs Lane church. She and Annie were only going to church once on a Sunday now instead of three times and it was quite a walk away. But, even more than that, something in her rebelled against the idea. Church, church – doing everything Father's way all the time? No! She could not face up fully to how angry she felt with her father, how hurt by his betrayal. She would not do this – follow his rule, his confining path, even when she was far away from him. They had these weeks away – and now it felt as if there was so much more of life to find out about!

On Saturday morning, after Annie had gone to do her cleaning at Masters, Hogg & Co., Margaret was in the office as usual with her aunt and uncle, and Susan and Bridget. Their employees were also in the workshop, cleaning. There was no particular rush on this week and at dinner time they were all going to knock off for the weekend.

All was quiet and industrious in the office. Margaret was writing envelopes for invoices. The only sounds came from the street or from Aunt Hatt's scratchy pen, Bridget spiking a completed order form or Susan's occasional sniffing – except when Uncle Eb, wearing his overall, came billowing in like a small tornado before disappearing again.

On his next appearance, Aunt Hatt looked up at him with an expression that dared him to disturb them as he started picking up and laying down some of the post received that morning. Margaret continued writing on an envelope.

'Ah,' she heard her uncle say. 'Germany, eh? Well, well. Not somewhere Georgie's been lately, is it?'

'That's unusual,' Aunt Hatt murmured, head still bent over her work, not wanting to encourage him. A moment later, the fragile peace was broken by a snort.

'Feller called von Titz – with a z!' Eb let out a bellow of laughter which set Susan giggling. Aunt Hatt looked disapprovingly at her husband over her spectacles, though her mouth was twitching.

'Ebenezer Watts, you should be ashamed, in front of your niece,' she said.

Margaret, having no idea what this was all about, looked at them, bewildered.

'Oh-ho – von Titz! That's a good one . . . Now . . . Hmmm . . . What does *he* want?' Uncle Eb's laughter subsided as he got caught up in the correspondence, stroking his beard. 'Well, I'm blowed – two of them. There's two orders in here – this is from . . .' He read slowly, his eyes widening. 'Ah – they're related. A Mr Friedrich Schmale. Says he's in London . . . South coast . . . blah blah . . . Coming to visit – in a couple of weeks' time! Well, I'm . . .'

'What does he want?' Aunt Hatt looked up at last. But Eb was already in a flurry of action.

'Margaret, young wench,' he said, arms waving. 'Go next door, will yer, and see if Caleb Turner's still knocking about. Get him in here, soon as 'e can . . .'

'Of course,' Margaret said. She made a mental note to ask Aunt Hatt later what was so funny about the name von Titz.

She stepped out into a golden morning, squinting in the slanting, smoky light. Sure enough, Daisy Tallis was perched on the step next door. The moment Margaret greeted her, the young girl raised her head eagerly.

'Are you watching life go by again, Daisy?' Margaret said kindly. Her uncle was in a hurry as ever, but she did not want to push past without a word. After all, the Germans were not on the doorstep at this moment.

'Yes.' The girl nodded. Her head was bare today, the curtain of thick, honey-coloured hair down her back. A little smile teased at the corners of her mouth.

What a lovely child, Margaret thought. She often found herself wondering about Daisy's mother. Aunt Hatt had told her that the woman's name had been Florence and she had died giving birth to another child, which had also left this world before its life had even begun. Equally mysterious was Daisy's father. Even after living here for a few weeks, Margaret had never, so far as she knew, set eyes on him.

'Do you know if Mr Turner is still in, Daisy?' Margaret asked. 'I've a message for him.'

'I think so,' Daisy said.

I can't miss Caleb Turner if he comes out, she thought. It wouldn't hurt to stand and talk to Daisy a little longer. She was just searching for something to say when she saw a tall, bearded man striding along the road in a long black coat, an unusual black beret-like hat tugged down lopsidedly on his head. In seconds his purposeful walk brought him level with them and he turned in energetically at the gate. The man gave Margaret a brief nod and swooped down upon Daisy to touch her cheek, just for a second, with teasing affection.

'Hello, Miss Daisy!' he said jovially. 'Is your pa about?'

'Yes, Mr Carson,' Daisy said, shuffling aside to let this whirlwind of a person in. He vanished at high speed into the house and Margaret heard him call, 'Morning, Mr Henshaw!' to the man in the front office.

'Goodness,' Margaret said. She had stood back to let him pass and only caught a glimpse of the dark beard and moustache and vivacious, smiling eyes. 'Who was that?'

'Mr Carson,' Daisy said.

This did not enlighten Margaret any further.

'He teaches at the jewellery school – with Mr Cuzner,' Daisy said, adding fervently, 'Mr Cuzner makes *lovely* things. My pa has known him all his life.'

'I see,' Margaret said. The sense of wonder that often overcame her in this place only increased. And she could not ignore the effect she felt from the man who had just dashed into the house, so bright-eyed and vigorous. Instantly she thought of Charles Barber and this brought only disgust and deep pain. Had she not been affected like this by Charles as well? All those exciting, shameful feelings – her obsession with him, her desire. It had only brought her punishment. Never again would she fall for the charm of a man! She was better off on her own.

'Do you like drawing, Daisy?' she said, with an effort to escape her churning thoughts.

'Oh, yes – I do!' Daisy said, seeming to light up at this.

'Well – why don't you come and see me later,' Margaret said, pleased. 'If your father will let you. And we'll see what we can do.'

Noting to herself that she must buy paper and pencils, she went into number twenty-four. The door of the front office was only open a crack now. Stopping in the dark hall for a moment, Margaret listened, curious to find out if there was any sign of the lively visitor, or of Daisy's father, but the middle door was closed. She could hear the low rhythm of male voices from behind it, but there was nothing to see, so she headed up the dusty staircase to Caleb Turner's workroom.

'I think it's a job for someone in Germany,' she told him. 'Well – perhaps two jobs, Uncle said.'

Caleb Turner turned from his work table to look impassively at her and said, 'Oh, ar? I'll be over in a tick, then.'

Margaret departed downstairs wondering what exactly *would* excite Caleb Turner.

The hall seemed a fraction lighter than when she had come in and, reaching the bottom of the stairs, she saw that the door to the middle room was standing open. It seemed whoever had been in there was no longer and all was quiet. Perhaps the men had gone to the workshop at the back, she thought – including that Mr Carson. She saw him again in her mind's eye, striding along the street.

She glanced at the front office, the door still just open a little. No one seemed to be moving about, and in a moment of curiosity, she stepped up close to the middle room. This must be where Daisy's father works, she thought.

Through the gap in the doorway she could just see the fireplace and, at the far end, under the window, a bench with tools scattered on it. Beside them rested something bright, its curves accentuated by the light falling on it. She felt herself take a sharp breath and gathered her arms in, one hand going to her neck. To her astonishment a lump rose in her throat and a prickle of tears in her eyes.

There was something in the shape that made her move closer, narrowing her eyes to make it out. The object was a silver bowl, eight or nine inches across, the rim of which had been skilfully turned out and flattened. Even Margaret's unpractised eye could see from the way the mottled surface of it caught the light, that it was hand-beaten. It rested on a silver base about half an inch deep.

The thing was magnificent – its shape, its proportion and simplicity, its subtle sheen – so beautiful that she could not stop gazing at it. How lovely, how very lovely, her mind kept repeating. She felt full of joyous excitement, as if she had been offered a revelation of something divine – beauty for the sheer, celebratory sake of it; a testimony to loveliness in the world. It was an object into which someone had poured their very soul.

Nothing in her life outside of nature had offered her beauty of this kind before. That anyone could fashion such a thing from a bare metal, using their hands, seemed a miracle.

She was tempted to slip into the empty room, to look closer, to cup her hands round the lovely thing. But the bang of a door closing somewhere at the back of the premises sent her scuttling towards the front door and out on to the street, in a turmoil.

Were these feelings all another snare of the devil, like Charles Barber, or was such beauty truly a working of the divine?

At dinner time, all the talk was about the Germans. Uncle Eb divulged that the two men were cousins. Herr Schmale was apparently in London: he had seen a gold bracelet in a shop in Hatton Garden and enquired as to the maker of it, since it was not the name of the jeweller under which pieces were sold, but rather the retailer.

Herr Schmale made it clear that he had been enchanted by the piece and was also interested in the process. He was keen to see how things were made and even to have a hand in the design of something unique for his fiancée.

While he was at it, his cousin, Herr von Titz, also wished to place an order – for individual framed portraits of his seven daughters. He would apparently be sending photographs for this purpose. Evidently Caleb Turner had accepted the possible challenge of creating dies for this order in his usual quiet way. Oh, ar, most likely, Margaret thought.

Annie, who had been working hard all morning, was silenced by hunger, eating Mrs Sullivan's liver, gravy and potatoes as fast as a hungry dog. But during a gap in the conversation, Margaret could not resist asking about the stranger she had seen go into number twenty-four. Could it be he who had made the beautiful bowl – or was it the work of the mysterious Mr Tallis?

'There was a man next door when I went to see Mr Turner,' she said. 'Rather a . . . noticeable sort of person . . .'

'Like a ship in full sail?' Uncle Eb said, charging his fork with potato. 'Coat-tails? Queer hat?'

'Yes. Exactly like that,' Margaret said, smiling. 'The little girl, Daisy, called him Mr Carson.'

'That's the one,' Eb said. 'He'll have come to see Tallis. He's one of them from the jewellery school – in Vittoria Street. There's a couple of 'em come back and to, wooing Tallis. Not that it gets 'em anywhere.'

Annie polished off her last mouthful and fixed her gaze longingly on the remaining potatoes. Aunt Hatt laughed and spooned two on to her plate.

'Healthy appetite you've got, wench, I'll say that for you,' she said. 'Look at you – tiny thing. I don't know where you put it all.'

Annie was too busy eating to reply.

'Wooing him? Why?' Margaret said.

'Ask me another,' Eb shrugged. 'Blessed if I know. I

hardly see the feller. He's a retiring sort, but he was about more before his missus passed on – that's a good while back now. Nice lady she was, weren't 'er, Hatt?'

'Florence Tallis? Oh, yes – quite a character she was. Made some of her own things too.'

'You mean she was a silversmith?' Margaret asked.

'Now and then,' Eb conceded, rather grudgingly. 'Not like a real professional smith, but a few of the ladies like to sort of have a go, you know.'

I'd like to have a go, Margaret found herself thinking – to her own surprise.

'But this Mr Carson,' she said. She felt a blush moving through her cheeks and even Annie, hearing something in her voice, had stopped gazing solely at the food and was looking at her. 'Who is he?'

'As I say, he teaches at Vittoria Street,' Eb said. 'It only opened a few years back, but a lot of them do their training there now. Come to think of it, his wife's some sort of smith an' all.'

'You didn't train there yourself then, Uncle?' Margaret asked. She was somehow relieved to hear that Mr Carson had a wife.

'Oh, no – there weren't nothing like that. Learned off my father, I did. He never had a big shopping like we've got here.' She could hear the pride in his voice. 'But he taught me what I know, all right – no need for some bloomin' school and all them fancy ideas.'

'Well, you obviously learned well,' Margaret said carefully, hearing the defensive pride in her uncle's voice.

'You ask Mr von Titz – he likes my work!' Eb sat back and chuckled again.

'Aunt Hatt,' Margaret went on quickly, 'I asked little Daisy Tallis if she would like to come in for a bit of drawing or something this afternoon. Would it be all right for me to go out and buy a few pencils for her?'

'Course you can, dear,' Aunt Hatt said. 'I always feel that no one does enough for that child, with only the maid and that odd father of hers. Now there's a kind thought if ever there was one.'

Twenty-Two

Daisy Tallis sat waiting that afternoon, seeming lost in her thoughts. But as soon as Margaret spoke to her, she jumped to her feet and Margaret saw the eager gleam in the girl's eyes.

'Come along, dear.' She held out her hand, looking forward to spending some time with a child again. 'I've some paper and pencils. Did you ask your father?'

Daisy nodded. As they went into the house, Margaret said, 'I don't believe I've ever met Mr Tallis.'

But Daisy was distracted, looking curiously about her as they went to the back room. She seemed amazed by it, seeing all Aunt Harriet's knick-knacks, the tasselled lamps and velvet draping on every possible surface, as if she had never seen such a room before.

'It smells nice in here,' she remarked.

'I know – my aunt always uses a lovely polish on the furniture, and look –' She pointed to the jar of lavender. 'She says with all the chemical smells from the workshop she doesn't want her home smelling like that all the time as well!'

Daisy nodded, still staring about her. She stood with her hands folded in front, her light hair falling down her back; she was wearing a dusty-pink dress, rather loose on her slender frame, but the colour suited her. Margaret thought again what a lovely child she was and wondered who decided on her clothes. She did not want to keep bombarding the child with questions, though.

'Come, Daisy – sit here with me. And Aunt said we may have some cordial and biscuits a little later.'

She had bought plain paper, lead pencils, coloured crayons. Daisy looked at them in wonder.

'What do you like to draw?' Margaret asked. 'Your friend, perhaps? Do you have a best friend, Daisy?'

'My best friend is called Lily,' Daisy said. 'She is in my form at school.'

'That's nice,' Margaret said carefully. 'Having a friend to talk to.'

'Oh . . .' Daisy said, only half paying attention. 'I talk to Miss Johnson and Miss Allen in the office as well.' She was staring at the lavender vase, a ceramic thing, pink roses on a black background. 'I'd like to draw that.'

She settled, absorbed, with the vase in front of her. Margaret sat beside her. As soon as Daisy started to draw, she was astonished by the girl's draughtsmanship. Her strong fingers held the pencil as if she was born to it, and the curved, symmetrical lines of the vase, its shape, light and shade, appeared skilfully. The children Margaret had taught in the village could usually only draw the most rudimentary of pictures.

'That's beautiful, Daisy!' she said. 'Do you do a lot of drawing at home?'

Daisy looked seriously at her. 'I draw the things that Pa makes. Sometimes he makes the things that I draw as well.'

'You mean you design things for him?' Her astonishment increased.

'Sometimes, yes,' Daisy said, turning back to her work in her self-possessed way. 'Pa says that things must be beautiful as well as useful. So I try and make them beau-

186

tiful.' She put her head on one side. 'That vase is *quite* beautiful. But the pink is a little bit . . . harsh.'

Heavens, Margaret thought, feeling suddenly out of her depth.

'I make things as well, sometimes.' Daisy held out her arm and showed a silver bangle, its surface hammered so that its tiny dimpled planes gave back the light. 'I make the shape in my size on the mandrel and solder it and then I can make patterns if I want.'

'It's lovely,' Margaret said.

'I've made other things – other bracelets, a bowl . . .' She was matter-of-fact about it. 'I can teach you, if you want.'

Margaret felt a pulse of delight. Could she really do something like that? But she must be careful not to pre-sume. She had no idea what Mr Tallis might think of any of this.

'Your father teaches you, I suppose? And what do you want to do when you grow up, Daisy?' It was not a question she often asked children, because with so many of those in the village it was obvious their future would be to work in the fields and farm cottages. But here things were different and she could see a talent before her. Another aloof look met her.

'I want to be like my mother,' she said.

Margaret smiled, and was trying to decide what to reply when the door opened and Aunt Hatt's smiling face looked around it. She wore a deep plum-coloured dress with a black shawl over it and, as ever, looked very fine.

'Ah – there you are. Hello, Daisy.' Her voice was warm and welcoming. 'Would you like some cordial?' Aunt Hatt seemed pleased to spoil the girl a little.

Daisy nodded and Aunt Hatt retreated to the kitchen

just as Annie appeared as well, pink-cheeked, as if she had been hurrying.

'Hello!' She greeted Daisy with pleasure. Both she and Margaret were very used to the company of children, to guiding and teaching. She put her head on one side. 'My goodness – what a marvellous drawing!'

'D'you want a cup of tea, Annie?' Aunt Hatt called from the back.

Soon they were all settled together. Aunt Hatt brought in a tray with tea and lime cordial and shortbread biscuits. Annie had come back from the cleaning session at the factory, bolted down her dinner and hurried out again. Now she was munching on a biscuit as if famished once more.

'I must say,' Aunt Hatt remarked as Annie swallowed her mouthful, 'I've never known anyone so small eat so much.'

Annie grinned. 'It's because I move very fast, Auntie,' she said.

'Well, you certainly do that.' Aunt Hatt sat back in her chair, relaxing with her tea.

As Annie chatted about her morning, Daisy continued drawing. Each picture was of an object or shape – the vase, symmetrical shapes, curves and spirals and curlicues – as if the draughtsmanship of the jewellery trade was bred into her as closely as breathing. She seemed happy to be there, sitting in the company of women, and sometimes as they chatted she looked up from one to the other of them, gave a little smile and went back to her work.

'How's your father, Daisy?' Aunt Hatt asked.

'All right, thank you,' the girl said, not raising her head.

Aunt Hatt rolled her eyes affectionately, as if to say

I'll never understand these people, and relaxed even further, closing her eyes.

'Have you been to see the Pooles?' Margaret asked Annie. 'How's the baby?'

Annie had been giving them bulletins each evening as to how the family were getting on. As she asked the question, she saw Aunt Hatt open her eyes again. At first their aunt had been baffled and worried as to why Annie was calling on a family in some run-down backyard. Gradually, though, Aunt Hatt had been drawn into concern for and sympathy with the Pooles' troubles – especially when she heard about what had happened to Mr Poole, and about the poorly baby, Nellie.

'Yes – she's come through it,' Annie said happily. 'She's taken some milk today and she's starting to eat again. She's a lovely little thing. Course, now it's the end of the week they've got Lizzie's wages.'

'And yours,' Aunt Hatt pointed out.

'Well, yes – but mine have gone on paying off what they owed,' Annie said, frowning.

Margaret watched her sister's intent face, thinking with a painful pang of their parents. Here was Annie, a born missionary who somehow did not want to be one – or at least, not the way the Church defined it. Margaret was the one who had assumed herself to be cut out for mission work. But she felt put to shame, often, by Annie's passion on behalf of others. And now, increasingly, she felt cut adrift from all that had gone before, from what she had thought she was destined to be.

'I just don't know how they're going to go on,' Annie was saying. 'The younger children are so little and even the boy, Den, is only nine. He's small for his age but he looks a tough little nut. The parish won't help, with Lizzie working, and so much falls on her. But if Mrs

Poole went out to work there'd be no one to look after the children.'

'What about her mother?' Aunt Hatt asked. 'Can't she lend a hand?'

'She died in the workhouse, when Mrs Poole was born,' Annie said. 'I don't think she has any other family.'

Aunt Hatt's face sobered even more. 'Dear, dear,' she said sorrowfully.

Annie shook her head. 'It's all wrong. It's as if they're being punished for being alive – for all sorts of things they can't help.'

'Well, they can't rely on you for ever,' Aunt Hatt pointed out. 'However kind you are to them.'

'We must pray for them, Annie,' Margaret said, because she could not think of anything else to offer.

She heard her aunt make a small 'huh!' sound, but she sat back and did not argue.

'Auntie?' Now seemed a good opportunity to ask. 'Can you explain to me – I don't understand why every-one thinks that German gentleman's name is so funny. Mr von Titz?'

Aunt Hatt's head shot round, startled. She found three sets of eyes watching her – not only Margaret's and Annie's but Daisy's as well – all waiting for an explana-tion.

'Well,' she said, apparently thrown into confusion. Margaret realized that the added pink in her cheeks was not just from the fire. She looked away and then turned back to them, and Margaret was even more confused when she saw that her aunt was trying not to laugh. 'You girls really are innocents, aren't you? D'you really not know?'

Margaret and Annie exchanged baffled glances. 'No,' Margaret said.

'All right,' Aunt Hatt said. 'I suppose it won't hurt this one to hear it as well.' She nodded at Daisy. 'His name is another word for – you know . . .' She ran her hands descriptively down the top half of her body.

'Bosoms?' Annie said.

'You got it,' Aunt Hatt said, laughing. Daisy started laughing as well.

'Von Titz,' Margaret said, a blush rising in her cheeks. 'Oh, dear – I see what you mean now.'

It was growing dark outside and soon Aunt Hatt said to Daisy, 'You'd better get off home now – your pa'll be missing you.'

Daisy got up obediently. She could easily have run back next door on her own, but she held out her hand to Margaret.

'Come and see my things?' she said. 'The things I've made.'

Margaret was touched at this girl, who seemed so self-contained and grown up, suddenly asking like a child. The two of them went out into the smoky dark.

In the hall of number twenty-four there was a smell of meat cooking and the only crack of light came from the middle room, the door ajar. Daisy trotted along and pushed it open. Suddenly Margaret felt nervous.

'Hello.' She heard a deep, fond voice from within. 'Have you been next door all this time? I should think you've worn out your welcome.'

'No!' Daisy sounded happy. 'And Miss Hanson has come with me – I said I'd show her my things.'

Too young to think about introducing her guest, she

disappeared excitedly into the room, presumably to look for her 'things'. Margaret thought she had better show herself.

The room, which she could see was the living room of the father and daughter, occupied the same space as Aunt Hatt's next door, but could hardly have been more different. A simple oval mirror hung over the mantelpiece, on which rested a very few objects; there was the workbench at the far end on which she had seen the silver bowl, a table for eating and two easy chairs by the fire. In the gas light she saw that the walls were papered in a parchment colour, strewn with delicate, rust-coloured leaves. It felt lighter and simpler altogether than next door.

A man had got to his feet from one of the chairs. She took in a tall, burly figure with a head of fuzzy, barely controlled dark brown hair and a thick beard. He was dressed mainly in brown, except for the cream shirt under his waistcoat, sleeves rolled up to show thick, strong-looking forearms. Above the beard, large eyes within a fleshy face – serious, sad, did she imagine the sadness? – were looking unwaveringly at her. Overall, this large, unusual-looking person, who had not yet uttered a word, affected her. Something about his sheer presence had a force to it.

'I'm Margaret Hanson,' she said, as her hand disappeared into his massive, muscular one; it gave hers a brief but bracing shake before releasing it again. She heard a tremor in her voice and felt foolish. What on earth was the matter with her? There was something overwhelming about Philip Tallis, his gaze, like that of his daughter, disconcertingly direct. 'Daisy has been with us next door this afternoon – as I hope she told you.' She tried to regain her natural way of talking. 'Doing a little drawing. She is very gifted at it.'

She smiled at Daisy, who was looking up at her, radiant. The girl was holding a number of silver bracelets and a little dish which she raised to show to Margaret.

'I made all these!' she said.

'Oh, aren't they lovely!' Margaret exclaimed. The bracelets were silver and of various patterns and textures. She took the bowl to examine the dimpled textures of the beaten silver, and the shallow, curving shape, primitive but effective. 'You are a very clever girl, Daisy.'

The large presence beside her had cleared his throat gently, watching them, but still had said nothing, so Margaret turned to him.

'I'm glad to meet Daisy's father at last,' she said, so brightly that she immediately felt foolish. But then, damn it, why did he not say anything? She was taken aback by her own irritation.

'Yes.' His voice was gentle. 'Philip Tallis.' Like the sudden and unexpected cleaving open of a rock, he smiled. 'Nice for Daisy to have women for company. I'm grateful to you.'

'Oh, it was a pleasure,' Margaret said. Somehow in Philip Tallis's presence she felt light, wispy almost, and disconcertingly female. 'She's a lovely girl and very talented. You're welcome to come again, Daisy.'

'Thank you, Miss Hanson,' the girl said formally.

Margaret said goodbye to them both and Philip Tallis saw her to the door.

'Goodnight,' he said.

And his voice, like his smile, affected her. Was it he who had made that thing of utter beauty that she had seen before? Outside, she stood for a moment in the chill evening, remembering. Am I so susceptible? she thought.

Only yesterday she had been curious about Mr Carson. They were both men who seemed to exude character. They each had a power to them.

But for heaven's sake! she thought. What was she thinking – after all that had happened, after *him*? The pain of it all filled her again; the way Charles Barber had taken and trounced her hungry young heart.

I must guard myself well, she thought, stepping back into number twenty-six. Men are not to be trusted – we are better off remaining spinsters and finding useful things to do.

Twenty-Three

As the months passed, Charles's attention had become increasingly fixed on Margaret – and hers on him. By the summer, they had shared many walks and conversations. Her health rapidly improved and she started helping in the village school again and teaching in the Sunday classes at the Zion chapel.

She sat through services in the chapel on bright summer Sundays struggling to discipline her thoughts to prayer. But Charles, sitting sideways at the front of the church, was all that filled her mind and her besotted heart. She spent whole hours trying to conceal the fact that her gaze was fixed on his profile, the pale skin, dark hair and solemn expression of one who has deep knowledge of the spiritual. Charles had a way of rolling his eyes heavenwards as if possessed of unearthly visions.

'Well, that's a good trick,' Annie said once, irreverent as ever. 'I'm surprised Father doesn't have a go at that. It makes him look awfully holy.'

'Annie, you're so . . .' Margaret swallowed her rage. Annie was so cynical! *She* believed Charles was holy. He was the most astonishing person she had ever met. And her father was also deeply involved with Charles Barber. Charles, passionately devout, was to be the son he had lost; was to fulfil the visions of service that her father had hoped for himself.

'Just because you're *mad* about him,' Annie retorted.

'It doesn't mean he's perfect. I wouldn't have him boss-ing me about the way he does you.'

Margaret had to leave the room before she lost her temper. She was so utterly caught up in Charles by now that she would have done anything he said. It was true that Charles had some odd ways with him. But she was so eager to comply with his wishes that there was never any quarrel between them.

Now that she was surfacing from her long confine-ment, though, she noticed changes in her father. He had aged. His face was more lined and set in an expression of granite-like severity which he must have attempted to soften when he visited the sickroom. She saw now, as she had never quite seen before, how much of a happy and gentle influence their mother had been. Leah had been kindly and open-minded, enjoyed life and laughter, even wearing the odd piece of jewellery. And their father had once been easier going. Now, something in him had hardened and become rigid.

In the summer, after a long period of restrained talk, things changed between Margaret and Charles. They were out walking one lovely June evening. It was near dusk and a warm breeze gently moved the willow fronds along the river. She had asked him to tell her more about his family. All she knew was that he was from London.

'My mother and father are no longer with us,' he said stiffly. 'He died of consumption, she of influenza. My only remaining relative is my grandmother. I have no brothers or sisters.'

Margaret was surprised. She had somehow imagined him as part of a large, loving family, or at least hoped that he was. She thought he was not going to say anything else, and when she turned to look at him she saw on his face a dark expression she had never seen before, just for a second, like a passing cloud.

'My mother was the pattern of all a woman should be,' he said. 'That's the only way I can describe her.'

'I see,' she said, somehow feeling put down, against this woman whom no one could match. 'And your father?'

He drew in a sharp breath. 'In my family, the men are either lions or mice,' he said. 'My father was a mouse.' There was such a bitter tone to his voice now that she found him forbidding and did not like to ask any more.

They had walked on, ascending the hill again, and paused to look out across the valley. Margaret's heart had only just stilled from the brisk climb when Charles caught her hand.

'Come,' he commanded. His eyes met hers, with a new intensity. 'It's time.'

Puzzled, she followed him back into the line of trees, he still holding her hand, which he had done only a few times before. Once they were under the canopy, he turned to face her, laying his hands on her shoulders. Seeing the look in his eyes, her legs went weak. It was not just her own heart that was captured. She could see in his eyes that he was full of a fierce emotion and that moved her further still.

'My dear Margaret,' he said. 'All this time we have been growing in friendship as godly brother and sister. You are so much younger than me but I sense that you feel as I do – that there is a bond stronger than death which has formed between us. You are mine – I am certain of it.'

The words pierced her to the core. She stood trembling, looking up into his eyes. Her future unfurled before her. They would marry, she would be the wife of a distinguished and passionate man of God. Charles had talked many times of his sense of calling to the mission field in the wider world. Her life would open like a flower, serving the Lord and caring for this extraordinary man.

'You feel it too, don't you?' he said.

'Yes,' she whispered, her pulse so fast that she almost thought she might faint. And she did feel it – sensations that vibrated through her because he was close to her and was affected by her.

Charles suddenly put his head back and drew in a sharp breath. Then he looked at her again with a strange shrewd expression, as if warily assessing her. Margaret's blood seemed to slow for a chill second, as if she had done something terribly wrong.

'God, woman – you have no idea just how lovely you are, do you? How alluring? You test my will every day – seeing you . . .'

He drew her to him, planting his lips upon hers so suddenly that she almost cried out. She was overpowered by his body, the sound of his breathing, his tongue, the way he pressed her close against him. Was this right? Was this what a man did? She had so little idea about anything. She and Annie had no mother to ask about such private things. But she was overcome by the emotional force of him as well as his physical strength. After all her years of sickness and uncertainty, God had answered her prayers in the form of this wonderful man and his overwhelming need of her.

'We must marry – very soon,' he said when he drew back, and his eyes burned into hers.

Margaret was reeling from the suddenness of this. 'I don't think Father will allow me to marry until I am twenty-one.'

'Twenty-one?' His voice was tense, almost angry. 'But you are only nineteen, are you not? That is an age away!'

'But if we are promised . . .' She began to protest gently. Surely that was enough? She found herself rather afraid of his passion. They could wait two years and then marry – they had their whole lives ahead of them!

They began to make their way back down the grassy hill. Charles had gone quiet.

'My dear,' he said, after a while. 'I am not sure I could bear to wait for you so long, my need of you is so great.'

Margaret was moved by this, but at the same time baffled. In her innocence she could not see what real difference it made whether they were married or not, if they belonged to each other. Even after Charles's kiss, physical relations between men and women were a vague, distant thing to her. Animals were really the only thing she had to go on and even then, she just did not believe that human beings really did exactly as she sometimes witnessed beasts of the field doing.

'But I must be restrained,' he was saying. 'Perhaps it is best if I do not touch you again. I must keep my distance, Margaret. I am a good deal older than you – I shall speak with your father and see whether he might allow us to marry sooner. I believe he has some faith in me so he might be prepared to bend.'

Within the month, without any consultation with Margaret, William Hanson conceded to Charles Barber that the two of them might marry after her twentieth birthday which would be in February the following year – 1905.

'Do you really want to get married?' Annie asked as they went to bed that night.

Margaret sank down on her bed. 'He is a good man,'

she said. She was hardly acquainted with her own will. It never stood alone. It was entwined with her father's, with Charles's, with that of the Lord God Almighty. 'Together we can do a great deal, I think.'

Annie looked seriously at her. 'I know you don't believe me, but I think he's . . . I'm not sure. There's something about him I don't like. He's too sure of himself. Too . . . I'm not sure what the word is – bossy.'

'Bossy?' Margaret laughed. 'That coming from you!' She flared up suddenly. 'How can you say that? You saw what he was like when he came. He was a broken reed . . .'

'If you say so.' Annie turned away, reaching for her nightdress.

'Well, you'd better start liking him a bit more,' Margaret said frostily. 'Since he's going to be my husband and your brother-in-law.'

Even saying this sounded strange and unreal. No doubt in time she would get used to it.

Charles kept to his word for the next few weeks. The two of them still visited in the village together, walked and talked, though she was aware of a certain strain between them. He did not seem to open his heart to her in the warm, confiding way that he had done before. She wondered if Charles was angry with her. He was often moody and curt.

'Is there anything wrong, Charles?' she asked nervously a number of times, willing him to come back to her.

'Not in the least,' he would say politely, giving a forced smile that hardly reassured her. Just when they were promised to each other, when they could be at their closest and most loving, he had become cold and impossible to understand, almost as if he was punishing her for something. Miserably, she searched her memory for anything she might have done wrong.

Twenty-Four

That warm Sunday, the first in August, they had been to the evening service.

William Hanson had conducted it, but Charles was there. Margaret, sitting beside Annie, watched him uneasily for the hour they were in the chapel as the day reached a gentle, summer end. He sat very still, looking forward. She sat wretchedly, wondering what he was thinking. She was so anxious to make things right with him.

The light outside was mellow, the sun sinking as the service ended. Charles stayed long on his knees after the congregation left. The farmers among them paused for a while in the balmy evening, catching up on local news before collecting their mounts from the stable. Their low voices drifted in through the open door and the air was sweet with the smells of harvest.

Margaret waited, her troubled heart making it hard to sit still. Charles remained in prayer, a lone, fraught figure, his face tilted back so that the copper light of evening bathed his features. The sight of him put her in turmoil. She remembered his kiss, the force of him, his body tense against her. Her feelings were a mixture of tenderness and disquiet that she could not make sense of. All she knew was that this man affected her like no one else.

She wanted to pray, to find God's counsel in this confusion, but all she could feel was Charles Barber's presence like a pulse across the cool space of the chapel. A strange feeling came over her, as if an actual force was coming from him, the bowed head and hunched shoulders – as if he was calling to her, trying to bewitch her. It was so strong that she felt pulled in, frightened by some magnetism in him. Her heart pounded faster and faster. What was this feeling she had of terrible wrongdoing which had made him distant? And yet he was calling to her in some way, compelling her. Her breathing was ragged and she wanted to get up and leave, but it was some time before she could force herself to move. At last she got to her feet and began to tiptoe out, leaving him to his prayer. But as soon as she moved, he followed.

Outside, the sound of the last horses' hooves was dying in the distance. Meadows stretched away to the south, green and sweet smelling, the paler acres of stubble beyond. The air was gentle and scented. Between herself and Charles, however, was not sweetness but something painful and tense.

'What a lovely evening,' she said, trying to make things feel lighter and more normal.

'It is,' he agreed. He was looking around him. It seemed that everyone was gone and it was quiet. He turned suddenly and took her hand. 'Margaret.' He stood in front of her and laid his hands on her shoulders. 'I have been thinking. Throughout the service, all that was in my mind was you, despite all the straining of my heart to pray. I want to ask you something.'

Her heart thudded, her chest compressed. Don't ask me anything, she thought. Please – don't make anything more happen, nothing new. I can't keep up with you. We are engaged to be married. What more can there be to ask?

'Come,' he said suddenly. Again he took her hand and she found herself being led along. To her surprise, instead of a walk along the lane which she might have expected, he led her towards the stable.

'I want to say a few words in private,' he said. As usual she was in his power.

There were no stalls inside, just an open place with a few rings fixed in the wall for tethering the horses, some straw on the floor where now there were horse droppings, a rough oak stool for mounting and a couple of old halters hanging from nails. It was gloomy and smelt of horse urine, rat droppings and mustiness.

She was expecting some plan, perhaps a proposal that they take off to foreign climes and the missionary field; something momentous and alarming to which she could not give an answer. She would have to delay and say she needed time to think; she would disappoint him again.

'I can't stand it,' he said, the moment they were inside. His face was white and strained in the gloom. Again, he took her by the shoulders, staring intensely into her. Quite roughly, with his right hand, he stroked her cheek. In that second she felt, in terror, that he hated her. 'You are my torment, Margaret. The sight of you . . . You must stop this – stop your wantonness.'

His voice was furious suddenly and she gasped as if he had slapped her. What kind of woman did he think she was? What was he saying?

'Because of the way you are, I find myself thinking about you every second of the day, whether you are there or not. The very sight of your body fills me with fever! I cannot see God. I cannot pray. I can only see you. You have bewitched me with your . . . your womanliness. For God's sake, stop it – I beg you. Release me!'

He was gazing at her with a coldness that cut her to the heart. It was as if he had turned into someone completely different – a frightening stranger.

'But how?' she said, flinching as his hands gripped her shoulders.

'How?' he said. '*How?* Like this, you whore, with your wiles, with your eyes, your *shape* . . . How do you expect a man to . . . Like *this* . . .' He shoved her against the rough wall and was tearing at her clothes so violently that she was taken completely by surprise. 'Do the thing you're made for – that you've been forcing on me all these weeks!'

'What are you doing?' she cried. Who was this man with hot, panting breath, grabbing at her? To her horror his hands were hauling on her skirt, fingers hooking painfully into her underclothes, yanking and tearing. She was so shocked, so ignorant, that while she was trying to struggle and could hear herself sobbing, protesting, she still had no precise idea of what he was trying to do. He had just gone mad.

'Charles!' She called his name, trying to shock him back into the person she knew instead of this crazed force, assaulting her.

His hand slapped her face so hard that she thought he had displaced her jaw. His face came close to hers, the eyes hostile, terrible.

'Don't speak, you whore! You Jezebel! I know you – I know what you want, you filthy deceiver; like all women, you are – however much you pretend to be holy.'

This was worse even than the pain. She felt all strength leave her as he tore away her underclothes. With one hand, he seemed to be trying now to loosen his own clothes as he forced her down on the stinking straw. It went dark, his suffocating shape pressing on her, blocking the light. To her horror she felt him trying to force her legs apart, fingers jabbing at the most private parts of her, and she tried to clamp her legs together.

'No!' she moaned, eyes closed, trying to escape in any way she could. 'Charles, no . . .'

'Don't speak,' he panted. 'Don't open your filthy whore's mouth. You *will* submit to me.'

There came a mighty cracking sound. Then another. A third. The iron force of Charles's body went limp and collapsed on her. Margaret opened her eyes. She lay for a second, stunned. She could hardly breathe under his weight and began to try to shove him off. She realized someone was pulling at him, easing her task.

'Maggie? Oh, Maggs! What has he done?'

Annie flung herself down, pulling Margaret into her arms. Margaret felt her sister's wiry form panting with fright and exertion, and found herself shaking all over, her teeth beginning to chatter. She clung to Annie, never loving her more, never more grateful for her little sister.

'I . . .' Margaret struggled to speak. 'I don't know . . . Where is he?'

Both of them looked round in the gloom. Charles was a long, inert shape beside them. Blood ran in a black line down his cheek.

'Annie – oh, heaven . . .' Margaret gasped, dragging herself to her feet. 'What have you done?' Her voice rose, a different terror filling her now. 'What did you do?'

Annie pointed at the heavy stool, upturned on the stable floor. One of its legs had come off. 'I hit him.' The rage rose in her voice. 'Hit him and hit him. He's like an animal – a filthy, rutting animal.'

'Oh, my . . . He's . . . He's not moving . . . Oh, Annie,

oh, Blessed Lord – what have you done?' Margaret's torn underclothes were bunched about her ankles and she dragged them off her so that she could get up. She managed to make her shaking legs work well enough to creep towards Charles Barber's prone body. He was so still, so silent.

'Is he dead?' Annie, still kneeling, spoke in a calm, flat voice.

Margaret crouched beside him. He seemed so big, lying there, so strange. In her shaken state she could not think. Dead. He was dead. She listened for breath. Confused, she could not decide if she could hear his breath or her own. In a second of insight, she remembered . . . pulse. You had to feel for the heart's pulse.

Dreading to touch him, she reached for his wrist, her fingertips searching for that beating moth wing of life . . . And there it was, the steady rhythm of it, the blood still moving. He made a slight sound in his throat.

'Oh, thank God!' She bent over, sobbing with relief. 'He's alive. Oh, God, you could have killed him, Annie. I thought you'd killed him!'

It was Annie now who seemed stunned. She just sat where she was.

'We must get help,' Margaret said. 'Father – we must fetch him.'

It was only as they got up together to go and fetch help that she felt the nakedness of her most intimate parts under her skirt. She was sore from his gross poking. Full realization of what he had been doing was coming to her now. Her trembling grew worse and sobs began to rise in her.

'You saved me, Annie,' she said through chattering teeth, as they stumbled arm in arm across to the house. 'I feel so . . . so soiled . . . But thank God he's still alive.'

Annie's voice throbbed fiercely through the dusk. 'You're not the one who is soiled. He's a beast. He'll burn in the eternal fires of hell.'

Their father brought a candle with him. He stood over Charles Barber, his shadow monstrous above him. The girls watched from the doorway. Margaret was still weeping quietly and shaking so that she could barely stand.

William Hanson did as they had done, stopping to feel the man's pulse, looking at the wounds on his head. He turned to them and his face, the strong features more emphatic in the candlelight, wore the most terrible expression Margaret had ever seen.

'What have you done?' His voice was low, like a storm about to break.

'He attacked Margaret,' Annie said. 'He had her down on the ground. So I hit him. He was trying to . . . to have his way with her.'

Their father walked slowly across and stood over them, his manner so terrifying that both of them cringed against the doorframe. He looked about to lash out. Instead, in a voice laden with quiet fury, he said, 'Go into the house.'

Single-handedly, their father had carried Charles Barber's prone body inside. He told Margaret and Annie that he was to be put to bed in the very small back bedroom beside the one they shared, which had once housed them as babies. Charles was to be cared for here. For an hour, their father bathed and tended to the invalid himself, issuing orders to the girls to bring water and soap and rags; he saw to the wounds and made him comfortable.

Margaret and Annie sat silent in the parlour. Annie made tea and handed Margaret a cup laced with sugar. She sat with it in both hands to try and hold it steady. Annie sat beside her and stroked her back. Margaret saw clearly then that for all her fire, her sister possessed a deep kindness and sympathy.

Eventually they heard their father's tread, slow on the stairs. He appeared at the door and to Margaret he seemed taller that night, his hair thicker and wilder, the nose more crooked, eyes more intense. He stood there, arms at his sides, and gazed on the pair of them.

'I'm waiting,' he said. 'What is the explanation for the abominable events of this Sabbath evening?'

They tried to tell him.

'How *dare* you say such a monstrous thing!' Their father towered before them, his eyes blazing with rage and disgust. 'I don't know from where you could have dreamt up such a wicked and vile idea! You, Annie – I have warned you against the kind of reading material you indulge in – yes, don't think I don't know. And you, Margaret – I thought you were good and pure. Perhaps you are still sick after all – much sicker than we realized!'

Margaret bowed her head under these verbal blows, so full of pain she could find no words.

'But Father!' Annie clamoured at him. 'I was there. I *saw* him – he was—'

'Quiet!' he roared. 'How *dare* you take issue with me like this? Nothing would have induced a man like Charles to stray from the path unless it was the work of a woman, toying with his fancy. It's not the first time this has happened – he is the sort of man who has an effect on women. But I would have thought you were stronger, better . . .' His face twisted with revulsion and he turned away.

'*No*, Father,' Margaret wept. 'It wasn't like that . . .' She was trembling with shock, too weak to defend herself. And the extent of her father's rage – the father whom she had idolized – crushed her.

'The trouble is,' she sobbed to Annie in their bedroom, 'he can see no wrong in Charles. He'll *never* see.'

'What did he mean?' Annie said. 'That it's happened before?'

'I don't know.' Margaret had hardly taken this in. She was so hurt by the betrayal of both these men that in her shocked state she felt it like a physical injury. Nausea rose in her, she felt bruised between her legs and her body ached with sorrow. 'Charles is like Father's son, isn't he?' she wept. 'He thinks Charles is like him and he wants to set him on his way to the great mission that he feels cheated of himself.'

William Hanson was adamant. He saw the world as a battle between darkness and light. She was at fault. She was the temptress; Charles, injured and felled, the innocent party. And his accusations instilled in her the most agonizing doubts, with which she had been wrestling ever since. Had what happened been her fault, somehow? Was she ill and flawed in some way?

They told the Davises, in whose house Charles lodged, that he had been taken ill at their cottage and they had thought it best to care for him there and then. No one was allowed near him except William Hanson, who nursed him like a son; not even Alice Lamb, their housekeeper.

Margaret was distraught. That their father expected them to exist under the same roof as her attacker – the man who was supposed to love her – was too much to bear. Each night the girls pushed the chest of drawers across the door and lay uneasily, knowing that he was breathing yards away. He had not asked to see Margaret. There was no offer of an apology.

She still waited for her father to soften to her but there was no change in his granite-like manner, nor apology for his injustice towards her. *Love is not love which alters when it alteration finds.* Annie quoted Shakespeare to her. And the second night, Annie suggested writing to Uncle Eb and Aunt Hatt.

'We've got to get away from here,' she said. 'If Father can't admit that he has wronged you – wronged both of us – we shall have to show him.'

Margaret felt a mixture of awe and horror towards Annie for what she had done, but her clear sight was a help. She tried to cling to Annie's reassurances that she had done no wrong. And during those days, in her pain, Margaret hardened her heart against both her father and Charles.

They had an answer from Birmingham by return of post and they were already packed when they told William Hanson where they were going.

'I can't stay here,' Margaret told her father coldly. He was standing close to his desk, facing the window, hands clasped behind his back. 'Not with that man here and with your blame. I do not think –' here her voice trembled as she struggled not to weep – 'that I have done anything wrong, but you have sided with him against your own flesh and blood. So long as he remains here, we shall not come home. And you must promise not to tell him where we are.'

'Yes,' her father said in a strained voice. 'I shall not tell him.' He still would not turn and look at her. She was speaking to his broad shoulders and he could not see the tears running down her cheeks. There was a long silence and she turned to go. As she was closing the door of his study she heard him say, 'Best if you go. If you stay here, I'm afraid of what any of us might do.'

II

Twenty-Five

October 1904

Annie hurried through the steel-grey morning, head bowed against the rain. It had been blowing a gale all night and even now she had to hold her hat on, its brim already dripping. The pavements were giving off the dull sheen of water and the gutters were gurgling. Broken tiles crunched under her feet.

I can't be late! She tore along the street. Just as she got to the gates of Masters, Hogg & Co., someone held the door for her and she dashed inside.

'Oh – we just made it.' It was another young woman from the workroom, called Mabel, looking at her with a wry smile as they hurried along the corridor. Mabel worked up at the other end of the room from her.

'Thank you,' Annie panted, taking off her poor straw hat and shaking it. She was encouraged by Mabel's friendliness. 'Let's hope so!'

They dashed up the stairs and into the stamping room just in the nick of time. Miss Hinks glowered at them as they ran in and quickly closed the door as if she thought they might try to escape out through it again.

'Eh, Mabs,' Dora bawled along the room, 'nearly lost yer tail there, dain't yer?'

'And you, Annie!' Hetty turned, seated at her press.

For a second, Annie took this as a criticism, before

seeing the grin on Hetty's face. It was the first time Hetty had ever really spoken to her in a normal way and she felt a glow spread through her.

'I'm surprised you dain't get blown away, little tiddler of a thing like you,' Doris said.

Annie looked round in surprise. 'I nearly blooming well did!' she said, grinning.

If Doris was teasing her – or even speaking to her – things really had come on. She was getting used to all the bravado, the Marie Lloyd songs, all delivered with as filthy a slant to their meaning as possible. And now they seemed to be talking to her as if she was one of them. She had learned that teasing was a mark of affection. No one had teased her and Margaret at home since their mother died.

Lizzie was already at her work station and just as Annie sat down the bell rang. Everyone was off and instantly the room was full of the thumping of the presses.

'Go on, Doris – give us a song!' someone called out.

'What d'yer want then?' Doris shouted back, never missing a second's work. Her hand flew back and fro, feeding in the metal strip, swinging the press, bringing it down with a thump. Annie knew that Doris had worked here for over thirty years, never seeming to feel the need to move to a more skilled department.

'Just give us summat cheerful, bab!'

Doris started singing, la-la-ing the words she couldn't remember, but the chorus came loud and fervent from all along the bench, '*A little of what yer fancy does yer good!*'

Annie, whose upbringing had taught her the exact opposite of this sentiment, did not join in, but she couldn't help smiling at the song, and at Doris being in such energetic voice at this time on such a grim morning. Then she noticed that Lizzie wasn't singing either and that her face looked pale and strained.

'You all right, Lizzie?' she asked, wondering if the girl was sick again.

Lizzie turned, then went quickly back to her machine, making a face. 'Nearly caught my finger then!'

There was a saying in the workroom that if you still had all your fingers you weren't working hard enough.

'It's the others – Den and the twins. They're both sick now. Mom's at her wits' end.' She stopped working for a second, a desperate look on her face and her eyes filling with tears. 'Will you come and see 'em, Annie? The neighbours are kind – well, Mrs Blount is. But Mom's a bit . . . I mean, you always seem to know what to do better'n I do.'

'Of course I will,' Annie said, glad to be of use. 'Are they poorly like you were?'

Lizzie nodded miserably. 'Den's really bad.'

When Margaret came with Annie's dinner, Annie told her she would be going to see the Poole family after work.

'Let me come too,' Margaret said, to Annie's surprise. 'And I'll ask Auntie if she's anything she can spare for them.'

'Won't she mind?' Annie said, remembering Aunt Hatt's shudder at the idea of even looking into one of the backyards.

Margaret gave Annie her gentle smile. 'Auntie's kind really – you know she is. She just isn't sure about people she doesn't know. If it's someone with a name and she hears what they're suffering, I'm sure she'll be sympathetic.'

The streets were smudged with fog again as workers poured out of Masters, Hogg & Co. at six o'clock. Among the crowd, Annie recognized Margaret's curvaceous silhouette in the dim light of the street, in her long coat and a wide-brimmed hat, lent to her by Aunt Hatt.

'Margaret said she would come and lend a hand,' Annie told Lizzie, who nodded and gave a faint smile. She seemed reassured, as if the two of them were like older sisters giving her help, and Annie was warmed by this.

Margaret greeted her kindly and the three of them set off. Night was drawing in, the air damp and acrid. Around them, a lot of passers-by were coughing and they heard hawking sounds of people full of catarrh. Annie's own throat was very sore and she hoped she was not going to go down with something.

'Do you know the way back after?' Margaret murmured apprehensively to Annie. Many nights back home they had set out together, to Watery Lane and other parts of the village, with a basin of broth here, advice about medicine there. They were used to helping people – that much felt familiar. But at home, they knew the dark lanes of the village like the back of their hands.

'It's not far,' Annie said, though she sounded doubtful. Though she had visited Pope Street in the daylight, now, in these dark, fog-blanketed streets, it was easy to lose your bearings.

'It's all right – I'll take you back,' Lizzie said. 'Den can't today, I don't s'pose.'

They bought bread and tea from Mrs Willis, who

made sarcastic noises suggesting *oh, she could actually afford it this time, could she?* when Lizzie produced her coins. Annie managed to hold back from delivering a lecture about being such a sour, uncharitable old lemon.

The entry was dark as pitch. Annie felt Margaret reach for her in the dark, placing her hand on Annie's back to follow her along. The yard was a pool of dirty yellow fog in the feeble lamplight and as soon as they drew near, they could hear Nellie howling again.

'Oh, dear,' Lizzie said, sounding distraught. She pushed the door open. 'Mom? I'm back. I've got Miss Annie with me – and her sister.'

A low, dismayed exclamation came from inside. Mary Poole was sitting at the table carding buttons. Nellie had pulled herself to her feet beside the chair and was yanking at her mother, crying and coughing. Lizzie went and picked her up.

'Good evening, Mrs Poole,' Annie said, stepping inside with Margaret following close behind. Mary Poole looked at them fearfully.

'Lizzie said that your other children are poorly now,' Annie said over Nellie's wailing as Lizzie tried to pacify her. The child's nose was running and she looked the picture of woe. 'So we came to see if there was any help we could give you. This is my sister, Margaret.'

'Hello, Mrs Poole,' Margaret said. Her smile and gentle voice were reassuring.

'Oh, I wasn't expecting –' Mary Poole pushed herself to her feet, looking even more scrawny and exhausted than Annie remembered. 'I don't know if I'm coming or going . . .' She recovered herself. 'Nice to meet you.' She peered at Margaret, then said to Annie, 'Ain't you both pretty? She your big sister?'

'Yes,' Annie said, looking around. Lizzie, with the baby on one hip, went to stoke up the range. The room had a dank chill to it. 'Where are the little ones – upstairs? May we go and see how they are?'

Mary Poole nodded. 'Den's been bad today. I think Ivy's a bit better, but they've both been poorly. I don't know what to do for 'em . . .' She spoke rapidly, sounding close to tears. Annie felt terribly sorry for this poor woman with too much on her plate for anyone to manage. 'Give Miss Hanson a candle, Lizzie . . . I dunno what to do for the best.'

Annie had realized, after spending time with Mary Poole, that while she was well intentioned, she seldom did know what to do for the best. She would stare at Annie with her childlike blue eyes, looking ever bewildered by life. Annie understood the effect on Mary Poole of never having had a mother or anyone else to show her how to manage.

'I'll make some tea,' Lizzie said, eager to be obliging. She seemed more capable than her mother. She had learned things from kindly Mrs Blount and the other neighbours, Annie realized.

Their boots sounded loud on the bare treads, their shadows looming on the walls of the narrow staircase. At the top was a tiny, dark landing and the doors to two rooms. Annie pushed the nearest one open, with the apprehension she always felt on entering a sick room, not knowing what you might find.

The bed took up almost all of the small room. There was just enough space to step round the bedstead on which, bundled up under a mess of bedding, lay the two little girls, with Den across the foot. As she made her way round to the far side, Annie's boot kicked against a metal pail, from which was emanating the filthy, acidic stench filling the room. The children had all been lying there in the gathering dark, with no light to guide them. She wondered what state the floor was in.

The sisters stood each side of the bed, Annie holding the candle. Two pairs of eyes peeped above the bedding at the top.

'Hello, Ada, Ivy,' Annie said. 'Are you feeling poorly?'

One of them whispered, 'I'm not being sick now.'

'Well, that's good,' Annie said. 'Perhaps you could come downstairs for bit, d'you think? Are you Ivy?'

The little girl nodded. Ada lay very listless and Annie stroked her forehead. She cast Margaret a worried look. The little girl seemed very weak. 'You could do with some water, I'm sure.'

There was a sudden eruption at the bottom of the bed. Den, who had been lying quite still and seemingly asleep, pushed himself up, reached out to scrape the bucket across the floorboards and leaned over it, retching, his skinny frame racked by the heaves. There seemed nothing much to come up except a thin thread of liquid. He spat, then lay back with a little moan, his eyes closed.

Annie's heart went out to him and she saw Margaret's face twist with pity.

'Oh dear, you poor thing,' Margaret said in her soothing voice, sitting herself on the edge of the bed close to Den. Annie watched. She knew she had always been good at organizing children, but Margaret was the one they usually turned to for a softer fondness. She was glad her sister was there.

'I'll get Lizzie to give me some water,' Annie said. Returning with two cups of cooling water, she found Den looking more awake.

'He says it's getting a bit better,' Margaret said, smiling round at Annie.

Den's pinched face looked suddenly much younger, Annie thought.

She went to the little girls, and Ivy, who was obviously recovering, sat up and was the first to sip some of the water. She was a sweet, tousle-headed little thing. Ada needed help to sit up and she flopped back like a rag doll.

'Here you are, Den,' Margaret said, taking the other cup of water from Annie. 'You must try and drink some of this.'

It was the first time Annie had seen Den as a child instead of a hard, sad little man. He sat up, reaching out. Margaret put an arm round his back and helped him drink.

'It'll stop soon, dear,' she said in her gentle voice. 'And then you'll feel better. There's nothing worse than being sick, is there?'

Den slowly took some water before lying back again. Margaret laid her hand on his forehead and stroked his hair back from his face.

'There,' she murmured. 'A night's sleep and I'm sure you'll feel better.'

Den gazed solemnly up at her. Annie could see something in his eyes, something intense, hungry.

'Will we feel better?' Ivy asked.

'Yes,' Annie said. 'I think you're on the mend, aren't you, dear? We just need Ada to get better now. We'll come and see you again. This is my big sister, Margaret,' she told the twins. But Ada's eyes had already closed.

'Margwit,' Ivy said.

'We need to go now, but we'll see you soon,' Annie said. As she came round the end of the bed, she saw

Den's stick-thin wrist outside the covers and his hand covered by Margaret's. Slowly, his eyes closed.

'You will try and make sure Ada drinks some water, won't you?' Annie reminded Mary Poole.

She nodded, wide-eyed. 'I did try, only I'm that busy . . .' She looked round helplessly. 'They're getting better though, ain't they?'

'Ivy is,' Annie said. 'She might be able to get up soon.'

They drank tea with Mary and Lizzie, before Lizzie led them through the streets towards home.

'Just take us to the end of Tenby Street,' Annie said. 'We'll be all right from there.'

Once Lizzie Poole, clutching her shawl about her shoulders, had disappeared into the murk, the two of them linked arms to make their way along the uneven pavements to Chain Street.

'That poor little boy is missing his father, isn't he?' Margaret said.

'They all are,' Annie replied. 'It's a terrible thing, what happened to him, and then just going off. I wonder if they'll ever see him again. And she's so . . . I don't know. She means well, but . . .'

'She's a bit like Meg Parsons,' Margaret said. 'Only more so.' They laughed. Meg Parsons was a young woman in the village who seemed to be forever in a pickle of one sort or another. Their father had done a lot of head-shaking over Meg Parsons.

They turned into Chain Street. Even seeing the name, on the black-and-white sign, now made them feel at home. After a moment, Margaret said, 'That little lad wouldn't let go of my hand.'

Twenty-Six

10 October 1904

Margaret kept busy in the daytime, but at night there were the dreams. The face close to hers, the eyes, his breath on her neck . . . The terror she had felt as he lay there afterwards, that he was dead . . . And each time, on waking, the desolation and shame . . .

She opened her eyes, her heart pounding. Something had happened. She sensed it, though she had no idea what it might be. What was the dream and what reality? The darkness gave no clue, but she had felt something strange, a tremor that was not a part of any dream.

Reaching out a hand she felt Annie's bent knee beside her. Her sister was deeply asleep. Annie did everything thoroughly and fast – even sleeping. Margaret did not want to wake her. Annie's days at the factory were exhausting.

But something had happened. Something that felt wrong – outside the house somewhere. How near, she could not tell.

Margaret slipped out of bed and dressed in the chill darkness. Feeling about in the dark she could only find one of her stockings, so she slipped out of the room bare-legged, carrying her boots downstairs.

She had no idea of the time, but in the autumn darkness it still felt like the middle of the night. After pulling her boots on, she stood in the hall, listening. A faint movement came from somewhere outside, but nothing more. Yet she knew something had happened. She opened the front door and stood on the step, her arms folded, feeling the damp, billowing air seeping into her. There was only the faintest light in the sky.

'Did you hear it as well?' a man's voice said.

Margaret gasped, so startled she almost fell off the step. She made out a large, dark shape to her right.

'Oh, my goodness,' she said, heart racing. 'I didn't see you there!'

From the voice and his presence at number twenty-four, she realized the man must be Philip Tallis. She pulled her cardigan protectively about her, trying to sound calm.

'I wasn't imagining it then?'

'No, you weren't,' he said. 'I was awake – I heard it.'

He looked up and down the street, clearly uneasy, though there was no sign of any disturbance. He seemed to be fully dressed, a dark jacket over his shirt. In the gloom she could just see the pale window of his face between hair and beard. She became acutely aware of having no stockings on, of the chill air against her naked legs. It brought back the foul association of the last time she had stood close to a man, shaking, naked about the legs. But this time she felt no threat. The man beside her was solid, with a stillness to him like a mountain.

'Do you know what it was?'

'Sounded bad.' His voice was deep, but soft. 'Summat big's gone up, I'd say. Must be a good way away, I suppose, but I thought I'd come out and see.'

'The ground shook,' she said, still shaken herself.

There was a silence for a moment, then Philip Tallis,

with another look back and forth said, 'Well, we aren't going to find out anything standing here.'

But he did not go inside. For a moment, they stood in silence. Something seemed to happen in the air between them, so that her blood moved faster. She thought she could hear the rhythm of her heart inside her.

'So – you're staying with Mr and Mrs Watts?' he asked hesitantly.

'Yes,' she replied, liking him somehow for his respectful gentleness. 'They're my uncle and aunt.'

Philip Tallis nodded.

'It's good of you to spend time with my daughter,' he said eventually.

'She's a lovely girl,' Margaret said. 'And she must miss her mother terribly.' The moment she had spoken she felt horribly clumsy. What a thing to say – as if the poor man were not also missing his wife! From all she had heard about Florence Tallis, it seemed the two of them were a devoted couple – perhaps no one could ever take her place.

'Yes.' He stood quietly, searching for words, but whatever they were, the words would not come and this moved her more than anything he might have said. He glanced at her, then out at the street, where a man had appeared and was moving along, putting out the lamps. Dawn light had begun to appear over the rooftops.

'Anyway . . .' he said, as if his mind had moved on to other things. With sudden formality, he added, 'Good day, Miss, er . . .'

'Hanson.'

He paused, and in the uncertain light, for a second he seemed to be looking directly, searchingly, into her face. With a nod, he disappeared indoors. The street felt abruptly abandoned, as if the lamplighter had doused more than the little flares of gas.

Margaret went in as well, shivering. It was not worth going back to bed now, she thought. She might as well dress. She thought about Philip Tallis going back into his room in number twenty-four, of Daisy fast asleep upstairs, their lives all lived so very close together. For a moment she found herself wrung with pity for Philip Tallis. He must be lonely without his wife, she thought, and having to bring up Daisy all alone.

She interrupted her own thoughts angrily. Weren't these just the kinds of feeling she had had towards Charles Barber – a tender sorrow for his suffering? And where had that got her? A shudder passed through her at the thought of what Annie had saved her from. How could she be thinking anything soft and kind about another man – *ever*, after that?

Once the news spread, everyone was talking about the explosion at Saltley Gasworks. In the early hours, someone working there had lit a cigarette. The explosion smashed windows all around the surrounding area. There were deaths – a few. The figures were uncertain.

By breakfast time, Caleb Turner had come in and told Uncle Eb what he had heard.

'How terrible,' Annie said, eating porridge at high speed. 'I wish we could go and help.'

'Help?' Aunt Hatt said irritably, as if despairing of ever understanding her energetic niece. 'How exactly are we supposed to help?'

'Well . . .' Annie's spoon paused for a second. 'There must be people injured.'

'But you're not a doctor or a nurse, are you?' Aunt

Hatt sounded impatient now. She was bustling about in her apron. 'Why do you always feel you have to get so involved in other people's business, Annie? Everyone should look after their own, that's my way of thinking.'

Annie stared back at their aunt as if this was a question quite foreign to her. 'But *someone* has to help, don't they?' she said. 'If everyone took the view that it was always up to someone else . . .'

'Yes,' Aunt Hatt said crisply. 'But it doesn't always have to be you, does it? We've got quite enough going on here with that German coming today.'

'Mr Schmale?' Margaret said, forcing down her porridge. She found it rather repulsive but did not like to say so and dutifully ate it every morning – except for Sundays when Aunt Hatt served up eggs and bread rolls. And they were all struggling with exactly how to pronounce the German gentleman's name. *Shmarler*, Uncle Eb thought.

'I won't see him, I suppose,' Annie said indifferently, taking her bowl to the scullery. 'I'm going to see Mrs Poole,' she said, emerging again. 'I've realized that in general she seems not to have a clue.'

Aunt Hatt frowned at her, but said nothing, since she had already long realized there was no point.

Margaret watched her sister leave with the usual mixture of pride and exasperation. As the elder of the two, she felt she should keep an eye on Annie. But keeping an eye on her was one thing – trying to argue with her was quite another.

Herr Schmale bounced into their lives at midday.

There was an energetic knock at the door and Susan, at her table in the office, visibly jumped.

'Oh, my Lord, that must be him!' she said, breathless.

'Well, don't dither – answer the door to him.' Aunt Hatt sounded equally dithery herself.

Margaret and her aunt waited as the door was opened and a bassoon-like voice boomed, 'Ah! Zis is the working premises of Mr Vatts – am I right, madam?'

'Yes, sir,' they heard Susan say, her voice high and nervous. 'Please come in.' Margaret and Bridget exchanged glances and Bridget pulled a comical face which made Margaret smile.

Aunt Hatt stood up to greet the visitor. Margaret got to her feet as well.

From the sound of the voice she was expecting a tall, imposing person. Instead, round the door bounced a plump little man in a dapper, pearl-grey suit. He was pink-cheeked with curling brown hair and an impressive waxed moustache which made his smile look even broader. His hat was in his hand and he used it to add a flourish to his bow.

'Good day, ladies!' His voice reverberated round the walls. 'I am Herr Schmale.' It seemed Eb had guessed the pronunciation about right. 'Vhich means "small" or "narrow" –' He stroked his rotund belly. 'I am Freddie Small – vich as you can see, I am not!' He gave a long chuckle. 'You are expecting me?'

'We are indeed,' Aunt Hatt said, going to shake hands. She seemed relieved at the sight of this jolly-looking arrival. 'I am Mrs Watts. This is my niece, Miss Margaret Hanson – and Miss Susan Franklin and Miss Bridget Grey who are on our staff. Margaret – would you please go and fetch your uncle?'

Margaret hurried out to the workshop. The glazed tiles of the yard gave off a glow in the grey morning. Several of the men looked round as she walked in amid

the smells of acids and gas, one or two with an apprecia-
tive look on their faces, though the presence of the boss
stopped them saying anything. The place was filled with
loud male voices over the thump of drop presses and the
hammering of metal. Uncle Eb was standing behind one
of the pegs, leaning over to watch one of the men as he
worked with his blowpipe.

'He's here, Uncle,' she said quietly. 'Herr Schmale.'

As they left she heard one of the men say, 'Shame it
ain't that von Titz bloke.' She suppressed a smile, hearing
the guffaws of laughter which followed.

Uncle Eb and Herr Schmale, or 'Freddie' as he insisted
on being called, seemed to hit it off very well. He told
them, as they all stood in the office, that he had been in
London visiting a fellow publisher, and had taken the
opportunity to enjoy a holiday on the south coast.

'But ven I was valking the streets in London, I saw
such beautiful jewels.' He pronounced it 'chewels'. 'Freddie' seemed a man of boundless enthusiasm. 'And I say
to myself, only such fine jewels are sufficient for the
finest lady of my life. So I am asking where zese things
of loveliness are made. And my cousin, Klaus, whom I
mentioned – Klaus von Titz?'

They all nodded with studied solemnity.

'He has already been saying to me that he would like
to have making some lovely portrait of his daughters. He
is, you see, twenty years my senior. Zo, I thought – I will
come to ze horse's, er . . .'

'Mouth?' Aunt Hatt suggested.

'Just so!' Herr Schmale bowed, beaming with infectious enthusiasm. 'It is my pleasure to see how sings are
made – not only to buy coldly from a shop.'

'Well,' Uncle Eb said, clearly encouraged by the prospect of a handsome order from their visitor. 'You'd better come and see.'

The two of them disappeared for the afternoon and Margaret assumed that that was the last she would see of the German visitor. But the two men had got along so well that to Margaret's surprise, Herr Schmale was to dine with them that evening.

'Do not make of any different arrangements,' Herr Schmale urged a very flustered Aunt Hatt. Appetising smells were seeping through the house, as Mrs Sullivan was preparing a huge fish pie, and Herr Schmale showed every sign of being delighted. He seemed to want company, to be part of the family. 'It vill be much more pleasurable than sitting in ze sterile rooms of an hotel!'

Margaret helped Aunt Hatt lay the table with her best white linen cloth and finest cutlery, including bone-handled fish knives. They lit red candles in the candelabra and Uncle Eb managed to find a bottle of port.

'Ooh, port,' Aunt Hatt said, making a face at Margaret as she placed six table napkins round the table. Georgie had been pressed into staying as well. 'That usually only sees the light at Christmas.'

Herr Schmale produced a bottle of white German wine called Riesling and the five of them settled down at the table, the deep red curtains swathing the back window and the fire lit. At that moment, they heard the slam of the front door and Annie's boots in the passage before she came flurrying in. No one had time to warn her that there was a visitor.

'Oh!' She stopped at the door. Having yanked her coat and hat off, her hair was a mess and she wore her old grey work dress. Her impish face was pink from the cold, eyes full of urgent things to tell them. All in all, she gave off an infectious life and energy.

Margaret realized, later, that she saw it happen in those seconds. Herr Schmale looked up from pouring wine to take in this new apparition. He lowered the bottle and gazed with a hypnotized frankness at her sister.

'This is my other niece, Annie,' Aunt Hatt said. 'Annie, this is Herr Schmale, from Hamburg in Germany.'

'Ah – but you must call me Freddie!' Herr Schmale got to his feet, walked round the table and bowed over Annie's hand, clicking his heels together.

'Er, how d'you do?' Annie said, bemused.

'Enchanted.' He did not release her hand and gazed on Annie with such intensity that she turned away as if in search of help.

'Sorry I'm late, Auntie,' she said, extricating herself from their visitor. 'I should really go and brush my hair . . .'

'No, no!' Herr Schmale objected. 'Please. Everysing is quvite perfect!'

Margaret watched him as he returned to the table, his enchantment plain to see. This is strange, she thought. Didn't Uncle say he was engaged to be married? Surely there had been mention of a fiancée?

She decided that she would never in her life be able to understand men and perhaps she would not take the trouble. But just to contradict this, the thought of Philip Tallis strayed once more into her mind before she banished it again.

'Eb,' Harriet said, much later, as they went tipsily to bed after more wine, topped off with port, than they ever had

232

on any normal weekday. 'That Herr Schmale is a nice man – but he's got you all wrong, hasn't he?'

Eb sat forward and gave a little belch, before frowning up at her. 'What – with all that talk about Arts and Crafts?'

'Yes.' Harriet peeled off her dressing gown to reveal her curvaceous figure swathed in a large white nightdress. 'All those . . . you know, William Morris and the Guilds and all of them arty lot. He thinks you're one of them.'

Her husband lay back, chuckling. 'I didn't let on though, did I? Good job or he'd be off next door to see that Tallis feller. There's no need for that – I can do what he wants easy enough.' He gave a huge yawn, lumping about to get comfortable. 'Come to think of it – why did Margaret have to mention Tallis? I dain't know she knew anything about any of this.'

'I don't know,' Hatt said, frowning. 'You don't think . . . ? She went a bit pink in the face when she spoke of him . . .'

'Could've been the wine,' Eb said.

'Oh, they didn't drink any of *that*. It's against the Bible, remember?' She giggled, then frowned in a confused way. 'I've never understood all that side of it. I'm sure Jesus Christ had a drink or two – He did, dain't He?'

'Ooh, I dunno.' Eb's eyes were closing. Through an immense yawn, he said, 'It's all beyond me.'

'And did you see the way your man was looking at Annie?'

'Ummm?'

'Eb?' She leaned over and gave his nose a playful tweak with her lips. 'D'you fancy – you know?'

One eye opened. 'What – now?'

Harriet giggled. 'Well – we could . . .' she said coyly. 'If you like.'

Suddenly her husband was very wide awake indeed.

Twenty-Seven

Margaret was already eating her breakfast the next morning when Uncle Eb came bouncing down the stairs, booming out, '*Nita! Juanita! Ask thy soul if we should part!*' with a cheerful soulfulness. He scraped out the porridge pot – '*Lean thou on my heart!*' he finished, head back as if howling at the moon.

Margaret laughed. She was getting used to Uncle Eb and loved his cheerful, optimistic nature.

'Our mother used to sing,' she said. 'You remind me of her.'

Their mother had been the less conventional of their parents, and the one who lived with most joy. Tears filled Margaret's eyes without her expecting it and Eb saw as he turned to her.

'Well,' he said kindly, sitting down with his bowl of porridge. 'That's to be expected, I suppose. She was a good'un, your ma. We had some happy times growing up here together, Lil and me. I missed her when she went off and lived over there. But it was what she wanted.'

'When you've got more time, one day – will you tell Annie and me more about when you were young and you worked for your father?'

'Ar – I'll have a think.' He smiled. 'Memory lane – seems a good while back now. Though when you come down to it, nothing much's changed – in terms of the job, what we did then is what we do now.'

235

He set about his porridge, looking up at her with such an appearance of twinkling joy that she laughed.

'You're very cheerful,' she said. 'Has Herr Schmale definitely put his order in – and the other gentleman?'

'Herr Schmale?' Eb plonked his bowl on the table, looking for a second as if he had no idea who either of the German customers were. 'Oh! Yes – we've got started on the design of Freddie's brooch. Von Titz is sending photographs.'

'That's wonderful news.' She ate her last spoonful. 'Uncle – may I ask you something?'

'Umm?' he said amiably.

'I don't quite understand – about the Arts and Crafts people. What's – I suppose I mean, why do you not see yourself as one of them?'

'Oh,' Uncle Eb said, sitting back. 'Well – I suppose I am. But that doesn't mean *they* would see me as one of them. Too much of a rough diamond, me. They're all very purist – everything by hand. Division of labour – *the enemy*. Machine-made things – *the enemy*.' He mocked with a solemn expression. '*Filthy lucre*. Trouble is, it takes them an age to make anything and hardly anyone can afford it when they do. And I think, well, a man's got to make a living and why shouldn't . . . Let's say the girls working in the pen factory with Annie . . . Those girls are never going to earn much, but why shouldn't they be able to afford a bit of finery as well? The purists might call it tat, but a bit of gold on a woman never goes amiss, even if it's nine carat.'

'So you would be seen as just commercial?'

'I *am* commercial. Churning it out, that's how they'd look at me. You know what they say, "Give a Birmingham maker a guinea and a copper kettle and he'll make you a hundred pounds of jewellery." I put my hand up to that. Some of it's tat. But what we make is a treat to look at as well.' He grinned. 'That lot're just worried that blokes like me'll put 'em out of business!'

At last she got round to uttering the name that so fascinated her. 'What about Mr Tallis? He seems to do both.'

'Oh –' Uncle Eb got to his feet. 'Tallis is a purist at heart. But a man has to make a living – and he's one of the best. But he's on his own, Tallis. Good for 'im.' He turned, leaving his bowl on the table. 'Them lot in the Guilds and that – very queer. Vegetarians and such.'

With these damning words, he set off to work.

The premises of Watts & Son were buzzing with activity. Herr Schmale had requested that he might be able to take his brooch – an expensive item – back to Germany with him. Yesterday there had been furious sessions of design and redesign. He wanted flowers, then he wanted leaves. Then flowers and leaves. Or should he have a fierce sunburst of colour, wrought in enamel instead of jewels? He seemed bedazzled by all the possibilities.

But by the end of the day, the design had been settled on an opulent combination of leaves and berries – emeralds, rubies and diamonds – which would all be cradled into the gold setting by Sid Cole and his helper, another fine and experienced gem setter. Caleb Turner had worked through the night carving out the die. When he brought it into the office, squinting from exhaustion and from working in poor light, Margaret looked at it in wonder. It never ceased to amaze her, the beauty that emerged from the mundane grime and stink of the jewellery quarter.

'It's going to be very lovely,' she told Caleb Turner, smiling up at him.

'Ar. Well,' he said, his expression not changing a jot.

'Get some sleep, Caleb,' Aunt Hatt instructed. 'You've done a fine job there.'

Some of the workers were carrying on with other orders, but a select number of them were fixed on getting Herr Schmale's brooch finished in time for him to leave the following day.

That afternoon, as the light was beginning to fade, there was a knock at the front door. Everyone in the office looked up.

'I hope that's not Freddie Small come already,' Aunt Hatt said.

Bridget went to the hall. She returned a moment later, a perturbed expression on her round face.

'There's a lad out there,' she said. 'Poor little thing. Asked for Miss Hanson. I don't know which one but Miss Annie's not here.' She lowered her voice. 'He's got nothing on his feet – and he's filthy. Shall I send him packing?'

'No.' Margaret got up. It sounded as if someone was in need. Going to the door she peered out into the fading light and saw a scrawny figure outside holding a bundle of something over one shoulder. He wore a cap, trousers that came halfway down his calves and a shirt far too big for him which hung out, reaching almost to his knees. It took her a moment to see his face properly and realize who it was.

'Is that . . . Den Poole, isn't it?'

He stepped closer. Gruffly, he said, 'Can yer buy some of my firewood, miss?'

Margaret went out on to the street. 'Are you feeling better now, Den?' she asked. The boy raised his free arm to rub his nose against his sleeve, then nodded. She felt how cold it was – and here he was with no shoes.

'Come inside, Den,' she said. 'Of course I'll buy some of your firewood – but come and get warm.'

Den obeyed, but with a proud tilt of his head. As they went back into the house, Margaret saw that the door of number twenty-four was open and Daisy Tallis was looking out, her hair hanging like thick curtains over her shoulders. Margaret smiled at her. She saw the girl look curiously at Den Poole before she returned Margaret's smile.

'Who . . . ?' Aunt Hatt was in the hall, a look of horror on her face. 'Who's this . . . ?' She managed not to say *ragamuffin*.

'This is Den,' Margaret explained. She was moved by his appearance at their house. She knew he had come to find her. 'His sister is Lizzie Poole, who works with Annie. May I give him a cup of tea, Auntie?'

'*Tea?*' Aunt Hatt erupted. 'He needs a darn sight more than tea by the look of him. Lad looks as if he needs a square meal, a bath and a delouse! Get Mrs Sullivan to give him what's left of today's dinner.'

'Oh, Auntie, thank you!' Margaret burst out in relieved amazement. 'It's true what my mother said – people here have hearts of gold!'

Mrs Sullivan's heart seemed slightly less gilded, however, and her face was sour as gone-off milk as she spooned some of the day's stew into a pan to heat. But as soon as Den was seated at the table in the back room, eating stew and boiled potatoes with silent intensity, Margaret saw a gradual unwinding in the child as he grew warmer and his belly filled. He picked up the plate and licked off every morsel and she did not like to correct his manners in the face of such hunger. He was so thin, she could see the tiny bones moving in his grubby jawline.

'Are your little sisters feeling better too?' she asked as Den picked up his cup of sweet tea with both hands and held it to his lips.

'Ivy is.'

'Not Ada then?'

Margaret felt a stab of real worry. It was days now. And would poor Mrs Poole have any idea what to do? She wanted to question the boy more, but she could see that now he had eaten his fill, his attention was fastened on the room around him. He looked all about him, seeming awed.

'There's a lot of things in 'ere,' he said. 'Is this a shop?'

'No, Den – it's my auntie's room,' she said. 'She likes her bits and pieces. Pretty, isn't it?' In truth, she found the room stiflingly overcrowded. She was used to something simpler.

'What about this poor boy's feet?' Aunt Hatt said as she arrived.

'What happened to your shoes, Den?' Margaret asked.

'I 'ad boots but I growed out of 'em,' he said. 'They'm too big for Ada and Ivy yet.'

'I've nothing here,' Aunt Hatt said, almost to herself. 'Anything of Eb's or Georgie's would be far too big. I wonder if Clara's brother . . .' She drifted away to speak to Georgie at the back and returned. 'Clara's got young brothers. We can't help you tonight, young man,' she said. 'But we'll find something for you, if your mother can't. Poor little soul – and it's only going to get colder.'

Margaret found a few coppers and relieved Den of his firewood before she sent him home. Once again she watched him disappear off into the dark, heading back with the sureness of a homing pigeon.

Annie, heading in the opposite direction from Pope Street, caught a glimpse of the lad, trotting along the pavement.

'Den?' she called to him, realizing who it was, but he was already gone.

Margaret was waiting for her.

'Have you been to the Pooles'?' she asked as Annie took off her coat. 'We've had Den here.'

Annie turned to look at her, hanging her coat. 'Oh – I saw him. What on earth was he doing here?' She realized only now that she was tetchy with hunger after her long day.

Margaret explained and as the two of them went into the back, Annie thought, this is like home. Talk always of people in the village, of their troubles and cares. It gave her a warm feeling. It was more like when their mother was alive. Of course they had had such conversations with Father, but it was never quite the same.

'That little one really needs to see a doctor,' Annie said. 'Little Ada. Mother Poole doesn't seem to realize. She hasn't the money, of course.' She sank down at the table. 'Should I get someone?'

Margaret joined her. 'She's only a scrap as it is. I think we should. We'll have to pay.'

She was about to offer to make Annie some tea when there came a loud knocking on the door again. Margaret got up to answer it but stopped, hearing that Aunt Hatt had already opened it. They heard a familiar booming voice, then Aunt Hatt came in with a peculiar expression on her face.

'Annie. You'd better come. I'm not quite sure what's going on.'

'*Me?*' Annie got wearily to her feet, frowning. 'Who is it?' It had sounded like that German man, she thought.

For some reason Jack Sidwell was also standing in the hall, probably on his way home.

'Hello,' he attempted.

Annie brushed past, ignoring him.

When she reached the front step, she found Herr Schmale still outside, half hidden behind an enormous bouquet of flowers, his beaming face peering out between fronds of vegetation.

'Ah! Miss Annie!' he exclaimed, stepping in a little closer.

Annie's bewilderment only increased. What on earth was going on here?

'My dear . . .' he began.

Her alarm accelerated swiftly to outrage when she saw Herr Schmale sink down on to one knee.

'Ever since I saw you yesterday, my heart has been in an ecstasy of certainty! Never have I been so sure as ven I first vitnessed your beautiful face. You are voman of such perfection – such a voman as I never expected to see. I am but a humble man, though I have the means to keep you in good style. I have come tonight, before I have to return to Germany – to entreat you to become my vife.'

He leaned back, still balanced rather unsteadily on one knee, as if throwing himself upon her mercy.

Annie glared at him. Her hands went to her waist. '*What?*'

She heard a gasp behind her and knew Aunt Hatt and Margaret were witnessing this bewildering encounter.

'Whatever are you *talking* about?' she said. 'We only

242

met for the first time yesterday and I hardly know you. We had a conversation about trams – that's hardly the basis for getting married, is it?'

Herr Schmale began to look crestfallen.

'Are you crazy?' Now she had started – her general irritation not assisted by her being extremely hungry – she seemed unable to stop. 'Aren't you supposed to be marrying someone else? I thought that was the whole point of why you're here at all. And you're wasting your time, in any case,' she finished definitively. 'I'm not going to marry *anybody*.'

She turned and stalked back into the house, pushing past the stunned audience of her sister, her aunt and a gaping Jack Sidwell.

Twenty-Eight

'What in God's name *possessed* the man?'

Annie had never seen Uncle Eb look so distraught. He paced back and forth in front of the fire in the back room, one hand raking his bushy hair until it stood on end. They were all trying to come to terms with the evening's bizarre events.

'So he just went away again?'

'He . . .' Aunt Hatt seemed close to tears. 'Well, it was terrible. He *looked* terrible. As if someone had hit him. He just took his flowers and . . . Like a whipped dog . . . Annie was a bit harsh with him, but . . .'

'What was I *supposed* to say?' Annie protested. She had her arms folded tightly, still feeling shaken herself. She did regret being quite so brutal with Herr Schmale now – for her uncle's sake, at least. 'That I'd marry him? He's out of his mind.'

'No, wench.' Uncle Eb sank down on to a chair. 'Of course not. I just can't imagine what got into him. He's engaged to some woman – Hilda, wasn't it, Hatt?'

Aunt Hatt shrugged. 'Something like that.'

'I can't believe it really,' Georgie said, standing in the corner near his father. He had been in the workshop and not witnessed these events. 'It doesn't sound like the same man.'

Eb shook his head, leaning forward, elbows on his

knees, one hand still raking through his hair. 'The feller must be off his rocker, as you say. I wonder if . . .'

Annie could see he was thinking about his deal with Herr Schmale, the costly brooch they had all rallied round to make as fast as possible. Would Freddie Small cancel the order now?

'I'm sorry this has happened,' Uncle Eb said. He looked up at Annie. 'I mean, last night when he was sat here, he seemed normal enough, dain't 'e?' He rubbed his head again for a moment. 'Well – can't be helped. We'll just have to wait and see.' He straightened up, giving Annie a sudden mischievous grin. 'You sure yer don't want to marry 'im?'

'Uncle!' Margaret protested, shocked by his sense of humour.

'Ebenezer Watts, for heaven's sake!' Aunt Hatt said.

Annie could not hide her scorn. '*Quite* sure,' she blazed at him. 'I don't want him anywhere near me after that. Or anyone else, for that matter.'

Herr Schmale appeared the next morning, every line of his body expressive of abject apology. He seemed altogether smaller.

'Vere is your sister?' he asked Margaret when he appeared in the front office.

'She's out – working,' Margaret told him warily. She certainly wasn't going to tell him where. 'She has a job.'

'A chob?' He turned the word about as if this was a new concept. His dejection increased. Aunt Hatt, who had let him in, placed herself behind her desk with quiet tact. Susan sat and Bridget stood, both very still, as if worried that if they attracted attention they might be asked to leave the room.

'I am ze vorst kind of fool,' Herr Schmale said. 'I am ze lowest of vorms, of stupid beetles . . .'

Margaret was not sure if she was supposed to contradict him. She indicated a chair for him, but he shook his head.

'No – I must stand. I want to offer Miss Annie my heartfelt apologies. I was for one night a man who had lost his senses, his bearings.' He looked solemnly round at the three of them, then shrugged, as if to say, *Well, here goes.*

'You see, my fahter introduced me to my fiancée. He feels it is high time – high time, you say zis? – zat I vas a married man. And Hilde is a fine woman, her family very vealthy in making soap powders. Soon vill be our marriage.' He spoke in tones of gloomy inevitability. 'Hilde is one year older than myself. But . . . When mine eyes fastened on to Miss Annie, oh . . .' He clasped his hands together. 'So fresh, so full of passion . . . My heart sprang up and said, *Yes! Zis is the lady viz whom you must join your life! Zis lady is perfect, if only she vill agree to be my vife!*'

He smiled round at them, though his eyes were large and sad. Margaret felt truly sorry for him.

'I'll explain to her,' she said gently. 'We realized that you were not feeling quite yourself.'

'Ah!' He shook his head. 'Unfortunately I vas more myself in that hour than I have ever been. But I see zat Miss Annie does not vant me.'

'She's only seventeen, sir,' Margaret said.

He looked astonished, but seemed a little reassured by this explanation. 'I see. So young. I had not realized. She is a small lady – but so much fire.'

'Will you still be wanting the brooch, Herr Schmale?' Aunt Hatt stood up. 'I believe it is almost ready.'

He hesitated, then nodded with resignation. 'Yes, of course. Thank you. You have been to a great deal of trouble for me.'

Aunt Hatt gave a formal nod. 'It's been an honour,' she said pleasantly.

Annie had hurried to work at the factory, feeling as if the previous night's events had been a dream. Sometimes she cursed having a pretty face. Their mother, Leah, a much plainer woman, had said to her daughters more than once, 'A pretty face can lead to a hard life. Looks aren't everything.' Somehow, Annie thought, men don't seem to look beyond.

She was still thinking about this when she got to her workplace amid the women's morning chatter while they waited for the bell to ring. Lizzie was already there and when Annie surfaced and looked round, she saw that Lizzie's pale face was lit up with excitement.

'Annie,' she hissed. 'Guess what – my dad came home last night!'

'Did he?' Annie was astonished. 'Well, that's a nice surprise, Lizzie. How is he?'

Lizzie's face clouded a little. 'I don't really know yet. He's never been right since the accident. But he's here – and he says he's going to go and get a job! Mom's ever so pleased.'

'Of course she is,' Annie said.

'Will you come and say hello to 'im? I want you to meet 'im.'

'Well, not today, surely?'

Lizzie shrugged. 'Today's all right. Why not?'

Annie was just about to ask about little Ada when the

work bell rang. She swivelled on her stool, picked up her strip and fed it into the press.

Mary Poole seemed a changed woman. When Annie walked into the house with Lizzie, she found Mary with her hair combed and fastened back instead of hanging in rat's tails round her face. The dismal little room had been tidied and there was a tasty smell of meat cooking and an air of celebration. By the smell of things they had blown all Lizzie's wages on a 'welcome home' feast.

'Mom – I brought Annie in to say hello to Dad,' Lizzie said.

Annie saw the lank brown hair at the back of a man's head as he sat on the chair closest to the fire. Den was sitting on the floor opposite the man, watching him, an intense expression in his eyes. Little Ivy was on the peg rug in the middle. There was no sign of Ada.

'Oh, Miss Annie,' Mary Poole greeted her, her eyes more full of life than Annie had ever seen them. 'Wilf – this is the lady who's been helping us. She's been ever so kind. And now he's back, ain't yer, Wilf?'

Her husband did not get up. Annie walked round and saw a gaunt, pale man. His hair hung in greasy hanks round his neck and he was very dishevelled and dirty-looking. He was in stockinged feet, with white-potato heels and toes, and by the hearth sat a pair of black boots whose uppers had almost completely cleaved away from the soles. As he looked up at her she saw a face with grey eyes like Den's and which looked both very young and very old all at once. Unlike Den's piercing gaze, Wilf Poole's appeared vague and distracted.

'How do you do,' Annie said, holding out her hand.

'All right?' Wilf Poole raised a gaunt arm and gave her

hand a limp shake. 'The missus says you've been helping 'er.'

'Just a little,' Annie said.

''Er's been marvellous,' Mary said. She seemed full of animation and anxious to be hospitable. ''Ave a cuppa tea with us, will yer, bab?'

'Oh, thank you,' Annie said, feeling it would be bad manners to refuse. Mary seemed so happy to be able to do something for her.

'Sit down,' Lizzie said, suddenly a host. She pulled a chair out from under the table. Annie could feel Den watching her.

'I see you're better, Den – and Ivy, aren't you, dear?' She smiled at the little girl. 'Where's Ada, Mrs Poole?'

'Oh – 'er's upstairs,' Mary Poole said. ''Aving a bit of a sleep.'

Annie felt a clutch of worry inside her. The little girl had been sick for what felt like a very long time now.

'Is she no better?' she asked, trying to contain her worry.

'She is a bit,' Lizzie said. But her eyes were worried. ''Er's not being sick any more. But . . .' She whispered, ''Er messes 'erself.' Lizzie, too, slept in that crowded bed. 'If she has anything at night, to eat, like.'

'Oh, I think 'er's on the mend,' Mary said. 'She's 'ad milk. 'Er likes 'er milk.'

'May I go and see her?' Annie asked cautiously. 'I won't wake her if she's fast asleep.'

'If you want,' Mary said as Annie headed for the stairs. 'I've got yer a cuppa tea 'ere, bab.'

'Thank you. I'll be down in a moment.'

The dark, mouldy house oppressed her more than usual today. The wall beside her had a clammy feel and the distemper was crumbling off it. She heard someone following her up the stairs and saw a flickering light and turned to see Lizzie behind her carrying a candle. The girl gave her a solemn look, communicating more worry than she had admitted to downstairs.

Annie pushed open the door to the children's room. A rank smell was the first thing in evidence.

'She keeps messing herself,' Lizzie whispered again, in apology. 'In the night, I mean. It's all sort of watery – it's hard to clean up the bed.'

Lizzie held the candle up and in its light, Annie saw Ada lying amid the muddle of bedding, looking very small and alone. She leaned down to touch the little girl's forehead, hoping she would wake so that she could see how she seemed and question her. With a shock, expecting feverishness, or at least warmth, she felt an unnatural coldness.

'Oh, no.' Frantic, Annie pulled back the covers. 'Oh, Lord in heaven, no!'

'What's happened?' Lizzie cried, almost throwing the candle down on to the chair. 'Ada? Ada, babby, you got to wake up now.' Her arms made helpless movements. 'What's up with 'er, Annie?'

Annie felt frantically for Ada's wrist, hardly able to believe the child's stillness, the cold desolation of that little body. She lay her head on the fragile chest, listening for the beat of her blood, but there was nothing, only a terrible silence. There was no rhythm of life left in her.

'No . . .' she could hear Lizzie saying over and over. 'No – Annie, make 'er wake up. Ada – wake up, babby!'

She came and knelt on the bed and snatched Ada from Annie's grasp, pulling her sister into her arms. 'Ada!' Sobs wrenching from her, she shook the little girl's body. 'You got to wake up now – Ada! Please, oh, please . . . You can't . . .'

'Lizzie, no, stop it!' Annie grasped her shoulders. It was terrible to see her shaking the little girl. 'Stop – Lizzie, please!'

At last Lizzie heard her. She held Ada pressed to her for a second, then, as if taking in that she was holding something dead, something foreign to her, she let her go, pushing her back on to the bed, and put her hands over her face, her shoulders shaking.

Annie reverently lay Ada's body straight. She had ministered to the dead before, but this time she had a terrible feeling of unreality. Her hands trembling, she hesitated before covering the little girl's face, as if it was the wrong thing to do, as if Ada might at any moment open her eyes. The only sound in the room was Lizzie's quiet weeping.

There was no sheet and she chose the softest cover, a threadbare candlewick counterpane, and lay it softly over Ada as she lay there, still as stone. At last she stepped back, whispering the first words that came into her head.

'The Lord bless thee, and keep thee: the Lord make His face to shine upon thee, and be gracious unto thee: the Lord lift up His countenance upon thee, and give thee peace.'

As she ended with an *'Amen'*, she heard Lizzie softly join in. Then Lizzie looked up at Annie, a terrible expression on her face, and said, 'Who's going to tell our mom?'

Twenty-Nine

'I never knew! I never knew 'er were as bad as that – honest! If I'd known . . . I were just busy and she was laying quiet, so I thought . . . I never done 'er no harm!'

Mary Poole sat beside the little coffin in the Pooles' cramped room, rocking back and forth, tearing at her hair, repeating the same words over and over. She seemed unable to hear what anyone said, she was so lost in her distress.

Margaret and Annie had arrived for the funeral to find the household in disarray, so they hurried to arrange things in time. The family seemed stunned. When they arrived, Den was feeding Nellie from a bowl of bread-and-milk slop. Little Ivy stood near her mother like a lost soul and Wilf Poole was hunched by the unlit range on a chair, smoking Woodbines, lifting one foot then the other from the floor, his face twisted and his body squirming as if in torment.

'That's very good, Den,' Margaret said, going over to him.

The boy looked up at her with blank, terrible eyes. Nellie, who was too young to know what was going on, accepted mouthfuls with a wide-eyed, wondering expression.

'Mrs Poole,' Annie said, touching her shoulder. 'They'll be here soon.'

Mary Poole let out a howl and flung herself forward, curling in agony.

'Don't let 'em take my little Ada – they always take my babbies away.'

Annie looked across at Margaret, too appalled for tears. Startled, Margaret knew she had never seen her fiery sister look more helpless or distraught. Before Ada's death, it had been a few days since Annie had seen the Pooles. She had not known how bad Ada still was. Mary Poole did not know what to do and in the excitement of Wilf coming home, they had not seen how bad Ada was. Despite all this, Margaret could see that Annie blamed herself for not having called in a doctor.

Among all the joys, sorrows and human passing they had seen working in the village, none had felt as heart-rending and despairing as this.

Mary Poole could not take it in at first. She had torn upstairs that evening when Annie and Lizzie came down, taken the chill body of her little girl in her arms and shrieked at her, pleading with her to wake up.

''Er can't've gone!' she cried. ''Er was just 'aving a rest!' She looked wildly round at Annie. 'I thought 'er was getting better! I never knew, miss – I dain't! Don't go telling anyone I done wrong by 'er!'

'I won't, Mrs Poole,' Annie said shakily. The idea that Mrs Poole might think she would report her to the police for this awful tragedy came as another shock on top of this terrible thing that had already happened.

Downstairs, Wilf Poole sat, stunned. Already a man of few words, any that he had left had dried up.

Over the following days, when Annie and Margaret

came to help arrange the funeral, it soon became clear that the Pooles had no remaining funds.

'I'm cast right down,' Mary Poole sobbed. 'We used to pay in, like, but I've lost that many babbies – four of 'em, between them that lived.'

Looking at Mary's thin frame, Margaret could hardly believe that her body had been able to withstand any of it.

'Dain't we, Wilf?' she appealed to her husband. 'Penny fund for funerals . . . but . . .' She shook her head and lowered it hopelessly.

The sisters looked at Wilf Poole. He nodded. Margaret could see that he had once been a nice-looking man, with a job and a family that was managing. His lips had the look of once having smiled, but they never smiled now. He must be about thirty-five, she thought, shocked. He looked fifty, his body bent, the greasy brown hair fading to grey.

'But we ain't got nothing now. I'll 'ave to 'ave 'er buried on the parish.'

'No, Mrs Poole, we'll help you,' Annie insisted quietly.

Margaret was struck by the way she spoke to Mary Poole. Annie had always had a rather commanding, 'we know best' sort of tone before. But now she spoke humbly, gently. She reached out for a moment and touched Mary Poole's trembling hand. 'There's my wages . . . And my uncle will help, I'm sure, won't he, Margaret?'

Margaret caught sight of Den's face, watching them. She saw a look of intense, desperate feeling. Seeing this family, she felt her heart might actually melt with sorrow.

'Yes,' she said, trying to hold back her tears. 'Of course.'

The funeral was of the most simple kind: one small carriage in which Mary and Wilf, Ivy and Nellie rode to the general cemetery at Key Hill. Den walked there with Margaret and Annie.

The Pooles had very little in the way of clothes fit for the occasion, but it was a cold, windswept Monday morning and all were covered by shabby coats. Den, in a pair of boots from Georgie's young brother-in-law, walked straight-backed into the cemetery, silent, not looking at anyone, but sticking close at Margaret's side.

They had made sure that Ada had her own grave, beside her siblings. As the chill wind blew, Ada was laid to rest in her bare coffin and the minister prayed over the tiny grave. Margaret longed to kneel and take the little girl's suffering brother in her arms. But Den was forbidding, his face flint hard as he watched his gaunt, heartbroken parents bury another of their children.

That Friday evening, Margaret and Aunt Hatt were working late in the office. Bridget and Susan had gone and in Susan's place sat Daisy Tallis. She had asked if she could come in again. 'Of course you can, Daisy,' Margaret had said. As they were busy, she added, 'But we've got a bit of a rush on. We had a special job to do last week for the German gentleman and we're catching up on the rest of the orders now. But you can come and sit with us and do some drawing if you like.'

Daisy settled happily with paper and pencils, her face

bent earnestly over her drawing. Flowers and beautifully shaped vases with ornate handles emerged on the paper.

'Go on, Daisy,' Aunt Hatt teased her, looking in admiration at the picture. 'Draw a portrait of me for once – or Margaret!'

Daisy smiled up at her, shook her head and went on producing symmetry and complicated decoration under the light of the lamp.

Soon they heard Annie come back from work. She closed the door quietly and must have been hanging her hat and coat in the hall.

'Hello, Annie,' Margaret called. She saw Daisy look up between her thick curtains of hair and smile faintly.

Annie appeared round the door. Her eyes seemed hollowed, face almost as pale as the white collar of her dress.

'Good heavens, Annie, you look terrible.' Aunt Hatt launched into her usual reproaches about how Annie must give up that job immediately, she was overdoing it and what would their mother have said? 'D'you think you're coming down with something, dear?'

Annie was already shaking her head.

'No, Auntie, it's not that.' Annie sank down on to Susan's chair. Margaret felt her heart pick up speed. She could see that whatever news was on the way, it was not good. 'It's Mr Poole,' she said. 'He's disappeared again. Lizzie came into work in a terrible state.'

'Oh, no,' Margaret said, all the sadness facing the Poole family hitting her with renewed force. 'When?'

'Yesterday.' Annie shook her head. 'You saw, Margaret – he's a poor thing. I don't know what he was like before the accident, but he used to earn a living all right. He can't seem to manage anything now. I suppose he's taken to the road again.'

None of them could think of much to say. Aunt Hatt

looked very dismayed. She and Uncle Eb had been kindness itself over the funeral. Annie's wages and more had gone into meeting the £2 needed for all the humble proceedings – an impossibly huge sum for the Pooles to have to find.

'That poor woman,' Aunt Hatt said in the end. 'Whatever are they going to do?'

Margaret saw Daisy listening to the conversation, her head raised, a look of sad sympathy in her eyes.

But by the next day there was worse news still.

'Lizzie could hardly manage at work today,' Annie said when she got back. 'She was in tears nearly all morning. She's such a brave soul normally.'

This time it was Den who had gone missing.

It was the talk of the table in the Watts household, night after night. Margaret could see that her aunt and uncle, whose normal teatime conversation was the business, their house, or Georgie and little Jimmy's goings-on, were being drawn in to the heartbreaking situation of the Poole family. Once again a great deal lay heavily on Lizzie's shoulders.

'I suppose the lad's gone to look for 'is father,' Uncle Eb said, sitting back after his steak-and-kidney pie and lighting up his pipe. The sweet smoke whorled about the cosy room.

'He's only a little nipper himself,' Aunt Hatt said.

'Mrs Poole thinks he's run away to sea and she'll never see him again,' Annie said. Her eyes were wide with a sad tiredness that was new in her. Margaret felt concerned about her little sister, as if her heart had been scoured by the Pooles as by no one else. She knew the situation made Annie feel utterly helpless, and it was not something Annie found easy to tolerate.

Later, when they were in bed, she said, 'You seem to have become very deeply involved with the Poole family. Is that wise, d'you think?'

Annie turned to her, and Margaret saw her sister's eyes reflect the spots of candlelight from the chest of drawers beside her.

'It's not wrong to want to help others in their suffering, surely?' But she sounded upset, rather than argumentative.

After a moment, Margaret said, 'I keep thinking about that boy.' She kept remembering the moment, once the funeral was over and they were walking away through the whirling copper leaves, when Den had caught hold of her hand. His thin fingers grasped hers and squeezed, tight, just for a few seconds before he let go, as if not allowing himself more comfort than that.

'He's grown attached to you,' Annie said.

'Has he? It's hard to tell with him.'

After another silence, Annie said, 'It's different here. It's what I wanted, I suppose, but it's hard. In the village we're "helping" always, as if we have something other people don't. And of course we do have things that the Pooles don't. But it feels different, working next to Lizzie every day, almost feeling every second of her worries and her grief coming to me . . .'

Annie's voice was thick with tears. Margaret was astonished.

'Oh, my dear,' she said. She shifted towards her sister and took her in her arms. Annie began to cry, her forehead pressed to Margaret's shoulder.

'Everything is so awful for them,' she said, her voice muffled. 'As if the whole world is against them just because they're so poor. Why does God let things like this happen?' She raised her wet face and looked into Margaret's eyes. 'Father always taught us that God is always in everything, working to the good. But why does God help some people more than others? They don't stand a chance, these people, and it's not *fair*.'

Margaret thought of the old adage, *God helps those who help themselves*. But that seemed no help either.

'It isn't,' she said, feeling feeble at the thought of this great city about them, and this one single family with whose troubles they had become acquainted. 'I don't know what we can do except be kind where we can.'

'She's terrified she'll end up in the workhouse,' Margaret said to Aunt Hatt. Annie was bringing home daily bulletins of the Pooles' misfortunes. Mary Poole was in a terrible state.

'Well, she will, if she has much more trouble,' Aunt Hatt said, her eyes wide with sorrow. She looked across at Margaret. 'I s'pose I've not really known all this close up before.' Like Eb, she seemed shaken by the harsh lives of people around her who she did not normally see.

'She didn't have a very good start,' Margaret said. 'She's got no one else in the world – that she knows of, anyway. I know her husband's not well and he can't help it, but she must feel very let down by him.'

Margaret and Annie visited the family – or what remained of it – most days, taking anything they could think of in the way of help. Lizzie came to the factory red-eyed and worked her press all day as if she was a machine herself.

'All I can do is keep working,' she said helplessly to Annie, as they sat together one dinner break. Her hands, chapped, red with rash, were never still. 'I don't know how to help our mom. And poor Ivy – 'er's like a little lost soul without Ada. 'Er's hardly said a word since . . .' She put her head in her hands and wept, her fragile frame racked with sobs.

Annie did her best to comfort her, when there was so little comfort to be had.

And still, no one knew where Den had gone.

Thirty

'Margaret.'

Someone was shaking her shoulder, a hand on her arm. It was him again, pawing at her, his eyes boring into her . . .

'No! NO! Get off me!' She sat up, lashing out feverishly.

'Margaret! It's all right. I never meant to startle you, bab.' Aunt Harriet was standing over her, holding a candle, her hair in a long plait. Her nightdress was covered by her long plum-coloured dressing gown. She looked startled by the violence of Margaret's reaction.

Margaret sat up, shaken, but fully awake now. 'I'm sorry, Aunt. What's wrong? What time is it?'

'It's late, gone half past eleven,' Aunt Hatt said. 'But you'd best come. No one else'll do, apparently.' She looked Margaret up and down. 'Get covered up. Mr Tallis is downstairs.'

'Mr *Tallis*?' Margaret felt immediately disturbed, her heart picking up speed. 'What d'you mean? Why?'

'He's got the boy . . . Look, get some clothes on quick and come down.' Aunt Hatt leaned over with her candle to light the one on the chair beside Margaret.

As Aunt Hatt disappeared downstairs again, Margaret, not possessing a dressing gown, half dressed once again, threw on her skirt, blouse, long cardigan and boots. Her hair was already fastened in a demure plait. She smoothed

261

it back and fastened a button on the cardigan, eyeing Annie as she did so. Annie, needless to say, had slept through all this.

As she made her way downstairs, she could hear quiet talk from the back room; the low rumble of Philip Tallis's voice, and Aunt Hatt's replies. The voice vibrated through her. She found herself thinking that he seemed a pure soul, Philip Tallis. Something about him gave her a sense of safety. In comparison, she felt soiled by all that had happened with Charles Barber, by her lingering shame that it had been her fault, made acute by her father's blame of her. She folded her arms and, feeling intensely self-conscious, stepped into the room.

But all such thoughts were pushed from her mind when she saw the little figure standing by the dying fire, between Aunt Hatt and Mr Tallis, his head hanging, also as if in shame.

'Den!' She hurried to him. 'Oh, my Lord, Den, dear, where've you been?' She laid her hand on the boy's shoulder, almost tearful with relief at seeing him. He had been away for over a week. He was holding his cap in his hands and his ragged clothes were even more filthy than usual. He smelt terrible. But he was still wearing the boots Clara had given her for him, scuffed and muddy.

Den raised his head to acknowledge her. Margaret could feel Philip Tallis quietly watching, holding his own hat. His presence seemed to fill the room and she was acutely aware of him.

'I'm boiling some milk,' Aunt Hatt said. 'The child looks starved.'

'Where did you find him?' Margaret asked Philip Tallis. Her eagerness to know what had happened overcame her shyness. 'What happened?'

'I was coming home, just now,' Philip Tallis said. 'The

lad was outside here, lying up against the house – under your front window.' He looked directly at Margaret then and she saw a questioning tenderness in his eyes. 'He asked for you – wasn't interested in anything else. It's late, I know, but I thought I'd best bring him in here.'

Margaret laid her hand on Den's back, could feel the boy's scrawniness through his clothes.

'Thank you,' she smiled at Philip Tallis. He gave a faint smile in return and did not look away immediately.

'Oh – the milk!' Aunt Hatt cried, hurrying to the kitchen. 'I'll cut some bread and butter.'

'Come and sit down, Den.' Margaret pulled a chair out from the table. 'You must be hungry.'

Den nodded. Although there was no need for Philip Tallis to stay, he lingered.

'Children seem to like you,' he observed. 'You're good with them. Daisy's taken to you.'

'I suppose I'm used to them.' She smiled up at him for a second, then helped Den push his chair in. She was glad of having the boy to busy herself with. 'In the village, where Annie and I come from, we both work with the children. Our father is the minister there, you see.' She frowned, looking down as all the pain of the rupture with her father rose in her. How normal it all sounded – this is where we live, this is what I do, as if all was as it should be.

'So what brings you here?' Philip Tallis asked, puzzled.

'Oh – it's a long story.' A horrible flush of shame passed over her that she was sure he must be able to see. Why had she said anything about home? It had all slipped out without her thinking. It was where she came from, who she was – or used to be. This thought came with a jolt. She held on to the back of Den's chair. The boy had leaned forward to rest his head on his arms, seeming utterly spent.

'We're just here for a little change.' She made her voice light, managing a brief smile. 'Annie wanted to come especially. She was always hungry to see more of the world.'

'I see.' He fingered the edge of his bowler hat. Did she sense disappointment in him at this? 'Well, Daisy'll miss you if you go again.'

'Yes.' Margaret wished she had never ventured into this now. 'I'm not sure how long we'll be staying. Until Christmas, I think.' She looked up at him, unsure what else to say. Despite her discomfort she found she did not want him to leave but she did want to change the subject.

'I . . . A while ago,' she stumbled on, 'I saw a bowl – a silver bowl – on the table in your room. The door was open, I mean . . .' She blushed, thinking how nosey she must sound. 'Daisy said you made it.'

'Yes,' he said. 'I do some things of my own, when I get the time.'

'Oh!' Her heart was beating fast. 'I would love to see some of your work!'

Almost immediately she regretted it. Would he take this the wrong way? She floundered inside. How were you supposed to talk to men if they always got the wrong idea? She had a horror now of appearing fast in some way, of giving off a message that she had not intended.

'Well – sometime, perhaps,' he said, seeming uncertain. 'Good. Right then.' Looking at Den, he moved closer. Above the beard, the strong features, she saw how big his eyes were, and how full of a sad sympathy. 'Poor lad. How long's he been living rough like that?'

'A few days.' She spoke barely above a whisper,

although Den was obviously asleep. 'My sister Annie works with his elder sister at Masters and Hogg, you see. His family have had a very unfortunate time lately. One of his little sisters died, and then . . .' She explained briefly about Wilf Poole, the accident and what had followed. She saw Philip Tallis's expression darken.

'My God,' he said angrily. 'What is he –' he nodded towards Den – 'Daisy's age?'

'I believe he's a little younger.'

'Will you put him up here for the night?'

'I think that might be best.'

Aunt Hatt swept in with a tray. 'Oh!' she said, seeing Den fast asleep at the table.

'I think we should give him something,' Margaret said. 'Who knows when he last ate? He'll go back to sleep afterwards.'

'I'd best be going,' Philip Tallis said.

Margaret saw him to the door, intensely aware, in the dark passage, of his sturdy form behind her. In that moment she was filled with an exciting awareness of her own femininity which in the next moment was clouded with shame.

'Here we are,' she said, for something to say, when she reached the door. She pulled it open.

Philip Tallis paused. Faint light reached them from the lamp along the street. Their eyes met in the almost-darkness. She did not want him to leave, nor did he seem to want to go. There was a fascination in him, a charge which drew her. Heaven help me, she thought. This man . . . What is the matter with me?

'It's all right?' she forced herself to say. 'My coming in with Daisy?'

'Yes,' he said simply. 'Of course. Come – whenever

you like.' He hesitated, then nodded, before stepping outside. 'Goodnight.'

In the seconds she was in the passage before returning to her aunt, Margaret gave herself a stern ticking-off.

Whatever are you doing? *No men.* Stop it . . . Remember how it was with Charles? No. And this one is even older – stop being so ridiculous . . . You'll just give him the wrong idea. In any case, we've got to go home . . . She composed her face.

They woke Den for just long enough for him to wolf down some bread and butter and the warm milk. He was asleep again almost before he reached the floor in front of the fire where they settled him with a pillow and a thick old eiderdown.

'His poor mother must be worried to death,' Aunt Hatt said. 'But I'll tell you summat – he's not leaving here before he's had a bath.' She wrinkled her nose. 'He stinks like a midden. And I'll see if I can cobble together something else for him to wear.'

Margaret rose early to find Den still fast asleep, curled on his side in a tight, cowering position. She knelt to look into his face, breathing in the bitter coal smell and the sharp, animal odour of the boy. His lips were parted slightly. His face, tide-marked with grime, had relaxed into sleep and he looked, for once, like a child.

'So this is the little urchin, is it?' Uncle Eb appeared behind her, overall already on. He looked at Margaret. 'I don't know.' He shook his head, though with affection. 'You wenches.'

'Aunt Hatt says he's got to have a bath,' she said, getting to her feet.

Eb chuckled. 'I should think so, by the look of the lad.'

'There's water on already – for tea first.'

'*Bath?*' Den said, looking completely horrified.

'No bath, no breakfast,' Aunt Hatt said, looming, hands on hips. 'And I've got bacon.'

At this, Den could hardly get his clothes off quickly enough. Within an hour he was bathed, reclothed in old garments of Eb and Georgie's, legs and sleeves rolled, and had his hands full of thick wedges of bread and butter with fried bacon pressed between them.

Margaret told him that she would take him home.

'Were you out looking for your pa, Den?' she asked as they walked to Pope Street. She was carrying a basin of soup that Aunt Hatt had insisted she take to Mary Poole, 'the poor woman'. Margaret had smiled at her – Aunt Hatt just could not help being kind, whatever she thought about it all.

Den nodded his head, then shook it as if in denial. His face was hidden under his cap, the one piece of clothing of his own that he had refused to give up. Margaret, her heart aching for him in all his sadness and confusion, wanted to reach down and take his hand. But the boy was shut in on himself – a hard little man again – and she knew he would shake her off.

As they crossed the mucky yard in Pope Street, the Pooles' neighbour Mrs Blount and two other women were out with a mangle, near the brew house. Steam was curling out of the little building from the hot copper of water and they had their sleeves rolled for wash day.

'Where've yer bin, yer little bugger?' Mrs Blount

shouted at him "'Ad yer poor mother worried to death, you 'ave.'

'Morning, Mrs Blount,' Margaret said, wishing the woman would button her lip and leave Den alone.

Mary Poole must have heard her because she came rushing out of the house. With her hair scraped back she looked even more whippet thin, her gaunt face and pale blue eyes alight with strained emotion.

'Denny!' She tore over to him and began slapping him about the arms and shoulders, sobbing. 'Where in God's name've yer been? Where *were* yer all this time? 'Ow could you go off when . . . everything's . . .' She folded helplessly in on herself, sobbing.

Margaret saw an instant's glimpse of agony on the boy's face before he assumed his usual look of blank sullenness.

'Let's go inside, shall we, dear?' Gently she steered the weeping Mrs Poole to her house then worked to give her and the little girls Ivy and Nellie what comfort she could, boiling a kettle for tea, leaving the soup for them.

'Annie will have told Lizzie that Den's back,' she told Mary Poole as she left. 'She saw him before she left for work.'

Mary Poole, seated at her table, nodded, so dazed with grief and worry that she seemed unable to move.

Thirty-One

'Here's the post,' Susan said, peering through the office window at the blurred figure of the postman who had appeared in the fog of that November morning. Bridget went to open the door. Margaret had been amazed when she arrived at the quantity of post that came in and out of twenty-six Chain Street.

Seated at her desk, writing out a receipt for the bullion dealer, she heard Susan speaking to the postman. The routine was soothing. Two weeks had passed with little event. Both she and Annie continued to visit the Pooles and to offer what help and comfort they could. And Den sometimes came round with various excuses for a visit – would they buy his firewood? Could he leave a message for Annie? – which they knew he could have done just as well through Lizzie. Margaret could see that the boy had become attached to her and was as kind to him as she was able to be.

Susan came in, shivering, with a packet and several envelopes. 'Ooh – it's cold out. This is for you.' Susan dropped an envelope on the blotter in front of Margaret.

With a shock like a bolt of electricity, Margaret recognized her father's handwriting. She slipped the envelope onto her lap and continued working. Aunt Hatt paid no attention. She was opening the other post, making little piles of enquiries and invoices.

'Oh, look!' She pulled some thick papers from the

packet that had arrived. 'That German has sent the pictures of his daughters. Oh, my goodness . . .' She sheaved through them. 'They're all very . . .' She gave a stifled giggle. 'They're rather stout! Margaret – I'll show Eb when he comes in, but I know what he'll say. Go and ask Caleb to come in, will you?'

'Yes, Aunt.'

Managing to hide the envelope behind her skirts, she slipped into the hall, tore it open and quickly read the short letter inside as she went to the door.

'My dear daughters,' her father had written.

> I am now of a mind that you should return home. You have imposed upon the hospitality of your aunt and uncle quite long enough. The situation is resolved here. Charles Barber has long been lodged once more with the Davis household and in any case will soon be installed in his new position. This unfortunate situation has been allowed to continue for long enough. I am, of course, disposed to forgive you for all that is past, as is Charles. He is confused and distressed at the idea that he caused trouble in some way. (See enclosed note.) It is time that we restore order to our household and that you both take up your work in the village again. The school needs you, certainly.
>
> Please make arrangements for your immediate return. My thoughts and prayers are of course with you.
>
> Your father,
> William Hanson

With it, she found another sheet of paper covered in bold, copperplate handwriting. As she held this with trembling hands, her eyes raced to the signature and it was a shock to see the words, 'With my enduring respect and affection, Charles'.

Standing behind the door, she scanned the letter.

My dear Margaret,

I hardly know what to say to you. During all these weeks I have been battering my memory, trying to recover that evening . . . Since childhood I have been subject to occasional fits and each leaves my mind in a numb and hopeless condition. I rarely mention this to anyone – even to you, my dear – as it is a cause of mortification to me. It is as the thorn in my flesh of which St Paul writes – I believe it to be a form of epilepsy which afflicts me, leaving my mind, for some hours after each crisis, with an irrecoverable absence of the time when it happened.

What I long to convey to you is the depth of my sorrow and shame. Whatever happened, whatever I did that frightened you so much, I write in humble and abject apology. Unwittingly, I have thrown into doubt all our precious friendship, our vision and pledge of a loving future together, devoted toilers in God's vineyard. My soul aches with the thought of not having you by my side as you had promised, a promise which I considered sacred.

All I ask, Margaret, is that you come home for a time, so that I might speak to you in person, to try and explain myself. I beg you to find forgiveness in your heart for a loving man who holds you in nothing but the highest regard, but who is at once and the same, a weak vessel.

She gazed at the ornate handwriting, rage like a flame leaping to life in her. Her first impulse was to screw up both letters and throw them into the gutter outside. But she had to let Annie see them first. She could well imagine Annie's wrath. He has no recollection of what happened, she thought. Well, how convenient for him. She slammed the front door as she left. Her father's words angered her even more than Charles's own. *I am, of course, disposed to forgive you . . .*

Forgive *me*! she raged inwardly. All the conflicting, painful feelings rose in her, almost stopping her breath. Her sense of guilt even though she knew, really, that she was not in the wrong, her feeling of being soiled, betrayed, wrongfully accused and – by her father – loved less than Charles, this man who he had taken to him as his son and whose word he had believed before that of his own flesh and blood . . . It was her father towards whom she felt the most hurt and rage.

She was glad of a job to do; something to try and keep her steady.

Hands trembling, she let herself into number twenty-four. As she went to the stairs, her eyes were drawn immediately to Philip Tallis's half-open door. She could hear voices – both male. But Mrs Flett was pushing her broom along the hall and Margaret did not want to be seen hovering. With the letters folded tightly in her hand, she hurried up to Caleb Turner's room.

'The pictures have arrived,' she told him. 'From that German gentleman.' She could not bring herself to say the name, even to Caleb Turner.

He looked round at her from his workbench, eyebrows raised. 'Those wenches of his, eh?' he said. 'All right – give us half an hour and I'll be round.'

Margaret leaned down for a moment to admire the die

he was working on – something floral, complicated – before leaving. Mrs Flett had disappeared from the hall and as Margaret went downstairs, unable to help herself, she paused halfway down. There was a silence, then hushed voices, as if whoever was in there with Philip Tallis was leaning over to examine something. She heard a few muffled exchanges and was about to carry on down the stairs when a voice came louder, as if the man had straightened up.

'Come on, Philip. This is exquisite – you know how good you are. Umm? What's all this mulishness about? All this grand isolation? Why not come and meet some of the other Guild members. They're a lively bunch – you could learn from them and at the same time teach them a thing or two, no doubt. Come and join us, eh?'

Margaret wondered if it was the dashing man she had seen in the strange hat. She heard Philip Tallis's patient voice.

'I've told you – I prefer to work alone. And I've my daughter to care for.'

'Bring young Daisy along with you – she's a talented little thing. She could learn a lot from it. You can't go on moping for ever, man. It'd take you out of yourself. You could do some teaching at the jewellery school – I'm sure we could arrange a session or two for you.'

'I'm not moping.' There was a flinty determination to his voice now. 'I just prefer to do things the way I do them, that's all.'

'All right – have it your way!' The man laughed. 'Hide your light under a bushel if that's what you want. You always were a stubborn creature.'

Margaret was burning with curiosity but she was afraid that someone would emerge from any one of the house doors and see her eavesdropping. She hurried away down the stairs.

Caleb Turner leaned over the desk. In front of him, laid in careful lines, were the photographs of Herr von Titz's seven daughters. They were plump, double-chinned girls in high, lacy collars, their hair taken back in complicated arrangements, heads sprigged all over with ribbons, except for one who had a rose pinned over her ear.

Caleb's usually impassive face was pulled into a frown.

'What the hell'm I s'posed to do with these?' he said woefully, scratching his head. 'They all look the flaming same!'

Margaret had only seen Daisy in passing during the past week. Sometimes the girl seemed to retreat from her and become distant, as if she was frightened of having something that would once more be snatched away. But that afternoon, she called at the door after school, wrapped in a grey wool coat. Even at her young age, Margaret thought, Daisy managed to look stylish.

'D'you want to come today?' she asked as they stood in the dark hall. Margaret could see the gleam of Daisy's big eyes looking up at her. 'Pa says I can teach you something if you like.'

Margaret felt immediately nervous, then cursed herself for being so. Sid Coles had spent a short while one day showing her how he set gems. She had loved having a chance to sit at his 'peg', the leather pouched across her lap, and have him guide her as she very slowly set a ruby into a gold clasp. This was just the same, wasn't it?

'That's all right – you go,' Aunt Hatt called from the

office, before she could answer. Aunt Hatt had a soft spot for Daisy. 'There's not much for you to finish off here.'

'What about the post, Aunt?' Margaret called back.

'Not to worry – Bridget can do it today.'

Daisy clapped her hands under her chin, apparently delighted. 'Come on then! Pa said he'd help us today – he's not too busy for once.'

Before Margaret could gather her wits, Daisy had seized her hand and started hauling her out of the door. Margaret was glad the child could not sense her pounding heart. Did this mean that Philip Tallis was going to teach her?

'Pa!' Daisy ran along the hall next door. 'Miss Hanson's here!'

Margaret could hardly breathe. For heaven's sake! She was furious with herself for the state she was in, expecting Philip Tallis to appear any moment. But instead, Mrs Flett, their housekeeper, came along the hall.

'Yer father's out the back,' she told Daisy. 'I s'pect he'll be in in a moment.'

'Never mind.' Daisy beckoned Margaret into the room. She felt strangely like a trespasser even though she had come at the girl's invitation. 'I can show you something.'

As Daisy pulled her coat off with a child's impatience and threw it on a chair, Margaret glanced around her again at the simple room with the workbench up at the far end under the window. Smoky light seeped through the pane. As with their own back room, the light was limited by the proximity of the workshop outside. But the fire was lit and the room warm and comforting.

'Here – I'll show you how to do something *easy*,'

Daisy said loftily. 'Pa's teaching me how to make a bowl – but why don't you make a bracelet? You'll need something on.'

She went to the back of the door and produced an overall in a milky brown colour. Margaret wondered uneasily, as she buttoned it over her dress, whether it had belonged to Daisy's mother, Florence Tallis.

'Here . . .' Daisy produced a length of what looked like wire, in a gleaming golden colour. 'It's better to practise on copper. Pa lets me practise with this – it's cheaper.' She tried it in a vague way against Margaret's wrist. 'Now – you have to shape it. This is a mandrel . . .'

There were several of the strange, tapered wooden things lying on the bench, looking like large root vegetables with sawn-off ends. Daisy, with the ease of experience, fixed one sideways in a clamp at the edge of the bench and showed Margaret how to fashion the piece of wire around it according to its size and hammer it into a round shape.

'You can do it oval as well – see?' Daisy held up another, different-shaped mandrel. She was alight with enthusiasm.

'You'd make a very good teacher,' Margaret said to her. 'Would you like that?'

Daisy shook her head dismissively. 'Oh, no – I want to make my own things. Now – you see the two ends are close together. Now you have to solder them. But first we have to put a flux on it – it makes the solder stick.' She seized hold of what looked like a lump of stone with a flat end, which she rubbed, in a shallow layer of water, against a stone surface. 'It's borax,' she said. 'D'you want to have a go?'

Margaret was beginning to enjoy herself. She was just

reaching for the conical piece of borax when she became aware that someone was watching them at the door. She jumped, then hoped it had not been obvious.

'I see she's put you to work,' Philip Tallis said.

Thirty-Two

Margaret returned his smile, realizing, in that second, how glad she was to see him. Even though she hardly knew him, his presence affected her. And any awkwardness there may have been was made easier by Daisy being there. Daisy was the reason for her own presence in his room and this made everything more relaxed.

'She's very enthusiastic,' Margaret said.

'Can I show Miss Hanson my bowl?' Daisy said.

'Paint the flux on the bracelet first.' Her father came over, still in his own overall. It hung open to reveal his shirt and brown weskit. She could smell the chemical smells of the workshop, the way her uncle smelt.

'You can show her while it dries. Oh –' He took hold of the curved piece of wire. Margaret saw his nails, wide and flat, the large hands gently skilful. 'You need to smooth the ends off first. Did you forget that, Daisy?'

He asked her in mock reproach, his face crinkling humorously. Margaret watched. She could not have said what colour his eyes were – a dark greenish-grey, perhaps – but she liked their quiet warmth and the hint of mischief they held today.

'No-o-o,' Daisy said, her own eyes wandering. 'Can Miss Hanson have a cup of tea?'

Margaret started to protest, but Philip Tallis said, 'I could certainly do with one.' He glanced at her. 'Will you join me?'

Once she had thanked him and he called the request to Mrs Flett, he went to a cupboard and brought out a silver item, obviously unfinished.

'That's my bowl,' Daisy said. She seemed younger this afternoon and eager for attention and praise. 'It's not finished yet.'

'So, Daisy.' Philip Tallis seemed more at ease talking with his daughter. 'What do we do first?'

'We take a disc of . . .'

He held up a finger. 'Before that.'

'Oh – make a drawing.'

No wonder she's so adept at drawing, Margaret thought, listening, fascinated.

'And then?'

'Calculate the size of the blank we need – the diameter of the bowl plus the height and then,' she spoke in a sing-song tone with impatient speed, 'we use dividers and then we cut it out and file the edges, otherwise there's blood *everywhere*!' She giggled. 'And then we put it on the head and we go bang bang bang!'

She pointed to a stump-like thing on the side of the bench.

'We shape it on there.' Margaret almost jumped as she realized Philip Tallis was actually talking to her. 'And, Daisy, what do we *not* do?'

'Go – too – fast!' Daisy recited, as if she had heard this a thousand times.

Her father cuffed her affectionately about the head and Margaret laughed.

'No trying to run before you can walk, eh, Daisy?' he teased.

Daisy made a face. 'Anyway,' she said. 'That's just part of it.' She recited, 'Metals are malleable, fusible and ductile. They are crystalline in structure and you sometimes have to heat them up which is called annealing, to make them soft again so you can work them properly.'

'Heavens,' Margaret said, genuinely impressed. 'You are already a little expert.'

'She's lived and breathed it,' Philip Tallis said.

Margaret was about to say, *I suppose she learned a lot from you and her mother*. But she did not say it. She found she did not want to mention the late Mrs Tallis, both for his sake and her own.

Mrs Flett came in then with a tray of tea.

'Hooray, cake!' Daisy said. 'That's because you're here, Miss Hanson.'

'Anyone'd think you never had cake,' Mrs Flett said drily. Margaret saw that despite her gaunt, almost sour look, she was a good soul.

'Not usually with jam in,' Daisy said, eyeing the sponge greedily.

'Thanks, Mrs Flett,' Philip Tallis said as the stiff-looking lady left the room. He laid a hand on his daughter's shoulder. 'You pour, Daisy,' he said. And as he did so, Margaret, watching them, found herself moved to tenderness. You need love . . . It was directed at both of them, her heart running startlingly ahead of her more balanced thinking. I could love you . . .

'Shall I show you the file for smoothing off these ends?' Philip Tallis was saying to her. 'Come and sit here.'

She moved towards him, feeling a blush spread up her neck. She forced herself to concentrate on the loop of copper as he handed her a file. Again she saw the wide nails, the index finger of his left hand blue with bruising.

'Just take the rough edges off. The ends need to fit flat together. Yes . . .' He stood respectfully a little away from her, but bent to peer closely as she started to move the file around the rough metal end. She was enjoying herself, the feeling of using her hands to make something. She could hear his breathing not far from her ear. 'That's good,' he said after a moment.

She looked round as he straightened up and their eyes met, friendly, smiling. His face seemed to her somehow inevitable, as if she had always known him, or known that she would meet him some day. As if something entirely new was happening to her which felt quite different from Charles, when her life had not felt her own. The letter from Charles was tucked under her mattress. In that moment it all felt distant, as if none of it mattered.

'That's fine,' he said. 'Come and have some tea and then I'll show you the soldering. After that I'll have to get back to the workshop.'

Daisy handed them tea and they sat in the chairs by the grate, Daisy perched on the arm of her father's.

'Did you grow up in the trade?' Margaret asked him.

'To a degree, yes,' he said. He sat back, relaxed, his knees spread wide. Father would never sit like that, Margaret found herself thinking. William Hanson always sat straight as a ramrod, as if he was in a wooden pew even when he was at home in private. 'My own father was a clock and watch repairer and I learned a certain amount from him. That's what really started me off. But my brother took on his business and I was apprenticed as an engraver to start – not in Birmingham though – out in Alcester. I wanted to learn more so I came into Brum and got a silversmith to take me on.'

'So you're from the country too!' she said, pleased.

'It's a small town,' he agreed. 'The countryside's never far away – though I've been here a good while now.' He took a sip of tea, the cup looking small and faintly ridiculous between his large hands. He looked up at her and, with some hesitation, said, 'Will you be going back to it soon?'

Margaret looked down, unable to stop her blushes again. Any mention of her being here brought back all the reasons they had come and those letters . . . 'I'm not really sure,' she said. 'We hope to stay until Christmas time at least.'

'Oh, you can't go away!' Daisy cried. 'Don't go – stay here for ever and ever!'

They both laughed, and Philip Tallis, with tact, changed the subject. 'How's that lad – the one that turned up the other week?'

'I haven't seen him for a few days,' Margaret said. With a sigh, she added, 'That poor family. If only the father would come home – even if he's not well, it's better for them having him there, I think. He's taken to the road again, I suppose. The poor man looked so sick and broken down.'

Philip Tallis shook his head gravely. 'Terrible.'

'He should come and learn with us,' Daisy said. 'The boy, I mean. You could teach him, Pa, and then he could get a better job and they wouldn't have to worry so much.'

'He's only nine, I think,' Margaret said. 'Or perhaps ten by now.'

'Well, *I'm* only ten as well!' Daisy said. 'I was ten on October the tenth,' she added grandly.

'I think –' her father got up, putting down his empty teacup – 'it's time we showed Miss Hanson how to solder this wire. And then I must go.'

He lit the gas jet and invited Margaret to seat herself at one of the pegs at the bench. In fact it was a half-bench, with three pegs, the flat side pushed against the wall.

'Take your time,' he said.

They had balanced a tiny snip of solder on the gap between the two ends. She held the copper loop with tweezers and he showed her how to heat round the whole circlet of wire before training the flame precisely on the solder.

'That's good,' he said encouragingly. All the time, she could feel him close to her, over her shoulder. The light was fading outside and he stepped away to light the gas lamps.

'I'd best get back to the workshop before they all knock off,' he said, but he spoke with an air of reluctance.

'I like teaching Miss Hanson,' Daisy said. 'Can she come again, Pa?'

Philip Tallis smiled. 'If she can stand being bossed about,' he said drily, looking back at Margaret from the door.

'Oh, I think I'll survive,' Margaret laughed. 'I've enjoyed it so much – thank you.'

He nodded, then departed. Margaret felt a second's bereavement as he left the room. The feeling was so strong it frightened her, as if he had been part of the light in the room.

I don't know myself, she thought, tidying away the tea things. I don't understand myself. With a sudden pang she thought of Charles Barber, of how she had been drawn so close to him and how she had loved that closeness. Perhaps there's something wrong with me, needing such things? she worried. The anger she had felt when the letter arrived was dying and now the rift with Charles saddened her. He was sorry, she thought. Perhaps she should be more forgiving.

'So,' Daisy was saying, 'now we have to put it in the

pickle and then when you get it out you polish it and you can hammer it . . .'

'Daisy,' Margaret said, jolted out of her thoughts. 'Perhaps I should go home now and help my aunt? Could I do it tomorrow, or another day?'

Daisy smiled in delight. 'Yes! Yes! Come tomorrow!'

That night, as she left Masters, Hogg & Co., Annie stepped out into the foggy street among a crowd of other workers, all hurrying, talking, coughing, gobbing catarrh into the gutter. With mild surprise she realized she had become quite used to all this. No one was immune to colds and coughs and she was streaming herself, having to blow her nose every few minutes. She was looking forward to being at home in the warm and eating her tea.

As she hurried towards Chain Street, cutting along Regent Street, a small figure passed, hastening ahead of her, a cap pulled low over his face. In a moment he had disappeared and only then did she realize that the boy, who looked much like so many other lads, was Den Poole. Or she was almost sure he was.

'Den!' she called after him, but he did not come back.

Annie frowned, hurrying after him. Where can that little scallywag be off to? she thought, managing to get him in view again in the gloom of the street. At first she thought he might be heading towards Chain Street, but he scurried past the turning, hugging close to the buildings. She saw him each time he reached the pool of blurred light round a lamp, then would lose him to the dark between. She was not sure why she felt compelled to follow, except that the boy looked somehow shifty, not answering her call, and he worried her, scampering about the streets like that.

It was not long before she found out where he was going. Further down on the right, Den stopped on one corner, at a public house called the Rose Tavern. She moved as close as she dared, not liking to hover near such a place. What might people take her for, lurking about the street corner outside a drinking den? She crossed the road from where she could just make Den out, in the faint light from the pub's windows. She pulled her scarf tighter round her neck, coughing. Winter was drawing in and within a moment the damp cold settled clammily about her.

Den stood outside the pub looking back and forth, his feet constantly shifting as if he was ready to run at any second. After a moment, Annie saw a burly man with a hat pulled low over his face move into view. He seized Den roughly by the shoulder and dragged him back into the shadows. Words were exchanged that she could not hear. She narrowed her eyes, sure she could see Den taking something from under his jacket and handing it to the man, who appeared to put something into Den's upturned palm. Then the man nodded and walked quickly back the way he had come.

'Oi. Where d'you think you're off to now?' Annie caught Den by surprise as he came tearing across the street. She grabbed him by the collar and he squirmed and hit out at her with vicious force.

'Gerroff me! Let me go!' He twisted away from her, taking off along the street.

'Den – it's me – Miss Hanson.'

He slowed and turned round to look at her. Hurrying towards him she could just make out his hostile features in the gloom.

'What's going on, Den?' Taking his arm she pulled him aside, up close to the wall. 'Who was that man?'

'No one.' He put his head down.

'Den – tell me the truth.'

But he shook his head mutinously.

Annie thought she had better try a different tack. 'Fancy something to eat?'

There was a pause before he looked up at her again, slyly.

'I happen to know that Mrs Watts has a great big steak-and-kidney pie on the go tonight.'

He sat shovelling food into his mouth. The others were all waiting for Uncle Eb to finish out in the workshop, but Aunt Hatt found Den a plateful straight away before retreating into her office. Annie and Margaret sat watching him eat, like a ravenous little wolf.

'Den,' Margaret said, 'would you like some jam suet and custard?'

The boy looked agonized. 'Can't,' he said. 'I gotta go. Gotta go *now*.'

Annie and Margaret looked at each other.

'We just don't want you to come to any harm.' Annie let Margaret do the talking. She had a gentler way with her and Annie knew that Den had a special feeling for her sister. 'Won't you tell us what you were doing for that gentleman? What was it you gave him?'

Den swallowed and looked resentfully at them both. 'Gems,' he said. 'I can't stop 'ere – I gotta take the money or the bloke'll finish me.'

'What bloke?' Annie said.

Den shrugged. 'The bloke. In Tenby Street.'

'How much did he pay you for delivering them?' Annie asked, beginning to get the picture. The gems must be stolen, she thought, or at the least irregular in some way. She had no clear idea of how these things worked.

Den lowered his head. 'Four bob.'

Margaret gasped. It would take Mary Poole hours of her toiling work at home to earn that much.

'I dunno anything about the bloke or what they're for,' Den said quickly. 'I gotta get the four bob for our mom.'

'Have you done this for the man before, Den?' Annie asked.

He shook his head, then, looking down, said, 'Once.'

It certainly beats selling firewood, Annie thought. She was taken aback at the immorality of her thoughts. The boy was turning into a little criminal! But she wondered if she would do the same in his position.

'All right,' she said. 'You'd best go and finish the job. But Den, you've got to stop this – you could get into terrible trouble.'

'I know it's good money, but you don't want to end up in gaol, do you?' Margaret spoke very seriously. 'Then where would your mother be?' She looked into his face. 'Is it any good me coming with you?'

'No!' Den said in alarm, shoving his cap back on his head. In a moment he had run out of the house. Annie sank her head into her hands.

'I hope he's going to be all right.'

'He should be,' Margaret said. 'So long as he just does what he's been asked.'

'He must never, ever do it again,' Annie said fiercely. She gave Margaret a surprised look.

'You don't seem shocked. You would have been – before.'

'So would you. I *am* shocked – and it's got to stop, but . . . Yes, not how I would have been once, it's true.'

They both smiled, then Annie yawned, stretching her stiff back. 'Oh – it's been a long day.'

'There's one more thing,' Margaret said. Annie could see from her expression that she had been saving this up to say all day. A feeling of foreboding grew in her as her sister reached into the waistband of her skirt and drew out a letter.

'From Father,' she said. She had decided not to show Annie the one from Charles – not yet, anyway.

Thirty-Three

'I can't go over all this again,' Annie said later, furiously. She lay with her hair strewn over the pillow as Margaret stood by the bed, brushing hers. 'Whatever is it that Father thinks he's got to forgive *us* for? He does have the most astonishing way of turning things about to suit himself.'

Margaret looked at her, brush in hand, grateful for her sister's conviction. 'Every time I hear from him – or think about it, I ...' She trailed off, looking in the mirror, where she could see Annie lean up on one elbow, her face fierce in the candlelight.

'You what? Think it was all your fault?'

Margaret sank on to the edge of the bed with a deep sigh. She thought of that other letter, just beneath her now, under the mattress, tugging at her feelings, throwing her into confusion again. 'No, not *all*.' She parted her hair roughly in two at the back and drew the left portion over her shoulder to plait it. 'But I just ...' She paused a moment, looking across at the candle's flickering shadows on the wall. 'He was so ... confused. Charles, I mean. And I was ...'

'Innocent is what you were.' Annie flung herself back on to the pillow. 'Maggs – he may have been confused, but he *attacked* you.'

Margaret sat silently doing her hair.

'We can't just stay here for ever,' she said miserably,

289

after a time. 'And don't you want things to be better – to make it up with Father? It's like an open wound. I can't just . . .' Her anger of that morning seemed to have withered away and now she could feel the tears rising in her, her self-doubt returning and the cold formality of her father's letter wounding her all over again.

'What I want, just at this moment,' Annie said, pushing up on to her elbow again, 'is to go to *sleep*. But yes – I do want to go back there. For a bit, anyway. It's our home. I miss the village. I miss the people – well, some of them. We need to grant forgiveness – but only when he *apologizes*. And I tell you another thing I've decided.'

Margaret looked at her, startled.

'I don't want to go back and live there and be expected to be a teacher and find some pious man to marry. I don't *want* to marry. So even if I do go home, I shan't be staying. God speaks to *me* – and not through Father or anybody else.'

Margaret stared at her, astonished.

'I shall be eighteen next year. I think . . .' She said it as if she had only just thought of it. 'I might become a nurse – like Miss Nightingale. I think . . .' She spoke with increasing conviction. 'I – think it might be the thing I'm best at. I'm not . . . I know now I'm no preacher. I'd rather preach by *doing* – by helping people.'

Margaret felt a moment of panic. Annie, going off to do something so daring, so full of risk! Annie, leaving her alone! But she was not sure whether to take this seriously. Annie was always full of madcap schemes.

'Heavens,' she said, not wanting to indulge this too much. She began plaiting the other side of her hair. 'You're certainly full of ideas.'

Annie frowned at her and lay down again. She was asleep before Margaret had even got into bed. When she did so, she lay with her mind in a tumult. Perhaps I should go home alone and see Father, she thought. But the idea of travelling back to the village to confront him, the fact that Charles Barber was still there, filled her with panic. He had at least tried to apologize . . . Suddenly her mind was flooded with all the good, tender memories of Charles: his vulnerability when he first arrived, the hours they had spent together walking, talking and at last daring to exchange kisses. The way her thoughts had been filled with him, his personality and ideas, almost as if she was possessed – a feverish possession she had believed was love. Had it been? Love *was* a fever – or so the poets seemed to tell her. And then . . . The other Charles, the hateful, animal face of a man she could scarcely recognize . . . What was it she had done to bring that out in him – bring on one of these fits he talked about? Was she wicked in some part of herself, and had she turned him wicked also?

Her mind strayed helplessly back to that afternoon and the sweet feelings of being in the presence of Philip Tallis. Not fever – but a calm. A tender calm. She saw his eyes again as he had looked at her, and the way he had lingered in the room, seeming not to want to leave. And how she had not wanted him to, as if his being there completed things.

Oh, my Lord and Saviour, she prayed, *amid this whirl of conflicting feelings, have mercy on my soul and let me walk ever in Thy ways.*

As if to chime with their conversation, Uncle Eb told them jubilantly after the post had arrived the next morning, that a letter had arrived from the builder, estimating that they could take possession of the new house in Handsworth in early February.

'February,' Aunt Hatt said, lighting up with excitement. She was at her desk in the office. 'Oh, Eb – how marvellous. We'll have to buy a carriage as well!'

'We shall,' Eb said, pulling back his shoulders in a sober manner so that his tummy bulbed further out at the front. Margaret could almost see the appearance of a top hat on his head. Uncle Eb was becoming a man of substance in every way.

But there was another uneasy thought. February was only a few weeks away.

'We'll have to take our leave of you,' she said, wanting to reassure her aunt and uncle that she and Annie were not to inflict themselves upon them for too much longer. 'You've been so kind to us.'

Eb and Hatt exchanged looks.

'It's been a pleasure having you,' Aunt Hatt said warmly. 'You're like daughters to us now, the pair of you.' Her dark eyes were full of fondness. 'And we've seen you come out of yourself, little Margaret. I'd say she's come out of herself quite a bit since she's been here, wouldn't you, Eb?'

'Oh, ar – quite a bit,' Eb agreed.

Margaret felt close to tears at her aunt's sweetness. But she could also see the question that lay under Hatt's kind expression. They had never fully explained the situation and why they had come – Margaret just could not bring herself to.

'Of course . . .' Aunt Hatt went on uncertainly. 'We shall have more space in the other place, if you needed to be with us for longer . . .'

'No, Aunt,' Margaret said firmly. In the daylight now, she was full of a new strength of purpose. 'We must make sure that we resolve our problems at home before Christmas. I know my father is expecting us back.'

'Oh, stay for Christmas!' Eb said. 'Our last Christmas in the old 'ome! We'll make it a good'un!' He held out a hand expansively. 'Porter and plum puddings!'

Margaret smiled at his enthusiasm. Aunt Hatt had spent one Saturday afternoon boiling pudding basins with muslin tops in the steam-filled kitchen and they were stored on a shelf in the pantry. She thought of her father in the little house in the village, alone apart from the ageing Alice Lamb, and her heart ached with sadness. 'We'll have to see, won't we?'

There was a curt knock on the door and Caleb Turner came in, balancing three heavy dies in his arms. With a look at Eb which said, *Criticize at your peril*, he plonked them, one by one, on the desk.

'Right – I've done five o' them German wenches. I'll get the other two in a tick.'

They all gathered round. The dies had been carved so that the oval patterns on them were each about three inches high. These heroic portraits of the German girls were to be stamped out in relief, enamelled and placed in gold frames set with gems.

'They look marvellous, Caleb,' Aunt Hatt said.

Margaret, who found it very difficult to distinguish the pattern on any die and how it would appear, and was also looking at them upside down, thought it better to say nothing.

'Well,' Caleb said gloomily. 'I defy you to say which one's which. I just hope *he* flaming well knows. I'll get the others – the rest'll be done by Wednesday, I should think.'

'What about the colours?' Aunt Hatt said.

'He said he dain't mind,' Eb told her. 'Just wants them

to look nice. So long as they're different colours, we'll be all right.'

Hatt looked up at him with a doubtful expression. 'Is Jack going to do them?'

'He's got toothache,' Margaret said. Jack Sidwell had been appearing with his face swollen and wearing an agonized expression.

Eb chuckled. 'He'll have more than toothache if 'e works on these. No – Jack's a badge-and-button boy – I'll send them over to old Sam Lieberman. In fact . . .' He scratched his head. 'P'raps we should've got it done with . . . Well, it's too late now. You've done the dies.'

'What?' Caleb Turner said. 'You mean, *cloisonné*?'

Eb sucked in air through his teeth and thought for a moment.

'No . . . You're all right,' he said, exhaling. 'Sam's very experienced at either – he's the best.' He clapped Caleb on the shoulder. 'Fine work, old mate.' He saw Margaret's puzzled face. 'Most of the enamelling round here's done on metal stamped out from the dies – like these, see? You lay the enamel powders into the different bits when it's stamped out and then fire it . . . It's called *champlevé*. With *cloisonné* it's a case of making the shape in wire instead and laying it on the top. Very fine work . . . But we'll go with it as it is. No one'd make a better job of it than old Sam Lieberman.'

Caleb Turner's look of doom increased. 'Well,' he said, turning to go. 'We'll see, won't we? Oh – and if that lad wants his tooth seen to, send 'im up to me. I'll soon whip it out for 'im.'

Thirty-Four

'Is that young Daisy again?' Aunt Hatt looked up from her accounts, hearing a tap at the front door. Susan got to her feet to answer. 'It's about that time.'

Margaret, at her own desk, had been musing on Charles's letter. The very fact of the letter now enraged her. It felt as if her father had once more placed himself on Charles's side. Yet, at the same time, how was there to be any resolution, any forgiveness? In calmer moments, she wondered whether, sooner or later, she would feel it the right thing to reply, but at Daisy's arrival this was chased out of her mind. Her heartbeat picked up speed and she blushed, feeling Aunt Hatt's eyes on her, as if her aunt could see into her head and know how often her thoughts now turned to Daisy's father.

'She's growing fond of you, Margaret.' It was said this time with a note of reproach, as if to say, *You'll be gone soon. Is it fair on this poor motherless child to allow her to fix on you only to lose you all over again?*

They heard Daisy's young voice, her feet hurrying in the passage.

'This one's here again,' Susan announced at the door. For some reason she had decided to be sniffy about Daisy's now daily appearances. Bridget, however, was a warm-hearted soul and always treated her very sweetly.

Daisy had her hair tied back austerely in a long bunch at the back, a black hat pulled down over her ears. From beneath its stiff brim, her eyes were looking out in their intent way.

'Hello, Daisy,' Aunt Hatt said kindly and Margaret smiled at her too.

'Are you coming for your lesson?' Daisy said to Margaret, in a voice so commanding that Aunt Hatt made a face as if to say, *Well, this one seems to think she's the boss!*

'Go on,' Aunt Hatt said, as she had said every day that week. 'There's not much more for you to do here, Margaret. You might as well learn a few things while you're here!'

'Thanks, Auntie,' Margaret said, laughing. But on the inside she was trembling with anticipation. Her heart soared. She knew she was doing Daisy a favour, giving the child some attention. But every day now, when Daisy showed her a few elements of silversmithing in between chatting to her – of which she also did a good deal – they were never alone together for very long. Philip Tallis always found a reason to call into the room. Daisy would be showing Margaret the right hammer to use to flatten a silver bangle, or to make tiny round wounds in the metal which then sparkled with light; or Margaret watched as Daisy moved her bowl slowly round and beat it into shape . . . And soon they would hear his footsteps along the passage.

Tea was often the pretext – a ritual almost as key in this household as in Aunt Hatt's. Mrs Flett would bring in a tray with tea and bread and butter or a plain cake, and he would often linger in the room talking, even after the cups held only cool dregs . . .

'I've finished the bowl!' Daisy announced as they crashed in through the door of number twenty-four that afternoon. 'Now Pa says all I need to do is fix it on to the stand and it's done!'

'That's wonderful,' Margaret said, infected as ever by the strength of the child's enthusiasm. Was it right, she kept asking herself, to be so enthused by the material world? Daisy showed no signs of religious interest. Margaret had asked her once or twice whether she would like to attend the church at Carrs Lane with her on Sunday, but she was met with a look of blank incomprehension.

'But Sunday morning's the time when Pa and I go for our walk!' she said. And Margaret saw that this Sunday habit was sacred to Daisy, the way fashioning things of beauty was sacred. And Margaret was pulled up short, confused by the thought that anything could substitute for church and still be of God . . . But what she saw between Philip Tallis and his daughter and between the two of them and their creations, was love. And what is that, she thought, if not part of that greater Love?

'Since Thou art Being and Breath,
And what Thou art may never be destroyed.'

She had loved Emily Brontë's poems when she was growing up, even though her father did not approve of them, since they were written not only by a woman, but one too young for him ever to take seriously. Emily Brontë's volume of poems was one of the books that she and Annie read secretly.

Father would say things such as, 'The sacred and secular are not to be parcelled into separate compartments – everything is sacred.'

But – Margaret recalled this in the seconds during which she entered the room with Daisy – he did not behave as if he believed this. And she thought back with both pain and affection on the narrowness of the lives they had led, which her mother had chosen out of love and faith and which she had cheerfully lived. If their mother had not died, would it not have all been very different?

Mrs Flett appeared immediately and said, 'I suppose you'll be wanting tea again, Miss Daisy?'

Margaret wondered if she imagined a slight air of disapproval, which could not surely be about the tea, an everyday thing. Was it herself, visiting so often, that Mrs Flett disapproved of?

'Oh, yes, please!' Daisy said. 'I'm ravenous. Is there any of that cherry cake left?'

Mrs Flett's bony face smiled in spite of itself. 'Oh, I think I can find a crumb or two.'

Daisy was bustling about, bringing her bowl with its lustrous surface out of the cupboard at the bottom of the dresser, when, as if drawn by a second sense, Philip Tallis appeared in the doorway. Margaret knew that he always tried to have a break at this time to see Daisy when she came home from school. But immediately he looked behind the door to where Margaret was sitting by the table, as if he was expecting – hoping, even – to see her there.

'Ah – good afternoon. Time for classes to begin, eh?'

'I think I'll just be watching,' Margaret said. She felt herself blush a little, wondering if it was so obvious that the reason she was here, had been here every afternoon this week – and it was now Friday – was because of him as much as Daisy. She was drawn by the work, the loveliness of it all, and by Daisy's need of company. But that was not all. There was the pleasure and excitement of his company that she could not resist.

'Pa – you'll show me how to solder this on here, won't you?' Daisy enthused. 'Now? You promised!'

'I will,' Philip Tallis said. 'But let's have some tea first

– I'm parched.' He came to the table, as Margaret had known he would.

'How are you today?' he asked quietly, removing his overall and seating himself.

'Very well,' she smiled. 'Would you like me to pour?'

He nodded, placing his hands, with their big, square nails, flat on the table.

'Are you very busy today?' she said, handing him his tea.

'Not too bad. Steady, you know.' He smiled, and with a definite twinkle in his eye, added, 'How's the German order coming along?'

Margaret had told him about Caleb Turner's struggle to make the dies representing Herr von Titz's daughters. When she had begun the tale, Philip Tallis said, 'Oh, yes, I can imagine Turner – "What'm I s'posed to do wi' these then?" He imitated Caleb Turner's lugubrious voice so accurately that Margaret was reduced to fits of laughter, despite feeling vaguely guilty.

'Have you ever met Mrs Turner?' she'd asked.

'Oh, yes – she's quite a cheerful body,' he'd said, with a mischievous glint in his eye. 'Enough for both of 'em, I think.'

She loved sitting and drinking tea with the two of them. Daisy dashed back and forth to the table, never still, taking sips from her cup and wheeling away to do other things. She was what made things easy. Once or twice, when she left the room for a few moments, the atmosphere between them had become fraught with a need to say something, and when neither of them quite knew what and could not meet each other's eyes, it was a relief when Daisy came swinging back in again.

Once the tea was over and Philip Tallis was about to

begin on Daisy's bowl, there was an urgent hammering at the front door. Daisy looked up and rolled her eyes.

'Oh, *no*!' she said, slouching against the table with annoyance. 'I can guess who *that* is. That's Mr Carson.'

Philip Tallis rolled his eyes as well. 'All right – go along and save Mrs Flett's legs, will yer, Daisy?'

A moment later, Daisy opened the front door to be met with a roar of greeting which made Margaret's eyes widen.

'Ah! Miss Daisy Tallis! What a marvellous sight to greet me on such a dull afternoon! Is your pa about?'

Philip Tallis looked round at Margaret, seeming about to warn her as he got to his feet, but it was already too late.

'Where is he? Ah – Tallis, you ridiculous old curmudgeon, you!' The tall gentleman came in like a whirlwind in his sweeping coat, a black beret pulled to one side of his head over tousled dark hair and dashing moustache, waxed and pointing upwards at the ends. He brought gusts of cold air into the room. 'Thought I'd pay you a call as you never seem to stir yourself to come and see us. How's . . . Ah! A visitor! Whom do I have the pleasure . . . ?' He yanked the beret from his head and gave a theatrical bow.

Margaret got blushingly to her feet. She had not seen this man since the time he called at the house in the early days. He was so strange and alarmingly vigorous that she felt shy and on her guard.

'That's my friend – Miss Hanson,' Daisy said. She seemed to have no shyness towards Mr Carson.

'Ah – *your* friend,' Mr Carson said meaningfully. 'I see. Well – good afternoon, Miss Hanson.'

Margaret responded as her hand was shaken vigorously, and his dark eyes bored into her. She remembered the effect this man had had on her the first time she saw him. Close up, she found him rather strange. It came to her that beside the inner glow of energy that she sensed in Philip Tallis, all Mr Carson's outward flurry seemed to her rather exaggerated.

'Tea, James?' Philip Tallis asked. 'There's a drop left.'

'Yes, yes – ooh, *cake*, yes, please! – Now listen, Tallis. I've come to drag you out with me – and Daisy – soon, *tonight*. No, no –' He waved a hand at Philip Tallis's attempts to refuse. 'I know you don't think you go in for the Kyrle Society or the Guild or whatever you want to call it. But there's something rather special tonight. We've a visiting speaker – a lady, moreover – and you're coming even if I have to drag you bodily to Great Charles Street. You must bring Daisy – and this young lady as well. No one should miss it!'

Daisy was listening now with avid attention. 'What is it? Tell us, Mr Carson!'

'First of all –' Mr Carson squatted down and spoke very solemnly to Daisy – 'you must promise me to get your old man there by hook or by crook.'

'Oh, for goodness' sake, James, spit it out,' Philip Tallis said, picking up Daisy's half-finished bowl as if he had better things to be doing. 'Daisy will need her bed – she has school tomorrow.'

'No, I don't, Pa,' Daisy said. 'It's Saturday tomorrow!'

'Daisy,' Mr Carson announced pompously, standing upright again, 'will need no other schooling after this. Not only is the speaker a woman . . .'

'Oh, tell us, Mr Carson!' Daisy was hopping up and down. Margaret was beginning to feel overcome by suspense herself.

'The lady is a Miss Hoyland,' Mr Carson said. 'A

remarkable woman – a pioneer in the new colour photography. I have already heard her this afternoon, giving a talk about her work. But even more remarkably, she has travelled all the way to the United States of America . . .' He spun his story out like a fairy tale and Margaret was almost as hooked as Daisy, whose mouth was hanging open now.

'Miss Hoyland – Miss Jacintha Emily Hoyland, being the woman's full appellation –' he smiled, mocking his own pomposity – 'has brought back colour photographs which she has taken of some of the work of Mr Tiffany in Fifth Avenue, New York.'

Margaret heard a small gasp, not from Daisy, but from Philip Tallis.

'Yes. You see! You do want to come!' Mr Carson did a little jig of triumph, hands on his waist, looking so funny that Margaret and Daisy both laughed. 'You see, Miss . . . er . . .'

'Hanson,' Daisy said, smiling as Mr Carson turned to Margaret.

'This fellow, here, Tallis – if ever there was a perverse and foolish old trout of a person, it is he. D'you know, this fellow has sold pieces of his work to Asprey's in New Bond Street, no less!'

'James –' Philip Tallis's face darkened and he sounded genuinely annoyed. 'Will you for pity's sake stop going on?'

Margaret watched, confused. She had no idea who or what Asprey's was, who Tiffany was or quite what was going on. Mr Carson took in her look of bewilderment.

'Mr Tiffany is one of America's finest designers and makers of artistic jewellery, stained glass, windows, lamps . . . Objects of extraordinary beauty and technical brilliance.'

'Can we go, Pa – can we?' Daisy was quivering with excitement. 'And can Miss Hanson come with us – *please?*'

Margaret was about to protest that she could not possibly go as her aunt would need her home. But a cross-current of deep, hungry excitement filled her. She wanted this – to know about it, to see things of 'extraordinary beauty and technical brilliance'. And if it was the evening time, Aunt Hatt did not really need her for anything . . . She looked at Philip Tallis, not realizing the desperate appeal that had come into her eyes. She saw an answering look in his that seemed to soften him.

'Well,' he shrugged, with a defeated smile. 'It seems I am far outnumbered.'

'Magnificent – well done, Daisy! And Miss Hanson! I knew we'd get him there one day – somehow. Now –' Mr Carson fished out a watch on a gold Albert chain and squinted at it. 'We must get moving before too long. It gets under way at half past six.'

Thirty-Five

Margaret walked holding Daisy's hand, following behind Messrs Tallis and Carson as they hurried along the darkening evening. The lamplighter was out, working his way along the street.

'Have you ever read Mr Charles Dickens?' Margaret asked Daisy.

'No,' Daisy said. 'Or at least – a little bit. I read *Oliver Twist*. But his books are very *long*.'

'It's true, they are,' Margaret agreed. 'But they're so good – the way he captures things. There's a little bit in *Dombey and Son*, when he says, "The lamplighter made his nightly failure in attempting to light the street with gas."'

Daisy giggled and Margaret saw Philip Tallis turn his head for a moment, as if to see what she was laughing at.

'Imagine if you could have lights so bright that the street was the same at night as in the day,' she said.

Margaret felt a sudden heady happiness, walking along behind the two men, as if she was on an adventure into the unknown. She had hurried into number twenty-six to see Aunt Hatt.

'May I go?' she'd said, after explaining the nature of the invitation. 'I think it would be very good for Daisy.'

Aunt Hatt stared at her with what seemed a glimmer of amusement. 'You don't really need to ask my permission, do you?' she said. 'Go on – we'll keep your tea for you. And Margaret,' she called after her, 'you'll need your hat!'

Margaret had been in such a fluster she had almost dashed out bare-headed and came close to knocking her uncle down in the passage.

'Where's 'er off to?' she heard Uncle Eb say in the back room as she pressed the black hat her aunt had lent her over her hair.

'The Guild – with Philip Tallis and Daisy.'

'Oh,' Uncle Eb said, in meaningful tones which brought a blush to Margaret's cheek in the dark. '*Is* she now?'

Mr Carson led them to a high building with, so far as Margaret could see in the gloom, an extraordinary number of windows in it. Other people were approaching and turning into the building and a few greetings were exchanged in the chill darkness.

As they went in, Mr Carson suddenly called Daisy to him to tell her something and Margaret found herself beside Philip Tallis as they moved towards the stairs. Glancing round her, she saw signs offering what seemed to be workshops in Ecclesiastical Metalwork and Pottery and Glazed Tiles. She would have liked to stop and look further, but the stream of people was carrying her onwards. Upstairs, they entered a room where a few curved rows of chairs were set out expectantly facing the same direction. The four of them sat together – Margaret between Philip Tallis and Daisy, who had Mr Carson the other side of her. Both the men removed their hats, revealing Philip Tallis's bushy curls and Mr Carson's dark waves of hair.

'And from where do you hail, Miss Hanson?' Mr

Carson asked, leaning across Daisy. But he spoke more softly than usual, as if sensitive to the fact that Margaret was not used to his hearty style of address.

'Oh – from a village,' she said, flustered. 'You won't have heard of it. It's not far from Bristol.'

'I see – and you're a niece of Ebenezer Watts, I gather?'

Margaret was nodding to this when someone tapped Mr Carson on the shoulder and, to her relief, took his attention. She found him rather overwhelming. The chairs were filling, though there was not a huge crowd. Some of them seemed to be rather outlandishly dressed in comparison to what she was used to. More than one of the men wore berets and she saw a small, dark-haired woman in a bright red embroidered cloak. Like Little Red Riding Hood, she thought, smiling at this odd garb. She sat back in her chair, conscious that she was very close to Philip Tallis, who had shrugged his coat over the back of his chair so that one flap of it had fallen across her leg.

'What beautiful windows,' she said, looking up at the curved shape with many panes in it, each reflecting the lamps.

'Yes,' he said. She could feel him looking at her. 'It's a fine building.'

'But you don't like to come here?' The words were out of her mouth before she could think.

Philip Tallis shrugged. 'I don't feel the need,' he began to explain, but at that moment there was a flurry of activity and a ripple of anticipation went through the room. Two men came to the front and with them, a very small woman, her hair fastened back severely from a middle parting, at the sight of whom everyone began clapping. One of the men, who was carrying a large portfolio, opened it on a nearby table and made a brief introduction. Everyone clapped again, then waited for Miss Jacintha Emily Hoyland to begin.

Margaret had expected something rather grand, a lady dressed in flowing silks at the least. Miss Hoyland, middle-aged with a thin, tired-looking face and plain clothing, seemed rather disappointing. An odd little body, Margaret thought. She looks as if she might have just removed her apron and be about to peg out her washing. Wasn't she supposed to be an artist? Daisy was wriggling this way and that to take a good look.

When Miss Hoyland began to speak, though, a rich, well-spoken voice rolled out into the room, which, coupled with the woman's wrung-out appearance, soon drew Margaret in with fascination. Above all, she was astonished by the confidence with which Miss Hoyland addressed a room full of strangers, most of them men.

'Let me begin by saying to those of you not here earlier, that it has been my immense privilege to address this Guild once already this afternoon – this place which is a cauldron of ideas harnessing beauty, innovative thinking and, most importantly, the deeply felt expression of our human soul, put to admirable social use.' She spoke briskly, as if keen to get to the main meat of her talk.

'It has been my privilege to voyage to the United States, where I was able to make a number of photographic reproductions of Mr Tiffany and the work of his staff. I break no confidences in showing you elements of the work itself, which is, of course, already recorded in the company's catalogue. However, I have also been able to photograph some of Mr Tiffany's workshops, to see the creation of these extraordinary pieces being carried out . . .'

She went on to say that while she had developed the

photographs to as large a size as possible without losing the best production of colour, nothing could of course match the reality of the original objects. However, her audience might want to move a little closer in order to catch the best of them. After due amounts of shuffling had taken place, she began to hold the photographs up one by one and talk about them.

Margaret was lost in whatever she was saying. Before her eyes moved a display of beauty which, even in the soft gaslight, brought her hand to her racing heart. She had to remind herself not to sit with her mouth gaping open. Miss Hoyland showed them pictures of stained-glass windows of exquisite colours, portraying landscapes and patterns, trees whose every leaf and flowers whose every petal had been wrought in coloured glass; a peacock, its tail aflame; lampshades of coloured glass, patterned with the iridescent bodies and wings of dragonflies; a shade fashioned as a trailing glory of wisteria, like cascades of blue drops of water. And jewellery: brooches of butterflies and snail shells, fine gold necklaces like webs set with stones, more glass, bright, singing colours of flowers . . . By the time Miss Hoyland was drawing to a close, Margaret felt half drunk on the beauty of it.

There were a few pictures of the workshop, a woman bent over a bench. Margaret watched, fascinated. Imagine doing such a thing – making these astonishing designs!

'This is one of the glass-cutting departments,' Miss Hoyland was saying. Margaret felt her attention sharpen even more as she went on. 'What many people do not realize is that much of the creative vision and skill behind most of these pieces is the work of one woman – Miss Clara Driscoll. In this workshop she oversees a good many young women who implement her designs – such as the Butterfly lamp and the Wisteria lamp that we have seen. And last year's exquisite Peony shade.'

She held up another astonishing picture of lush pinks and greens. What must they look like when you really see them? Margaret thought, exchanging a delighted smile with Philip Tallis. She drank in Miss Hoyland's words.

'These girls – whose backgrounds are very widely varied – are known as the "Tiffany girls".' Her voice took on a dry note. 'All these items are listed for sale under the name Tiffany, that of course being the company name. But in fact most of the lamps which have come to appear as familiar Tiffany creations were designed by Clara Driscoll.'

By the time questions had been asked, more applause given and they had filed back down on to the street where everyone set off in their own direction, Margaret was still in a daze.

'Come along, Daisy,' Mr Carson said. 'You take my hand and tell me all about it.'

'All about what?' Margaret heard Daisy say, and Mr Carson laughed.

'Will he be going out of his way?' Margaret asked Philip Tallis.

'Oh – no,' he said easily. 'He lives just round in Vittoria Street.'

They set off again. The streets had filled with fog and Mr Carson and Daisy were already ghostly figures ahead of them.

'Look – take my arm,' Philip Tallis said. 'I know the way all right.'

Surprised, but realizing this was only practical, Margaret laced her arm through his. It did not feel over-intimate – it would have been a struggle to stay together without it, and she knew it was what he would have suggested to Daisy. It felt safe and companionable.

The constraint Margaret would have felt walking with him was also pushed into the background by her excitement.

'I'm so glad we went!' she said. 'I've never seen anything like that stained glass. So beautiful – I had no idea there were such things in the world!'

Philip Tallis gave a low chuckle. 'I'm glad you liked it. But you must have seen stained-glass windows – in churches?'

'Well, once or twice – but not in ours. Our church is very plain. And never like those – so . . . Oh, like windows into heaven! We never really had very beautiful things at home, you see. Because we're such a religious household they were looked upon as . . . superfluous. Vain. We never thought about it, I suppose. We did have the beauty of nature around us – but there were always so many things to do. Even though my mother was from here . . .'

'Was she?' Philip Tallis sounded surprised. Margaret was gratified that no gossip seemed to have reached him.

'Yes – she was Uncle Eb's sister. In fact, she worked for their father here for a time. And she did wear jewellery sometimes, even though she was religious! But that was how she met my father.' She glanced round at him. 'But our mother died when I was thirteen.'

'I see,' he said. 'No wonder you have a feeling for Daisy.'

'Yes,' she said, 'though I was lucky enough to have my sister Annie.'

They walked in silence for a moment, Margaret still awash with all that she had seen, and was somehow drawn out of herself.

'Beautiful things like that *change* you,' she said suddenly.

'Yes,' he agreed. And though that was all he said, by the tone of it, she knew he understood what she meant. 'We'll cross now,' he added.

They were soon home. Mr Carson said his goodbyes and headed cheerfully into the night. Margaret was about to do the same and began saying her thank yous, when Philip Tallis stopped her.

'Just one moment.' He opened the front door. 'In you go, Daisy – scoot up to bed quickly now, it's late.'

'Goodnight, Pa, goodnight, Miss Hanson!' Daisy said and disappeared inside.

Once more they were out on the front step. The street was mostly quiet, except for Mr Carson's receding footsteps.

'Margaret,' Philip Tallis said. She could not see his expression but he sounded nervous. He stopped.

'Yes?' Her heart kept up a thump, thump that she was suddenly aware of, as if everything, its sound and feeling, were suddenly exaggerated.

To her surprise, she heard him let out a sharp sigh.

'You're so young. How old are you?'

'I'm nineteen,' she said. 'Twenty in February.'

'Well, I'm thirty-four.'

She was not sure what to make of this. 'That's not so very old,' she said, unsure how else to reply. There was a moment's silence, before she heard him say, very quietly, 'Do you think it's too old for you?' Before she could set this straight in her mind he had stepped towards her and said stiffly, almost angrily, 'Heaven help me, I'm a fool. But you've . . .' It came out in a rush. 'You've disturbed my heart, woman, that you have.'

He was close, a looming shadow in front of her. Her

body was palpitating as the blood pumped round it so hard she thought he must hear it. She must say something. *I'll love you . . . I can love . . .* No, not that – that sounded ridiculous.

'And . . .' she managed.

His hand came to her chin, very gently, tilting her face up to look at him through the darkness.

'Have I spoken out of turn?' he said humbly. 'I can't stand the thought of you going.'

She shook her head. 'I was trying to say . . .' She swallowed. Was it safe? Was *he* safe? Hadn't Charles seemed safe? But this was now – she must take this moment, the way she must let beauty and all it implied into her life. And what she meant to say was, *You have disturbed my heart too. Every time I see you or I am close to you, you disturb me with tenderness.* But what she said was, 'You're beautiful.'

She heard a faint sound come from him, a chuckle, no, a sob.

'Beautiful,' he said. His voice was choked with emotion. 'Well, I've never been called that before, you lovely, lovely girl.'

He drew close and looked down at her, seeking her permission to draw her into his arms. Very gently he removed her hat and handed it to her, before bringing her head against his chest with his hand, so tenderly that it made her want to weep.

Thirty-Six

The dinner bell rang out along the passageways of Masters, Hogg & Co. Within a second, all the women in the stamping room downed tools and the sounds of thumping presses were replaced by that of feet hurrying towards the door.

Annie made her way out beside Lizzie, as usual, though one or two of the others looked her in the eye with what appeared now to be friendliness. She noticed that Lizzie's young face appeared pinker than usual, as if a flush of happiness had permeated her skin. And the girl's pale eyes had a new light in them. She clutched Annie's arm.

'I've got summat to tell yer,' she said excitedly as they hurried along the corridor, two little ripples in the river of women. Beyond the windows, the tall chimneys blackened the already lowering sky with smoke.

Unable to hold back until they were outside, Lizzie said, 'Someone's seen our dad! Mr B came and told us last night. 'E was working near the cut over Ladywood way – and he saw Dad in the road.'

'Oh, that's good news,' Annie said, trying to sound as if she thought it was. But she wondered why, if Wilf Poole was so close to home, he didn't come and see his family. 'Did Mr B speak to him?'

'No,' Lizzie said. ''E said 'e only saw him in the distance, like, but 'e was sure it was him.'

They stepped out into the day. Everything about it was grey and bitterly cold. But as ever, Margaret was waiting near the factory gates. She approached with a smile, holding the basin of food which Aunt Hatt had requested Mrs Sullivan to fill to the brim every day, so that there was always extra for Lizzie Poole. They were determined to make sure the girl had a good feed at least once a day, with all the burdens she carried. Annie was deeply grateful to Aunt Hatt for this.

'Hello, Margaret,' Lizzie said, lifted out of herself by the good news. 'You look ever so nice today.'

'Oh – thank you!' Margaret smiled and Annie noticed that her sister was looking radiant in a way she had not seen in a very long time. She did not have time to think about this because Margaret was handing her the basin and two spoons and asking after Mrs Poole. One or other of them always tried to call in at the Pooles' house at some point in the week, but neither Annie nor Margaret had seen Mary Poole for a few days.

''Er's going along, ta,' Lizzie said, though her face fell a little. ''Er's had a bit of a cold, like.'

'See you later then,' Margaret said, turning in her stately way and disappearing down the street. Annie watched for a second. It was at moments like these that she felt proud of having a sister like Margaret, so upright and calm and attractive-looking.

'She's lovely, your sister is,' Lizzie said as they took their seats in the dinner room. 'I wish I had a big sis.'

'Yes,' Annie agreed, unwinding the muslin cloth that Mrs Sullivan had tied round the top of the basin and unleashing a delicious smell of warm gravy. 'You could do with one, with all you've got on your plate. Or a big brother – someone else to go out to work and not just you.'

'If only Dad'd come home,' Lizzie said, her face clouding. Her eyes filled with tears. 'I know it'd make all the difference to our mom. I mean, I know he can't go out to work any more – he ain't right in himself. But just having him home . . . And maybe . . .' Her eyes wandered a moment. 'If he could just stay home with Nellie, and our mom could get a job . . .' She wiped her eyes and took a mouthful of the stew and potatoes. 'Oh, this is nice,' she said dreamily. 'You're ever so kind, Annie, you and your auntie.'

'You just eat,' Annie said. She felt very protective of poor Lizzie. 'You've got to keep your strength up.'

'What I got to do,' Lizzie said, looking troubled again, 'is move up – learn so's I can do piercing or slitting – so I can earn more.'

'I'm sure you could,' Annie said. 'Have you asked Miss Hinks?'

'No.' Lizzie's face fell further. 'I think she'll say I'm too young. But I'll do it – one day.' She looked puzzled for a moment. 'Why don't you move up, Annie? You could do that work.'

Annie smiled. 'Oh – I don't know how long I'll be here,' she said.

'You're not leaving, are you?' Lizzie said anxiously, poised with her spoon over the basin.

'Not yet,' Annie said, not wanting to worry her.

'One day, when I'm bigger,' Lizzie said through a mouthful of beef, 'I'm gunna get a really good job and then I can keep our mom and 'er won't need to work. And we'll live in a nicer house and . . .' She trailed off as if something in her had deflated. 'I just wish our dad'd come home.'

*

Daisy Tallis stood on the step the next morning, her feet neatly side by side. It was a Saturday and Annie was back at the factory. Margaret opened the door. Gravely, Daisy issued her invitation.

'Pa says, will you come with us for our walk tomorrow morning?' Her face then broke into a childish grin and she wrung her hands together. '*Please*,' she wheedled. 'Say you will!'

Margaret was about to dismiss this out of hand. Tomorrow morning was Sunday. Every Sunday she and Annie walked into Birmingham to Carrs Lane to attend the Congregational church. 'But . . .' she began.

'Please,' Daisy said sweetly. 'Pa wants you to – and so do I.'

In those seconds, Margaret felt as if her father and all the church elders, not to mention God, were breathing down her neck. Sunday! Church! Nowadays they were only going once on a Sunday which was bad enough – not like the twice- or thrice-daily Sunday services of child-hood. A battle took place, briefly and violently, inside her. Philip Tallis wanted her to go. Daisy also. She quizzed herself sternly. Where did the duty of love lie?

'All right.' She could hardly believe she was saying it. She felt a wondering burst of inner excitement. Philip Tallis wanted her to go . . . Philip, who had held her so close and tenderly after the meeting on Thursday. Who, ever since, had flooded her mind and heart.

'You'll come!' Daisy jumped up and down, her hair flying. 'Oh, goody goody! I'll go and tell Pa!'

'What time?' Margaret called after her.

'Oh . . .' Daisy said vaguely over her shoulder. 'You know – morning time.'

*

Whether by coincidence or not – Margaret never decided – later that day Aunt Hatt came into the back room, holding against herself a skirt in a wool weave the colour of crushed raspberries.

'Would you fancy this, Margaret?' she said. 'Only, I'm getting a bit broad in the beam these days and . . . Well, it might do you nicely if you alter the waist a bit and you can let the hem down. It'd look very nice on you, I'd think.'

'Oh!' Margaret said, her heart picking up speed with pleasure at the sight. 'How lovely! But . . .' She was used to wearing drab greys and black and all her clothes were so old now, that the thought of wearing such a bright colour felt rather sinful.

'But what?' Aunt Hatt said. 'It'd suit your colouring. Go on – try it on.'

'Well, it would go very well with my cream blouse,' Margaret said, feeling a smile creep across her face.

'Here you are then.' She handed the lovely soft thing to Margaret. 'Pleased to see it go to a good home. Our Clara's far too thin for anything of mine.'

Margaret spent a happy hour sorting out the waist and hem and pressing it, excited at having something so new and lovely to wear the next day.

'What d'you mean, you're not coming to church?'

Annie stood by the bed, fastening the buttons of her deep blue Sunday frock, a scandalized expression on her face.

Margaret was sitting on the bed, still in her nightgown, hair in a thick plait over her shoulder. She bent her legs up towards her, wrapping her arms round them. She felt defensive and flustered as Annie's gaze burned into her.

'It's just for once,' she said. 'Daisy asked me. Said they wanted me to go. It's the only time they really get some leisure together.'

'But why not this afternoon?' Annie said.

'I don't know,' Margaret replied, beginning to feel snappish with her sister. After all, it was on her conscience, not Annie's, wasn't it? And she did feel guilty, she couldn't deny it. 'They always go on Sunday mornings, that's all.'

'Well, *I'm* going to church,' Annie said, yanking the comb through her hair. Her chin seemed to look even more pointed in the mirror this morning. 'I never thought *you'd* be the one to break away!'

'I'm not breaking away!' Margaret argued. 'It's just this once.' Annie had an uncomfortable habit of being able to prod at her most uneasy feelings.

'Well,' Annie said sniffily, pulling her boots on with a clatter, 'please yourself. Run after every male who comes your way. *I'm* going to have some porridge.'

Margaret stayed on the bed, shaken. She was torn between fury with Annie and utter panic. Was Annie right? Was she weak and easily swayed? Was this some path to perdition that she was setting out on? Annie had witnessed what happened with Charles Barber. At the thought of him, Margaret's doubts mounted even more. How could she trust anyone ever again – or trust herself? Especially if what it meant was giving up her life's habits and commitments . . .

I didn't go to church very often when I was ill, she thought. And the sky didn't fall in.

'Heavenly Father,' she whispered. 'It's really just this once . . . To please a lonely man and a child . . . Not because I am abandoning You.' But her conscience nagged: *Will this man be the cause of you slipping away? . . . He does not hold fast to the faith. He is not one of us.* 'One of us.' A phrase of her father's. *He will lure you away, to a place where you don't recognize yourself.*

She thought about dressing quickly and following Annie to Carrs Lane after all. But another thought came. Charles had seemed the ideal, the pattern of faith, of all that she might hope for of love and marriage . . . For a second, despite everything, the memory of him seemed like a safe, familiar haven. Charles, the real Charles, not the ferocious brute she had encountered that night. Should she write back to him, reply to that letter in which he begged her forgiveness? She felt a moment of longing for all the old certainties.

Then the image of Philip Tallis came to the forefront of her mind, those large, gentle hands, his eyes, amused, caressing, the feel of him holding her and the loving words he had uttered. A melting feeling of longing filled her.

'Oh, for goodness' sake,' she said to herself. 'All this fuss about a little walk!'

Thirty-Seven

She put on the raspberry-coloured skirt, stroking the soft fabric almost in disbelief that she had something so lovely. The cream blouse went with it beautifully and a dark blue cardigan. She stood longer than usual in front of the glass, doing her hair.

I'm being so vain! she thought, bending to look in the little tilted mirror on the chest of drawers. Her grey eyes looked solemnly back at her. She wound her hair up, saw her strongly boned face, thick, waving hair piled in a becoming style and happy eyes looking back at her, and knew, though she tried to suppress it, that she was beautiful. It was as if now, aged nineteen, she had flowered suddenly and fully into womanhood. She looked strong, curvaceous, graceful, and this was exciting and alarming in equal measure. She smiled at her reflection, imagining that Philip Tallis was on the receiving end of that smile. Her eyes shone, and her face lit up with such joy that she felt panic-stricken by her own appearance.

Maybe I should stop all this vanity, take this skirt off and put on my usual Sunday dress, she thought. The dress was of a demure grey with a band of cotton lace at the neck. This inner struggle was ended by her realization that it was so cold out that whatever she wore would be largely covered by her coat.

'My, my,' Uncle Eb said, looking up from his porridge

as she came down. He too seemed to be seeing her almost for the first time. 'You off to church, wench?'

Annie had evidently left before he came down.

'Er, no – not this time,' Margaret said, taking a small portion of porridge and hoping she might force a bit of it down in her nervous state. 'I'm going out for a little walk with Daisy, and er . . .' She trailed off, blushing.

She could almost feel Uncle Eb's ear pricking up. 'And . . . ?'

'Well – Mr Tallis. He invited me as he realized that so far I have seen very little of the town.'

'Ah – did he now?' Eb was smiling knowingly. 'And just by the way – it's a city, is Brummagem. First to be called a city without a cathedral and all that church big-wiggery,' he announced. 'How about that?'

'Yes,' Margaret smiled. 'Mother told us that.' As Congregationalists, they had been pleased at this break with the Anglican Church which usually decided such things.

'Course, they're talking about making St Philip's a cathedral,' he said. 'But that's not why we're a city. We're a fine "city of a thousand trades" without all their carry-on.'

Margaret nodded enthusiastically, glad that this had diverted him from the subject of Philip Tallis. But it was momentary.

'So – walking out with Philip Tallis, eh?' he said. 'Who'd have thought?'

'Not walking out, exactly, Uncle,' she protested.

'Well, yer going out, and you'll be walking.' He looked at her with mock innocence. 'What else would you call it, bab?'

*

Daisy called for her, wearing a deep green coat with large buttons. It reached to her shins and was at least a size too big, but as ever, Daisy, young as she was, looked striking. Margaret was glad that Annie had already set off for church, as she didn't want any more caustic remarks from that direction.

'Are you ready?' Daisy said, excited. 'It's not a bad day and Pa says we'll go into Birmingham!'

'Yes – just let me get my hat on.'

Margaret already had her coat buttoned. She used the hat as an excuse for a last peep in the hall's rust-spotted mirror. She pushed the pin through the hat into her hair and thought, *Here goes*.

'Bye, Auntie!' she called. But Aunt Hatt was in the back making preparations for her Sunday bath ritual and there was no reply.

It was bright and cold outside. Philip Tallis was waiting. His shoulders looked very broad in the big brown coat and he wore a bowler hat over his thick curls. Suddenly Margaret was taken aback at how smart he looked and her pulse sped up even more. He tilted his head in a gentlemanly manner.

'Morning, Miss Hanson.' And Margaret realized, then, that he was as nervous as she was.

'Good morning.' She smiled uncertainly, glad that they had Daisy with them, but then he smiled back, his eyes lighting at the sight of her, and she was struck again by his face, the gentle seriousness she saw in him, combined with a touch of mischief.

'Oh!' Daisy exclaimed, looking Margaret up and down now they were in full daylight. 'What a lovely skirt, Miss Hanson! May I see how you look – will you unbutton your coat?'

'Daisy!' Her father said, horrified.

'It's all right,' Margaret laughed. She was secretly gratified that Daisy had noticed. She turned aside and unbut-
toned her coat for a moment. Daisy, her face serious,
studied the ensemble.

'I love that cream colour with it – like raspberries and
cream.' She clasped her hands under her chin as if the
matching of colour was a serious matter. And Margaret
knew Daisy was not a frivolous child. She was serious
about everything she did.

'It's so much nicer than the colours you normally
wear,' she said, sighing. Then added, 'Though you look
very nice in those too, of course.'

'My aunt passed the skirt down to me,' Margaret said,
buttoning her coat again. 'It is nice, isn't it?'

'Oh, Mrs Watts always wears lovely colours,' Daisy
said. 'Let's hope she gives you some more of her clothes.'

Philip Tallis and Margaret laughed at the brutal honesty of this.

'Have you quite finished, Daisy?' he said.

'Yes.' She walked off. 'Let's get going, shall we?'

'I thought you might like to see more of the town,' he
suggested. 'Daisy and I sometimes try to go out nearer
the countryside on our walks – but that's nothing new
for you, is it?'

'I would enjoy anything,' Margaret said lightly. With
you, she wanted to add. 'But yes – I've seen precious
little of Birmingham during my time here.' She thought
of her arrival in this bewildering place, her hot faintness
on the tram journey, the talk about hanging . . . It had all
felt so overwhelming then. She realized, with surprise,
how used she had become to being in the city, or at least
this busy part of it.

Bells were ringing as they set off and little groups of

people were moving towards the churches, spruced up in their Sunday best.

'I suppose we're keeping you from your Sunday, er . . . worship,' Philip Tallis said, rather gruffly. Margaret realized that it had only just occurred to him.

'Yes,' she agreed. 'But it won't hurt for once, will it?' She thought of Annie's scandalized expression and suppressed a smile.

'Well, I should hope the Almighty will treat you kindly,' he agreed, and she could hear his gentle teasing.

Daisy seized her father's hand, then Margaret felt the girl's other palm pushed into hers.

'There – we can walk like this!' Daisy skipped along happily and it gave Margaret a warm feeling, them all being connected like that, friendly and comfortable.

There were a good many children out playing in the chilly day as they passed along Graham Street, hearing the bells from the church in St Paul's Square. Further along, a group were gathered round a man in a top hat who was turning the handle of a barrel organ. It was only when they drew close that they could hear the flat tinkle of the music through the clanging bells.

'Oh, look!' Daisy skipped even more in delight, seeing the ornate little contraption, which was drawn along on wheels. 'He's got a monkey in a top hat!'

'So he has,' Philip Tallis said. Often the monkeys on the barrel organs wore a tiny red fez, but this one sat solemnly with the air of a very small, pale-faced businessman, in his miniature top hat.

'Gracious,' Margaret said. She had never seen such a thing before. 'However do they train them to do that? Don't they bite?'

'I wouldn't go too close,' Philip Tallis said as Daisy rushed in to see.

'Oh, Pa!' She hurried back. 'Can I give him something – a halfpenny?'

Her father put on a mock look of long-suffering and rattled change in his pocket. 'You'd have the milk out of my tea, you would, young wench.'

Daisy giggled and ran back with the money. The man tipped his hat to them and they stood a little longer, listening amid the crowd of jostling children. The church bells suddenly fell silent and they could hear the metallic little tune more clearly. Daisy was ahead with the other children and for just a second, Margaret saw Philip Tallis turn to her. Their eyes met and she felt him take her hand and give it a loving squeeze before releasing her again. Colour rose in her cheeks. The gesture was modest, but it spoke volumes of feeling and she loved him the more for it.

'Come on,' he called to Daisy. 'Or we shan't even get as far as Birmingham!'

He took them past Snow Hill station and St Philip's, the church at the heart of town. Margaret looked about her at all the tall, gracious buildings along the new boulevard of Corporation Street, then along New Street. All the shops and businesses were closed and there was a quieter, more celebratory Sunday-morning feeling to the place.

'It's not the liveliest time to see it really,' Philip Tallis said, as they turned down a sloping street with the elegant spire of St Martin's church rising at the end. 'This is where the outdoor markets are – you should see it in the week – packed, this area. The wholesale markets, like the meat market, are over there at Smithfield – and that's the Market Hall –' he pointed to a huge building, its entrance flanked by two columns. 'You'll really have to go in there one day.'

'They sell pets and everything!' Daisy said. 'Chickens and rabbits – and the most delicious *food*. Oh, roast pork and crackling! It's making my mouth water thinking about it!' she groaned.

'Never mind,' Margaret said. 'I'm sure Mrs Flett's making you something nice for your dinner.'

'Mrs Flett's not a *bad* cook . . .' Daisy began.

'Now, now,' her father silenced her. 'We're lucky to have the lady – she's been good to you, Daisy.'

Just then, a thin, poor-looking man approached them, nursing a little bundle close to him as if it was keeping him warm.

'Hot chestnuts, straight from the fire,' he murmured.

'Oh – Pa – can we have some!' Daisy cried. 'I'm so hungry!'

Philip Tallis hesitated, then dipped his hand into his pocket again. The chestnut seller was watching, teetering with expectation of a sale. Margaret could see how thin and ragged he was. She pulled her little drawstring purse from her waist.

'Here – I'll buy some as well,' she said.

'No, no . . .' Philip Tallis gestured for her to put it back and bought a double helping. As they walked away with their newspaper-wrapped cones of nuts, she saw the relief in the man's eyes.

'He looked as if he really needed the money,' she said, feeling the man's desperation. 'Here you are, Daisy.'

'Look – we can sit down, over next to Lord Nelson!' Daisy said.

Nelson's statue stood grandly, the figure with the hull of a ship to his right, surrounded by railings set in a low wall. The three perched in a row, Daisy in the middle, enjoying the hot, waxy nuts.

'He looked very poor, that man, didn't he?' Daisy said sadly.

Her father nodded. He leaned forward and rested his arms on his thighs. 'Is there any news of that lad's father – Poole, isn't it?'

'Wilfred Poole,' Margaret said. 'Well, yes – sort of. Annie said just last week that Lizzie, the sister who she works with, seemed very excited, saying that someone had seen him.'

Philip Tallis shook his head. 'It's a terrible thing, that. If only he'd just get himself home. Not that he's much use to them when he's there, I suppose.'

'It's moral support though,' Margaret said. 'Poor Mrs Poole – she's so alone. There seem to be no other relatives. We talk about it all the time at home, round and round, what can be done? Even Aunt Hatt's said she might come and visit her and see if there's more we can do. It's as if Mrs Poole's a widow while her husband's still alive – and either way, she's no better off.' She felt her anger rise. 'It's *wrong* that families should be put in this position. They're barely keeping above water with Lizzie's earnings and her mother's bits of outwork. And . . .' She was about to mention Den's activities after dark, but thought she had better not. 'What are the poor supposed to *do*? It seems as if the only options are either starvation or the workhouse.'

'That lad . . .' Philip Tallis said, shaking his head. 'A proper urchin. He's running wild.'

Daisy was listening intently. 'Can't you teach him, Pa?'

'But how old is he? He's not even ten, is he? The lad should be at school, not running about the streets selling firewood.'

'He's nearly ten, I think,' Margaret said. She peeled

another glossy brown chestnut. 'We keep encouraging him to go. He's got to until he's twelve – that's the law.'

'Have they not been round – there are people who check up, aren't there?'

'I don't know,' Margaret said. 'If they have his mother hasn't said.'

'Best to stay at school as long as you can,' Philip Tallis said. Margaret had thought that with his self-made approach to life, he would not be a great supporter of school. 'No progress without education.' He looked round at her. 'You seem surprised at me saying that.'

'Yes, I am a bit,' she said. 'But I agree. I missed a good deal of school because of illness. I was fortunate that my father had a lot of books, being a clergyman. But without those . . . And even so, I feel ignorant of so many things.'

'Yes,' Philip Tallis said, with understanding. 'I certainly do. I had the basics of schooling, but it was pretty poor.'

She was puzzled by him. They walked back up Spiceal Street among the slow-moving Sunday walkers, warmed by the chestnuts, though their breath clouded the air. Daisy went skipping ahead of them. Margaret dared to ask, 'Why is it exactly that you don't like going to the Guild? Mr Carson said your work is some of the finest . . .'

Philip Tallis shook his head impatiently. 'I've nothing against the Guild. It's full of sharing ideas and teaching people. I just don't . . .' He trailed off.

'What? Fit in?'

His head turned sharply at her bluntness, as though she had touched a nerve.

'Something like that, yes. Some of them are high-flown compared to me. And – having a business to run, a daughter to bring up . . .' There was an edge of bitterness to his voice. 'I want to develop, to learn. Mostly I've taught myself, looked at things, copied things, then . . . Well, thought of new things to do. It's not that I don't have the skills. But you have to keep working, trying, visualizing. I just find I'm better off on my own, that's all. In any case – I don't want to go to talks about embroidery or designing wallpaper. That's not what I'm about. Thing is, here in Brum, there's the metal-bashing work most people do, working in the quarter, and there's the Arts and Crafts lot with all their high-flown ideas. I just feel I'm somewhere in the middle – neither quite one nor the other.'

'Well,' she said simply. 'That seems reasonable to me.'

He glanced at her and she saw something in him relax, as if realizing himself understood. He gave a faint smile. Once again, briefly, he took her hand and she squeezed his as if to say, *You are right to be how you are.* Their eyes met again as they released each other.

'We'd best be heading back,' he said. 'I'll show you the Town Hall on the way.'

'Eb?'

'Ummm?'

Harriet Watts blew out the candle that night and settled beside her husband under the heavy covers, in the smell of waxy smoke.

'You still awake?'

'Well, I am now.'

Hatt turned on her side and rested a hand on his comforting belly.

'These girls don't half get us into some things, eh?'

'What – you mean you're saying you'll go with 'em tomorrow?'

'It's just – all these years I've lived here, I s'pose I've closed my mind to the way a lot of people live. You know – in the yards, and . . . Well, you see people on the street, but I've never thought they're anything to do with me.'

'You do what yer can, Hatt,' Eb said sleepily.

'Not much though, when you come down to it. There's not much help for people, is there?'

'Ummmergh . . .'

'Eb?'

Her reply was her husband's heavy breathing.

'D'you think that Philip Tallis is sweet on Margaret? I mean, that it's not just that she's kind to little Daisy? I mean, he must be nearly twice her age?'

'_____'

'Eb?' She poked him. 'Oh, for goodness' sake, Ebenezer Watts,' she mumbled, turning over. 'Just when I'm trying to talk to you . . .'

Thirty-Eight

'Are you ready?'

Annie was hardly back from work before she was nagging at them to go out with her, her head round the office door, hat still on.

'Don't you want a cup of tea first?' Aunt Hatt complained. She was alone in the office – Susan and Bridget had both gone home. 'I've a thing or two to finish.' She looked at Annie's pink, impatient face. 'Mrs Sullivan's put aside a pot of rabbit stew for them.'

Margaret saw Annie's face soften. 'I'll have a quick cup. It's nice of you to come with us. I just thought – you know, Auntie, with you being older. Maggs and I are just kids so far as Mrs Poole's concerned.'

She took off her hat and wiped her hands over her face. 'It's a filthy day.'

'Give me five minutes,' Aunt Hatt said grandly, from her desk.

They set off into the evening. It was already dark, a mizzling, icy rain coming down, and it seemed a bad choice of night for Aunt Hatt to come with them. But it was too late now – they had started off. They kept their heads down, shielding themselves under hat brims. Margaret and Annie took it in turns to carry the pot of stew.

Despite Aunt Hatt's muttering about why ever she was doing any such thing, they blessed her generous heart.

The gaslight in the yard in Pope Street seemed to give off even less illumination than usual. The rain had become heavier as they walked and they could just see its blurred fall in the feeble light.

'Oh, my,' Aunt Hatt said, looking around her with a shudder as they emerged from the entry and went to the Pooles' door. Even though there was very little to be seen of the dismal yard, it was still possible to feel the mean, cramped atmosphere of the place. The rain was falling insistently and they could hear the splash of water from a broken guttering somewhere further along.

Lizzie opened the door to Annie's knock. She gave a strained smile.

'Hello, Lizzie,' Annie said as they went in. 'I told you we'd come.'

'It's nice of you, Annie,' Lizzie said, opening the door. She sounded full of cold and kept sniffing.

Mary Poole was at the table, bent over a pile of boxes. The room smelt unpleasantly of the gum she was painting on them to stick their edges together. As she looked up, Margaret could see the exhaustion in her eyes, her thin face otherwise showing no emotion, as if she had no remaining energy for that. She, too, did not look well. Even in the dim light they could see the redness of her nose.

'Mrs Poole – my Aunt Harriet's come to see you, as well as Margaret and me,' Annie said and Margaret heard how gently she spoke.

Mary Poole looked up, seeming startled, but Aunt Hatt, uncomfortable as she was at being in this place, cleared her face of any dismay and spoke to her with a quiet civility.

'How d'you do, Mrs Poole? I'm Mrs Watts. No, don't get up. I'm sorry if we've taken you by surprise.'

'Lizzie,' Annie said quietly. 'We brought you some stew – it's rabbit. Is there any heat in the fire?'

The room was very cold and Margaret wondered if they had anything to put on the range. While Annie and Lizzie tried to get it going, she looked around. There was no sign of Den. Ivy, her hair a tangle as usual, was on the floor by the range with Nellie.

'What beautiful children!' Aunt Hatt said, going over to the two girls and bending down to them. 'Is this your little sister?' she said to Ivy, who nodded, wide-eyed. Nellie put her arms out and chuckled. She looked like a tight little parcel, wrapped in an array of grubby white knitted garments, and she had a lovely, round face.

Aunt Hatt picked her up and tickled her cheek, talking to her, as she brought her over towards the table. Margaret sat on the chair by the fire and reached out to Ivy, who came to her shyly. Poor little mite, Margaret thought. She's so lost without Ada. She took the child on her knee and began to say little rhymes with her. Still holding Nellie, Aunt Hatt sat down at the table beside Mary Poole.

'You're having very difficult times, I hear, Mrs Poole,' Aunt Hatt said. She seemed more relaxed, having a child to hold, and there was a warmth to her voice.

'It does for my back, doing this,' Mary Poole said plaintively, bending this way and that in her chair. 'It's all this sitting.'

Margaret was too caught up in talking to Ivy to hear more of their conversation, but a moment later the door opened and Den came in. He stopped, startled, and Margaret thought how wild he looked, how old, for a boy of nine. He was carrying a few remaining bits of wet firewood.

'D'yer sell any?' Lizzie quizzed him.

'Yeah. I got thruppence. And I got this an' all.' Digging into his trouser pockets, he brought out some nubs of coal.

'You been down the wharf, Denny – in this?' Lizzie asked, with a nod towards the dark, soaking night outside.

'Nah – these bits fell off of the cart.'

Lizzie took the meagre supply of wood and coal off him, her slim frame bending over the range, working to garner some heat. Den came and hovered near Margaret and Ivy. Margaret wanted to draw the little boy into her arms, but she knew he would fight her off if she tried.

'I'm starving,' he said, sniffing the air like a dog.

'I know – and Miss Annie, Miss Margaret and Mrs Watts've brought us some stew – but it'll do you more good hot,' Lizzie said. Margaret saw her glance at her mother and Aunt Hatt, and she seemed reassured, seeing the two of them talking.

The room gradually filled with the mouth-watering smell of the stew, heavily padded with potatoes.

'Can't we eat it now?' Den said fervently, moving from one foot to the other.

Aunt Hatt looked round, still holding Nellie. 'We'll leave you to eat in peace,' she said.

'It's good of yer to've come, Mrs Watts,' Mary Poole said. Though deferential, she did not seem overawed by Aunt Hatt, not any more at least. While it must have seemed grand to her, having the wife of successful businessman Ebenezer Watts walking into her house all of a sudden, Margaret felt great affection for her aunt's warm manner, which could put anyone at ease.

Aunt Hatt had put Nellie down and they were gathering themselves to leave, when they heard the rain-muffled sound of boots moving closer across the yard, followed by a sharp rap on the door. Within a second, Den vanished. Margaret had never seen anyone move so fast, like a shadow, sliding away somewhere so that he was invisible.

'Open up – it's the police!' a man's voice boomed from outside.

'Oh!' Mary Poole cried, aghast. 'What do they want? Denny . . . What've you . . . ?'

'I'll have to answer it, Mom,' Lizzie hissed frantically, going to the door. As she opened it the sound of the rain grew louder and Margaret saw two figures in black rain-capes.

'Yes?' Lizzie said faintly. She looked such a poor, defenceless thing, Margaret thought, her heart going out to her.

'We'll have to come in, miss,' a voice said. 'Is this the house of a Mrs Wilfred Poole?'

'Oh!' Mary cried, pulling her shawl tightly round her shoulders. 'Yes – Wilfred Poole's my 'usband. What is it? What's happened to 'im?'

Margaret felt a cold sense of dread course through her. She knew this was what Mary feared, every day.

The two bobbies entered, rain dripping from helmets and capes, seeming to take up most of the room.

'What is it?' Aunt Hatt said. She looked quite imposing, standing there in her hat and coat.

'Are you Mrs Poole?' one of the men asked, apparently confused. He had a thin little moustache. The other was more portly, with a round face. Margaret saw them glancing about the dimly lit room. It did not sound as if they were after Den, but he was still squirrelled away somewhere out of sight.

'No, I am,' Mary Poole said faintly, her eyes full of fear.

'I'm afraid we 'ave some bad news for you, ma'am,' the chubbier of the two said. 'You'd best prepare yourself.'

'Oh-h! What is it?' Mary brought her hands up to her face.

'Here, my dear – sit down.' Aunt Hatt, her eyes full of concern, brought up a chair and helped Mary on to it.

'Yesterday afternoon, a man was brought out of the cut at Farmer's Bridge . . .'

As he said it, Mary Poole let out a moan and started to rock back and forth. Lizzie gave a stifled cry and Annie went and put her arm about Lizzie's shoulders. Margaret reached out to touch Ivy's head as she was now standing close to her, wondering if the child understood what was happening.

'No!' Mary Poole cried, leaping up again. 'No – don't say it . . . Don't say any more!'

'Oh, dear Lord,' Aunt Hatt breathed.

'We have reason to believe . . .' the policeman ploughed on, obliged to force the words out.

'No – no, it can't be!' Mary cried. 'It's not Wilf! Why would you say it's my Wilf?'

'We have reason to believe that the deceased is Mr Wilfred Poole,' the voice said inexorably.

'Mrs Poole . . .' The one with the moustache tried to get through to her. 'Your husband was known to the force. He's been picked up more than once in Birmingham for vagrancy . . . I'm afraid there can be no doubt as to his identity.'

There was an appalling moment in which the only sounds were the rain and Mary Poole's broken cries.

'I'm afraid he'll have to be identified all the same,' the policeman continued. Margaret thought, what a terrible job. Was he sorry, she wondered, this burly young man? He did sound it, a little. And how had Wilfred Poole ended up in the canal? Was it some terrible accident?

'You'll need to come to Steelhouse Lane – that's where they've got 'im. Not now – in the morning will do.'

'No! Now – I want to go now. I don't believe you!' Mary Poole was screaming, beside herself. 'If it's 'im, there must've been some dirty business. Someone must've pushed 'im in! My Wilf would never've taken his *own* life – he was a God-fearing man!'

Out of the corner of her eye, Margaret saw Den appear silently from the shadows. In that reflex of his, the way he had disappeared, she could see how he had evaded the wag man from the school for so long.

'Listen, Mrs Poole,' Aunt Hatt was saying and Margaret could hear the emotion in her voice. 'I'll come with you. Margaret, Annie – you stay here with the children, get them fed. But save some for their mother. She's going to need it.'

And with that, to the astonishment of the sisters, their Aunt Hatt helped Mary Poole into her coat and the two of them stepped out into the rainy night with the two police constables.

Thirty-Nine

When Aunt Hatt walked into twenty-six Chain Street, much later that night, she sank down at the table in her wet coat, laid her head down on her arms and quietly began to weep. Margaret and Annie were soon crying as well, having held back their tears until they reached home, but needing release after the awful sadness of the evening that had just passed. Aunt Hatt had come back to Pope Street from the police station with Mary Poole, and then the three of them had walked home in a heavy silence.

Uncle Eb, who had in the first instant been highly indignant, wondering where on earth they had all got to, melted at the sight of his wife's grief.

'Eh, my little pet – whatever's the matter?' He hurried to her and stroked her back. 'Where've you all *been*? You're wet through, Hatt – you must get out of these clothes or you'll catch your death!'

But Aunt Hatt was not ready to be budged so quickly. Margaret, with tears on her own cheeks, managed to explain. Annie had her hands over her face.

'They got the right feller then?' Uncle Eb asked.

'Yes.' Aunt Hatt sat up, wiping her face with her hands. She looked dazed. 'There was no doubt. Oh, it was so horrible, Eb . . .' Her face creased again. 'That terrible gloomy room in the police station – and the poor man laid out stiff . . . That poor little wife of his – howled like a dog, she did. I thought she was going to go and throw herself in as well after she'd seen him.'

'You don't think she will, do you, Aunt?' Annie said.

'No – I don't suppose so. She's still got all those children. But . . .' She shook her head. 'He was . . . Well, he was dead, of course. No one knows how it happened for sure. But apart from that, he was such a poor, thin sort of specimen. You'd wonder how he'd managed in the world at all, by the look of him.'

'He didn't,' Annie said, wiping her tears away. She sounded utterly exhausted. 'Not really – not after the accident.'

Aunt Hatt nodded. She looked up at Eb and reached a hand out. He took it, raising it to his lips in a way which made Margaret feel even more tearful. She found herself longing for a pair of arms about her. If only Philip Tallis were here! She was startled by the strength of her longing for him.

'Oh, Eb,' Aunt Hatt said. 'That poor family . . . And the way they live . . . I had no idea . . . We're so fortunate.'

Eb, more sober than they had ever seen him, nodded, his eyes wide with sorrow. 'We are, that's for sure.' There was no hesitation. 'We must pay for that poor feller's funeral.'

Mary kept saying it was all an accident, though no one would ever know for sure exactly how Wilfred Poole died, whether by his own hand or another's. Mrs Blount came and sat with Mary and listened, as Annie and Margaret did, to her shock and her fears for the future. They helped support Mary through the funeral, once more at

Key Hill cemetery. Neighbours helped deck the house in black crêpe.

Wilfred Poole's body was buried in consecrated ground, close to that of his children, on a day so raw and cold that Margaret felt her own heart might burst with sorrow. It had been a similarly desolate morning when they buried their own mother, and for some moments she was a heartbroken thirteen-year-old again, her body aching with loss. But as she stood with Annie and Aunt Hatt behind Mary Poole and her children, Lizzie carrying Nellie and holding little Ivy's hand, it was the sight of Den that tore at her heart most of all. Now the man of the family, not yet ten years old, he stood stiffly upright beside his mother in a jacket of his father's, far too big for him, and his big boots, staring dry-eyed ahead of him as the vicar's voice carried words to them, thinly in the wind.

Wilfred Arthur Poole
Born, 5th June 1871
Died, 25th November 1904
Rest in Peace

III

Forty

December 1904

Margaret hurried out to the backyard. It was one of Uncle Eb's mornings up early to prepare the gold, stoking the furnace in the cellar. Rank fumes lingered on the cold air. Pushing open the door, she stepped into the other smells of the workshop. Despite the cold outside, thanks to the coal stove, its chimney curving up through the roof of the workshop, along with the flames of the gas jets and the bodies working side by side, there was already a warm, acid-smelling fug inside.

As usual, the place was full of activity, the pegs occupied by Uncle Eb's men who were bent over their tasks, some of them hammering away at strips of metal; the thump of the presses and loud bangs from the drop stamps at the far end, and the hum of the extractor fans. Georgie looked up from where he was talking to someone at one of the pegs and gave her a smile, and a few others said 'Morning' politely. Margaret, somehow yearning to belong, often wished they were not quite so polite, that someone might call, 'All right, bab!' to her as they might to one of their own. But she was the boss's niece, so they were all watchful and polite.

'You after Mr Watts?' One of the men, blowpipe in hand, removed his Woodbine from his mouth and set it down on the bench. ''E's up the far end.'

'Thank you.' Margaret smiled and walked slowly along the room. She loved coming in here, seeing all that went on. As she had grown used to the place, the more she loved the busyness, the drive towards production of what in the end were all beautiful things. She was still astonished by it. For a second she thought about Christmas, about going home as they surely must, to return to their old life. A bleak feeling filled her. Though she loved her home, the meadows and hills around the village, it all seemed rather quiet and slow now, compared with the life here.

Uncle Eb was talking with Tom Haines, one of the drop stampers, their heads bent over something that Uncle Eb was holding. Tom, a dark-haired, stocky man, had been doing the work for twenty-five years and he had the uneven gait of a drop stamper to prove it. Margaret felt self-conscious as the two of them looked up and eyed her coming towards them.

'All right, wench?' Uncle Eb said. 'Anything up?'

'It's just . . . Aunt Hatt says could you come into the office? Mr Lieberman has come in with . . . with the portraits for . . . Herr V.T.' She felt herself blush with embarrassment at the impossibility of saying the man's absurd – in English – full name.

'Oh – 'ere already, is 'e?' Uncle Eb said, handing the die they had been examining to Tom. 'I'll 'ave to go and see 'im, Tom. I'll be back.'

In the office, Sam Lieberman, a small, middle-aged man with a dapper appearance and neat moustache, opened a box and brought out the seven portraits one by one with impressively precise slowness, laying them on the desk.

'Oh!' Margaret could not help exclaiming. 'They're so beautiful!'

The men who had created them, Caleb Turner, other men who had stamped them out and Sam Lieberman, had worked a miracle from the tinted photographs. From each of the little oval shapes, set on a different-coloured pastel background, looked out the face of a young woman. While there was a similarity in their pale plumpness, the portraits each captured something individual: the sheen on the brown hair of one, the shape of the lips, angle of eyes; a bow here, the shading of a cheek and a different hairstyle there. Each wore a gown of a separate, gorgeous shade – a deep red, peacock green or golden yellow – colours, the very sight of which filled Margaret with an excited joy. And each of the young women surveyed the world with a sweet, blue-eyed expression all her own.

'My, my,' Eb murmured respectfully. He picked up each one and peered closely at it before moving on to the next. 'Well, Sam – you've done a fine job here, I must say. These are marvellous – some of the best I've ever seen.' He chuckled. 'I'll tell yer summat – these wenches look a darn sight better on here than they do in those photographs.'

Mr Lieberman, an old-world sort of gentleman, stood with his hands clasped together at his waist and gave a little bow.

'Thanking you, Mr Watts. I do think they look rather fine.'

'We'll have to get Caleb in to see them,' Uncle Eb said.

'His dies were the making of it,' Sam Lieberman said humbly. Too humbly, Margaret thought, gazing at the colours he had created, each picture a tiny alleluia of beauty.

'Right – well, we can get cracking,' Uncle Eb said. 'We've got the frames all set already – we'll get them fixed in today and we'll have them sent off to that German feller in good time for Christmas.' He reached out a hand and the two men shook on it. 'Marvellous job you've done there, Sam – thank you.'

'Is Den coming?' Daisy asked in her commanding way when she arrived after school that afternoon. She walked into number twenty-six and the office with all the confidence of a child who has grown up in the business.

'Hello, Daisy,' Aunt Hatt said. 'Are you teaching Den now as well?'

'I'm trying to,' Daisy said, rolling her eyes.

They all laughed.

'Don't forget, you've been doing these things all your life,' Margaret admonished her gently. 'Smithing may be like breathing to you but that's not how it is for the rest of us!'

It was nearly a fortnight since Wilfred Poole's funeral and things were not going any better for the family. Mary Poole had caught a chill in the cemetery and been brought low with it. Lizzie was also full of cold, but struggling on as usual. To add to the misery, the weather had grown very cold. Annie spent as much time helping as she could and Aunt Hatt sent her with contributions of food without fail, every day. They had managed to persuade Mary Poole that Den and Ivy must be at school, but that after school, Den could come over to Chain Street and learn some things from the Tallises. Uncle Eb said he might be able to think of taking the lad on in time, but at present he was just too young.

'If that young bossy-boots Daisy teaches him a thing or two, it'll keep him off the streets, any road,' Uncle Eb said.

And Daisy loved teaching people. Den had started to arrive in the afternoons, lured as much by the tea and cake and attention he was given in the Tallis household as for any educational reasons.

'I'll go to school if I can come 'ere after,' he'd said, in his gruff way. 'I'll wag it, else. There's no point in all that flother and them teachers bossing us.'

Daisy had begun teaching him some basic smithing skills and Margaret usually went in with him, Aunt Hatt being quite happy for her to leave the office by then. As if by a sixth sense, when she arrived Philip Tallis would usually appear and all of them would have tea together while Daisy bossily instructed Den. 'No – don't hold it like that. No – you have to hit it harder!'

That afternoon, when Margaret stepped out of the house with Daisy, they met Den hurrying along the street, his skinny form as usual swamped by his clothes.

This time, Philip Tallis appeared the moment they were in the house, soon followed by Mrs Flett, with tea and toasted crumpets. Margaret saw Den's eyes widen with glee at this. Mrs Flett was a kinder soul than her grouchy exterior would have you believe.

'Come on then,' Philip Tallis said. 'Tuck in. No good working on an empty stomach, is it?'

Den did exactly that, taking a buttered crumpet in each hand and cramming them into his mouth.

'Slow down, you'll choke!' Daisy said, waving her crumpet in the air. 'And it's rude taking two at once, Den.' Den carried on scoffing, unabashed. 'Miss Hanson, will you come out with Pa and me again on Sunday? *Please?*'

Margaret laughed. 'But I go to church on Sundays, Daisy.' For the last two weeks she had appeased her conscience and gone faithfully to Carrs Lane with Annie.

'But God won't mind!' Daisy reasoned. 'God's every-where, isn't He?' Margaret was taken aback. Despite Daisy's complete godlessness, which made her fear for the fate of the child's soul, she could not really argue with this logic. 'Please! Pa says you're leaving by Christmas and there's hardly any time left.'

Margaret felt a pang at this. It was true. They could not just stay here, endlessly, not making peace with their father, not resuming their normal lives. Mostly she was so busy that she pushed all thoughts of her father, of Charles's letter and everything, out of her mind. But she knew she was going to have to think about it because there was very little time left of this other, new life.

'Come this Sunday – please say you will,' Daisy said. 'You ask her, Pa – she'll listen to you.'

Philip Tallis laughed and looked bashful. 'Stop bully-ing the lady,' he said. Margaret could see that he did not like to ask. He was very reserved, very careful with her. And neither of them had made any firm declarations about the future. There was so little opportunity ever to be alone that it was difficult to talk about anything unless it was in front of Daisy.

'He wants you to,' Daisy said. 'I know he does. Don't you, Pa?'

'I'm always happy to have Miss Hanson's company,' he said carefully. He looked at Margaret with a faint smile. 'But we mustn't force her.'

'Yes, we *must*!' Daisy argued. '*Please.*'

'Enough now,' Philip Tallis said. 'Don't be rude, Daisy.'

'No, it's all right. I'll come,' Margaret said. Of course she wanted to! 'I'd like to.'

Daisy danced round in delight. 'I knew you would! You're coming! Now, Den – to work!'

As Daisy bustled about at the pegs on the workbench, her father quietly asked after the rest of the Poole family. Margaret told him all was not well, that Mary had a fever.

He nodded, a sober expression on his face. 'Poor woman,' he said. 'And now she's truly on her own.'

There was a silence in which Margaret felt he wanted to say something but did not know how to begin and the discomfort grew, so she spoke instead.

'That friend of yours, Mr Carson,' she said tentatively, 'was very complimentary about some of your work. He said you are one of the best . . .'

Philip Tallis waved a hand dismissively, seeming embarrassed. 'Oh, old Carson – he's a talker, all right.'

'But I'd love to see some of the things you've made,' she said warmly, remembering the beautiful bowl she had glimpsed.

He looked at her, seeming puzzled. 'But I can't show you them,' he said. 'Or not the real thing. They've been sold. I might have a few drawings knocking about somewhere.'

'Oh, yes, of course,' she said, feeling foolish. 'But aren't you making something else, now?'

'There's the odd thing, when I get the time. It's not easy, you see – what with the business and Daisy and being on my own . . . Often the only time is at night and then the light is so bad.'

Margaret blushed. 'Of course – I'm sorry.'

'You see, Daisy's mother used to take quite a hand in the business. Not just the paperwork – I have Mr Henshaw and the ladies to do that – but in the works as well.'

'I gather she was very skilled, your wife?' Margaret said, with a sinking feeling inside her. Everything she had heard about Philip Tallis's deceased wife made her sound extraordinary. It was the first time they had talked about

Florence Tallis, and she knew it had to be done. Even the thought of the woman made her push all her feelings towards Philip Tallis back into their rightful place. She could never fill the shoes of a woman like Florence Tallis, of whom everyone spoke so warmly.

'She did learn quite a bit, yes. She did some smithing herself – but she was very good on the business side.'

'It leaves you a lot to do,' Margaret said, the inner shrinking increasing. She looked away, feeling distant from him.

'Margaret . . .' He glanced at Daisy, who was bent over the bench with Den, showing him how to do something. Seeing the children occupied, he leaned towards her. 'Florence died more than five years ago. We had a good marriage, I won't say we didn't. But she is gone.' His eyes met hers, full of meaning. 'I am no longer married.'

She was embarrassed that he had read her feelings so easily, and looked down into her lap in confusion, pressing her finger into a loose grey thread of her dress.

'Since then there has been no one else. Not until I met you.'

The longing look in his eyes brought her feelings sweeping back.

'I love you,' he said, quietly and simply. 'I know I'm older – quite a bit older. But I wonder if you could get used to me?'

Margaret was overwhelmed. There was love – she knew she had the most tender of feelings for Philip Tallis – and there was fear, and confusion. She was afraid, after the shock and horror of what had happened with Charles Barber. Could she trust Philip – or herself? His world was so different from her own – this city, his lack of the faith she had been brought up to believe was the root and stem of her life. Added to this was the feeling that things were unfinished – at home with her father and with Charles himself. She had moved from what she thought was love to hatred of the man. Somewhere, she felt, there must be understanding. There must be peace, or she could not live with herself.

'I . . .' She looked at him, cheeks burning. 'I know . . . Oh, I do want to be used to you!' Feeling she had spoken too loudly she glanced at Daisy, but she was immersed in helping Den. 'I love you, Philip – I do. But there are things . . .' She looked away from him, her face hot with confusion. She could not tell him – not about Charles or what had happened.

'I must go home for a time. There are some things I just have to do – to resolve. I can't promise anything at the moment – even though . . .' She stopped, wanting to pour out the tenderness of her feelings towards him. But she did not want to make a promise that, in her own confusion, she might later break.

'But – you might come back?' He reached out his hand and she linked hers with his.

Forty-One

The wind was blowing so strongly the next day when Margaret set out with Annie's dinner that she had to clutch the basin under one arm and hold her hat on with the other. Waiting outside Masters, Hogg & Co. close by her was a pale, thin young girl with ginger hair, holding a bundle clutched tightly against her. Margaret had seen her there before over the past days. The girl could only have been thirteen or so. She cringed against the factory wall, wearing no coat, her ankles bare above a pair of worn brown lace-up shoes. Her head was half covered by a shawl and she was turned partly to the wall, trying to shelter from the wind. From her arms came the anguished cries of a very small baby. The girl kept jiggling from side to side, trying to quiet the little one.

'Why don't you come and wait here with me, dear?' Margaret said, beckoning her to a corner where the wall of the factory entrance extended further. 'There's a bit more shelter.'

The girl turned a thin, narrow-eyed face towards Margaret with a mistrustful expression. But she was shivering and looked so wretched that she moved over to where Margaret was standing.

'Is that your baby brother or sister?'

The girl nodded, still shaking the infant about to try and settle her. 'M'sister. Nancy.'

'I've seen you before. Does your mother work here?'

The girl nodded. 'I 'ave to bring 'er so's Mom can give 'er a feed off 'er titty – in the break, like.'

Margaret felt a pang of desperation for the girl and her mother. What a pitiless, endless struggle it all was. At least the woman had work, she thought. But then there was all the other labour at home, the endless physical toil of bearing and raising children. For a moment she was filled with horror at the thought of marriage and all it entailed.

She heard the dinner bell ring and moments later a tough, harassed-looking woman, her ginger hair screwed up at the back, emerged from the stream of other workers.

'Floss?' She rushed up to the girl. 'Come on – give 'er over, quick. My blouse is soakin'.' She pulled the howling baby into her arms and they hurried off along the street.

'Maggs?' Annie appeared then, hugging herself in the freezing wind. Her gaze followed Margaret's, after the woman and the girl.

'I don't know how some of these women do it,' Annie said sadly. 'I really don't.'

'Here.' Margaret handed over the basin. 'How's Lizzie today?'

'Not too bad. Says her mother's past the worst, thank goodness. I'll go round tonight. I'll come home for tea first, though. I don't want to keep inconveniencing Aunt Hatt.'

'All right – see you later,' Margaret said. She hurried back towards Chain Street, head bowed. The mizzling rain was swelling to fat drops, somewhere between rain and sleet. To her annoyance she realized her left boot was leaking, the wet seeping round her toes, and she walked even faster, thinking of chilblains.

When she was almost home, she suddenly realized that someone had fallen into step with her: chestnut-brown boots, a thick brown overcoat. She looked up, startled.

'I saw you from the other side of the road,' Philip Tallis said. His eyes looked down at her from under his bowler hat with their usual warmth, though as ever she saw his shy uncertainty. 'Have you been taking your sister her dinner?'

'Yes,' Margaret said, narrowing her eyes against the relentless wet blowing into their faces. She was just going to tell him about the woman and her baby, but realized it was not really a suitable subject to talk to a man about. The wind and sleet made it hard to keep her head up. So she said nothing else, which felt inadequate.

They walked on a few paces, dodging the busy crowds and swerving round basket carriages. The gutters were filling with muddy water. They turned into Chain Street and along towards the respective premises of Watts and Tallis.

'Margaret,' Philip Tallis said, rather abruptly, whether through haste or shyness she was not sure. 'Come in with me a moment, will you? I've something to show you.'

'All right,' she agreed, used to entering number twenty-four now, so much so that she gave it no thought. As they went up the step, it suddenly occurred to her that Daisy was away at school and she felt a tingle of excitement mixed with apprehension.

It was a relief to get inside, away from the big, slushy drops. Voices could be heard from the front office but the door was almost closed and there was no sign of anyone in the hall. Seeming worried that someone might come out and accost him, Philip Tallis led her quickly to

354

his room and closed the door, throwing his hat on to the table. Margaret removed her own as well and laid it on the back of the chair. The fire was alight and the room warm and welcoming, but for the first time since she had stood with Philip Tallis on the front step that dark morning, they were completely alone. She felt a pulse of misgiving. She had spent far more time alone with Charles and she had put all her trust in him, until he suddenly turned into someone terrifying, as if the very devil had entered him. She had always felt safe with Philip, but now she could not help her sudden misgivings. Her attention was quickly caught, however, by something on the workbench, gleaming in the dull light from the window, and she was immediately drawn to go and look.

It was a bowl, its rim shaped round into eight curves as if it were a flower opening. Its outer surface had a band round the top, engraved into shapes which gave the impression of leaves and flowers, and the indented parts of it were black. Below the band were even more dainty stripes of black patterning and to each side was fixed a handle, slender as a long, graceful S. She could see immediately that the piece had a rightness of form and dimension, an integration of pattern: sheer perfection.

Margaret did not touch it, but gazed in fascination. Philip came to stand beside her.

'D'you like it?'

'It's . . .' She struggled to find an adequate word. 'It's *lovely.' How do you even begin to make something so exquisite, so perfectly wrought?* she wanted to ask. But more prosaically she said, 'How do you get the patterns black and silver like that?'

Philip Tallis picked the thing up and held it to the light. She wondered how his large hands managed such fine work. For a second she wondered whether it was he that she loved, as a man, or the fact that he made such beautiful things, objects into which he had poured his soul.

'It's called *niello*,' he said. 'You make the bowl, obviously. I engraved the patterns and then you apply the inlay – it's a mixture of sulphides: copper, silver, lead – and charcoal. So that you have all the light and shade brought out.'

She peered closely at it. 'It's so perfect – the shape of it – everything.'

'I could teach you,' he said quietly, laying it down. He turned to look at her. 'I can see you have a feel for it.'

'Me?' She laughed. 'I could never begin to make such a thing!'

'Why not? You have a good eye – and a good hand, I'm sure. It takes practice, that's all.'

'Oh – and something else,' she said, unable to say what exactly that was. 'A feeling, I think.'

He smiled faintly. 'Perhaps, yes.'

In the same second, they became aware that they were very close together. Margaret felt as if her flesh had become sensitive all over with a tingling awareness. Philip Tallis reached for her hand and drew her back from the window, which looked out all too close to his workshop on the yard behind. And when they were standing close to the fireplace, in the dim winter light, her heart was running so fast she thought he must be able to hear it. He did not let go of her hand. Shyly, she looked up at him, but he must have seen some other misgiving in her expression.

'You're shaking,' he said. He examined her hand, caressing it lightly. 'Don't be frightened of me. You're not, are you?' He seemed wounded by the possibility.

'No,' she said, drawing in a deep breath. She knew the

fear was there: that this man she was beginning to know and care for would turn all at once, as Charles had done, into a terrifying stranger. Yet at the same time she trusted him deeply, and found herself longing to be with him.

'I . . .' He swallowed, seeming to lose courage. 'I hope you don't think I'm too rough a diamond, Margaret. I know there're some that think so.'

'Rough?' she said, astonished. It was the very last thing she had ever thought him. A man who had the soul and skill to make things of such beauty! 'No! Of course not.'

'I feel . . .' He gave a little laugh and looked towards the ceiling for a moment, as if looking for inspiration. 'I feel somehow rough next to you. And old. And . . .' He looked into her eyes again, fearfully, as if predicting rejection. 'All I can think of is wanting to *hold* you.'

Moved, she rested her hands lightly on his forearms. 'I'm sorry I'm not more . . . direct.' She looked down, a blush rising in her face. 'There have just been things which . . .' She ground to a halt, unable to explain.

'You mean, why you are here?'

She nodded. To her horror she felt approaching tears and had to swallow hard. Raising her face again she said, 'I need to . . . to resolve . . . certain things. Then I'm sure I shall feel clearer.'

There was a moment's tense silence. She knew she should resist him, but, seeing the look in his eyes, she could not. They moved forcefully into each other's arms.

'Margaret,' he said, in a wondering tone. She felt his breath on her hair as he spoke. 'Oh, at last – this is the first time I've managed to see you on your own.'

She moved back a little and looked at him. It was so much harder to be alone in a big town, she had discovered!

He smiled, appearing nervous, and drew in a deep breath. 'My heart – it's going like mad!'

She glanced round, afraid that someone would come in. 'What about Mrs Flett?'

'Not here at the moment.' He smiled, gazing on her, his eyes full of a hunger she could not misunderstand. He reached to stroke her cheek as if he could not believe she was really there with him.

His lips arrived on hers, the slight bristle of his beard against her chin. This kiss – for she knew it was a kiss; a kiss she longed for – was gentle, but there was a strength of longing in it which moved and excited her. Her emotions rose to meet his and she kissed him in return, her arms about his back, pulling him close. And he did not change into something violent and terrifying. He remained himself, Philip, this solid, rock-like man with whom she knew she was falling deeply in love. With him she felt safe and loved and full of love in return.

For a time they stood in each other's arms and he held her with her head against his chest as he had done before, his hand warm on her hair, tender, as if she were a child to whom he was giving comfort.

'I love you,' he said. 'All I want is you, here by my side.' And she knew he wanted her to reassure him, to say that she wanted the same. She stood in the warmth of him, feeling the rightness of this, while still full of so many uncertainties. She had not come here expecting this revolution in her life. She knew that she loved him, that he was, in an indirect way, asking her to marry him, to be a wife to him and a mother to Daisy. And it was a miracle – yet it felt overwhelming. She was still too full of ragged ends, of guilt and sorrow, to answer him directly.

'I do love you,' she whispered. 'I do.'

She pulled her arms more tightly round him, wanting

to answer by showing him, instead of making promises, until she was sure beyond doubt that she could keep them. And they stood in a loving embrace, until she remembered that Aunt Hatt would be wondering where on earth she had got to.

Forty-Two

'Oh, Auntie – that smells *delicious*,' Annie said, picking up her knife and fork before her plate was even in front of her. She had just come dashing in from the factory, her cheeks burning pink from the cold of this freezing night. Even Uncle Eb still had his jacket on.

The four of them were round the table, Eb and Hatt, Margaret and Annie. Georgie and Clara, who had brought Jimmy round to be doted on by his grandmother, had gone home, as by now had all the staff. The lamps were lit, the room cosy and smelling of coal, of Aunt Hatt's lavender water and of the delicious aromas from the big dish of Uncle Eb's favourite dinner – faggots and gravy – into which Aunt Hatt was dipping her spoon. The clock struck the half-hour – six-thirty – and the smoke-filled darkness had long fallen outside.

Aunt Hatt laughed. 'I can feel your mouth watering from here,' she said, passing Annie a well-filled plate. 'There you go.'

'Go on, wench,' Uncle Eb said. 'There's plenty of spud to go with it.'

'Potatoes, Eb,' Aunt Hatt ticked him off. She continued dishing out. 'How're they getting on with the German order?' she asked.

'Nearly done,' Uncle Eb said, reaching for the dish of cabbage. 'Beautiful job they've all done an' all.'

'I'm sure the German gentleman will be pleased,' Margaret said carefully. 'They're lovely – the pictures he's done, I mean.'

'Lovely – they're a flaming masterpiece!' Uncle Eb chuckled, sitting back. His fleshy face and the upturned ends of his moustache made him look very jolly. 'Did you see the pictures he sent of those wenches? All I can say is, if it's a case of life imitating art, life's got a fair way to go!'

'Oh, Eb,' Aunt Hatt said. But she sat down in front of her own plate of faggots, smiling mischievously. 'But old Sam Lieberman's done a flattering job, I'll say that!'

Annie had her head down, eating urgently. No one got much sense out of her until she had had her tea.

'You had that lad around today, Margaret?' Uncle Eb said. He took a reluctant interest in Den Poole.

'Yes – for a bit,' Margaret said.

''E any good?'

'I don't really know. You'd have to ask Daisy,' she said, guiltily aware that she had spent the whole of tea-time immersed in Philip Tallis, not watching how Daisy's lessons to Den were progressing. She had yet to broach the fact with Annie and the rest of them that she had promised to go out with the Tallises again on Sunday morning.

Eb and Hatt had started talking about other business matters and Margaret found her mind inevitably wandering to next door. They all lived so close together – only separated from the Tallises by a couple of walls. Walls which she knew, if she so chose, could become her own home. Home, in this place of what their father would call 'heathens', with no religion. A place of commerce and far from all she had known . . . As she relived the feeling of Philip Tallis's arms around her, his lips on hers, she was not aware of the blush that was rising in her cheeks. She was rapt, caught up in her fancy, so that she jumped when Annie sat up straight and said, 'What was that?'

'There's someone at the door.' Aunt Hatt pushed her chair back, frowning. 'I'll go.'

'Good God – what now?' Uncle Eb exclaimed with a groan.

Silence fell in the room except for Eb's fork against his plate, the hiss of the coals. They heard Aunt Hatt's footsteps, the door, muffled voices, more footsteps.

'Annie –' Aunt Hatt's head appeared. Her face was troubled. 'You'd best come. It's that young wench – the daughter. She won't come in.'

Margaret and Annie looked at each other and both got to their feet. As they reached the hall, Aunt Hatt watched from the doorway.

Lizzie Poole was just inside, looking ready to flee out again at a second's notice. She had a sodden-looking shawl wrapped over her head, and her white oval of a face looked distraught.

'Annie – it's our mom,' she burst out. 'Can you come?'

'Is she ill?' Annie said, reaching immediately for her coat.

'I'll come too,' Margaret said, pulling hers on.

'No – not ill exactly . . . 'Er's just sat there and 'er's gone all strange – won't say a word to me. And Nellie's disappeared – I dunno where she is!' Her voice teetered on the edge of tears, but she was intent on getting the message out.

'We'll go, Auntie,' Margaret said.

'D'you need me to come?' Margaret could see her aunt was reluctant and she touched her arm.

'We'll come back if we need you.' She mouthed the

word *sorry* before the three of them set out into another freezing, wet night.

'What's happened, Lizzie?' Annie quizzed her. 'Have you any idea?'

'No,' Lizzie said. 'I can't get a word out of 'er. She looks so queer. I told Den to look after Ivy. And he ain't been to school today – I know he ain't and he won't tell us where he's been . . .' Her worries came tumbling out.

In the mizzling rain they passed along the muddy streets to the yard in Pope Street. In the Pooles' house, they found Mary sitting on the chair by the range, bolt upright, staring ahead of her. Den had Ivy at the table and the two of them were eating the remains of a loaf of bread.

Margaret and Annie approached Mary Poole very gently. Margaret was surprised that Annie seemed uncertain and did not take the lead. She found herself going up to the young woman and saying softly, 'Mrs Poole? It's Margaret Hanson – and Annie's here too. Is there anything we can do to help you?'

For a moment she thought Mary Poole had not even heard her. She wore her usual old frock covered by her shawl and her pale hair was caught up scraggily on her neck. Her rigid back did not give for a moment, but stayed ramrod straight.

Margaret and Annie exchanged glances and Margaret looked at Lizzie, who shrugged desperately. Den and Ivy sat so still, it was as if they were scarcely breathing.

Margaret walked round in front of Mary Poole and knelt in front of her, taking her icy hands in hers.

'My dear Mary,' she appealed to her, looking up into her face. 'Can you not tell us what the trouble is?'

There was a silence, then Mary Poole's body began to shake. At last she broke into sobs, her head bowed.

Annie, eyes wide as if in horror at what they might be about to hear, laid a hand on Mary Poole's shoulder. Margaret kept hold of her hands and they let her cry for a few moments until she was able to speak. No one else spoke or moved and the only sound in the room was her thin, broken weeping.

After several attempts, Mary at last broke into speech.

'I can't go on! I just can't manage any more. I'd never've done it otherwise – I'd never!' Another storm of crying quenched her for a few moments. Terrible possibilities flooded Margaret's mind. Where was little Nellie? She had heard of the desperate actions of poor mothers, women pushed beyond the limits of their own strength and sanity. Surely Mary had not felt driven to such a desperate crime?

She looked round at Annie and was startled to see that her sister's face was contorted with grief, her cheeks already wet with tears.

'Mary,' Margaret said, a sternness creeping into her voice which seemed to get through to the woman. 'Where is Nellie? What have you done with her?'

Mary Poole stared back at her and her face filled with an enraged horror. 'No! No – it ain't that! You think I've gone and done 'er in, don't you? Of course I ain't! What d'you take me for? You think I did for Ada an' all, don't you and I never . . .'

'No! Mary, no – of course we don't think anything like that of you!' Margaret said, horrified. 'You mustn't think that! Ada was sick. She died because she was poorly . . . But what about little Nellie – where is she?'

Mary quieted and withdrew her hands from Margaret's, wringing them in her lap. She freed one for a moment to wipe her eyes in a hard, bitter gesture.

'It's only for a while – 'til I get on my feet. I can't

manage – no husband, only Lizzie with earnings, and me, if I do every day on them boxes and half the time I get 'em all wrong . . . And doing carding, but there's no money in it – not really . . .' She shrugged. 'I thought, if I can just get proper work, like, we can get back on our feet, but with Nellie 'ere – and I got no one – no mom or nothing . . . I can't do it. So I thought if I took 'er somewhere where they'd look after her for a bit for me . . . There's a place up Erdington where they look after girls. So I went . . .'

She collapsed into tears then, softer, grief-stricken tears. Margaret could hear Lizzie and Annie sobbing somewhere behind her.

'When I said goodbye to 'er . . .' She could hardly speak for tears. 'I dain't mean goodbye. There was this woman took 'er and 'er said 'er'd be safe there. It ain't for long – 'er won't remember it, will 'er? Little babby like that? I'll go and get 'er out of there . . . I will . . . I'll go and get my little babby back . . .'

'Oh, Mary,' Margaret said, her own voice choking. She leaned forward and put her arms round Mary Poole's painfully thin shoulders. She could see that Mary, in her desperation, was doing what she thought was for the best for her family, but all Margaret could feel was heartbroken for her and very afraid.

Annie had her arms round Lizzie and both of them were crying. After a moment, Margaret got to her feet, patting Mary's shoulder, and went to Den and Ivy. Ivy's face crumpled.

'Where's our Nellie?' she cried. 'I want 'er – and I want our Ada. I want 'er to come back!' She laid her tousled head on her arms on the table and wept, heartbroken.

Den sat with his jaw tight, fists clenched on the table, not looking at anyone.

'Nellie will be back, we hope,' Margaret said, though she felt great misgivings about promising anything. 'Your mother is trying to make things better for you all.'

She bent to put an arm round each of the children. Ivy sat up and rested her head wearily against her, but Den flung her off and got up violently from the chair. He went and sat on the floor by the fire, cross-legged, his back rigid, staring straight ahead of him.

Forty-Three

This time, when Margaret told Annie on the Sunday morning that she was going for a walk with Philip and Daisy Tallis, Annie did not say a word. She got up silently and took herself off to church, which Margaret found almost more disturbing. The past weeks had changed Annie. Always so sure, so fiery and argumentative, she had grown quieter, as if a deep, more uncertain conversation were going on inside herself.

Margaret had noticed this especially since Friday night and her storm of tears at the Pooles' house. Yesterday she had gone into the factory for cleaning as usual, then wandered off for most of the afternoon. In the evening when Margaret asked where she had been, all she said was, 'Oh, just walking.'

Margaret allowed herself to lie in bed for a few more minutes than usual, the blankets pulled up to her chin, cosy in her thick nightgown, even though there was a rime of ice on the windows and she could feel the cold of the air in her nostrils. Annie had pulled the curtains and the day looked bright and crisp. The Sunday street was quieter, without the clatter of hooves and clamour of voices. A bell was tolling somewhere and the calm rhythm of it soothed her. She lay thinking about Philip Tallis, a warmth spreading through her as she remembered how he looked at her, the gentle, caressing way he spoke to her. Under the gruffness he showed with some people, she knew he was a man of deep feeling, kindly, a lover of beauty. She knew she could love him – did love him. But uprooting her life to stay here in Birmingham? It was something that would never in a thousand years have occurred to her when she first left home.

There would be ice in the ruts of the muddy tracks around the village today. Longing filled her as she thought of all the beauty of the countryside. She could imagine golden light on the trees, the clear, mirror-like surface of the winter river, reflecting willows, the flight of rooks scattering in the air . . . A powerful pang of homesickness went through her. Was that no longer to be where she belonged?

But then the reality of it drummed its way into her. Father. The rigid routine, which could feel heaven blessed if you chose to think of it that way: church three times on a Sunday, the school, the visiting and living always in the line of duty. All the things she thought she had been born to do, and yet which, as a young woman, her sick body had refused to let her participate in, as if it bore a different message to her, one she could not directly inter- pret. And how strange it was, the rush of excitement she felt at the sight of colour, of the objects of beauty made by Philip and others, the way they set her heart pound- ing, a thrill going through her that was almost like . . . She could not form the word. The word for what the body might feel for a man . . . And were all these instincts wrong? The texture and beauty and colour and love that living here had given her? Or was it all a trap, in a glittering disguise, the way Charles had been a trap? Was it God testing her – or his adversary?

Heart pounding with the tension of it all, she sat up and swung her legs out of bed. It was not too late to throw on her clothes and follow Annie to Carrs Lane –

to turn her back on all this newness of feeling, the temptation it offered, and return to the straight and narrow.

And then the thought came, blatant: how straight and narrow my life was after Mother died, and how ill it made me!

She sat on the side of the bed, staring at the winter light from the window.

They took the tram to Soho Road, even though the day was cold and turning blustery, to walk in fresher air. Daisy was wrapped in her warm coat and hat, a thick scarf wound round and round over her long hair, and her eyes lit up as they reached the wrought-iron gates of Handsworth Park.

'I love it here,' she said. 'Pa – can't *we* move out to live here, like Mr Watts?'

Margaret had told them that the new house was just up the road from here.

'Oh, I don't know,' Philip said, with a comic air of exhaustion at all Daisy's demands. 'Give us a rest, young miss – it's Sunday.'

Daisy laughed and skipped ahead. The ice was melting on the grass and the sky was now thick with fast-moving clouds so that the sun came and went like a winking eye. Margaret walked beside Philip Tallis and they chatted, she telling him what had happened on Friday, what Mary Poole had resorted to. He looked appalled.

'What a choice,' he said furiously. 'For a child to be orphaned like that when she still has a mother. It's a stain on our country that this woman is in such desperate straits.'

'It's having young children that does it, isn't it?' Margaret said. 'Now Nellie is not there she can go out to work. She's no family to help. It's women with little ones who are the worst off. And those other poor children of hers. Little Ivy has lost her two closest sisters. And I really don't know what to do for the best for Den.'

'You do all you can,' he said. 'Soon as he's old enough he can get some proper training – but it's not in line with the law now. I can't employ a lad that young . . .'

'I know,' Margaret said. 'No one was suggesting you should. And you've been very kind. His being able to come to your house and learn things off Daisy means a lot to him.'

'He's not the sort of lad that would come if it didn't,' Philip Tallis agreed. 'Though mostly I think he comes for the food!' They laughed.

'Well, for whatever reason,' Margaret said, 'he's learning things. He likes it, I think.'

She breathed in, looking across the frozen green of the park towards the church. Walking here, out of the hubbub of the close-packed place where they lived, and seeing trees and water, and being here with Philip, she was filled with a sense of bliss, of which she found herself questioning and being suspicious. Even though she knew she had seldom been this happy, somehow confusion was never far away.

'D'you ever think,' she said to him, as they walked at the edge of the little boating lake, 'that feeling happy is wrong?' Even as she said it, she thought how odd it was that her father seemed to have instilled this into her and how perverse it must sound.

Philip turned to look at her, frowning. 'Wrong? No. Why would it be wrong? There's enough goes against it in this life. You have to make the most of it while you've got it, to my mind.'

She nodded, staring at a brown mallard drifting on the water. His hand reached for hers. She wore gloves, but his large hands were bare.

'Are you happy now?' he said.

'Yes.' She looked at him in confusion, feeling she owed him more honesty. She turned and took his hand in both of hers, looking into his eyes. 'I am. I'm just . . . Before I left – well, this is why we left – I had a falling-out with my father. He's not an easy man but he is a good man, at heart. It's just not always easy to . . . Anyway, I don't think I can be properly happy until we have resolved things.'

Philip frowned slightly. 'An apology?'

'Yes – from him. The trouble is, I don't know if we shall ever get it. And if we don't, I'm not sure what to do about it. It's in my nature to apologize – even though I know really I am not in the wrong – just to make things better. But Annie . . .'

'Feels differently?' He seemed amused.

'She does, yes.' She thought of Annie for a second, her quietness lately. Was her sister all right? There seemed so many challenges that she felt suddenly tired. Releasing his hand, she turned to the little lake again. A few brown leaves floated on the murky water.

'We'll go back for Christmas, I think,' she said. 'And hope to make things right then.' With Father and, she thought, somehow also with Charles. She knew she could never settle fully if she was at loggerheads with anyone.

Philip was silent, staring ahead of him. She could see that he did not want to ask again whether she would return.

'Just for a while,' she said, trying to feel quite sure of this. She squeezed his hand.

'Come on, Pa!' Daisy called. 'Let's go to the bandstand!'

It was too cold for boats and bands that morning. All the walkers were muffled up tight and the air grew damper, threatening rain. But there were a few hopefuls in the park with barrows, selling hot potatoes and chestnuts. Daisy looked longingly at them, but her father took her hand and she did not argue. They were all beginning to feel the cold and a drizzle had begun.

'We'd best not stay too long today,' Philip said, 'or we'll be in for a soaking. Let's walk back to the tram stop, eh?' He looked hopefully at Margaret. 'And you could come back home with us for a cup of tea?'

'So where've you been?' Aunt Hatt asked when Margaret slid into her place at the Sunday dinner table only just in time. Delicious smells of roasting beef had drifted from Mrs Flett's kitchen as they sat next door and Philip asked if she might stay.

'I'd best not,' she said. 'I think Auntie would be annoyed. She's bought some pheasants specially today.'

Her aunt had not seen her go out that morning, but Annie was already at the table, having been back from church for quite some time.

'Oh – just out for a walk,' Margaret said, rearranging her cutlery.

Aunt Hatt put her hands on her hips. 'Who with?'

'Well – with Mr Tallis and Daisy.'

'I see . . . No, Eb – let them stand a bit, don't cut straight in . . . Mr Tallis. You seem to be seeing rather a lot of him.'

'He's a nice man, Auntie,' Margaret said. She knew her aunt and uncle felt responsible for her and that they were concerned at what might happen, that Philip Tallis was so much older than her. But she also knew they were a bit funny about him because he was somehow different from them, which did not impress her.

'Yes,' Aunt Hatt said, busying herself with the roast potatoes. 'Well – I suppose he is. But I'm not sure that means you need to spend so much time with him.'

Forty-Four

The next week, the densest of all fogs descended, filling the streets and barely lifting even at midday. It seemed to muffle the sounds, almost as if the horses wore sacks over their hooves; it added an air of mystery to the distant cry of voices and pressed against the windows of Watts & Son as if waiting to be invited in. At night, the light from the street lamps took on a feeble, exhausted air and the daylight arrived as if filtered through an old dish clout. The lamps burned all day in the workshop and office as everyone strained their eyes over their tasks of page or peg.

Enclosed as they were in this murky world, unable to see out to any degree, everyone concentrated on what had to be done and crawled thankfully to bed once the day was over. And they were busy days.

Sid Cole and his assistant gem setters finished the work of arranging the daughters of Herr von Titz, and when they were brought into the office and everyone stood round admiring, they were the brightest thing that happened all week.

'Well, I hope he's pleased,' Aunt Hatt said, arms folded as she looked down at them, smiling. 'They are lovely, aren't they, Eb?'

Uncle Eb seemed very pleased. 'Well, if 'e don't like them, dog bite 'im, is all I can say.'

'Ooh, aren't they pretty?' Bridget breathed, peering short-sightedly at them.

Each of the frames stood out around its picture, each a slightly differently wrought twine of leaves, buds and flowers; an ivy here, an acorn there, set with gorgeously toning colours of emerald and ruby and other less precious, though no less vivid, stones: garnet and jasper, malachite, topaz and rose quartz. The collection, laid across the desk, glowed in the gloom, adding a majesty to the faces of the seven German sisters. The sight of them lifted Margaret's spirits.

'Right,' Uncle Eb said. 'We must get them packed off and sent today.' And he gathered them up as if they were tea plates and disappeared.

Margaret sat back at her work table. 'Haven't you ever wanted to learn to do all these things, Auntie?' she asked.

Aunt Hatt turned to her, her lovely face wearing a gentle smile. 'Oh, yes – and I did, a bit. From my father. But it's all a man's world really, that side of things, and someone's got to run the business. Eb's not very good in the paperwork department. He never got on with that side of things. So . . .' She shrugged. 'There it is.'

'Women just do the chains – and the polishing and such,' Susan put in, in a tone which suggested that this was the unchanging law of the universe. 'Oh – and the pen nibs, like your sister.'

'I see,' Margaret said, a little discouraged by this, thinking of Philip's offer to teach her. She smiled. 'Well – you're a very good team, the pair of you.'

Annie came home with news that Mary Poole had come back to Masters, Hogg & Co. looking for work, but there were no vacancies at the time so she had been taken on in the piercing room at Brandauer's in New John Street West.

'Well, that's good,' Aunt Hatt said, though sounding doubtful. She still could not get over the fact of Mary Poole handing Nellie over to the orphanage, even though she could understand that the woman had been at her wits' end.

'Yes.' Annie's voice was sad. 'Lizzie said they're all feeling a bit more hopeful now there's another wage coming in, even though the house feels terrible without Nellie. She says as soon as they've picked up a bit, they'll be able to get her back.'

'But won't that mean Mary having to stop work again?' Margaret asked. 'Or finding someone to look after her?'

Annie nodded. Her face looked pale and strained. 'I didn't like to ask. It was nice to see Lizzie looking a bit more cheerful and not having to provide for all of them by herself.'

When they were preparing for bed in the attic, Margaret chose a moment when Annie had slipped into bed first, as usual, leaving her hair all over the place, while Margaret was still plaiting hers. It seemed the best time to broach the subject, when they were alone in the candle-lit room. With her back to Annie, passing the brush through her thick hair, she said cautiously, 'You don't seem quite yourself. Is anything the matter?'

She expected Annie to snap back at her, as she would often have done in the past, that she was perfectly all right, thank you very much, and wanted to be left alone. Instead, she sighed.

'I don't know.' She sounded small and deflated, not like the old, always certain Annie. Margaret turned and came to sit on the bed, still plaiting her hair.

'It's all got me down a bit, I suppose. I used to think there were answers – sure answers – if only you worked hard enough and had enough faith. Mary Poole doesn't go to church but she has faith of a kind, if you talk to her about it. But in the end –' she looked directly at Margaret, really seeking her opinion – 'what difference would it actually make if she had the faith of ten? She's still as poor as a church mouse, and there's no help other than the parish – and they're so cruel. She told me all about it – these hard faces looking down on you, making you feel as if you're wicked because you're poor, and not giving much help anyway.'

'Well, you're helping her,' Margaret pointed out. 'And maybe it is the faith she has that keeps her going.' She trailed off, not certain of anything herself either. 'Something helps her keep going, anyway.'

Annie lay back and stared at the ceiling. 'Yes, maybe it is. She loves her children – that's what it is really . . .' She looked up at Margaret. 'I just thought God was *there*, waiting to help if we'd only ask. But . . . It's only us that can do anything, isn't it? God works through us – not in any other way. Because if there was a God who was not like that, who could just sort everything out and make it better, you'd have to wonder why He doesn't do it – why would He be so cruel? There's just something *wrong* that people are living like that.'

'Yes,' Margaret said, with a helpless feeling. She could hear that Annie was close to crying and she felt tearful herself. She wanted to offer one of the old remedies – God as the ever-listening ear; why didn't they pray together? – but all their certainties were being prised open into doubt and she felt just as shaken herself. She got up to put her brush down and lifted the bedcovers to get in beside Annie, blowing out the candle.

'Maggs? D'you think . . . ? Am I good with people?'

'Yes. I think so.'

There was a hesitation in her voice that Annie caught. 'But?'

'You're very good when you're not being too bossy, that's all. You're sympathetic and practical and you genuinely care for them.'

'D'you think I could be a nurse? I think more and more that's what I want to do. Look after people – make sure it's done properly. At least, that's something I feel right in doing,' she added quickly. 'Without being *too* bossy.'

In the darkness, Margaret smiled at this new humility.

Until now, Den Poole had turned up in Chain Street every so often. But that week he appeared every day, after school. He arrived looking sullen, said very little and ate as much as he could. With Daisy he did not need to say a great deal as she chattered on regardless and showed him things to do with his hands, which she said he was 'getting quite good at, really', in a tone of superior astonishment.

On the Friday afternoon, when Margaret was round at number twenty-four, to her surprise Den said, 'Can I come tomorrow?'

'But it's Saturday tomorrow,' she reminded him.

'I know – but in the morning, like. Can I bring Ivy?'

Margaret realized suddenly that Mary Poole and Lizzie would both have to go into their factories for cleaning and Den would be alone with Ivy. She looked at Philip Tallis as if to say, *It's not my place to decide.*

'Yes, you can,' Daisy said, seeming pleased at the

thought of Ivy's arrival as well. 'Just for the morning because then Pa needs a rest,' she advised him.

Margaret and Philip Tallis looked at each other and he rolled his eyes.

'Well, all right,' he said. 'This once, anyway. I'm starting to feel we're running a school here.'

Margaret had a number of jobs to do for Aunt Hatt for a lot of that Saturday morning, and it was nearly dinner time when she went next door to number twenty-four. Nodding to Mr Henshaw as she passed the office, she could hear from the laughter in the Tallises' room that Den and Ivy Poole were still there.

Putting her head round the door, she was surprised to see the three children playing with little puppets. They each had one, or in Daisy's case, two, all roughly sewn little animals, on their hands. Noises of goats and pigs, a cockerel and a donkey, were all being made at once. Margaret watched as Den, who had the cockerel on his hand, with a floppy red comb on its head, was pretending to peck off Ivy's nose, rather too violently Margaret thought.

'Cock-a-doodle-doo!' he shrieked. Ivy, though giggling, was squirming to get away from him.

Tears rose in Margaret's eyes. She realized it was the first time she had seen either of the Poole children smile, let alone laugh. Mary Poole must have cut Ivy's hair, because it was now a little blonde pudding-basin shape around her ears, and her face looked rounder and very sweet.

She hardly liked to interrupt, but she slipped into the room, sat on the chair behind them and watched.

'Hello, Miss Hanson,' Daisy said, after a while, getting to her feet. 'Can you do dog noises? You could have this puppet.'

'Oh, well, I don't know about that,' Margaret laughed. 'Please!'

So she joined in as best she could, yapping and woofing like one of the little Jack Russells in the village even though the puppet was a brown mongrel of indeterminate breed.

'You're very good!' Daisy said, and all of them laughed and played on.

After a while, Margaret said, 'Now – you heard what Daisy said about Mr Tallis needing a bit of peace and quiet after his dinner. So if you two come next door with me, Mrs Watts said you can have a little bite to eat before you go home. She's got some very nice-looking sausages.'

Den and Ivy leapt up, hearing this.

'Are you coming with us for a walk tomorrow?' Daisy said to Margaret with big, pleading eyes.

'I think tomorrow, Daisy, I shall be going to church with Annie,' Margaret said. 'But I'll see you very soon. Have you got your cap, Den?'

She led Den and Ivy next door, taking Ivy's hand. To her great surprise, as they went into the hall of number twenty-six, Den caught hold of her other hand and held it, seeming unsure.

In the bustle of getting into the house, she did not at first register that something was different. From the back room, she could just hear the murmur of voices.

'Right – it smells as if the dinner is ready,' she said, leading the children along.

She pushed the door open. In a second her body went rigid. There was a tingling at the back of her neck as if the hairs were standing on end and she was suddenly grasping the children's hands so hard that Ivy gave a whimper and pulled hers away. Margaret had to remind herself to breathe and her heart was pounding.

'Hello, Margaret dear!' Aunt Hatt got up, with a smile. 'Well, here's a lovely surprise for you – a visitor.'

She indicated the figure who had been sitting by the fire and was now getting to his feet. There, only a few feet away, apparently unchanged in every detail, was Charles Barber.

Forty-Five

He was so utterly familiar: the old Charles, the charming, friendly man whom she had thought she loved, walking towards her, a smile breaking over his face.

'Margaret.' His tone was full of gladness and he held out his hand. She let go of Den, feeling no option but to shake his hand in return. He took it gently, lifting it to his lips, and made a little bow over it, before raising his eyes to hers.

She felt dizzy, disorientated, her heart thudding as if to warn of great danger. During those seconds she saw him and nothing but him. Then she returned to the room and was aware of Den and Ivy still close beside her, of Aunt Hatt beaming at the pair of them.

'How . . . How did you know where we were?' she asked faintly.

'Oh –' Charles stepped back tactfully, releasing her hand. He spoke in a light tone. 'Your father told me. He said that before I leave for my post, it was time for us to resolve our little difference and part as friends – wouldn't you agree?'

Our little difference? Her sense of betrayal by her father deepened again into rage. He had promised not to tell Charles, ever, where she and Annie had gone.

'And besides,' he said, his eyes looking at her with a humble longing, 'we have both missed you so very much. Your father is rattling about that house alone except for the housekeeper, and is desperate for you and Annie to return home – though of course he finds it hard to say so. And I . . . Well, we must make peace, Margaret. I know I have done you wrong somehow, for you to have reacted in such an extreme way.'

Again, he made a small bow. Just behind him, Margaret saw Aunt Hatt's face taking in the look and manner of Charles Barber, the man Margaret had told her she wanted to marry but that her father had opposed it. The man she *had* wanted to marry . . . Looking at him again now, here, as lively and engaging as he had always been, her heart ached. For a crazed moment she wondered if she had imagined that night in the stables. Had it been him – or another man for whom she had mistaken him? Or was it a dream? He still seemed to have no recollection . . . Had she been mad in some way?

'Come and sit down, both of you,' Aunt Hatt was saying. 'It's ever so nice that Mr Barber has come, isn't it, Margaret? Annie won't be back for a little while yet, but . . .'

'Of course – how lovely!' Charles said, with another bow of acknowledgement. 'I'm so looking forward to seeing little Miss Annie again.' Charles appeared convincingly as if there was nothing in the world that would give him more pleasure.

Margaret watched him with a dizzy sense that she was slipping into a reality that was not as she remembered it: that she was being compelled to remember it differently. The old feeling, with Charles, of being forced, came back to her. And she had not told Aunt Hatt anything, so her aunt could not contradict . . . But Annie would never forget. And when Annie walked through the door there would be all hell let loose and everything would be dragged into the open – which also felt more than she could bear. Somehow she had to resolve this situation, so that she could have peace.

Aunt Hatt was beckoning Den and Ivy to the table, putting plates in front of their eager faces. 'I'm sure I shall have the pleasure of seeing Annie later,' Charles said. 'But . . .' He turned to Margaret and with all the appeal and charm she remembered, he said, 'Very shortly I shall be taking up my new appointment in the church at Banbury. I should very much like to show it to you, Margaret – for you to come and meet some of the people there. I know they would love you. It's the work of an afternoon by train, if we were to set off promptly. And . . .' He lowered his voice a little. 'It would give us an opportunity to talk for a time. To . . . make peace with each other.'

'That sounds a lovely idea!' Aunt Hatt said. 'It'd do you good to have an outing, Margaret, after being here in the office all this time. Why don't you go and see?'

Margaret could tell what Aunt Hatt was up to and could not help being amused by it. Charles had worked his charms on her. Aunt Hatt thought she was going to come back engaged to be married! What a lovely man – who could resist? And in her own heart there was a deep longing for peace; for all the pain and bitterness of the last months, the division between herself and her father, and between herself and Charles, to be resolved. In those moments, Charles brought her old home back to her, the village and their ordered life of religious love and service. It felt pure and good and she ached with longing for it.

'You'll need some dinner.' Aunt Hatt had left the room, returning a few moments later with two steaming bowls which she set in front of Den and Ivy. 'Why don't you stay and have a dish of soup – it's a hearty one with pearl barley . . . And I've some sausages . . .' Den had already shovelled several mouthfuls in before she had finished speaking, cheeks bulging. 'Slow down, young man – no one's going to steal it off you.'

'I'm afraid that if we are going, we should leave at once,' Charles Barber said.

Margaret was not aware that she had agreed to go, but as before, with Charles, she felt herself swept along. Where was the harm? She knew he meant nothing to her now and they would be in company at all times. It would be much easier to talk away from here, without Aunt Hatt close by.

'Well, then – I'll cut you some bread and cheese,' her aunt said, bustling into the kitchen.

There was a moment's silence in the room, broken only by Den's hurried slurping.

'Margaret.' Charles's voice throbbed with appeal and he spoke with apologetic humility. 'You will come? I should so hate us to part not as friends after all we have meant to one another.' He stared intently at her, a gentle, encouraging smile at the corners of his mouth.

She looked back into his eyes, those intense, passionate eyes, knowing he was right. They must find a point of meeting. He would apologize, away from here, for the terrible lapse in his behaviour. She could try to understand, to forgive him, and things might be repaired. And then it would be over.

'Yes,' she said softly. 'All right. If you think we can do it in an afternoon.'

'Oh, I'm sure we can,' he said. 'The trains are very good.'

*

Soon they were on the tram, wrapped in their winter coats, with a parcel of bread and cheese. For once there were seats available and they sat close beside each other.

It felt strange to be sitting at his side again as she had done so many times in the days when she had felt enlivened and comforted by him. Though it was not pleasant exactly, it felt right to be trying to resolve things.

'It's so very nice to see you,' he said. His eyes radiated into hers. 'It's been very bleak in the village without you there, you know.'

'I've missed it,' she said, smiling quickly before looking down again. She knew this was true – yet also, only intermittently. She had been caught up in this busy new world, in all the daily routine of Watts & Son, her aunt and uncle and Georgie, and all the other goings-on with the Pooles, with Daisy and Philip Tallis . . .

As they made their way into Birmingham she asked after the village, some of the families and church members, and their conversation grew easier, focused as it was, and had so often been before, on practical things, on their religious duties. This was not the moment, she knew, for the deeper, more painful conversations that they must have, that he would surely begin, in which he would explain himself. She asked after various neighbours, and after the Davises with whom he had been lodging. She could not bring herself to ask after her father.

'Allow me to pay for the tickets,' Charles said, as they approached one of the booths in Snow Hill station's marbled booking hall. 'This must be at my expense, of course.'

'Thank you,' Margaret said. Until that moment she had not thought of the expense of the tickets, though she had brought a small amount of money with her.

As they moved through the busy station she became aware of the pressure of his hand on her back, steering her through the crowds towards their platform. For a second she felt a moment of panic and tried to ease herself away from its control. But she told herself not to be so foolish – he was only trying to help, so that they did not become separated in the crush. She decided that his hand also felt reassuring, as if it was part of his way of trying to make peace.

Forty-Six

'We're in luck!' he cried, as they hurried down the steps to the platform.

Steam was hissing from the huge locomotive waiting behind them and a sleeve of smoke hung in the air. Along with the other hurrying passengers, they made their way to the small carriages which ran along a corridor.

Charles ushered her into one of them and they settled side by side, Margaret sinking into a seat next to the window, still holding the packet of bread and cheese from Aunt Hatt. The compartment filled up and moments later the engine shrieked and there came the whoomping sound of it getting up steam and they eased off along the platform. Charles stood to remove his coat and flung it up on to the luggage rack.

'Yours?' He held out his hand.

'I'm still chilly,' she said. 'I'll keep it on for now, thank you.'

As he stood there close to her, reaching up, she remembered him acutely, his figure, the strong legs which had always walked so urgently beside her. She remembered the way he had held her in the early days, their first timid kisses. A pang of confused longing and dread went through her. As if sensing her thoughts, Charles looked down at her between his arms. He gave her a long, meaningful look which went right through her. Without removing his gaze, he sank down beside her again.

'I've missed you so much,' he said. He spoke softly, for only her to hear, but her face coloured and she looked round at the other half-dozen people sitting with them. The couple opposite were quite elderly and still fussing over their things. Beside them was a woman with two young children and on the other side of Charles sat a man hidden behind a newspaper. She could tell none of them were eavesdropping but their presence did make it difficult to talk.

Charles turned towards her a fraction, as if to enclose them in a cocoon of privacy. His closeness brought him back to her even more: the way his thick hair lay across his forehead, the beard, neatly trimmed, and the way his eyes, tawny in this light, seemed to look deeply into her. His mouth was curved upwards, amiably. She felt the hairs rise on her flesh. She was here again, with him, with his intense look that seemed to gather her up and carry her along with him, as if there was nowhere and no one else in the world. Charles, the real Charles whom she remembered. Then for a second she recalled his face, the feverish, terrible way it had changed on that night, and a shudder went through her.

'Are you all right?' he asked, full of concern.

'Yes.' To distract him, she handed him Aunt Hatt's package. 'Perhaps you could put that up as well?' She eyed the rack. 'Until we want it?'

He nodded politely and did as she asked, before sitting again, and in those seconds she calmed herself, straining for a balance. All she was doing here, with him, was taking this brief opportunity for explanation and apology, for healing. That was all. She thought of Philip, the loving look in his eyes, but at this moment he belonged to another world. First, she had to do this – the old world had to be settled.

'So,' Charles said pleasantly. 'How have you been spending your time in Birmingham? Your aunt seems a very nice person.'

'She is,' Margaret said, relaxing a fraction at this positive appraisal. 'And Uncle Eb. They've been kinder than we could have expected. I've been working in the office with Aunt Hatt. I've learned such a lot about the business and all the things they make. You should see Uncle Eb's workshop – the "shopping", he calls it – at the back. It looks all grimy and workmanlike and the men in there hammer and drill away and work with chemicals that burn your nostrils. And then, out of the end of all that come these things which are so fine, so beautiful! It's astonishing.'

He was watching her, listening, eyes gleaming with a certain amusement at her enthusiasm.

'And Annie – has she been working there too?'

'Annie?' She laughed, feeling more at ease now they could talk the way they used to. There was a pleasure in simply talking to someone who knew her and her family well. 'You know how headstrong she is. During the first week she went off and got herself a job at one of the pen factories. I mean, they make pen nibs – thousands and thousands every week. There are a great many factories making them in the district – some of them very famous, like Gillott's. You must have heard of them? Between them they provide the means for people to write, all over the world! You've no idea how complicated it is making a pen nib. Or at least –' she corrected herself – 'I had no idea before I came here. Anyway, Annie – in the interest of the Lord's mission in our great cities, you know what she's like – wanted to see how it is to work in a factory.

390

To see what people's lives are like. And she's been there ever since.'

'I imagine it must be gruelling,' Charles said.

'Oh, it is. I should never have survived it. They're there from morning 'til night on those presses, banging out bits of metal at an astonishing rate. Annie says there are some ladies there over seventy years of age, still working. They're very tough – but then so, it seems, is Annie. And she has involved herself with helping various people . . .'

'Well, I'm glad to hear that Annie, at least, is so devoted to God's work,' he replied. Margaret was taken aback, thinking she heard a barb of sarcasm in his voice, but he was still smiling and she was left confused. Darkness invaded her mood for a moment and she pulled herself up short. The Charles who had attacked her, who had tried to . . . do those unspeakable things to her. Where was he? Was there to be an apology? But she could see that here, in this quiet crush of people, there would be no opportunity.

They were leaving Birmingham, green fields all around. She sat back and took a breath.

'How long does it take to reach Banbury?' she asked.

'An hour or so, I believe,' he said.

'I'm looking forward to seeing it.' As she spoke she wondered why she felt the need to appease him, as if she, somehow, had long ago slipped into the wrong and been the cause of all their troubles. 'Your new church. Will you be the sole incumbent?'

'No.' He looked down, unable to hide the bitterness in his voice, and his face pulled into an angry frown. 'They have not seen fit to do me that honour. In fact, I am to work with two others.' He gave a stiff smile. 'We all have to serve our apprenticeship, even those of us not working in the more material trades. Mine, it seems, is to be prolonged.'

Silence fell for a moment. Charles adjusted himself in his seat. He seemed preoccupied. She wondered whether he was feeling the weight of his conscience.

'Do tell me,' she said, 'about home.' Swallowing her hurt, she said at last, 'Tell me about Father. About the work. The Lord's work.' The words felt rusty in her mouth and she realized, with something that was almost panic, how little she had been talking about these things lately.

Charles also sat back, giving the impression of being appeased by this. As they journeyed south, stopping at Warwick and Leamington Spa, he gave her news of their little church. Though he talked about their work in the village, the progress of the word under himself and her father as shepherds of the flock, she thought she heard a bitter edge to his voice, a touch almost of scorn. She realized that he had been hoping for more, to be sent back to a large mission in one of the great cities – Birmingham, Manchester or London. And it had been decided that these were not the right places for him. Who had said what to whom? she wondered. Had her father, although not able to confront the truth directly with her, spoken to someone, hinted, or more than hinted, at Charles's lingering instability?

The more he talked, the more she felt an attitude of disapproval towards her coming from him. So, to convince him that she had not spent her time in Birmingham mixed up only in worldly matters of commerce, she told him about the Pooles.

Charles shook his head on hearing this, in a manner of pastoral sadness and concern.

'The life of the poor is endlessly hard,' he said. 'It is our task and our mission field.'

'At least at home people can more easily keep live-stock and grow a little something,' she said, wanting to impress her new knowledge upon him. 'In the quarter where the Pooles live, the houses are in a most dire state, all crammed together amid smoke and fumes, and there's not a house which has running water and scarcely a blade of grass or a garden to be seen. Although –' she smiled – 'there is a man in the next court of houses to the Pooles, who somehow manages to keep a pig!'

Charles smiled politely. 'Gracious me. Though I did see such things when I worked in the city myself.'

'Of course,' she said, still trying to appease him. 'You have had so many experiences of ministry.'

'Not enough, apparently, to warrant having my own congregation.' The bitterness was now very clear.

'Oh, Charles, I'm sorry,' she said. 'I know that's what you would most like. Perhaps they think you need one more stage of preparation before being given such a heavy responsibility?'

'There are those younger than me charged with greater responsibilities,' he said sulkily.

'But you were unwell. You ...' She stopped. 'You were not fit.' It sounded too cruel. But she felt for him, felt his misery and sense of disgrace, when she knew him to be gifted and devoted. And yet ... How could such a man, a man who had attacked her, be allowed to ...

All the darkest of thoughts invaded her mind. Thoughts she had forced away, tried to deny. The things her father had said, his blame of her ... It was she who had been made into the problem! In a career otherwise unblemished, it had only been with her that Charles had run aground. Only with her – because of something in *her* – had he become an animal who could not be trusted. A twisted, self-hating sense of guilt welled in her. *The curse of Eve!* Father said . . . He said she was to blame . . . In those moments, she was infected with self-disgust . . . But then had there not been a mention of something else happening – another incident . . . ? She had never been told what.

'Ah, well – yes,' he was saying. 'It's true – I was a little exhausted.'

He became gentle suddenly, smiling again, touching her hand for a moment. 'I have to remind myself not to be impatient. Or ambitious, for that matter. The Lord sees and measures our achievements very differently from the world.'

'Yes, indeed – though I'm sure He sees your dedication,' she said. The words sounded trite, even to her.

Charles glanced out of the window. There was the beginning of a town. Turning to her, he spoke very softly. 'It would all be so much easier to bear if I had you at my side, as before.' He looked down, apparently tormented and contrite. 'Margaret, my dear Margaret,' he murmured softly. 'I know I have wronged you. I have caused hurt and confusion between yourself and your father. I . . .'

A spasm of pain passed over his face. 'I still do not know of what I am accused. I woke and found myself lying in a bed in your house and since then all has been confusion and desolation. Whatever it is – I . . . I regret to the very heart of my being that I have no memory of it.'

They were moving so close to it, to that night, and her pulse was uncomfortably fast, blood banging in her ears. Rage boiled up in her. Rage and shame and confusion. Not remember? Had the blow Annie gave him genuinely injured his memory? How could he *not remember*? And if he did not remember, how could he take responsibility?

'I don't . . .' she began to say. But the pound of her blood, the distraught tears which wanted to pour from her, her longing to beg him to remember, to apologize properly, to be honest and true, all stopped her speech.

She put her hands over her face, so that the slowing of the train, the stirring of the other passengers and their reaching to find their belongings was all lost to her. She had no idea whether they could hear her and Charles's conversation, but it seemed not to matter. It was as if there was no one but him; he was sliding through her thoughts, possessing her as he had before, and she longed with all her soul somehow to make things right.

'Margaret – my dear . . .' He sounded distraught. 'Please, say you forgive me – for whatever I have done.'

She removed her hands from her face, wiping her eyes, about to say, *How can I forgive you, if you say you do not know what you have done?* But as she surfaced, hands limp in her lap, she realized that the train was sliding to a halt. Charles, his eyes boring into hers, grasped one of her hands, pressing it so tightly that she flinched.

The train jerked, brakes screeching, to a standstill, and a voice outside called, 'Banbury!'

'Oh!' she said, thrown into panic. 'We're here, look. We must get off!' She looked round, trying to gather their things. The mother and two children were already stepping out into the corridor.

But he gripped her hand harder. The look in his eyes had changed. There was something cold and forcing, which chilled its way through her. They needed to move, to get off the train . . .

'No,' he said, in a soft, smooth voice which was quite

unlike the chill look in his eyes. 'Not here.' He tightened his grip another fraction on her hand. She let out a small sound of pain and he relaxed the hold again slightly. 'Now, don't go making a silly lot of noise. Just be sensible. We are going to go a little further, that's all. There's someone I want you to meet.'

Forty-Seven

'Why didn't you tell me you wanted to visit your grand-mother in the first place?' She was furious after the panic-stricken moment of him gripping her hand, forcing her.

'Because . . .' He loosed the pressure on her hand as the train eased into motion again, a few newcomers in the compartment. A mischievous smile spread over Charles's face. 'You would never have agreed to come – and I wanted you to, very much.'

She glared at him. 'But why tell me untruths, Charles?' she hissed at him. 'D'you know – I may not be living among people who you would class as Christian, but they are more straightforward in truthfulness than you are!'

He gave her a crestfallen, little-boyish look. 'Don't be angry. I just wanted you to come. I knew you would think Oxford was too far away – when it isn't really very much further. I have not seen my dear grandmother – Elsie is her name – for far too long and I know she would love to meet you. She is my late father's mother. As you know, my mother is also a widow, and she has gone back to live with her own mother in Enfield. It is rather far, so I do not see her often. But Elsie was always very kind to me and I hate to neglect her.'

'Well, that's all very nice,' she said, angry and jarred by the fright he had given her. 'But you really just should have said so. And what about Banbury – are you really moving there?'

'Oh, yes, I am!' he reassured her. 'And I would like you to see it. Now – let me ask you. No secrets or ruses now, I promise. If you like, we can turn about tonight and go straight back from Oxford. Or – and this is your decision, dear Margaret – we might stay the night at my grandmother's house. It's quite central. I know she will be very reluctant to let us leave. She is over eighty now, and I never know each time I see her whether it is the last. We could easily take in Banbury on our way home tomorrow.'

'But Charles – my uncle and aunt are expecting me back tonight! What on earth will they think if I don't go home? And how much anxiety we should be causing. You don't seem to stop to think!'

'Of course, of course – I'm so sorry,' he said miserably. 'I'm so caught up with the excitement of seeing you again. Dear Margaret –' he took her hand again. 'There have been so many times when I have wanted to write to you and plead for you to come home so that we could talk to each other and set right whatever was wrong. But your father strenuously advised me against it and of course his word has been my rule. I'm sorry for getting carried away. Banbury will have to wait for another time.'

'All right,' she said, almost recovered from her fury. 'We'll stay for a couple of hours now we seem to be here. But you must just be straight with me.'

'Shall we have the bread and cheese?' he said, jumping up. 'It's getting late and there's just time.'

The fog that had taken frequent possession of Birmingham was not in evidence in Oxford, but the sky was like a steel grey helmet as they set off to walk from the station into the town. It was already the middle of the afternoon and Margaret felt irritated with the whole project. They would scarcely have reached his grandmother's house when they would have had to turn round again. What on earth had he been thinking of?

'We could cut along Walton Street,' Charles said. 'But you have never been to Oxford before, have you? I'll take you along through the heart of the town so that you can see.'

'All right,' she said. 'If it's not far.' She was interested to see this city of learning, but her irritation was further increased by the way Charles was holding her elbow, as if steering her.

'Would you mind?' She stopped, extricating herself from him. 'Please let go of my arm. I should prefer us to walk separately.'

He shrugged and smiled and said, 'Of course,' as though he had not noticed that he had been bearing her along like this. They passed a wall with a keep, the remains of a castle, and went on to the middle of Oxford and the soot-encrusted stone of the ancient colleges.

'Do you know any of their names?' Margaret asked. She thought the place looked rather dour and intimidating in its grandeur.

They stopped, having reached a crossroads.

'Well – along there is Christchurch,' he said. 'Behind are others – Merton, Corpus Christi . . . But we need to go this way.' Once again, he took her arm. As soon as she could she pulled away.

'We must not stay long,' she said. 'I must be sure to get home in time so as not to alarm them.'

'Of course,' Charles said. 'In any case, she is an

elderly lady – she will not be able to stand company for too long. Perhaps a quick cup of tea, that's all.'

As they walked along a street of shops, the rain began, soft at first, then more heavily.

'Heavens, we shall be soaked,' Margaret said, lowering her head to shelter under her hat brim. 'Is it much further?'

'A little way, not too far . . .'

They were walking past a church and she plunged towards the door. 'Let's go in here – just to shelter from the worst,' she said.

'In *there*?' he protested. But she had already gone in, the heavy door giving way to her hand.

They stood in the smell of stone and mustiness, looking about them with a kind of horror.

'Is it Catholic?' she said, afraid. 'I thought it was the Church of England.'

'It is – in the Catholic style,' he said, the disgust plain in his voice. 'Look at it – signs of the whore of Babylon all about us. Let us go . . .'

'No,' she said. 'It's too wet.'

She shared his sense of skin-creeping distaste, because that was what she had been brought up to feel. Roman Catholics and even the Church of England were both remote to her and alien, over-ornate and worldly; in everything showy and deeply mistaken. She had never ventured even into the simple little church in the village, let alone one such as this.

No one else was inside and she began to walk along the aisle between rows of carved wooden pews, in turn flanked each side by stone arches rising to a point at their centre. Ahead of her, dull light straining through them, were windows, framed in a similar Gothic shape, ornate and stained in gorgeous colours. Almost ashamed, she felt her heart begin to beat with pleasure.

She was standing in front of an altar, of the sort that her own denomination would deem overwrought and idolatrous. Upon its gold-and-white altar cloths, stood a huge cross and tall candlesticks, all shining brass, each holding a long white candle. To the right, hanging from the wall, she could see a light flickering in a ruby holder.

For a moment, she sank down on the seat at the front, gazing at the sight before her. Those candlesticks – just the sort of thing they would make at Gibson & Franks nearby in Chain Street, she thought. But Uncle Eb could make them if he was asked to. And Philip . . .

Her heart seemed to swell. It was strange and foreign in this place, but it was beautiful. It was like the time she had first seen the silver bowl on Philip Tallis's workbench: the feeling of being lifted, through her senses, to an intimation of something sublime. Beauty, she thought, *beauty is truth, truth beauty* . . .

In that moment she was filled with longing for Philip Tallis – a feeling of homesickness at being here in this strange place, away from him. Philip was not religious, but his love of beauty linked hands with what she saw here in front of her; it lifted the spirit above the mere materials, the hammering and soldering. And whatever it took for her to adapt herself, she knew with a passion in those moments, that she loved Philip. That quiet, brilliant, tender man – he was her love. And she would return to him and make a life with him. The thought filled her like a burning warmth of conviction.

Here she was with Charles, who had deceived her even in bringing her here, when she had come for the best of reasons, to try and make peace. Yet she was still waiting for an apology.

She heard his footsteps walking along towards her, clipped and brisk, as if dissociating himself from this place which had warmed her soul.

He has deceived me, she thought. And where is the apology, his making an account of himself? Where is his truth and courage? The remaining hours of the day with Charles were something to be passed through so that she could go back to her real life. She felt peaceful, as if a tight string inside her had been cut. He came and stood beside her and she looked up at him coldly.

'Let's get out of here.' His face was twisted as if having eaten something sour. 'I feel a sense of pollution. You're welcome to my coat as well as your own, if you like – but I can't stand being in here.'

'Is it too powerful for you, all that beauty?' she asked, her sarcasm unmistakeable. She had a feeling of certainty, of triumph. 'So much more powerful than the words of any sermon you could come up with?'

'What can you mean?' he snapped as they stepped outside. 'The place looks like a . . . a bordello.'

The door thudded closed behind them. It was still raining, though less heavily. He was hurrying her now, furiously, the hand once more grasping her elbow.

'Charles . . .' She stopped. 'For the last time, would you please let go of my arm?'

'Yes.' He seemed to recollect himself. They were turning into a street of terraced houses. Observatory Street, she read. 'In any case – we are all but here.'

He stopped in front of a simple two-up-two-down house and rapped on the wood.

There was a pause, then a sound of muffled movement before the door swung open and a stooped little woman with a crushed, suspicious-looking face appeared, dressed entirely in black, a grubby apron tied at her waist.

'Yes?' She seemed crotchety at being disturbed.

'Grandmother – Elsie – it's me, Charles. Edward and Jane's boy. I've come for a visit – with my friend, Margaret. It's been such a long time – and such a pleasure to see you!'

Margaret saw a flicker of something in the old lady's eyes which she could not decipher. She did not break into happy greetings but instead said cagily, 'What is it you want?'

Charles laughed, seeming baffled by this question. 'Just to see you, Grandma. Is that such a strange thing?'

The woman did not look unconvinced that it *was* in fact rather strange, but faced by a member of her own flesh and blood, after a moment she shuffled backwards and held the door wider.

'You'd better come in then.'

Forty-Eight

It was a cramped little house and once the front door was closed, the narrow hall was almost in darkness except for a crack of light from a room further along. They seemed to be treading on a gritty linoleum, though it was too dark to make out anything much.

'Come through,' Elsie Barber said, shuffling ahead of them. She had the painful, rocking gait of someone with bad hips.

'Let me take your coat, Margaret,' Charles said. 'We can hang it to dry.' His voice, in the gloom, sounded warm and reassuring after his grandmother's rather frosty reception of them.

Gladly she slid her coat off and Charles shed his. He opened the door beside them.

'I'll drape them over the chairs in here so we don't have damp things hanging all around us in the back. Do go through.'

He indicated the room at the back into which the old lady had disappeared, and carried the coats into the front.

Margaret found herself in the small but cosy room in which Elsie Barber evidently did most of her living. So much so, in fact, that there was a makeshift bed along the back wall of the room away from the window instead of a couch. Elsie was hurriedly pulling at it to make it more respectable. The top cover was a very old, sandy-coloured blanket. The head of the bed just fitted in next to the range to the left of the window, and there was a small table, two wooden chairs and an armchair. Elsie's few crocks and pans were piled higgledy-piggledy around the foot of the range. The room smelt of cooking, of urine and of some slightly rancid food.

'I've nothing much for you,' she complained.

'Please don't go to any trouble,' Margaret said. 'After all, we came unannounced and we shall not be stopping for long.' She would have liked to be able to give a proper explanation of their sudden arrival, but was aware that she did not have one.

'Can't manage the stairs these days, with my hips being as they are.' Elsie Barber turned from the bed, gathering her shawl about her. In her pale, watery eyes, wispy white hair and the boniness of her face, Margaret saw a vulnerable, uncertain old woman looking back at her. She felt immediately sorry for her. Elsie Barber had the look of a countrywoman and reminded Margaret of various elderly women she had known in the village at home.

'May I help you in any way, Mrs Barber?' she said.

'You can fill the kettle in the scullery and set it on.' She pointed and Margaret went to collect the kettle. She jumped as she turned, finding that Elsie Barber had come up close behind her.

'I have to live in 'ere, see,' she whispered. A strange, suspicious expression had come over her face which Margaret found disturbing. 'There's odd people about, see. I'm all right in this room of a night – lock myself in, safe as houses.'

'I understand,' Margaret said, her heart pounding with alarm, though she was not sure why. But the woman's wild look frightened her. 'That's very wise of you.'

'It is.' Elsie backed away. Her face softened, as if

relieved that she had been understood. 'Some of us know things, see.'

Margaret took the kettle into the little scullery in the back corner, where there was a tap and a stone basin. As the water trickled into the kettle she heard Charles come into the other room.

'Well, why didn't you tell me if you wanted to come, boy?' Margaret heard Elsie Barber say irritably. 'Years pass and not a word – and you turn up like this.'

'I'm very sorry, Grandma.' Charles's voice had taken on its appeasing tone. 'It was something I thought of on the spur of the moment, to be truthful with you. Margaret and I were travelling south – to see my new church at Banbury. And I thought – why not? I so wanted the two of you to meet each other.'

'Why?' Elsie said, with undisguised scepticism.

Charles laughed. 'Because you're my grandmother, of course, why else! I have very fond memories of you.'

'Huh,' Margaret heard, returning with the kettle. Elsie Barber pointed her to the range and she positioned it on the heat.

Charles, perched on one of the upright chairs, was saying earnestly, 'I know I've been very poor at keeping in touch with family. It's part of the nature of the ministry – it's so demanding that one can feel quite devoured – and the family was not very near. But soon, when I am at Banbury, I shall be able to visit you more often.'

Margaret turned from the range to see Elsie Barber give a nod of what could only be called lukewarm enthusiasm at this prospect. She sank into the easy chair by the fire as if her legs would no longer hold her. Margaret saw that her ankles were very swollen, her feet pushed into loose tweed slippers. The wooden-cased clock on the mantel struck a mellow four times as she did so. Already, the light outside was fading.

'There're a few biscuits – in that tin.' She pointed Margaret to a pale yellow tin on the table, which said 'Peek Frean & Co.' on the lid. 'If I'd known you were coming . . .' She didn't elaborate on what she might have done had she been in possession of this foresight. 'Sit down, girl.'

Margaret took the other seat by the little table and Charles looked across and gave her a strange, confiding smile, which she returned, momentarily touched. *I know this place is not much*, his smile seemed to say, *but this is my family and I want to share myself with you.* And his grandmother's house humbled him in her eyes. It was a lowly place.

She looked around the room while they waited for the kettle. It was very simple – the bed, the range and chairs, the dingy, butter-coloured paint on the walls. There were no pictures or memoirs of family that she could see. She wondered if these were in the parlour at the front.

'So – how's your ma?' Elsie asked.

'Oh – she's well, I believe,' Charles said. 'Though her own mother is ailing and takes a lot of care.'

'Ah, well,' Elsie said fatalistically. 'At least she *has* someone to care.'

'True, very true!' Charles laughed.

'And you're getting on all right, being a vicar?'

'I'm not a vicar, Grandma,' Charles said testily. 'I am a Congregationalist, remember?'

'Oh,' Elsie said, seeming unimpressed. 'Yes. Well, same difference.'

The kettle was hissing. There was an air of desperation about the conversation and Margaret looked uneasily at the clock. They would have to start for home as soon as they had drunk their tea and she was already impatient to be off. This whole, strange day felt like a waste of time – a day removed from the real life which she now knew was hers. There was to be no proper healing with Charles. Now she simply wanted to be away from him.

At last tea could be made and drunk. Elsie posed half-hearted questions. He asked after her two sons, who, according to her, turned up now and again. 'All the men in my family are lions or mice,' she remembered him telling her. She wondered about Elsie Barber's sons and how he would describe them. The tea was warming and she ate a couple of plain, stale biscuits and started to thaw out.

Once they were down to the dregs, she began to stir and try to catch Charles's eye, though he kept looking away, bringing up little topics of conversation. The clock struck five.

'Charles,' she said eventually. 'I'm afraid we really should be on our way. My aunt and uncle will be worried. It's quite a journey back to Birmingham,' she explained apologetically to Elsie Barber.

'Birmingham,' she repeated, in tones which suggested that Timbuktu would not have sounded further.

'Right you are – of course. I'll fetch our coats.' He jumped up, then cried out, his face contorting in pain. 'Aaagh!' He bent over, rubbing fiercely at his calf.

'What's wrong?' Margaret asked, hearing his moans of pain.

'It's nothing – just a cramp – it'll pass in a moment.'

'Don't worry – I'll fetch the coats,' she said, keen to be away.

'If you wouldn't mind,' he said, muffled. 'I really will be all right in a moment.'

She went out into the hall, which felt chill after the

warm back room, and felt her way into the room at the front. It was almost dark but there was just enough light to see, in blocks of grey and black, the furniture in the room. It felt cold and unlived in.

Why ever didn't he bring the coats in to dry by the fire? she thought, irritated at his lack of practicality. Feeling her way about, she could make out that he had just thrown them in a pile on a chair near the window. She tutted, feeling the soggy wool. The damp had just seeped between one and the other and they were no drier at all.

She was gathering them up into her arms when she heard the door close, very softly. As she walked towards it, there came the sound of a key turning in the lock.

In the first seconds, her mind did not take this in. She heard the sound but could not connect it with the present. Going to the door, she turned the handle. There was no movement. She pulled, yanked the handle, dropping the coats on the floor, then banged her hands on the wood.

'Charles! Charles – I seem to be shut in here! Come and let me out!'

Trying to make sense of it, her heart pounding, she was full of confusion. The old lady had talked about locking herself in. Was she more crazed than she looked? Had she come and turned the key for some deranged reason of her own?

'Charles!' her voice rose to a wail. They had to go – they must go and catch the train! 'Come and let me out – I'm locked in.'

But the house was strangely silent. And no one came.

Forty-Nine

She stood by the door in the darkening room. Disbelief and confusion swiftly turned to panic and rage. Locked in – a prisoner! Who had crept to the door like that and turned the key? Was it the old lady, or had it been Charles? What was going on? Why did no one answer and come and let her out?

Raising her hands, she hammered and hammered on the door until the palms of her hands and her fists were sore.

'Let me out!' she called. 'How dare you lock me in here!' Her emotions swelled and boiled over. She began to shout and scream more than ever in her life before. 'I want to go home – let me out of here!' She was full of desperate longing to be away from here, to be back with her aunt and uncle. Why in heaven's name had she agreed to come with Charles, and what was going on in the other room? Did the old lady have some hold on him? Was she as mad as she had looked when she spoke to Margaret? Or was it he who had brought her here, scheming all the while?

When there was still no response to her pleading shouts, she went to the window. There was something in the way, hard against her knees. A chest of some sort. Leaning across it, she looked each way to see if there was anyone to whom she could plead for help. The lamps were not lit yet, though she thought it was not long before the lamplighter must come out. But she could see no one in the narrow street. In desperation she began to bang on the window anyway, trying to release her feelings, to alert someone, anyone, please, dear Lord, please . . .

'Help me!' The pane shuddered under her hand. She tried to force up the sash but it did not budge. 'I'm locked in. Someone let me out – help!'

At that she heard a sound outside the room. She stilled.

'Margaret.' It was his voice, low, outside the door.

She tore towards it. 'Charles! Let me out! What's going on?'

'You must stop banging on the window.' His voice was soft and persuasive again. 'Stop that noise, now. You wouldn't want anyone to get any ideas in their head, would you? You sound . . . unstable. Anyone seeing you, might begin to think—'

'Let me out!' she shrieked. 'What d'you think you're doing, locking me in here like this? Let me go home. You said . . .' Her voice, to her fury, began to break into sobs. 'You said we should go home this evening.'

'I did, I know,' he said reasonably. 'But I don't think you are in any fit state to travel now, are you? Let us wait a little and see if you feel better in the morning, shall we?'

'In the morning – no-o-o!' She was wailing. 'Why have you done this? You're . . . you're a terrible, wicked man . . .' She was about to continue telling him what he was, but fear gripped her. She was in his power here. She must not say anything to enrage him. She stopped abruptly.

'Wicked, am I?' The soft voice again, through the wood of the door. 'Why – what did I do, Margaret? I

411

have no memory of anything other than that I was hit over the head by some deranged person . . .'

She stood, trembling, behind the door. He *was* wicked. Even more wicked than she had ever believed. And she had thought that things might be made right, that there could be understanding, forgiveness. Tears ran down her cheeks. She was angry, but even more, now, she was frightened. Even in her upset state she realized, with cold rationality, that she must not insult him. What else might he do if she said the things she really wanted to say?

'I've tried to believe the good in you,' she managed, attempting to control her voice so he would not hear that she was weeping. 'I came with you because I wanted us to make peace.'

'Peace? Well – you are the person who can perhaps explain why we needed to make peace in the first place. You were a sick woman when I first met your family,' Charles said. His voice was dry, objective. 'I was kind to you, always, so far as I remember. I would have said I did you a lot of good. But you always had a vivid imagination – fed by too much time alone, pretending to be an invalid, I should imagine . . .'

Pretending? She gasped. '*I was not . . .*' she whispered.

But she could see it was no good pleading with him. She sank to her knees behind the door, oblivious to the hard floor, the horror of the situation seeping through her.

She heard his footsteps moving away, into the back room. What was he telling his grandmother? Because she knew now that the old lady was not to blame, had nothing to do with this, odd as she was. And that Charles, the charming, vulnerable man to whom she had given her hungry young heart, was two people – the outward man

412

of charm, and this calculating, soulless man of steel. And she, with all good intent, had placed herself in his hands.

Overwhelmed by her own foolishness, at having been so taken in, she bent over, curling up, weeping in the darkness.

It was very cold. The only remedy she could see were the damp coats and she pulled them around her, repelled by the thought of wearing any garment of Charles's. But I'll use it if I must, she thought savagely. I'll use it to keep warm, if it serves.

She felt her way round the room, wondering if there was any way she might light the place. There was a dim glow now from a lamp along the street. As a distraction from the sick rage and dread that crouched in her, she moved slowly about the room by feel. A firm armchair, leather upholstery by the feel of it. Another the same, the other side of the fireplace. There seemed to be very little in the room. Elsie Barber had moved anything she needed for her comfort into the back. There was some sort of rug by the hearth.

Groping round the fireplace, her fingers searched for a candle, for matches – matches especially. There must be a gas mantle somewhere in the room . . . But nothing in the way of a matchbox came to meet her questing hands. All she could feel was an empty coal scuttle and the wiry hairs of a hearth brush. She wondered whether the coal scuttle might be heavy enough to break the window, but when she lifted it she found it was a light, tinny thing.

The only other object was the chest. Feeling her way to it, she lifted the lid, seeing, with a sense of horror, the dark space inside it. She was reluctant to put her hand in. The chest gave off a stale, old smell of camphor. Don't be ridiculous, she told herself. What could possibly be in there that might be harmful? Nothing, most likely. With her heart racing, she plunged her hand down with a gasp. Nothing. Except, right at the bottom, what felt like a very worn, old scrap of blanket. It was something. Taking the coats off and wrapping the blanket about her, she put her own coat back over her shoulders.

She thought about moving the chest in front of the door, but when she tried lifting it, it was so light and paltry that she realized it would not keep the door from opening. The only thing to do was to drag one of the chairs over to the door and sit on it. As quietly as she could, she pulled the nearest one across the floor, ramming it as close as she could up against the door knob.

I must be calm, she told herself, feeling a fraction safer as she sat on the chair, wrapping the blanket about her. I must think what to do.

From next door, she made out the faint sound of the clock chiming the half-hour. Was it half past five – or six? She had lost track of how long she had been here. Her mind felt unsteady, jittering with panic.

A moment later, she heard the footsteps again. They stopped outside. She could hear the bang of her own blood.

'Margaret?' The voice was calm, with a patronizing smoothness. He was so close, just inches away on the other side of the door, and she gripped the arms of the chair, hardly daring to take a breath.

I hate you. The thought came to her, hard and clear as a diamond. You are wicked and I hate you with all my heart. She wanted to get up and scream at him. Yell and howl her loathing of him, her rage at having fallen into this trap through her own good intentions. But she would not answer him. Would not let him have any satisfaction. Because now she could see, horribly clearly, what satisfaction he gained from controlling, imprisoning, both mind and body.

'Margaret, my dear?'

She sat quite still, her breathing shallow, saying nothing. She tried not to think about what would happen if he managed to force his way into the room. She would try and stop him, but he would win in the end. And what might he do? He might do what he had tried to do before. He might do anything.

The footsteps moved away. She could breathe again.

She sat back in the chair, her mind utterly awake and on alert. Dear God, sweet Jesus, help me, please! Help me get out of here! Seldom had prayer felt so heartfelt.

The most obvious thing was somehow to break the window and escape along the street. But if she was to do that, he would hear, long before she had succeeded. If she waited until much later, that might be possible, she thought. Surely he must sleep? But then she would be faced with the dark, unfamiliar streets of a town she did not know – and where could she go?

Panic rose in her. She took deep breaths, trying to calm herself. If she waited until the next day, mustn't this be resolved? Charles could not just keep her here for ever, and the daylight would surely bring him to his senses? Or she would find some way out? She could see that his grandmother was no use to her – she was frail and Charles would easily overpower and intimidate her. She owed Margaret no loyalty, in any case.

Hugging herself, she gathered her freezing feet up under her and crouched in the chair, alert in every sense and to any sound which might mean he was coming back. She said the Lord's Prayer over and over again, longing for sleep, to escape this night lying ahead.

Fifty

There was a clock out in the hall which struck the half-hours. Sometimes the minutes between each strike felt aeons long; at others they raced. Seven, half past seven, eight.

She became aware of the need to relieve herself, which grew into a humiliating, insistent pressure in the lower part of her body. Every so often, Charles made a visit to the door. He would turn the key but the door would open only half an inch before jamming against the back of her chair.

'Margaret?' He said nothing else, just called her name several times, as if he needed to know she was there. She did not answer.

But now, she wondered, should she call out? She had no need of food – it would have sickened her. But the thought of calling out for a chamber pot was too awful to contemplate. She waited, the cold making the problem more acute. I'm not asking *him*, she thought.

It had struck nine when she gave in. Stiff and frozen, she got to her feet.

There's nothing for it, she thought, energized by her rage. Why should I sit here in all this discomfort? She felt her way to the coal scuttle and with fumbling and difficulty, managed to relieve herself into it. For some reason, as well as the immediate relief it gave her, this felt rather satisfactory, as if she had struck a small blow of revenge.

Just as she was pulling Aunt Hatt's skirt back down, she heard sounds coming from the next room, and she dashed back to the chair to secure it with her weight. But the noises stayed in the room, Charles's voice raised angrily. Though she listened with every fibre of her being she could not make out the words, but their tone was angry. She heard Elsie Barber's voice, even more indistinct. There were some lesser sounds, thumps as if furniture was being moved. Gradually, it went quiet.

Margaret covered herself with everything she had, the old blanket smelling of moth balls, the coats. If only she might sleep, to pass through this night more quickly. But she was wide awake, every nerve inside her poised for any sound. Her body was like a cauldron of worry and fear. Whatever must Aunt Hatt and Uncle Eb be thinking? Especially when Annie came home and told them who Charles was, as she undoubtedly would have done. And however was she going to get out of here? Her mind kept returning to methods of escape.

Once, she got up and very quietly tried the door, just in case. Was it really locked? But it would not give. She was a prisoner. She imagined running out of here, along the street, to anywhere. She would walk all the way back to Birmingham if she had to . . . Back to . . . home. It felt like home. She sat thinking of Philip Tallis, his face, his arms around her on those precious few occasions when they had managed to snatch time alone, his gentle, reassuring manner.

I know now, she thought. Any doubts in her mind about the future of her life had been wiped away by these past hours. Her father must have told Charles where she was. And his deceitful intentions and her genuine desire for reconciliation had brought her to this. She boiled with rage. She knew who was worthy of her love and trust now, all right!

Time passed, unevenly tagged by the clock. The night took on a deeper silence. She soothed herself with thoughts of Philip. Comforted, she dozed, or thought she did. Each time she woke it was with a terrible pounding of her heart as she was shocked back into realization of where she was, of what she had allowed to happen to her.

The clock had struck two – she thought. One, half past one . . . ? It was hard to keep track. She heard the door open along the passage, the almost, but not quite, silent footsteps. Gripping the blanket round her, both hands fists, she sat absolutely still, her breathing shallow so that there was hardly a part of her that moved.

The key turned in the lock. She leapt up on to her knees, clinging to the back of the chair, forcing her weight down on it with all her strength. The door crashed against the back of the chair.

'Margaret. Are you awake?' His voice was so close: he was whispering in her ear. She waited on her knees, pulsating like a baby bird.

The silence went on for so long she wondered if he had gone.

'You know I love you, don't you?'

She waited, hardly breathing.

'I love you and I want you to be my wife. I don't know how else to get you to see what you mean to me . . . I've kept away from you, though I was longing to see you with every fibre of my being . . . Your father said . . . Look – can I come in? We must talk, properly. I need to explain myself to you.'

She let the silence after this go on. The first sound was a gasp, a cough almost. Gradually she realized he was weeping.

'You torment me,' he sobbed. 'I hardly know who I am when I am near you, Margaret, my love, my darling love.'

There came another long pause.

'Speak to me – please. I don't want to have to force my way in, but I shall, if you don't say something to me. I know you return my love. You tormented me then, with your body, your kisses. I was an innocent when I met you – innocent in love . . . And you . . . you made me feel things – for the first time in my life. You led me – you awakened me . . .'

He rambled on. She listened, staggered by the absurd self-deception of the man. Innocent – he was not far off thirty and she but a girl of nineteen! She had a hard, cold feeling now of certainty. Where before she had wondered so many times whether it had been she who was to blame, now she knew she was faced with something utterly self-centred and deranged. Though she was shaking with fear, this certainty gave her strength.

Eventually, in the face of her silence, he closed the door again and she heard the key turn, the steps receding. She slumped down on the chair, her chest heaving. He's mad, she thought. How did we not see it before? She tried to reason things out. He had not tried to force his way in. If she stayed here until the morning, then she must make something happen. In the daylight she might see if there was something with which she could more easily break the window . . .

Sinking back she fell into a light doze, only to be wakened again by the turning key, his voice sliding through the crack.

'You can't escape me for ever, Margaret. I could come in any time I please.' He slammed the door against the back of the chair several times, as if to flex his muscles. 'But I'm not the sort of man to behave like that – you know that, don't you?'

She could tell that he was foxed by her silence, her refusal to plead any more. He's going to keep this up all night, she thought, picturing him sitting, waiting and brooding, the other side of the wall while his grandmother lay in her makeshift bed. The fact that he was not immediately trying to force his way in was no reassurance. That was what he was like, she realized. He would wait, biding his time.

At last he retreated again. Soon, she heard the clock striking three.

Her senses woke her. He was coming back. She leapt up to kneel on the chair. The shock and the sudden drumming of her heart made her feel sick.

She could hear movement somewhere outside. Straining her ears, she sat absolutely still, unsure whether she could hear anything or not. There was something: a shuffling noise. With no warning, the key turned and she gasped, clinging to the back of the chair as if on a storm-tossed boat. Would he be able to push his way in this time? Or had he come to pour more vile nonsense into her ears?

'Miss?'

It wasn't him!

'Yes!' she hissed, leaping from the chair. Through the crack in the door she pleaded in a whisper. 'Yes – oh, don't lock it again, please don't!'

'Let me open the door,' Elsie Barber said. She seemed

to be speaking alarmingly loudly. 'You want to get out of here, miss.'

Hauling the chair from the door, Margaret thought, surely he can hear, he'll be out any moment! But she had to take this chance if it was being offered. If it was not a trick . . .

Elsie Barber stood in the darkness of the passage.

'Come on – out of the front.' Now that she could see Margaret, she was whispering.

'Thank you . . . Oh, thank you . . .' Margaret seized her coat and rushed out into the hall. Elsie Barber was shuffling along towards the front door. Margaret looked back fearfully as the old woman undid the bolt.

'It's all right,' she said. ''E's asleep at long last. And he's not going anywhere – I've locked 'im in.'

'But . . .' Margaret was hugely reassured by this. 'What about in the morning?'

'Oh, never mind 'im,' Elsie Barber said. 'I'll deal with 'im. 'E's another of 'em – just like my pig of a husband was. You want to get as far away from 'im as you can while you've got the chance.'

She thrust Margaret out on to the step with surprising strength. The street was almost invisible in the morning mist.

'Go on. 'E don't want anything off me – it's you 'e wants. You clear off out of 'ere. I won't be unlocking that door for a good few hours yet.'

'What time is it?' Margaret looked about her, confused.

'Gone four.'

'Which way is the railway station?'

'Down there and turn right – past the canal basin and on you go.'

'Thank you, Mrs Barber,' Margaret said. 'Thank you for helping me.' She felt sorry for the old lady.

But she was already shutting the door.

Margaret was so full of tense energy that she felt she could run and run endlessly. But even a hurrying walk away from that house, that street – from *him* – was all she could manage, since the mist was so thick and the dark still unbroken by dawn. But it felt wonderful to be outside, as if she had been locked in the little house for days instead of just a few hours. She walked as fast as she could manage, straining her legs, intent on getting as far away as possible.

It was hard to believe that he would not follow, that the old lady had really locked him in. It felt, as she hurried through the gloom, as if he might have the power to break out of any confinement and come after her.

Reaching the end of the street she turned as instructed, walked further, turned again and became unsure. Had the old woman left out a turning she should have made? They had come a different way before and she had no clear sense of the right direction. She slowed, feeling her way through the gloom. It's all right, she tried to reassure herself. He can't leave the house. He can't find you. And yet it still felt as if he was everywhere, might at any moment jump out on her.

She wandered, hoping for the best. Nothing seemed to matter now that she had got out of there. She was on her way. She would get home today!

Turning a corner, she heard the clopping of hooves moving towards her. A sturdy brown-and-white horse emerged out of the gloom pulling a cart.

'Please!' She raised her hand and hurried towards it. 'Could you stop a moment?'

'Whoa.' The middle-aged man reined in his horse. The animal's aroma was reassuring, damp breath issuing from its nostrils, as was the bitter smell of coal from the cart. Its driver was well wrapped up in a coat and muffler, above which a kindly, sagging face looked out from under a cap.

'I'm trying to get to the railway station,' she said. 'I've lost my bearings.'

'The railway station? Well – you're not too far.' He looked carefully at her. 'Are you all right, miss?'

Only then did Margaret realize that she still had Elsie Barber's blanket bundled round her under her coat which was hanging open. She pulled the sides of it together, realizing she must look very dishevelled.

'I . . . Yes. Thank you.' She tried to sound in command of herself. 'I need to leave Oxford.'

He stowed the reins and climbed off the cart. He had a fatherly air and she was not afraid of him.

'You won't get a train for a good while yet, m'dear,' he said. 'It's Sunday morning – I'm not sure if they run 'em, least not 'til church time is over.' She could see him wondering why a young woman like her was running about on the streets at this hour.

She stared at him. 'I'll just have to . . . to wait, I suppose,' she said.

''Ave you got your fare?'

She looked at him, this reality not having occurred to her. She had a little money, but she had no idea how much the fare was.

'I . . . I don't know . . .' She felt very cold suddenly and close to tears.

'Look – you could go and wait for a bit in my house

423

– my missus wouldn't mind. It's only just along there.'
He pointed back along the street.

'Oh – thank you. That's very kind. But no.' The
thought of entering another strange house filled her with
desperation. She needed to know she was on her way. 'If
you could just tell me the right direction?'

He pointed, explaining. Just as she was about to thank
him, he fished in his pocket. 'Here, miss – take this.
Can't give you more, but you look as if you could do
with it.'

He handed her a two-shilling piece, backing away
when she tried to return it, protesting.

'Go on,' he said. 'Good luck to yer.'

'Bless you,' she whispered as he flicked the reins and
the cart moved away. 'May God bless you abundantly.'
His kindness brought her to tears.

Fifty-One

The previous day, Annie had hurried back to number twenty-six from her morning at Masters, Hogg & Co. Aunt Hatt was clearing away Den and Ivy's plates so that she could lay the table for everyone else's dinner. The children had already gone home. Annie hung up her coat and hat, hungry as ever.

'Where Maggs?' she said, coming to the table.

Aunt Hatt looked at her, eyes full of coy meaning and a half-smile on her lips.

'Margaret,' she said, 'has gone out for the day with a gentleman – a very charming young man, at that.'

Annie frowned at her. 'What d'you mean? Who?'

'Well,' Aunt Hatt said, as if knowing she was party to secret information. She put a handful of spoons down on the table and began to lay them in their places. 'I know there's been a bit of a rift – your father not approving and all that. But I'm sure that can all be got over. He seems such a nice man.'

Annie's heart began to pick up speed. 'Auntie –' Aunt Hatt looked up, startled at her tone. 'Who was it? Who's the man?'

'Well – Mr Barber, of course. The one Margaret told me she wants to marry . . .'

'*What*? He came here?' She advanced on her aunt. 'Charles Barber? Where are they? Did she say she'd go with him? Where've they gone?'

Aunt Hatt took a step backwards in the face of Annie's urgent questions. 'Well, he said they were going to Banbury, to see something. He's going to a new church there, I think he said.'

'And she said she'd go – with *him*?'

'Yes. She seemed quite happy about it. It all sounded very nice, Annie – I don't know what you're in such a stew about. They'll be back later – they've only gone for the afternoon.'

'But Auntie,' Annie burst out, 'Charles Barber is a *terrible* man. I know he can turn on the charm and he's good-looking and makes everyone feel sorry for him and convinces them into thinking he's nice, but he's *not*. He's wicked. Why on earth did Maggs say she'd go? She's so stupid sometimes!'

'Eh, eh – what's going on in 'ere?' Uncle Eb said, coming through from the workshop for his dinner.

'Annie's getting all worked up . . .' Aunt Hatt began. She became aware of Daisy, still lurking at the side of the room. 'You'd best run home now, dear,' she said, in a voice that did not encourage argument.

'I'll tell you why I'm all worked up!' Annie erupted, as the front door closed behind Daisy. 'Margaret never told you the truth about what happened at home because she was – I don't know – embarrassed. She felt badly about it when none of it was her fault in the least – but that's Margaret for you. That man, that barbarian, Charles Barber, attacked her – tried to force himself on her in the stable behind the church. I could see something was wrong – he was . . . Anyway, I followed them and he was already . . . So I . . . I stopped him. I knocked him out.'

'You did *what*?' Uncle Eb said, looking back and

426

forth in total bewilderment, compounded by the fact that he had not even met Charles Barber.

'He was ... Well, I won't say what he was doing because it was too disgusting, but I hit him over the head ...'

'Annie! What with?' Aunt Hatt asked.

'There was a stool – heavy thing ... I just bashed it on his head as hard as I could and he was out cold.'

'You mean ...?' Her uncle seemed torn between concern and amusement at this description. 'You actually ...?'

'Yes. And what's more, Father wouldn't believe Margaret and he made us have Charles *in our house* until he recovered. That's why we left. But when he did come round he swore he couldn't remember anything because he's a *liar* and a *hypocrite*. And now she's gone with him again because no doubt, knowing Maggs, she's got some idea about forgiveness and everything being all right again ... For pity's sake – *anything* could happen.'

Once Annie had got through to them, her uncle and aunt swung into action. Just waiting was not enough, Annie commanded. Somehow Charles Barber had discovered where she and Margaret were.

'If it was Father who told him, then he's got to come and help sort this out – and *find* them. He never believed us about Charles – he can't face the fact that underneath all that flannel of his the man's a lunatic.'

Though Uncle Eb and Aunt Hatt were finding it difficult to take all this in, Eb hurried out to send a wire to William Hanson, asking him to come immediately. Once home again, he paced up and down, clutching at his hair. 'Should we be going to Banbury?' he said. 'Getting on a train instead of sitting here?' He took another turn along the hearthrug. 'I don't know the place, don't know where to begin. We could go to the police station . . .' Raking his hair again.

'Don't you think all this might be a bit hasty?' Aunt Hatt said. 'They might come back and no harm done.'

'He should never have been told where we were!' Annie turned on her. She was alight with worry and anger, though even she could see that dashing off after Margaret and Charles was not guaranteed to get them anywhere. 'The least Father can do is come and face up to all this. Why should we go back there after all this, as if we've done wrong when he can never, ever apologize for anything? He's so *arrogant* – he's always got to be right about everything. Maggs might be a little mouse when it comes to Father, but I'm damned if *I'm* going to be!'

'Well – you've learned a thing or two in that factory,' Aunt Hatt said, very taken aback by the force of Annie's bottled-up rage.

'Not just there, either,' Annie retorted. 'I've always been the one who's stood up to Father.'

They waited, trying to keep busy, kept saying the same things. As Aunt Hatt pointed out, by now the two of them could be anywhere and as Annie pointed out, Charles was most likely lying anyway and had taken Margaret somewhere completely different. The afternoon passed, evening fell and dragged so slowly it was as if all the clocks had stopped. Daisy knocked on the door, and then her father. Aunt Hatt told them, gently, some of what had happened. And still Margaret and Charles had not come back, and they wondered all over again whether they should have gone, should have done something more than summoning the girls' father.

'What do we do, Eb?' Hatt appealed to him, as they got ready for what would be a sleepless night together. 'I should have stopped her – I feel terrible!'

'Well, how were you to know?' he said, sitting down heavily on the side of the bed. 'We'll just have to hope to God this is all a storm in a teacup and the wench gets back here tomorrow sometime. Otherwise – well, it'll be the cops, I s'pose.'

'I don't even know if she took any money,' Hatt said tearfully.

'Eh – now then, old girl – don't you get all worked up,' he said, having been the one who was the most worked up all afternoon. He climbed into bed and put his arm round Hatt's heaving shoulders. 'None of this is your fault. That's it – you cuddle up to me.' He shook his head. 'It's all beyond me. Sounds as if Old Man Hanson's done those girls a great wrong . . . Always was a stubborn one, him. But all these goings-on – there's me thinking these God-fearing folk never get up to anything. I mean, that little wench knocking the feller out cold!' A chuckle broke from him. 'We'll 'ave to watch ourselves with that one!'

'It's not funny, Eb,' Hatt said crossly, wiping her eyes. 'I'm worried to death.'

'I know, bab.' He turned and looked at her, his eyes sober now with concern. 'Me too.'

To Margaret's relieved surprise, there was a train leaving Oxford for Birmingham at seven twenty. Thanks to the kind coalman, she had enough for a third-class ticket with only a farthing to spare. She said prayers of thanks for this miracle as she climbed into the carriage, immediately looking out to scan the platform in case he had come after her. Even once the train had pulled out of Oxford station, she was ill at ease, half expecting to see Charles Barber appear from somewhere. But time passed and nothing happened. She began to relax just a fraction and breathe more easily, sending up more grateful prayers.

Exhausted as she was, having eaten nothing for hours, she still felt electric with tension, longing just to get home and reassure everyone that she was all right. She could not get warm and kept the old yellow blanket on, disreputable as it looked. The journey passed surprisingly fast and by ten o'clock, the train was nosing its way into Birmingham. Margaret smiled with joy at the sight of the endless rows of chimneys and factories. Never would she have imagined herself so overjoyed to see them and regard this place as home!

By ten fifteen, they arrived at Snow Hill. It was only a mile to get home and she set off at a brisk walk, desperate to get there as fast as possible. She felt relieved and foolish and terribly apologetic towards her aunt and uncle – and Annie too. Though she had been away for less than twenty-four hours, it felt more like weeks.

As she turned the corner into Chain Street, a shock of sudden recognition passed through her. A man was walking along the pavement ahead of her, dressed in a black ulster, a broad-shouldered, utterly familiar figure. *Father.* William Hanson's walk was brisk, his head down. The sight of him caught her breath. He was heading for number twenty-six. Why was he here – had they summoned him? Could it be because of her?

He turned in through the gate, but before she had even reached the house, a little figure ran out from the front and, with her green dress and golden hair billowing about her, came tearing along the pavement.

'You're back! Oh, Miss Margaret . . . ! Den said you got on a train and he tried to follow you and they grabbed him and wouldn't let him go on the platform!' Daisy flung her arms about Margaret's waist and clung to her. 'He said he didn't like that man and he was going to get on the train. Oh, I'm so glad you're back – everyone's been worried to death!' She gave her a squeeze, and before Margaret could say anything, rushed back to the house shouting, 'Pa! Pa! She's here – Miss Margaret's come back!' Still shouting she tore in through their front door.

Within seconds Margaret, dishevelled, exhausted and bewildered, found herself face to face with two distraught-looking men: Philip Tallis, who appeared at his door, and her father, who was standing at the door of number twenty-six. She felt a clutch of dread at the sight of her father, at his grim expression. It came to her that he had always filled her with a sense of wrongdoing.

'Margaret!' Philip rushed down to the pavement and she saw the distress in his face giving way to relief at the sight of her.

'Philip – oh, my dear Philip!' It was not her father who had first claim on her loyalty, her gratitude and love. She knew now where she belonged. As she and Philip hurried to each other, and as she felt herself enfolded in his arms, sobs of pent-up tension and relief started to rise in her.

'I'm here,' she said, her cheek pressed against the rough weave of his jacket. 'I'm so sorry – I'm here, my dear love, I'm home and I never want to be anywhere else.'

'Oh, thank heaven,' she heard him say, hoarse with relief. 'Thank heaven . . . You're here.'

She recovered herself, not wanting to give in to all her emotion now. As they loosened their grip on each other and looked into each other's eyes, she could see how much the last hours had cost Philip in worry and uncertainty, along with all the tenderness he felt for her. He reached up a hand and gently stroked her cheek.

'Pa?' Daisy's voice was timid for once. They each reached out to draw her into their embrace – the embrace of a new family.

As they released each other, Margaret turned to find her father quietly watching them. He had removed his top hat, holding it to his chest in a way that seemed humble. She saw that his hair, still thick and strong, had faded to grey and that his expression was not that of a grim authoritarian. He simply looked older and distraught in a way that began to soften her resentment.

'So, Father,' she said. And she stepped towards him.

Fifty-Two

It was as she stood in front of her father, William Hanson, that something began to give way in her. She was suddenly overcome by a hot, faint feeling and her legs began to shake.

'Oh . . . help me . . .' She reached out to Philip who seized hold of her and ordered William Hanson to bang on the front door.

In seconds, everyone was around her – Uncle Eb and Aunt Hatt, Annie, her father, Philip and Daisy. As the heat and blur receded, she found herself seated in the back room, everyone still there, Aunt Hatt announcing sweet tea and Annie kneeling in front of her, gazing anxiously up into her face. She tried to force her lips into a reassuring smile.

'Maggs?'

She had never seen Annie so worried, or so tender.

'Oh, Maggs – thank heaven you're back. Are you all right?'

Margaret nodded, hardly realizing that tears were coursing down her cheeks. 'I'm perfectly all right – I am. I think I just need something to eat. It's been a long time since I had anything . . .'

As she began on the cup of deliciously sugary tea and a plate of bread and butter and jam that Aunt Hatt brought her, everyone waited, talking gently, though she was hardly aware of anything they said. She felt blanketed in everyone's love and concern, while they let her eat and gather herself without asking questions for the moment.

The food began to take its effect, and she felt herself grow stronger and calmer. She noticed, then, from her seat by the fire, that her father was seated on an upright chair, on the other side of the room. Aunt Hatt was fussing and giving everyone tea. Annie and Daisy sat either side of her while Philip was at the table and Uncle Eb stood somewhere letting out exclamations which included well-I-nevers at Margaret's abrupt reappearance and finding his house suddenly full of people . . . Soon Aunt Hatt could contain herself no longer. She came and stood in front of Margaret.

'Whatever happened, dear?' she burst out. 'I mean, I thought that young man seemed such a gentleman.' Blushing suddenly, as she realized that whatever had happened might not be something with which Margaret wanted to regale a room full of people, she added, 'Of course – if you can't say . . .'

'No – it's all right, Auntie. And in any case –' She felt strength pouring through her. Glancing across at her father, she went on, 'Everything is on his conscience, not mine.'

She told them exactly what had happened – the sudden change of plan, going to Oxford, the grandmother's house.

'Oh! Locked you in!' Aunt Hatt exclaimed, hands going to her face. She sank down on a chair at the end of the table. 'Oh, my Lord!'

As Margaret told them about the progress of the night, the sheer terrifying weirdness of all that had happened sank into her and she was trembling as she spoke.

But she wanted them to hear it – especially her father – in all its details.

'And,' she said emphatically, 'd'you know what the old lady said to me, as she let me out of the house? She said . . .' She turned very deliberately towards her father. '"He's another of them – just like my pig of a husband was."'

For a second she felt concerned that Daisy was hearing this. But then she thought, if I'd known a bit more at her age I might never have got into all that mess in the first place.

'*See*,' Annie said. She was not going to spare their father's feelings and looked directly at him as she spoke. 'That's *exactly* what he was – is. And someone should do something about it. We should get the police on to him. He *abducted* you.'

'I wonder if that old lady will be all right,' Philip Tallis said. 'I mean, if she locked him in?'

'I know,' Margaret said. 'I wondered too – though I couldn't do anything about it. When I got to Oxford station I realized that if she let him out it was the first place he would come looking for me. So I waited until I had found out the time of the first train and went away again – out along the cut, until it was time. I was scared stiff he'd be there waiting, at the station . . .' She turned to Daisy. 'What was that you said about Den?'

'He followed you,' she said.

'But why?'

'He said . . .' Daisy tilted her head to one side and suddenly put on Den's gruff voice. '"That feller – he looks like a bad'un. And when 'er saw 'im, 'er copped 'old 'o my hand so hard I thought 'er'd pull it off. It was 'cause she were frightened of 'im."'

Margaret's eyes filled with tears and when she looked at Annie, she saw the same emotion.

'What a boy,' Annie said, having to wipe her eyes.

'But why could everyone see it except me?' Margaret said.

'Well, I couldn't,' Aunt Hatt said. 'He seemed perfectly nice to me.'

'All that time – I couldn't see the bad in him. There *was* good in him – and I suppose I only wanted to see the good – I know that when I see it.' She smiled at Philip Tallis and he gave her a loving smile back.

'When he came along, I was so . . . And he has a way of getting inside your thoughts, burrowing in like . . .' She shrugged.

'An earwig?' Daisy suggested. Everyone laughed.

'Yes – a great big fat earwig,' Margaret said, putting her arm round Daisy for a moment.

There was a movement at the side of the room and they all looked to see William Hanson getting stiffly to his feet. Even the way he did this seemed the action of a man older than she remembered and Margaret felt a jolt of sorrow. Still in his black coat, he came and stood beside her and reached out a hand as if to put it on her shoulder, before, on second thoughts, removing it again. He stood with his hands clasped behind his back, bending forward slightly, and his stance silenced everyone else.

'I owe you an apology of the profoundest kind,' he said. Even though he was speaking quietly, his resonant preacher's voice resounded about the room.

'My dear Margaret –' She could see that it was costing him to speak, to admit how deeply he, but above all she, had been wronged and deceived by Charles Barber. 'And you, Annie – who can see through walls that confound

436

those of us less inclined to see. All I can say is that I was wrong. I looked upon Charles as a son – or perhaps, more perniciously still, as the man I might have been. I was blinded by my own need to believe in him, by his persuasive, insinuating ways.' Pulling back his broad shoulders, he shook his head sadly.

'Even now, it is hard to believe what he is capable of, what a serpent we had living among us, and how long he took to show us his true nature. I have to tell you, I am left stunned and wretched over this whole business. But I owe it to all of you to face the truth.' His speech was made in the stiff manner of a man seldom used to being wrong, but when he looked down at her, Margaret could see all the sorrowful love in his eyes. 'I owe it to you, my daughters, especially you, Margaret, who has been so wronged and endangered. And you, little Annie, who always fights for the truth.'

Annie nodded at him with grave dignity.

'And to all of you –' he looked round the room – 'who have been so kind and hospitable to my family, I want to give thanks and all contrition where it is due. I think, Harriet, you have been able to give them the love and guidance of a mother – something they have sadly lacked for so long.'

'Oh, Father.' Margaret stood up, unable to hold back her tears. She went to him and they gave each other a brief embrace. 'I know you only wanted to believe the best of him – as I did. But I was not lying to you. That was what hurt the most – that you could have believed that of me, of us.'

'There is none so blind as those who will not see,' said her father. He looked carefully at her. 'You look well, my dear – even after what has happened.'

'I am well,' she said, realizing that tired as she now

was, she had hardly ever felt better. She had found a life that suited her.

Releasing Margaret, her father looked round warily, 'And little Annie?'

'The thing is,' Annie said, not quite ready to forgive all yet. 'You really must believe us when we tell you things. Just because we're girls doesn't mean we have no judgement or insight. And in this, we had a good deal more than you.'

'You did,' Margaret said.

'Yes . . . Well . . .' She went to her father. He looked down at her with gentle fondness.

'I stand corrected, Miss Annie,' he said. They embraced stiffly, not being a family given to outward show.

Aunt Hatt stood up, looking tearful. Margaret even saw her uncle wiping his eyes.

'Will you have another cup of tea, Mr . . . er, Reverend Hanson?' she asked, getting in a fluff with the titles.

'William, please,' he said, smiling stiffly. 'And I must say – it is a pleasure to see you both again. It's been too long. Another cup of tea would be most welcome.'

'What are you going to *do* about him?' Annie demanded as they all sat down again.

'I shall take measures as soon as I get home,' he said. 'He is dangerous and must be stopped. He is unwell, I believe.'

'Unwell!' Annie erupted. 'He may be unwell, but he's a complete ba—'

'Annie's been working in a factory,' Aunt Hatt interrupted. 'I'm afraid some of it might have rubbed off.'

William Hanson looked astonished. 'Well, you always said you wanted to see more of the world. I am full of admiration.' He gave the creaking laugh of a man not often overcome by mirth. 'But now, girls, there is no reason for you not to return home, is there? I think we have all imposed on your aunt and uncle quite long enough.'

'Oh, no,' Annie said straight away. 'We're not coming home. At least – we'll visit, of course. Soon. But not for good. I'm going to apply to become a nurse.'

Exclamations of surprise rang round the table.

'Ooh, are you?' Aunt Hatt said. 'Oh, my – I couldn't do that.' She looked carefully at Annie. 'Come to think of it, if you really think that's what you want, from what I've seen of you, you'd be marvellous.'

This affirmation brought a beaming smile to Annie's face. 'Thanks, Auntie,' she said.

Margaret sensed her father looking at her.

'I'm afraid I shan't be coming back to live at home either, Father, though I look forward to visiting very much. I . . .' In confusion, she looked across at Philip Tallis. Holding her gaze very seriously, he got to his feet.

'Reverend Hanson,' he said. 'I know you don't know me and I hope that we can rectify that in the days to come. But I should like to ask you for Margaret's hand in marriage.'

'Ohh!' Daisy cried, jumping up and leaping about the small available space. She went to William Hanson, hands clasped in front of her chest. 'Oh, say yes, *please* – you've got to say yes!'

Margaret was beginning to feel genuinely sorry for her father, the number of shocks being inflicted on him in one day. He looked about him with an air of almost comic bewilderment.

'Well, I . . . What's your name, my dear?'

'I'm Daisy Hanson. And I would like your daughter to marry my father, please, if that's all right?'

'What do you say to that, Margaret?' William Hanson said. 'And is this all right with Miss Annie?'

'Oh –' Annie grinned at Philip Tallis. 'Yes. I think he'll do.'

Margaret looked from her father to Philip Tallis and back again, a smile growing on her face of utter certainty. 'I say yes, Father. Gladly – yes!'

Everyone in the room broke into applause – even, in a measured way, William Hanson.

'Oh, Margaret, bab – you'll be our next-door neighbour!' Aunt Hatt exclaimed, not even trying to hide her tears now. She seemed to have forgotten all about moving house.

'And you'll be my mother!' Daisy cried. Her face sobered. 'Not my real mother, of course.' She looked carefully at her father. 'But *like* my mother.'

Margaret walked round the table and put her hand on Philip's shoulder. 'I've found a truly good man, Father.'

'She has,' Annie said, serious now.

'Well.' William Hanson looked back at them all with a helpless smile. 'My Leah used to say that the people she came from here were golden-hearted – and from what I see, I believe it to be true. I bow to your judgement. I'm sure you know what to do for the best, my dears.'

Fifty-Three

'My goodness,' Aunt Hatt said, as Susan took delivery of a substantial parcel and laid it on the desk in front of her. 'That looks interesting.' She stood up and peered at it. It was thickly wrapped in brown paper and tied about immaculately with twine. The address was recorded in a precise, ornate hand. 'It's got German stamps on it.'

'You going to open it then?' Susan asked, with an impatience shared by Margaret, though she did not like to say so. The stamps looked foreign and interesting, with heads in profile and '*DEUTSCHES REICH*' printed on them.

'Oh, my – how do you say that?' Bridget said, peering at them.

It already felt like a day of excitement: Friday 23 December, the last working day before Christmas, which the girls were to share with Uncle Eb and Aunt Hatt – and Annie's last day at Masters, Hogg & Co.

'Shouldn't we wait for Eb?' Aunt Hatt said, looking up at them with mischievous eyes. Margaret thought, with a warmth spreading through her, how lovely her aunt was. And this – this place and this street were to be her home! She was full of happiness.

'Oh, he won't be in for ages,' Susan said, slumping down at her desk again.

'No,' Aunt Hatt said. 'I'm not opening that – it's addressed to Eb and it's for Christmas.'

Annie came home that evening rather tearful at having left the factory.

'It sounds silly, doesn't it?' she said to them over the tea table. 'It's such hard, boring work, but I'm glad I've done it. And I'll miss some of those women.'

'And others you won't, I can imagine,' Aunt Hatt said, carving up a meat pie with some vigour.

Annie grinned. 'Yes – that is true. But some of them were very nice to me when they heard I was going. And I'll miss Lizzie.' She looked at Margaret. 'I'm so glad you'll still be here to keep an eye on everyone – Den and all of them.'

'Did you tell them you were going in for nursing?' Uncle Eb said, pulling his sleeves up in happy anticipation of a good meal.

'No,' Annie said. 'No – I just said I was going home.'

'Which you are,' Margaret pointed out. 'For the moment.'

They had told their father that they would both return home after Christmas – Margaret just for a couple of weeks; Annie until she had turned eighteen in April and could apply to be accepted somewhere as a nurse, which, being Annie, she seemed quite certain she would.

Margaret would be returning to make her life in Chain Street. Daisy was wild with impatience about this.

'Why can't you just get married *now*?' she kept asking Margaret.

'Because we have to make a few arrangements,' she said. 'With the church, for a start.'

Daisy looked blankly at her. Margaret had told Philip she would like to be married, by her father, at Carrs Lane church.

'Margaret,' he said, holding her in his arms. The joy and sense of wonder she saw in his face lit her heart. 'Anywhere – on the moon, if you like, so long as you'll be my wife.'

They had decided to be married in the middle of January with Daisy and Annie, of course, as bridesmaids.

Now that the decision was made, Margaret was happier than she could ever remember. Each day she saw something new and loveable in Philip Tallis. There was only one small cloud in the sky of her happiness which she wanted to clear. The day before, she had managed to speak to her aunt alone in the back kitchen.

'Auntie.' She felt foolish, nervous. 'I . . . I really do love Philip, you know.'

Aunt Hatt came up and took Margaret's face gently in her warm hands. 'I can see that, Margaret. It's written in every line of you. You've blooms in these cheeks I've never seen before.' She lowered her hands, smiling. 'And I know we'll be living out in Handsworth – maybe you can persuade him to move out one day as well! But we'll be here with the business, and it'll be lovely to have you about.'

'It's just . . .' She looked down, twisting her fingers together. 'I have had the impression that you and Uncle Eb don't – didn't – really like Philip very much.'

'Margaret –' Aunt Hatt said earnestly. 'It isn't not *liking*. Mr Tallis is a good man – anyone can see that. He's just a bit different, that's all. He does things his way – and I respect that and Eb does too. We've just never got to know him. I don't think being a bit different has ever been a crime, has it? And anyway – I owe you an apology, my dear. My being taken in by that smooth snake in the grass of a man who turned up here . . .'

'You weren't to know, Auntie. Charles has always been able to turn on the charm. That's why everyone falls for him.'

'Except Annie.'

'Yes, well . . .' They laughed. 'She's mellowing,' Margaret said. 'I even heard her saying something nice to Jack Sidwell yesterday.'

'Poor old Jack!' Aunt Hatt said. 'He's got some young wench on his arm, though – I saw him the other day. He's no match for Annie.' Her face sobered. 'But you said your father's taking measures against that monster.'

Their father had returned to the village, happy that his daughters would soon be joining him. When Aunt Hatt had asked if he minded the girls staying for Christmas – 'I don't think Eb and I will get through all my puddings without some help' (though Eb said he thought he might, with a little application) – William Hanson agreed peaceably.

'Christmas is rather busy in the church,' he told Aunt Hatt. 'Which means I am not much present at home in any case. And I'm sure I shall be well taken care of by our members. I have a housekeeper – she won't let me starve.'

'Needless to say, Charles did not come back to finish his last few weeks as he was meant to,' Margaret now told her aunt. 'He should have been there over Christmas. I know Father said he has written to the Church administration to say that Charles should not be allowed to work for them again – and he's told the police. No one knows where he is at the moment.'

'Oh, I expect they'll get him,' Aunt Hatt said. 'He can't hide for ever.' She shuddered. 'Ooh, it gives me the creeps thinking about him.'

Margaret nodded. 'Me too. But I'm determined to keep him out of my mind – to banish him completely as soon as I can. He has taken up too much of my mind for too long.'

They saved the parcel from Germany to open after Christmas dinner. Georgie and Clara said they wanted to have their first Christmas dinner in their own little house but would be round later with Jimmy. So it was the four of them: Uncle Eb and Aunt Hatt, Margaret and Annie, and sitting round the table in the cosy room felt especially precious since they all knew it was soon to end. And it was the first time in a long while that Christmas had not been overlain by a pall of grief – their mother had died just before the season, and at home it could never feel anything but bleak and sad.

There was a little tree, perched on an occasional table in one corner, groaning with decorations made of papier mâché and glass, folded paper and bows. The ceiling was draped with paper streamers, the hearth almost invisible under the weight of red ribbons and greenery, adding to all the trinkets that decked the place every day of the year.

'Just think,' Aunt Hatt said, pink-cheeked, as roast beef with all the trimmings gave way to her brandy-soaked pudding and a generous tot of port, 'next year we won't be here. Oh, Eb – just think! We had Georgie as a baby in these rooms and we won't be here any more!' She teetered on the point of tears.

'Well, the business'll be here,' Eb said. 'You'll be back most of the day anyway – and think of that new bathroom.'

'Oh!' Aunt Hatt sighed dreamily. 'The bathroom. And those curtains for the bedroom . . .'

Once they were all replete, Eb sitting back, rubicund of face and convex of tummy and lighting his pipe, Aunt Hatt went into the office and fetched the parcel from Germany, and her giant pair of scissors.

'Come on,' she said. 'Presents in a moment – but first let's see what's in here.'

They cleared a space at her end of the table and all watched as Aunt Hatt cut the strings, pulling away the crisp paper, under which were layers of tissue. Eventually a rectangular box emerged, over a foot long, silver, decorated with scrolling leaves and patterns of flowers and birds all set with coloured stones.

'Well,' Eb said tipsily. 'That looks a bit of all right, whatever it is.'

Aunt Hatt was turning it this way and that. 'Look –' She tugged on the little silver knob at the front and a flap came down. 'I think it's a musical box.'

Margaret and Annie leaned in closer as she turned a little mechanism inside, which provoked the startling development of a flap on the top shooting open and a bright green bird appearing. It rotated, rocking back and forth to a twinkly tune. They all laughed in delight.

'Let's have a look, Hatt – pass it over,' Eb said. 'I bet we could make one of those.'

'Hold on, before you get on to that,' Aunt Hatt said. 'There's a letter with it.'

She opened a sheet of thick, butter-coloured paper and read it standing up, as if declaring an edict.

'Dear Mr Ebenezer Watts,' she read, tilting the paper towards the light.

> A thousand thanks for the exquisite portraits of my beloved daughters, which your manufactory has created for me with such artistry. My wife and I are full of delight at the sight of them, and such fine examples of your English craftsmanship add much beauty and joy to our home.

'Ah,' Eb said, looping his fingers in his braces and sitting back in satisfaction. "English craftsmanship". That's it.'

Aunt Hatt frowned slightly and said, 'Shoosh, Eb.'

> As a token of my appreciation, I am sending a musical toy from Germany – also, I think you will agree, most excellent in execution.
>
> My cousin, Friedrich Schmale, asked me to convey to you his fond regards. He is now established in a new home with his wife Hilde from where he runs his business but also delights in walking in the mountains.
>
> It is my hope that one day our paths will cross and that I shall be able to visit in person.
>
> I remain your grateful servant,
> Herr Klaus von Titz

'Shame,' Eb said woozily, 'going about with a name like that. Sounds a nice enough bloke, though.'

Aunt Hatt sank into her chair. 'Well, that's nice. And it sounds as if poor old Freddie Small has settled down, anyway.'

They all looked at Annie, who shrugged, blushing.

'Going about breaking hearts,' Uncle Eb teased her.

'Well, let's hope he has,' Margaret said, feeling rather sorry for him all the same.

Later, she went next door with a little parcel for Daisy, containing drawing materials and a bar of sweet-smelling soap. Knocking at the door of number twenty-four, she felt her spirits soar. Here she stood, light and joyful, released from all the burdens she had carried for so long. Looking up at the chipped black door, she thought, this is to be my new home – and any moment now, he will come, my Philip, and we shall be together!

The door swung open and Philip, dressed in his best Sunday suit, beamed at her, reaching for her hand. As soon as he had closed the door behind them, he drew her into his arms in the hall.

'A good moment to come,' he whispered. 'Little'un's out the back – she'll come charging in in a moment. Gives me a second to say happy Christmas properly.'

They kissed, briefly, then held each other tight.

'I'm so happy, she said, looking up at him. 'My dear, dear Philip. Happy Christmas!'

'And New Year and new life,' he said joyously. 'As long as you are here, Margaret. That's all I ask.'

She reached up to kiss him again. 'Oh, I will be,' she said. 'Of course I will – my dear, dear love.'

Acknowledgements

My thanks to the staff and enthusiastic volunteers at the following Jewellery Quarter Museums:

Museum of the Jewellery Quarter, Vyse Street; J. W. Evans Silver Factory, Albion Street; The Coffin Works, Fleet Street and The Pen Museum, Frederick Street.

Also to Grace King, Silversmith, for her smithing workshop, which gave me a few welcome experiences of metal-bashing.

It's always a pleasure to hear from readers, and you might be interested in looking at my website at:
www.anniemurray.co.uk

Or you can join my Facebook page at
www.facebook.com/Annie.Murray.Author

Or follow me on Twitter **@AnnieMurrayWriter**

Further Reading

My information came from a wide range of sources, but these were the main books:

Jewellery Making in Birmingham 1750–1995 by Shena Mason

The Jewellery Quarter, History and Guide by Marie Haddleton

Birmingham's Jewellery Quarter by Alison Gledhill

Jewels of Our City: Birmingham's Jewellery Quarter by Jean Debney

Hockley by David Harvey

Birmingham and the Midland Hardware District, ed. Samuel Timmins

Brief History of the Birmingham Pen Trade, Birmingham Pen trade Heritage Association

They Worked All Their Lives: Women of the Urban Poor 1880–1939 by Carl Chinn

Poverty Amid Prosperity: The Urban Poor 1834–1914 by Carl Chinn

Birmingham's Industrial Heritage 1900–2000 by Ray Shill

A History of Birmingham by Chris Upton

The Girl from Hockley by Kathleen Dayus

Seeing Birmingham by Tram by Eric Armstrong

Finely Taught, Finely Wrought: The Birmingham School

of Silversmithing 1890–1990, compiled by Barbara Newport

A Silversmith's Manual by Bernard Cuzner

The Edwardians by Paul Thompson

Lost Voices of the Edwardians, ed. Max Arthur

By Hammer and Hand: The Arts and Crafts Movement in Birmingham by Alan Crawford

The Arts and Crafts Movement in Britain by Mary Greensted

A New Light on Tiffany: Clara Driscoll and the Tiffany Girls by Martin Eidelberg, Nina Gray and Margaret K. Hofer

Online silver forums at http://www.925-1000.com/forum/index.php?